The Tau Ceti Diversion

Chris McMahon

The Tau Ceti Diversion

Chris McMahon

Published 2018 by Lanedd Press, an imprint of Pop & Top Publishers.
www.popandtop.com.au
Please direct all enquiries to the publisher at:
publisher@popandtop.com.au

ISBN: 9780980387049

PRINTING HISTORY
Severed Press edition published 2016

This is a work of fiction. Names, characters, places, and incidents are products of the author's imagination or are used fictitiously and are not to be construed as real. Any resemblance to actual events, locales, organizations, or persons, living or dead, is entirely coincidental.

Cover Art: Daryl Lindquist

Chris McMahon's website: www.chrismcmahon.net

This novel is dedicated to my wife
Sandra, for her continued love, support,
and unfailing faith in me.

Acknowledgements

Special thanks to Marius Hancu for his invaluable insight and advice on the manuscript. Marius, more than anyone else, helped me to give shape and polish to the book's final incarnation. Thanks also to all the people who contributed over the years to the final work that the Tau Ceti Diversion became, members of the Edge and Vision writing groups, and the amazing Marianne de Pierres who first saw the nascent manuscript at the enVision writer's workshop.

List of Characters

Starburst Officers and Crew

Andrai Wright	Lieutenant, responsible for onboard systems.
Bolan	Chief Warrant Officer.
Evelle	Lieutenant, responsible for biosystems, and Karic's ex-wife.
Gemma	Lieutenant.
Ibri	Lieutenant, and computer specialist.
Janzen Davis	Commander, ExploreCorp executive, and heir to the Davis fortune.
Karic Zand	Sub-Commander, engineer, designer of the *Starburst*, and original inventor of the *Starburst*'s stasis equipment.
Mara Montes	Lieutenant, and astronomer. Born and raised on the space-based Davis Industries Platform.
Resk	Biosystems technician.
Ryal	Lieutenant, and propulsion engineer.

Imbirri

Ember	Member of the First, and of the red caste.
Green Patch	Member of the First, and of the gold caste.
Munch	Member of the First, acolyte of Utar, and member of the purple caste.
New Bough	Member of the First, acolyte of Utar, and member of the gold caste.
Otla	Member of the First, acolyte of Utar, and member of the green caste.
Reth	Member of the First, and of the red caste.
Swith	Member of the gold caste, and most senior of the Gathered gold.
The Awakener	Spiritual leader and chief of the Imbirri, and member of the green caste.

Utar	Shaman of the Imbirri, known as Deepwatch, and member of the gold caste.

Fintil

Asthel	Newly born female Fintil.
The Fountain	Guardian of Fintil knowledge.

Glossary

AI	Artificial intelligence, specifically in computing systems.
AU	Standard Astronomical Unit of distance, based on Earth's orbital distance from the Sun, about 150 million kilometers.
Comband	Wrist-worn video and radio communications device.
Cru	Planet in the Tau Ceti system orbiting at around 0.55AU from Tau Ceti.
DavisCorp	Earth-based corporation owned by the Davis family with diverse off-planet interests, including industrial space platforms, and arms manufacture.
Deepwatch	Formal title of the shaman of the Imbirri.
Epsilon Eridani	K-type main sequence star 10.5 lightyears from Earth.
EM	Electromagnetic.
ExploreCorp	Earth-based corporation formed as a subsidiary of the Davis family corporation, DavisCorp, with a focus on interstellar exploration and colonization.
Fintil	Technologically advanced, winged natives of Cru, dwelling on the bright side of the planet.
First	A select group of Imbirri awakened to sentience directly by the Imbirri leaders.
Free Colonies	A coalition of colonies inside Earth's solar system comprising Mars, the Moon, and settlements on the Jovian moons.
Gathered	Imbirri raised to sentience by the First.
G-class star	G-type main sequence star varying between 0.8 to 1.2 solar masses and from white to yellow in color, of which the Sun is an example.
gee	Gravitational acceleration equal to one standard earth gravity.
IC	Integrated circuit.
Imbirri	Hairless, bear-like natives of Cru's dark side.

Odin	Optical data interface with integrated computing power, worn as glasses.
Redwing	Vibrant red-winged butterflies that hatch annually on Cru's dark side, and are used by the Imbirri to mark the passing of the years.
Shipcom	Artificial intelligence interface of the *Starburst*'s onboard computing system.
Singularity	Region inside a black hole where the laws of normal spacetime cannot exist.
Suspension	Human suspended animation.
Suspension field	Combination of electromagnetic fields used in suspension technology to suspend cellular biological action during stasis.
Stasis	Human suspended animation.
Tau Ceti	G-type main sequence star 12 lightyears from Earth.
Terminator	Planetary dividing line between night and day. The terminator is essentially stationary on a planet tidally locked to its star.
Tight-beam	High-energy focused laser beam used for interstellar communication.
Timezones	Registered communities whose members maintain the same relative aging in real time.
Transmission node	A mountainous, crystalline tower that provides heat and light on Cru's dark side.
XR32	A handgun equipped with small, rocket-propelled, high-explosive rounds.

Prologue

Utar knew that the intruders would destroy his people.

Even now, their starship sped toward Cru, the Imbirri home-planet, like a plague-ship. Within it, thirty-eight of these aliens slumbered. It was they who would wreak so much havoc on the timeless march of the Imbirri.

Over thousands of years, Utar had trained his mind to reach outward into Timespace, passing through the fabric into the potentials of the future — paths which would be, or could be. In all of his many visits to this strange realm of potentials, the paths of his people had stretched to infinity unhindered; yet now, the timelines representing the alien ship cut across every single Imbirri future, leaving only the blurred mass of the unknown. An event lay on their path — bloody like the instrument of death — followed by a cascade of changes that could destroy the Imbirri.

He sent his mind through the void to the tiny vessel that housed the intruders. A capsule of dull metal powered by the heart of a miniature sun. He could sense the travelers on the tiny vessel and felt no great evil. He now knew what they called themselves. There was one *human* casting his feeble spirit-eyes toward his, trying to understand his presence. Utar did not want to destroy the humans, but what choice did he have? He had killed before, in the name of the Imbirri, destroying the forbidden ones, the Changed ones. Were these weak-limbed humans any better than those fallen Imbirri? Those he had once loved?

Utar drew his mind back from the alien ship and reached out to the Unseen One, a massive device that orbited his planet's small yellow companion star. Slowly, the colossal bulk of the device resolved before his minds' eye. He was aware of the vast superstructure that contained it — more sensed than seen. Within it, was a black disk, the size of a small moon, surrounded by a hot ring of rotating gas. Its powerful sentience reached out toward him, filling his mind with a confusion of colors, geometrical shapes, and readings. A flood of information he scarcely understood. Many of the ancients' devices — mysterious artifacts left by that unknown, vanished race — he had fathomed fully, but no the Unseen One. It was too powerful and complex for his mind to conceive.

But that did not mean he could not use it.

As always, huge jets of superheated gas sped toward the Unseen One's dark heart from the yellow sun. The device hungrily consumed them, squeezing the matter so violently that parts of it escaped, particles and lethal radiation shooting back out into space. It was deadly, yet undirected. Delicately, he reached out with his mind. With a careful adjustment, he shifted the axes of the device into alignment. Now the fountains of radiation issuing from the gas ring surrounding the device would intercept the path of the human ship. Even as he watched, a new jet of gas detached from the ring and spiraled into the dark heart of the Unseen One. Much was consumed, yet some radiation spewed back into space, toward the invaders. He longed to speed with it, and see it strike, but exhaustion overwhelmed him.

Many seasons he had now spent in Farsleep — the longest he had ever dared. Time was the payment for work such as this. Any more time in this cerebral realm would risk his own life. Yet, he was content.

Soon the staccato buss of the starship's computer would cease. With silent screams, many of the humans would immediately follow. Their craft would be crippled, and those who survived the initial strike would be helpless to avoid their own deaths as the vessel drifted, broken, through the void. His calculations had been exact. The new timeline inevitable.

On Cru, his people awaited him. Now he would return in triumph. His heart warmed as he remembered the innocent Imbirri who sheltered under his protection.

Now they would be safe.

Chapter 1

Karic's mind reeled. He looked again at the image of the *Starburst* that rotated slowly above the interface projectors and gripped the chill metal of the console to steady himself. His mind groped through the data as he tried to understand how their meticulously planned voyage, his state-of-the-art spaceship had found themselves in danger. The high-resolution digital image of *Starburst*, assembled only moments ago from pictures taken by a small probe as it wove around the ship, was splashed with red, orange and yellow highlights. All those bright colors — superimposed on the dark gray and black images of the metal hull — were visual aids showing estimates of structural damage.

Translucent interface icons floated above the console, bobbing slowly out of the way then drifting back to position as the virtual *Starburst* continued to rotate. Beyond them, the big screens that lined the room were filled with diagnostic data. Over sixteen percent of their systems were on backup, their primary processes having failed outright. The failures were ship-wide. On account of the immense timescales of interstellar travel, the *Starburst* had been designed with multiple levels of redundancy, but this failure rate was way too high. A power unit on a hatchway and two remote systems had failed to respond to the AI at all. Taken in conjunction with the deterioration of the outer structure, it was all damning. The skin crawled on the back of his skull.

Karic, the sub-commander of the *Starburst* and Lieutenant Ryal, the officer responsible for the fusion systems, were the only members of the *Starburst's* crew out of suspension. The Shipcom had roused them seven months early to investigate the damage. The other officers and crew remained in long-term stasis. They might as well be blocks of stone for all the help they could offer. He had to rouse them all. He needed every scientist, engineer and tech he had to save the ship, the mission ... and their lives.

Karic took a deep breath and tried to quell the rushing flow of his thoughts. The air of the command deck was cold, sharp with trapped odors of plastic and ozone. He leaned back in the command chair, conscious of the quiet stillness, the empty workstations and darkened consoles. The flexible smart-metal of the chair molded around his back. Its chill had faded now, internal sensors heating it to match his body temperature. The silvered gleam of the fixtures was stark against the matte gray of the polymer-coated floor, and the curve of the hull beneath him was hardly noticeable here, on the outer level of the habitat ring.

The low hum of the interface projectors seemed loud in the silence, a rising counterpoint to the soft whisper of circulation fans.

Communication with Earth had failed.

They were alone.

The familiar solidity of the command center, its high-tech alloy and smooth, functional design, seemed a brittle thing now, like a polished facade concealing the unseen tension of stressed metal before its rupture.

"Shipcom. Begin the emergency revival process," said Karic. That would revive the thirty crew and six other officers in suspension, including Commander Janzen Davis.

"Unable to comply," responded the Shipcom in its flat, feminine voice. His mouth went dry.

"Give reason for inability to initiate emergency revival sequence?"

"Radiation levels are currently above the upper limit for programmed revival risk factors."

Karic's heart leapt into a sprint, a flood of adrenalin threatening to swamp his brain.

The revival process was tricky. The suspension fields had to be reduced precisely, otherwise severe damage could occur at the cellular level. Ambient radiation could cause the fields to surge. He must have completed his own revival sequence before the radiation levels exceeded the preset danger levels.

That meant those levels were climbing!

"Idiot!" shouted Karic, slamming his hand onto the console.

"Please repeat the command," replied the Shipcom, unable to interpret the context. Despite the advances in AI, in the 22nd century when *Starburst* was launched, they still remained only expert systems responding from a vast array of human-input decision trees. Syntax was crucial, and instructions had to be precise.

"Display the sensor feeds. Trend the radiation levels."

A multicolored graphic appeared on one of the screens. The radiation levels had been rising fast over the last few hours, primarily X-rays.

"Oh my God."

Neither the officers' nor crew's stasis decks would be safe in a radiation surge. The protocol was clear. All personnel had to be moved into the central hold. The big storage space was on the ship's axis, inside the habitat ring. There they would be shielded by the habitat ring's whole rotating mass as well as by the forward deflectors. But locked in suspension, none of the officers or crew could be moved. *A surge would kill them all.*

A vein in his temple throbbed.

It could take hours to bring someone out of suspension. If he waited — and the levels started to peak — there would not be enough time to move them. But if he brought them out of suspension now — overriding the presets — then he could be putting all of them at risk, since they were more vulnerable to the radiation in the revival process. His thoughts flew to Mara, then guiltily included his ex-wife, Evelle. The thought of Mara lying dead tore at him.

Karic had never felt about anyone the way he had felt about Mara. Their affair during the heady days of commissioning had been a whirlwind of excitement, technical triumphs, and snatched moments of passion. Only when it was over … when it was too late, did he understand how he felt. He never would have believed in those early days that a twist of fate would put his ex-lover and ex-wife on the same voyage.

Karic viewed the radiation levels critically. No one knew the suspension system better than he did. At the current levels, he was confident the revival would be safe. But how quickly could those levels change?

He scrolled through the system icons and isolated the computer controlling the crew's suspension equipment. He flicked the icon toward the main screens. Data flared to life. It was all functioning normally.

"What is the crew revival time?"

"Two hours," replied the Shipcom.

His hands clawed at the floating icons, drilling down to the systems controlling the officer's suspension equipment, completely separate from the crew's. Not for the first time, he cursed the lack of computing power in the dedicated systems. It would take *three hours* for the six officers. Anything could happen in that time.

He reached for a glowing red icon and dragged it into the center of the field. With a touch, it blossomed into a virtual keyboard. A message hovered over the input field in swollen red letters.

INPUT CODE TO DISABLE PRESETS

He grew lightheaded as the implications of the moment weighed on him. His decision now would change everything. Karic's fingers teased open the smart seam of his flight fatigue to find the St. Christopher medal on his chest. Gripping it between his thumb and forefinger, his thumb circled the smooth, ancient metal of the backing in anxious circles. The superstitious affectation helped him to relax. Karic tried to broaden his thinking, letting his mind fall into a free-associative state, searching for any other way out of this. *Starburst* was en route to Tau Ceti. Less than a year out. They had completed their original mission to Epsilon Eridani, then diverted to the small G-class star system, twelve lightyears from Earth. As the moments stretched out, no flash of inspiration came to save him. The evidence was clear, and reviving the whole crew was the prudent solution. Eventually, the pressure to *do* something became unbearable. He let go of the medal. The seam of his fatigues slithered closed, the two halves writhing against each other until the collar tightened against his neck.

Something danced at the corner of his vision.

"No. Not now!" Relaxing his mind had been a mistake.

Karic felt the fugue coming. In the fugue state, his mind would slide into a dream, while externally he presented as catatonic — immobile and unresponsive for up to hours. It was a legacy of altered genetics inherited from his grandfather. No one knew about the flaw, and it was vital it stayed that way. Each time he roused from suspension it seemed to be getting worse. Increasingly, he was using drugs to control it.

He reached for his pocket, his fingers clutching for one of the stim-stabs he always kept there, but he was too slow.

The unstoppable wave of the rising fugue state engulfed him.

Karic's mind expanded into space, stretching molecule-thin as it sought to fill the immensity. A distant sound, like a rushing river, roared through him. The stars boiled and the fabric of space hummed with energy as it shifted and stretched. He sensed awareness — a vast darkness, like a hand searching blindly, groping toward them. The fingers stretched like stilettos, each a razored knife seeking a fatal point of entry ...

"Awaiting Code," said the Shipcom.

Karic snapped out of his mental fugue.

He looked at his wrist. *Twenty-six minutes!* A trickle of cold sweat ran down the inside of his uniform. He put the stim-tab into his mouth and crunched it to powder, wincing at the bitterness. His heart began to thump faster, a new clarity flooding through him. He smoothed down his short, wavy light brown hair and tried to focus.

Karic expanded the 3-D graphic of the *Starburst*, zooming into the microstructure of the ship. The external surface of the main habitat ring had perished, particularly at the rear of the ship, which was not shielded by the forward deflectors. A cold feeling settled into the pit of Karic's stomach. The stasis chamber for the main crew — thirty men and women — and the biodome were back there. His original design had included additional radiation shielding for the crew's chamber, but the expensive shielding had been removed by the ExploreCorp Executive in a cost-cutting exercise.

It was a testament to her designers that the electronics, particularly the Shipcom, were holding up so well. Only the protection afforded by the forward deflectors had prevented wholesale systems failure.

Swallowing down the sick feeling in his stomach, Karic typed out the memorized code.

He stabbed at the input.

PRESETS DISABLED

Acting now would mean some people may die, but not acting might leave them in a situation too terrible to contemplate.

"Begin the revival process for the whole crew."

"Confirmed."

The silence left in the wake of the Shipcom's voice weighed on him, as though the air pressure had ramped to twice atmospheric.

"Give me the revival sequence for the officers."

Janzen and himself were first by priority, beyond that the order was randomly generated.

"Janzen and Andrai, Mara and Ibri, Evelle and Gemma."

He let out a long breath.

With a hand gesture, he swept the virtual interface away.

He had an hour before Janzen and Andrai revived. He tapped his knuckle on the console as he thought of his ex-wife Evelle, and Gemma, most at risk in the revival process.

Ryal was down the central axis at the main fusion plant. That was top priority for him when roused by a shift override.

Karic tapped the comband on his wrist. "Ryal?"

Ryal's thin face with its close-cropped reddish hair appeared on the screen of Karic's comband, the bulkheads of the fusion plant behind him. Ryal listened calmly as Karic outlined the situation.

"That explains the system failures," said Ryal.

"I want you back here. This could be bad," said Karic.

Ryal's mouth tightened into a thin line, and his eyes narrowed. Karic recognized the dour look, and knew that whatever Ryal was thinking, there would be no arguing him out of it. "I can't see any other option but to take the fusion drive back to standby. If we lose control of that while it's delivering thrust ..." He did not need to finish the sentence. The whole ship would become a hydrogen bomb.

It was suddenly hard to breathe. "How long?"

"At least two hours. Maybe more," said Ryal.

"OK. Get cracking," said Karic. "I'll check out the biodome, then get down there to help." The systems in the biodome filtered and recycled their air, and were critical to the crew's long-term survival. When it came to biological systems, there was no substitute for the human eye.

"Acknowledged." The comband's square screen faded to dull gray. For a moment, he saw his own faded reflection there in miniature, his deep brown eyes fierce and determined beneath dark brows, cheekbones prominent on an otherwise well-proportioned face framed with wavy brown hair.

Karic started to rise from the chair when he realized he had not watched the last duty log, the routine video record left by the last two officers on shift. He been too distracted by the damage to the ship and the threat posed by the radiation. The report was three months old, but even so, it was important he reviewed it — any piece of information may prove vital. Karic swiveled the command chair to face the wall screens. The last two officers on shift had been Mara and Commander Janzen, both now in stasis.

"Shipcom. Play last shift log."

The screen brightened and he saw the smooth, handsome face of Commander Janzen.

"Good morning, Karic," said Janzen, smiling to reveal a row of perfect, white teeth. He was wearing his trademark *odin* — optical data-interface glasses — the left pane opaque. "I'm always pleased to see you on-shift.

"The efficiencies have been a little low on the main drive train. You might want to pay some attention to the energy-use factors. I don't have to tell you how expensive those fuel pellets are." Janzen's eyes flicked to the left and went out of focus as he switched his gaze to the odin's tiny screen. "Mmnn. Andrai did report some deterioration in the outer structure, but — yes. That looks minor."

At a whispered command the odin contracted to a narrow yellow band below Janzen's carefully shaped eyebrows. He looked back to the camera, seeming to meet Karic's eyes. "Well. Mara has uploaded a more detailed update. Have a good shift. Next time I see you, we will be orbiting Tau Ceti." Janzen's voice was deep and rich, but there was no disguising his hunger for success. His family had financed the mission, hoping to find a habitable world and cash in on the immense profits of the colonization trade. The sort of world they were hoping to find orbiting Tau Ceti.

The commander ran a hand through his short blond hair in an unconscious gesture. "Maybe we can have that tennis rematch?"

Back on Earth he and Janzen had been keen players. Karic and Evelle had been invited into the elite circles of Janzen's family, the Davises, on two occasions, playing social doubles on a world-class court set into the immaculately landscaped grounds of their Long Island mansion. He and Janzen had even had the odd cyber-match in the habitat's recreation room while they completed their mission at Epsilon Eridani, but the pace of work had soon left little time. The keen disappointment of their first mission had also affected them all. The indications of a promising world in the habitable zone around Epsilon Eridani — as seen from Earth — had led to a Mars-sized moon orbiting a gas dwarf. A tortured world squeezed by tidal forces and bathed in radiation.

"Commander Janzen, out."

The screen darkened for a moment, then an image of Mara flared to life above him. In the recording, Mara was standing at the main console, her dark hair pulled back into a business-like bun, her slim, attractive face tight with tension, her dark brown eyes intent. Always detached and efficient — on the surface. It had been only at the end of their brief but intense affair that Karic saw firsthand the emotional intensity that boiled inside her.

"Morning, Karic," said Mara. It was convention to greet people at the beginning of their shift as though it was morning. "Everything seems to be pretty much under control here at the moment." *Three months ago.* "The only thing I'm a bit worried about is radiation. Up until now I've had all the sensors configured to get as much data on the planets around Tau Ceti as possible. I detected an intense X-ray burst from the direction of the star. We didn't have our sensors aligned to monitor it, so I can't tell for sure whether Tau Ceti was the point of origin." Their efforts had been particularly focused on a big planet orbiting Tau Ceti at 0.55 AU — a favorable orbit for life — which showed signs of both oxygen and water. Another, orbiting at 1.35 AU, which was even bigger, was also on the edge of the habitable zone.

Mara's forehead wrinkled. "I can't determine the cause of the X-rays," she said. For that moment, she had forgotten he would be watching her.

A memory of Mara, laying beneath him, her eyes unfocussed in ecstasy, fled through his mind, leaving a trail of longing in its wake.

"That sort of star shouldn't be producing anything remotely like this," continued Mara. "I am hoping that it's coming from a singular celestial event, way out beyond the system, and that the worst is past. But, if the source is in the vicinity, this could just be the beginning of a sustained burst. Anyway, I have aligned some of our sensors on Tau Ceti to gather data. Just keep an eye on it for me, will you? Wake me if it's anything critical." She clenched her jaw tightly and she leant forward. The video feed cut.

So there were signs of X-rays, even three months ago.

A redoubled sense of urgency propelled Karic out of the command chair and across to the hatchway. He touched the faceted diamond of the release sensor on the wall, which was lit with sharp highlights of red and amber that would still be visible through smoke and fume in an emergency. Such a simple piece of equipment, yet somehow smooth and reassuring beneath his thumb. The hatch shot open with the soft hiss of the broken seal and a muted thud as it hit its stops inside the wall. *At least that still works.* It shut automatically behind him with a dull thump. Outside, he followed a narrow corridor that ran down the length of the habitat section to the biodome. To his left and right, he passed the crew's day areas, laboratories, and workrooms, now out of sight behind closed hatchways. His breath came faster. The crew were helpless in stasis. If the worst came to pass, those spaces would remain as empty and silent as a mausoleum.

Here, as for all areas of the ship, the floors were covered with the ubiquitous gray polymer coating. Tough and durable, it deadened the sound of his footfalls, giving slightly under his weight, and helped to dampen vibration. It was functional and well-designed, yet it always brought up images of the overcrowded urban towers of Earth, and the gray, composite polymers used there for durability and resistance to vandalism and graffiti. As though even in this tiny capsule of human life the stark inequalities of Earth clung to them.

The walls and ceiling were lined with molded white plastic glowpanels, now softly lit. The crew's bunks and stasis chambers were in the low-g sections of the habitat, above his head and closer to the axis. The upside-down layout of a rotating habitat had seemed strange at first, but was now second nature. It was only the centrifugal force throwing his weight against the inside of the hull that gave the illusion of gravity.

Despite the danger they were in, he felt the visceral thrill of being here, on the first Terran starship. Based on reports that had reached them at Epsilon Eridani, nine interstellar craft had left Earth after them — some heading for systems that were not even considered likely candidates in 2157 when the *Starburst* set out, but had become hot targets based on new observations. The possibility of being upstaged by these newcomers made no difference to Karic. The *Starburst* was the *first*. Her voyage was a realization of his own lifelong dream.

Karic had been against the diversion to Tau Ceti. Within ten lightyears of Epsilon Eridani there were more than eight systems that looked just as promising. In just a few days of personal time, with each of the crew taking their turn out of suspension to monitor the ship, enough real-time would have elapsed for Earth's gigantic orbital telescopes to provide them with a much more thoroughly analyzed target system. A system with much lower inherent risk — and greater chance of success.

"The race is still on," Janzen had argued. "We may have been the first to leave Earth, but we have the oldest tech. If we want to be the first to find signs of alien life — or a habitable planet — we cannot wait for Earth's astronomers." Karic still remembered the warmth of Janzen's hand on his shoulder, and looking up into his handsome face, framed — as always — by his stylish odin glasses. *"This is our chance, Karic. We are at the frontier. We have to take the gamble."*

In the end, there was nothing Karic could say to alter what was, in fact, a command decision. Even if it had not been so, it would be hard not to have been swayed by Janzen's optimistic certainty. I guess when you were the son of the legendary Zin Davis, and heir to the immense Davis fortune, you had plenty to smile about. Not that Karic begrudged him his wealth — far from it. If not for Janzen and the backing of his company ExploreCorp, the *Starburst* would never have left Earth orbit.

That there had been no more news from Earth was even more worrying. The tight-beam from Earth had gone out of alignment at Epsilon Eridani, shortly before their diversion to Tau Ceti. The Earth orbital station should have been able to correct the transmission based on the *Starburst's* return broadcast, but there was still nothing.

Now they were facing their first major challenge. An unknown and deadly threat. He and Janzen would have to work together with the whole crew to deal with this crisis. At least he could rely on Janzen. The imposing commander respected Karic's expertise. They had worked hand-in-glove since the beginning of the project — when *Starburst* was nothing more than a dream. Janzen ironing out any snags in the finances and delivery of resources, Karic leading the design team and unraveling the technical problems as they arose. Both of them shared a vision and drive for space exploration that had overcome all obstacles to get them here. Their falling out over the diversion to Tau Ceti marked their only disagreement of the voyage.

At the end of the habitat section, the molded panels that lined the walls were in poor condition. Large sections were discolored, having disintegrated to a bone-white powder that dusted the floor. Three panels had failed to darkness, standing like rotten teeth against the creamy brightness of their neighbors. The results of the exterior scan showed the rear skin of the ship had taken damage, yet to see it like this also *inside* the ship was deeply disturbing.

Still, it was not possible to halt the attrition of decades. Even in a vacuum-sealed storage locker, the blue officer's stripes down the arms and legs of his uniform had faded almost to the blue-gray color of the jacket and pants. Only the sub-commander's bar still gleamed silver above the ExploreCorp logo on the left side of his jacket.

Karic thumbed the hatch release and entered the humid atmosphere of the biodome, blinking in the intense light. The specially designed glowpanels on the ceiling flooded the space with daylight ambience. He took a deep breath, imbibing the organic richness of the air like a tonic. A gardener robot bustled past, intent on some duty. The biodome took up the whole rear section of the outer level of the habitat. There were few true windows on *Starburst*, because of the structural problems and shielding issues. Instead, the rear wall of the biodome was lined with screens that could display the exterior starscape, giving a pleasant illusion. They remained dark now.

He set off on a circuit of the dome, studying the vegetation as he went. It was uplifting to be here, with sight of the walls obscured by the plant growth, the illusion of an Earthbound garden only ruined by the glowpanels above his head. He was amazed at the growth, but then, it had been more than three years since his last shift. Not all the signs were good. Here and there amongst the rows, plants had died. He had soon circled the whole floor to arrive back where he started. Then he walked to the rear of the dome where the control stations were located. He came across a robot methodically cutting and removing a dead tree. Karic knelt down and gathered a handful of soil. It looked rich and dark, and yet he wondered how many of the carefully selected bacterial cultures it had been seeded with remained alive. Evelle, who was biosystems officer, would have her work cut out for her.

He let the earth fall through his fingers.

Karic checked the logs and found that activity had increased dramatically over the past few months as the dome's AI struggled to replace those plants killed by radiation and keep the system running. Seed stock was low and three gardener robots had taken themselves offline in the past year.

Karic shut down the console. There was nothing more he could do. He had to get down to the axis of the ship and help Ryal.

Karic looked up whimsically at the darkened screens across the back wall. He would take just a moment, a brief pause to take a breath after all the tension of the last hours.

"Shipcom. Activate biodome screens."

One by one, the big screens that lined the rear wall flared to life.

"Exterior feed."

The Shipcom fed them data from the sensors on the ship's hull until a continuous starscape spread across the walls. Tens of thousands of stars crowded around him. Karic stood for a long moment, alone with space, allowing a sense of serenity to settle on him. From the earliest age, he had been drawn to the images of distant nebulae, galaxies that swirled with living suns, yet so far from Earth. The desire to reach these distant places had shaped his life, driven him first into fusion spacedrive research, then on to lead the team that made the crucial breakthrough in suspension technology — human suspended animation — reliable long-term stasis.

Something shimmered at the edge of his vision. For a moment, he wondered whether the biodome glowpanels had been damaged here as well. Two points of light in the vast starscape above him grew brighter, swelling into the shape of huge eyes. In rapid motion, thousands of snaking lines appeared in space, glowing lines connecting him and the ship with those luminous eyes. Each of the lines drew taut, stretched and snapped, the vivid colors dissolving into a dark mass of smoke, covering everything … except the eyes. They swelled, until they were titanic suns of hate, drawing a dark orb into orbit with them: a darkness within a swirling cloud that sang in tones of deadly color. Matter was drawn into that dark core, flashing with violence as it disappeared. The savage energies raced outward, like a blinding arrow, straight to the living human heart of *Starburst* …

"Karic, what is going on?" *Janzen.*

Karic snapped back to the present. A sweat of fear broke out on his forehead. His eyes flicked to his wrist. *Forty-six minutes.* He gasped, as an intense wave of nausea hit him. He looked back up to the stars. Everything was normal.

"Karic. What is the emergency?" It was Janzen's voice, small and thin as it issued from the tiny speaker on his comband. Janzen and Andrai had emerged from suspension.

Karic touched the screen. The commander's face was still drawn from the revival process, but his penetrating blue eyes met Karic's directly. His mouth was drawn in a thin line.

"We have a serious situation on our hands. Remember the radiation Mara was so concerned about? Well, the ship has taken a battering, everywhere from the microstructure to the biodome. Sixteen percent of primary systems have failed."

"You were right to be concerned. I have Andrai reviewing the data now," said Janzen. He took off his odin. "Although it does appear that the radiation has been nowhere near any lethal threshold."

"True, but the historical trend indicates a pattern of increasing intensity. We can't risk having the whole crew in suspension if the radiation levels peak," said Karic.

"I would agree — if the radiation were close to any intensity that would threaten our wellbeing. But the situation as I read it is that none of us were threatened. Even so, you altered the presets on the suspension equipment and put all of our lives at risk." Janzen's tone remained even, yet the implication stung Karic. Personnel *were* more at risk during revival, that was why the decision had been such a tough call.

"I know that equipment. No one's life was put at risk," said Karic.

"Not to this point, but the revival process is far from over," said Janzen.

"If the radiation is high enough to affect the revival process, then it's high enough to threaten us," said Karic.

"But nowhere approaching lethal levels," insisted Janzen.

"We have to get everyone out of suspension. Then we'll have options to deal with this," argued Karic.

"We need a lot more data before we can make a call like that." The commander's voice was tense, his usually cultured tones clipped.

"By the time we do that, it could be too late. Lives are at risk," said Karic. He did not understand why Janzen had rejected his precautions. When it came to technical decisions, Janzen usually deferred to him.

Janzen ignored the comment. He slipped his odin back on, then reached back up to fractionally adjust the fit. "I see no reason for the crew to be revived at this juncture. I have cancelled the revival sequence."

"You've what?"

Janzen gave Karic a disarming smile. "I can understand your concern on the radiation, but perhaps you are overreacting? We have limited resources out here. Bringing all thirty crew out of suspension at once would have a serious impact on food consumption. I am sure you appreciate that."

"The crew has minimal shielding. Based on the trend —"

"As I understand it … the Shipcom did not issue any alert," said Janzen, his voice smooth. "We are on track for Tau Ceti, with all systems functional."

Had he really misjudged the situation so badly? No. The risk was real. "Janzen, you need to see the data."

"The only data we need to assess is on the new system. I thought you of all people wanted to reach planetfall as soon as possible. Reviving us has wasted time and manpower, and taken us that much further from our goal."

Karic paused. The safety of the crew, the safety of the ship — their only home for hundreds of years in space — was more important than reaching Tau Ceti.

"What about the revival sequence for the officers?" he asked.

"I have left that running. We need all our heads on this one. As for shutting down the fusion drive — that was ill advised."

It was also impossible to stop. Once begun, Ryal would have to complete the turndown procedure. At least there would be no chance of a runaway reaction if the radiation peaked and destroyed the drive's control systems.

"When you finish in the biodome, make your way to the control deck. Janzen out."

Janzen had been an excellent commander so far, dealing with the crew well and displaying a good grasp of logistics. Both of them shared the same passion for success, yet at heart, his friend was an executive. Karic had noticed before that Janzen lacked the instinct of a good scientist or engineer.

The commander's confidence in the face of this threat should have reassured him, but instead it filled Karic with a deep disquiet.

Chapter 2

When Karic returned to the main control room, Ibri and Mara had also awakened from suspension. They sat at the main console with Andrai, their faces all colored by the floating icons of the graphical display. Karic looked immediately at Mara. A strand of her dark hair had escaped her hurried coiffure and fallen across the pale skin of her neck. The astronomer was oblivious, her forehead creased with concentration as she manipulated the icons in the interface with precise, controlled movements of her slim fingers. No doubt she was assessing the astronomical data coming in through the sensors and attempting to make sense of what had happened over the past year. He took a deep breath and let it out slowly, easing the tension in his chest. She was out of immediate danger.

"Morning, Commander," said Karic.

Janzen acknowledged him with a nod and a tight smile. He was pacing up and down the deck dictating notes into his odin. Janzen seemed to dominate the room, looming over them from his two-meter height. He only had the left eye-screen of his odin down, but he had activated the noise barrier. Although he talked rapidly into the little portable AI in the odin's frame, only the faint hum of dissonance could be heard, created by the fraction-of-a-second delay between his real voice and the broadcasted sound-dampening signal.

As usual, Janzen was dressed in a top-of-the-line version of the standard ExploreCorp uniform, tight-fitting blue-gray jacket and pants. The bright red stripes down the arms and legs and the gold diamond on his left shoulder denoted his rank as commander. The fabric gleamed in the cabin lights, looking soft and new, the colors sharp. Karic's own uniform — and the rest of the crew's — had long ago stiffened with age.

"Morning, Mara. Andrai. Ibri."

Andrai, in charge of onboard systems, nodded cheerfully to Karic. The tech's wide face was soft and pleasant, framed with an unruly mop of blond hair.

Ibri's eyes barely flicked in Karic's direction, the taciturn computer specialist no doubt annoyed at the interruption to his work. With his dark complexion, lean, lanky build, and short black hair, he could not be more different from Andrai.

"Good morning, Karic," said Mara. She looked across at Andrai and they shared a conspiratorial grin.

"Hit it?" asked Andrai, in a low tone.

Mara nodded.

Andrai reached up and flicked an icon. It tumbled forward, then disappeared. A moment later, one of the screens changed to a moving countdown in huge red numbers. The active countdown to Tau Ceti.

00c 00y 09m 22d 12h 43m 11s
00c 00y 09m 22d 12h 43m 10s ...

On their current inbound trajectory, they were less than ten months out of the Tau Ceti system and closing fast.

Andrai gave a whoop and he and Mara laughed as they clapped. Even Ibri paused in his work and joined them with his own subdued version of applause — hands coming together, but in such a desultory manner that they produced no noise. Checking the countdown was a ritual, something they always did when they were on shift together.

Janzen, focused on his dictation, flashed them a smile, then turned his back.

"That's a hell of a thing," said Andrai, looking at the countdown. "Although it would have been nicer to have woken up in orbit, boss." ExploreCorp had insisted on a military style command structure for the mission, citing a need for a clear chain of command. Yet despite the differences in rank, they were all indispensable specialists, and did not stand on ceremony.

"That would have been too easy, Andrai," said Karic.

"We all know Karic likes to do things the hard way," said Mara.

"Oh, yeah," said Andrai.

Karic grinned at Mara's reference to the commissioning of the *Starburst*. Karic had earned something of a reputation for rechecking every system, and reworking every analysis. He sobered as his eyes shifted to the live radiation display and he joined them at the main console.

Having been lead engineer for the design and construction of the ship, Karic knew the *Starburst's* systems intimately. From the beginning, it was he who ran the ship on a day-to-day level, making all the technical decisions. Janzen had never concerned himself with operations. The fact had never bothered Karic before. Yet now — with an emergency staring them in the face — he could not forget that Janzen had been absent from almost all the exhaustive training sessions that led up to their departure.

"Andrai, start reviewing all the systems on backup. I want to see which ones can be brought back to primary. And I want to know exactly how much damage the electronics has taken," said Karic.

"OK, boss," said Andrai, who began to methodically drill down through the interface icons. He was the best tech Karic had ever worked with. He was not big on conversation, but would happily follow a conduit for hours tracing a break in transmission, or spend a day problem-solving equipment breakdowns without a single complaint.

"Mara, any clues on the X-ray source?"

Mara leant toward him, the three silver bars on her uniform — indicating a rank of third lieutenant — glittering in the cabin lights atop the gentle swell of her breasts. Her forehead creased with the intensity of

24

her concentration. "I am running two prognostic programs. They might help to identify some of the more probable sources, but it's sheer guesswork at this stage. You know how long a proper study would take."

"How long until your program gives us some preliminary results?" asked Karic, his voice tight with strain.

"At least an hour," said Mara, chewing her bottom lip. A sign she felt the same pressure as Karic to understand their situation. "I have diverted as much computing power as I can."

"That hour will pass soon enough," said Karic.

"Yes," said Mara, her eyes drifting to the radiation display.

Karic brought up a report on the forward deflector and began scanning the data. Satisfied, he turned his attention to monitoring the suspension equipment. So far the radiation counts were not causing any problems.

The computer specialist, Ibri, was busy at his station, running thorough checks of the external sensors and the myriad smaller computer modules that were networked to the Shipcom — controlling everything from the fusion drive to the waste recycling units. With his long, lanky frame, he seemed to loom over his console.

Janzen gave a silent command and his data-glasses retracted to a thick yellow band, the faint dissonance disappearing as the odin's noise dampening field cut.

"Karic," said Janzen striding toward him. They shook hands. The commander gripped his upper arm with his free hand in an affectionate gesture. "Nice to see you."

The commander's smile was infectious. It was hard not be swayed by the charismatic man, with his classic good looks, or brought up short by his penetrating blue eyes. Karic could not even resent the fact they were the product of illegal genetic tampering by Janzen's hyper rich family.

"Do you want to show me this radiation trend you were concerned about?" prompted Janzen, releasing his grip.

"Right." Karic quickly navigated his way through the system to his analysis of the radiation data.

Andrai and Mara had both stopped work, eyes fixed on Karic and Janzen. Mara's face was tight with worry, Andrai's congenial smile strained. Both knew there was still time to revive the crew.

"Here you can see the prior radiation peaks. These give you some idea of the risks. Look at the variance. It's significant. If we got that same variance at the current intensity, we could end up *well* into lethal territory. That's why reviving the crew is so important. We need to be able to evacuate everyone into the central hold if the levels spike." Karic looked at Janzen expectantly.

Janzen nodded appreciatively. "I can see your reasoning. Yet we have no reason to predict a future trend based on a past one — not without more data." He leaned down toward Karic and lowered his voice. "I simply can't approve a revival of the crew with the presets disabled. Not based on this. It's against protocol."

"But the data ..."

Janzen raised his hands to stop Karic. "Look. I am happy to revisit the decision — but only when you have completed a full analysis of the ship and we have something more substantial to go on."

"Goddamn it, Janzen! The crew have hardly any shielding!" snapped Karic.

Janzen was silent for a moment.

"I would prefer it if you referred to me as Commander from now on, Karic," said Janzen, his voice low and smooth.

Karic swallowed. A pounding began at his temples. "Very well ... Commander." He forced himself to unclench his hands, which had curled into tight fists.

Karic looked up at Janzen, searching for the friend who had opened the door to his future with ExploreCorp.

"You have done good work, Karic. I support your decision to revive the officers — I told you that," said Janzen in a reassuring tone. "Complete the analysis. Meanwhile, I need to review our resources given the unexpected live time."

Maybe he just needed to trust Janzen's call.

Janzen sank into the commander's chair in the center of the room and activated the full-immersion mode of his odin. Both data-screens had now descended over his eyes, plunging him into a virtual environment. The telltale distortion of the noise-dampening field followed a moment later.

He felt Mara's cool hand on his. She never could get the heat to her extremities. "It's probably for the best, Karic. We really don't know if the radiation will trend up."

Karic could not articulate the urgency he felt. It was like he knew there was something coming.

Two eyes ...

He shook himself, wary of provoking a fugue state by trying to recall his prior experience in the biodome.

Karic turned to Mara and nodded. She swiftly withdrew her hand. The absence of contact nudged the emptiness inside him. He grimaced, unhappy to be reminded of his unresolved feelings.

"Ibri, how do the computer systems look?" he asked.

Ibri looked up at Karic, his dark brows drawing together in irritation. He watched him with dark, assessing eyes for a moment before replying. "Lost some external nodes. Seven sensors down. Lot of gear on redundancies." He spoke softly, almost at the limit of hearing.

So much damage. All over the ship, it was the same. Janzen had made the call, but the crew would be the ones to pay for it if he was wrong. With their lives. If the surge did come, it would leave them in a crippled ship — with a dead crew. Their mission would be over, and he and the other officers would be left drifting in a metal tomb lightyears from home, waiting to join the others in their final sleep.

"Andrai, what is the status of the fusion drive?" asked Karic.

"Ryal has almost completed the transition to standby." In the absence of the acceleration provided by the drive, *Starburst* would continue to coast toward Tau Ceti at the same velocity it had achieved when the thrust was cut.

"Good. Would it be possible to reconfigure the forward deflectors to give the rear of the ship more protection from the radiation? Could you extend the field past the laser?"

Andrai nodded. "Yes, we could, but we would need more power from the fission plant to compensate. It would also lower the deflection efficiency of the shield. And we would take a little more wear on the forward superstructure from particles." The *Starburst* had a closed-cycle fission reactor located forward of the fusion drive. It provided the colossal amount of energy required to create plasma in the fusion drive, and electrical energy for the ship's shields and systems, including the containment in the fusion reactor. The full output of the fusion plant was directed into thrust.

"Do it."

Andrai's eyes flicked back to Janzen and he hesitated. The commander's mouth was moving soundlessly, and he was oblivious to everything beyond his odin.

Karic followed Andrai's gaze. "Let me worry about Janzen. Right now we are heading toward an unidentified source of *intense* radiation. We need every edge we can get," said Karic.

"OK, boss. I'll start on the reconfiguration now."

The others continued to check the systems, slowly bringing the ship back to life.

"Karic," said Mara. "*Karic!*"

His head snapped up from his workstation. He looked across to Mara and saw her eyes fixed on the radiation count. It was climbing rapidly, the digital figures blurring into each other.

Mara's hand found his and gripped hard.

"Oh no," said Andrai. They were all watching the display, motionless. Karic had a sense of unreality as he watched it climb. *I didn't want to be right. Mother of God ...*

Karic flinched as the count of the radiation levels changed from black to red.

"My God. They're above threshold!" said Mara.

The voice of the Shipcom blared above them.

"Radiation levels exceed safety limits for personnel in the control room. Emergency revival of the crew and evacuation to the shielded areas of the ship is recommended."

Janzen jerked in the command chair. He exited full immersion mode and ran to their console. Like the others, he stared in shock at the rising radiation count. He activated his left data-screen, linking directly with the AI. His face grew pale.

"This … is not right. This cannot be right," said Janzen. "This is not the scenario."

"We have to revive the crew," said Mara.

Karic's guts twisted with a sickening realization.

"It's too late. The radiation levels will interfere with the suspension recovery process."

"But the Shipcom …"

"Only recommended that action because I disabled the presets."

Janzen was stunned. His jaw was slack as he watched the display. "This cannot be *right*."

Karic shook off the shock. Every second counted. "Back to the suspension room. *Everyone!*" he ordered. The additional shielding that surrounded the officer's suspension chamber would be enough — for now.

"Gemma and Evelle. The crew," said Mara, stunned.

Evelle!

Karic activated a link. "Ryal. We're evacuating to the suspension room. Is the standby sequence complete?"

"Almost. I need ten minutes," came Ryal's voice across the link.

Karic swore. "Get there as soon as you can."

"Roger that. Ryal out."

"Shipcom, we need to lock down the command deck," said Karic.

"Commander. Order confirmation?" queried the Shipcom.

"Yes. Complete lockdown," said Janzen. His voice shook, his blue eyes glassy.

The field of glowing icons vanished and the big screens deactivated.

"Everyone, follow as quick as you can," said Karic, running for the narrow hatch that opened onto the vertical accessway between habitat levels. The hatch slid into its recess and he slipped inside. As he gripped the chrome rungs of the ladder, they stung his fingers with a mortuary chill. He looked up the cylindrical shaft to orient himself, blinking in the harsh white light.

"We'll be right behind you," called Mara, before the hatch snapped shut.

The walls of the shaft up to the ship's axis passed in a blur of conduits

28

and cables. His speed increased as the induced gravity fell away. At the top of the tube were two hatches. One, above his head, gave access to the ship's axis and main dock; the other, on his left, to the lowest level of the habitat. He extended one arm above his head to brace himself for impact while his left hand reached for the hatch release. Karic timed it perfectly — the benefit of long practice. He hit with a thud and the hatch to the habitat's lowest level shot open. He sprang through. Outside the tube, he pushed off the walls of the habitat corridor, half-running, half-flying as he raced to the suspension room. Inside, a chorus of alarms jangled in unison, warning lights casting hues of amber and red over the darkened interior. The room, at the lowest level of the rotating habitat, was close to the axis of the ship, and the floor showed a noticeable curve. The gravity here was one-third of Earth-normal.

Both Evelle and Gemma were on stasis couches, their supine forms wrapped in the shimmering nimbus of suspension fields, as immobile as statues. Evelle's long blonde hair was carefully coiffed around her pale face, like some space-age sleeping beauty waiting for a magic kiss. Gemma lay straight and rigid, the posture so typical of the slim redhead, her severe, close-cropped hair standing in spikes as prickly as her combative personality. That much appeared normal. Yet instead of the usual whitish haze, the collapsing suspension fields were shot with ragged veins of blue, red and green, the surging fields skewed by the incoming radiation.

Careful to compensate for the lowered gravity, he closed the distance between the hatch and the workstation in two long strides, his feet lifting slightly off the deck with each step. He steadied himself on the console and switched the screen to the monitor feed from the crew's suspension chamber. Like here, the room was lit with flashing warning lights. The crew's suspension fields, not in the midst of a recovery cycle, were more stable. He panned and magnified the feed. A sickening taste of bile rose in his throat as he saw the burns on the motionless faces and hands. Their cellular tissue — held in a delicate state of enforced equilibrium — was being torn to shreds. The horror of it burned into his retinas. Soon, the suspension fields would be preserving nothing more than corpses, warped beyond recognition by the radiation.

For a long moment, he could not take his eyes away. He watched the face of Bolan, the chief warrant officer, char to black. Rotund, energetic, prone to pranks that endeared him to his shift crew, his voice would never be heard again. On the couch beside him was tiny Resk, a gentle biosystems tech who worked with Evelle, her slim hands curling like claws as they reddened. Her delicate face sinking into itself like a melting waxwork.

Evelle.

Karic tore himself away from the footage, turning back to Evelle and

29

Gemma. Their revival process was incomplete, but the suspension fields were doing untold damage, transforming and destroying cells they were designed to insulate and protect. The technology was an intricate synthesis of field theory and cellular biochemistry. Carefully configured fields interacted with the electrochemistry of each cell, targeting key organic molecules, altering charges, shifting every single cell into an enforced equilibrium where chemical and electrical potential was reduced to zero. Where there was *no* action. Stasis from the inside out. No metabolism. No corruption. Just matter — as stable as a crystal lattice.

Now, instead of carefully restoring the pre-suspension biochemistry, a cellular wrecking ball was loose. The delicate balance in each cell was being randomized with each radiation-induced surge, the chain of chemicals that drove the machinery of the body twisted beyond recovery. Cell death would follow, leaving a wild, unpredictable trail of biological destruction.

He had no choice but to halt the process early and hope they could be revived.

Karic's fingers flew over the keyboard of the suspension computer.

The fields cut.

The life-sign monitors for both Evelle and Gemma began to scream with warning tones, adding to the alarms that already blared through the confined space. Both of their hearts had failed to start, the interrupted electrochemistry of the cardiac muscles too out of kilter. Without hesitation, Karic took a set of defibrillators from beneath the suspension couch and began to work on Evelle.

He ripped open her jacket. Her two lieutenant's bars flew off the faded fabric, hitting the wall with a series of *pings*. He applied the paddles. The first shock lifted her from the couch, but failed to start her heart. He tried again. Then again. Finally, her heart started, and she started breathing. Her eyes flickered open.

Then she screamed.

Evelle's limbs turned blue. She writhed on the couch. *The internal damage must be immense.* Her eyes rolled wildly, focusing on him without recognition. He grabbed a vial of morphine from the medical kit, took her arm in a clinch under his own, and injected the drug.

Gradually, her pain subsided.

Janzen appeared at the hatchway to the suspension room, followed by Ibri. The commander pushed across the room with too much force, his long arms and legs thumping into the wall. He stabilized himself, his eyes quickly scanning the revival status.

"You have cut the sequence," said Janzen. The tall commander checked Gemma's vitals then grimaced. "No pulse."

Mara and Andrai took in the situation in an instant and went to work on Gemma, trying frantically to revive her. But there was nothing they could do. Gemma was gone.

One look at Evelle told them Gemma had been the lucky one.

Evelle was in shock. Every few seconds, a tremor passed through her body. His arms around her, Karic looked across the room to Mara.

"What are the radiation levels?"

Mara quickly checked the screen. Her hands shook. "Still rising!"

Karic touched the screen of his comband, bringing it to life. "Ryal. Where are you?"

"Almost there, boss. Two minutes."

"Head straight for the central hold when you finish," said Karic.

"Understood. Ryal out."

A hot rage built in Karic. How could this have happened?

Using every shred of his willpower to contain the emotional firestorm inside him, Karic slowly lifted Evelle. Andrai stepped forward to help, but he shook his head. He could easily bear her weight in the low-g.

"*Go,*" hissed Karic.

Janzen was first out the door, followed by the rest of the crew. Andrai stayed close to Karic and Evelle, his eyes wide with concern. They all made their way in bouncing steps down the corridor to the access tube. There they passed through the hatch into the vertical accessway, then up through another hatch into the ship's axis, which was stationary relative to the habitat's gravity-inducing rotation. Andrai helped Karic to gently lift Evelle into the zero-g. She was still in shock, and looked around her with glazed eyes. Her body grew taut with every tremor, and she whimpered in pain.

They pushed through the zero-g to the huge hatch of the central hold, then passed through it. As they drifted into the hold — a vast open chamber more than four-hundred meters long — Karic blinked in the dim lighting. For a moment, it felt he had entered some alien space. He had forgotten to activate the dock lights, and could not pause to issue a command to the Shipcom through his comband. Crates and machinery brooded here, draped in shadow, floating in a three-dimensional space that made a mockery of planet-learned spacial reasoning. Their breath, coming fast, frosted in front of them. Everything was chilled by the inexorable heat-sink of deep space.

He sprang lightly from a strapped-down storage crate and drifted through the center of the dock with Evelle in his arms; the others followed on the same trajectory. He pushed off again, gaining speed, and sailing past the seven capsule-shaped emergency reentry pods, each fully fueled and ready for deployment.

The heavy lander emerged from the gloom.

Karic looked down at Evelle's face, creased in pain. Her eyes were getting focused now, as the shock wore off. By the sound of her tortured moans, the pain was worsening. He bit the inside of his cheek in frustration, tasting blood. Her situation seemed hopeless, but at least inside the lander, they would be able to give her some rudimentary medical help. He gritted his teeth and fixed his gaze on the landing craft, his eyes searching out its familiar contours for the entry hatch, his mind groping for anything to distract himself from his grim thoughts.

The vehicle stored here was only the core section of the full landing craft, which would be augmented for planetary landfall with external tanks. It was a big craft. An aerodynamic vehicle that owed its design lineage to a long line of spaceships dating back to the old NASA Space Shuttle. Like the reentry pods, it was a miracle of lightweight metals and ceramic that could alter its profile in-flight.

Karic braced himself as he hit the heavy lander's airlock. He hit the release, and they clambered into the cabin, each of them taking hold of something to halt their forward momentum and anchor themselves in the zero-g. The interior was outfitted with many handles for that specific purpose, padded to reduce the risk of injury. Lights blared, triggered by their movement, outlining the off-white synthetic fabric of the walls, floor, ceiling and chairs, and gleaming from the silvered steel of the console. The lander's flight-deck was compact, built on a square frame, designed to seat eight personnel in comfort — ten in an emergency. It took them into its steady embrace, enclosed them in familiar technology. The vehicle was heavily shielded in its own right. It would afford them the best protection they could get from the intense X-ray radiation. Ibri leant across to close the heavy outer hatch, lean muscles poised.

"Wait for Ryal," said Karic.

Mara tapped her comband. "Ryal. Where are you?"

There was nothing but static.

Janzen's face flushed red. "Ibri, close the hatch."

Bracing himself on a handle next to the hatch, Ibri pulled down the locking lever. The heavy hatch shut with a deep *boom*. The finality of the sound was unnerving. The lanky tech touched the hatch sensor and the internal locking bars slid into place with a low whir and click, securing the outer hatch to the hull. A moment later, the internal hatch whispered from its niche and enclosed the tiny decompression space between the two doors.

What about Ryal? They turned to Janzen with the unspoken question.

"We'll open it when he's outside," said Janzen.

Evelle's tremors had ceased and she was becoming more lucid. Most of the cellular damage was to her thickset lower body, which was swollen and misshapen. Her soft round face and lustrous, long blonde hair were untouched. Her lips were terribly pale. Her green eyes glowed against her pallid skin. Karic brushed strands of her sweat-damp hair away from her face.

"Karic. What is it, Karic? What's happened?" She looked down at her lower body and broke down in tears.

"You can survive it. You can. As soon as the radiation levels lower, we will get you back into stasis. On Earth, they have the best facilities ..."

Evelle nodded, growing calmer, more certain. Fully aware now, she watched the lander's small screen with the others as the intensity of the radiation continued to climb to lethal levels throughout the rest of the ship. "Karic, the crew? What about the crew?"

Karic shook his head. He saw Resk's face again, burning to a withered husk.

"The biodome," whispered Evelle.

There was no hope that any of the stored biological material would survive this. Whatever happened, the dome was lost to them. That meant surviving on rations and relying on chemical purifiers for their air. But there was something deeper about the loss. Those living things had been a very real link to Earth.

Evelle listened quietly as Karic told the whole story, from his detection of the radiation levels to his decision to begin the revival sequence. But then the morphine wore off, and the tremors worsened.

"You did the right thing. The only thing you could have. If Janzen hadn't cancelled the revival. They ... they would be alive."

It was true. And if Karic had not acted as he had, only he and Ryal would have been able to make it to the safety of the lander. The surviving crew turned to Janzen, drawn by the shared realization. Mara's eyes were hot with accusation. Andrai was stunned, his gray eyes, usually lit with humor, now darkened. Ibri alone seemed unshaken. The tall tech's dark eyes were fixed on Janzen with a sort of hunger, an eager fascination with the horror of the moment. The commander remained silent, his blue eyes distant.

"Ryal, come in?" said Mara across the link. *Static.*

"Shipcom. What is the status of the fusion drive?" asked Karic.

"Fusion drive is now in standby mode."

Karic felt a heavy weight settle into the pit of his stomach. Ryal had sacrificed himself to save them. He could not have survived out there. He must have collapsed in some narrow accessway on his way back from the fusion plant at the rear of the ship — and died there. Alone.

Hours passed. There was no reply from Ryal and Evelle's condition worsened. She began to cough up blood, the perfect droplets making ghastly clouds in the zero-g that drifted inexorably toward them in the confined space. Mara worked in grim silence with a handheld fluid vacuum-cleaner to intercept them, but crimson splashed the walls where

33

the blood escaped her. Evelle's face grew deathly white, while her abdomen continued to swell. Her eyes took on a glassy clarity. Unearthly. Frightening.

"I won't make it ..." said Evelle, shaking with fear, pain and shock.

"You will, Evelle. You will," said Karic, but he knew she was dying. Bleeding internally. He sat beside her, holding her hand. Karic cursed the order of the revival sequence. But who would he have die in her place? Mara?

"Tell me ... love me," said Evelle. Blood rouged her lips.

Karic's heart tore with guilt. Throughout all the years of their separation, the long years when their marriage faded from love to a companionable distance, never once had Evelle spoken like this. His feelings for her had simply faded. When he had told her of Mara, she had seemed so understanding. He thought it was all the same for her. Only now did he realized how terribly wrong he had been. She had never, ever, stopped loving him. Letting him go was a sacrifice she had made: for him. Yet she had never said a word, supporting him even though he broke her heart. The crew's promotional tour must have been torture for her. The same torture he was experiencing now with Mara.

"God, forgive me, Evelle. Forgive me." The guilt and pain were overwhelming. Beside him, Evelle's body was cold. Strange. Now, only as she lay dying, did the years roll away to reveal the love he still felt for her. Once more they were two eager young scientists, sharing their life, their work, their dreams ...

Karic stared into Evelle's eyes. "I do love you, Evelle."

Through the pain, the terror of death, she managed to smile.

Evelle reached up slowly and touched his cheek. Sweat broke out on her brow with the effort of movement. Her eyes filled with pain, but the tremors slowed.

"Lead them home, Karic."

Karic's heart raced like a stallion, running in fear. "Just try and relax." She shook her head.

"... dying. Ship is dying. Not built to survive — this. Crew ... Biodome. Gone."

Her hand fell back to her side, lifeless. For a long minute, she concentrated on breathing, her eyes filled with determination. Bubbles of blood filled her mouth, and Karic gently wiped them away.

"This is not ... company field trip anymore. This is survival. Janzen cannot lead. Not through this. Must be you. Take command. Otherwise," she took a rattling breath, "no one will survive."

Not even at Epsilon Eridani, when he and Janzen had their first serious clash, had he considered taking command. He feared the power of ExploreCorp. They were one of the few corporations big enough to fund space travel. They had absolute power over their own operations, and would remove him from subsequent missions without a second thought if it suited them. He could not let his dream die, not that way. Not after all the sacrifices he had made. Yet, if he had taken command at Epsilon Eridani, thirty-three men and woman would still be alive. Evelle …

She grew increasingly lethargic. Overcome with pain, she began to cry.

"I don't want to die here. Not so far from home … hold me." Karic tightened his arms around her.

Evelle convulsed in pain. Her abdomen swelled to a huge size, then she collapsed. Her heart had stopped. Despite their best efforts to revive her once more, she was gone.

Karic knelt beside her, cold and empty. He had taken her for granted. What he had understood as an amicable decision to keep working with him must have been a desperate attempt to keep him in her life, at any cost. He was humbled. "She never said a word," whispered Karic to himself.

"The radiation is starting to level off," said Mara.

"OK," said Janzen, in an authoritative voice, "everyone prepare to get back to their stations. We will need a full damage report." He looked around at the silent crewmembers.

"A friggin' damage report?" snapped Mara. "What about Ryal!"

Janzen's eyes flicked rapidly between their stony faces. He raised his hands in a conciliatory gesture. "All respect to the dead, Mara. We need to keep this ship — and ourselves — alive."

"You make me sick, Janzen. What's the matter? Worried about the cost of the repairs? Well, at least there are thirty-three less people you have to pay!" Mara's eyes blazed.

Janzen tilted his head back and looked down at her. "Mara — I think that is quite enough."

Karic's pain and anger surged inside him. He wanted to strike out at Janzen. If not for him, those thirty-three people would be alive right now. Yet the commander was right. They had to stay focused. The intensity of his feelings burned away, leaving a numb acceptance in their wake. The fact that he had been right was no consolation at all.

"We have to deal with the situation, Mara," said Karic softly. "That comes first."

Janzen's gaze rested on Karic for a moment, where he held Evelle's still body. Droplets of blood floated from the corner of her mouth, leaking into the zero-g in a silent, incarnadine procession.

The commander straightened as much as the zero-g allowed, bracing himself between the floor and a handle on the roof. He lowered the left data-screen of his odin. "Everyone to your stations. We have a lot of work to do." Ibri left right behind Janzen. Mara hesitated, her body rigid with tension, then she followed.

Karic's blood pulsed at his temples, the air shimmering. Two whirlpools turned in his mind. Eyes that glowed with satisfaction. Huge, alien eyes. Karic shook his head.

Andrai drifted over to Karic, his body slouched in the zero-g. He stopped himself with a hand on Karic's shoulder. His hand tightened in silent support.

"I'll help you with Evelle," said Andrai.

Chapter 3

The observation bubble was hot and confined. Mara watched the flickering display of the radiation meter anxiously, fearing another surge. The shielding on the starship's hull would not help her here. If another X-ray burst arrived without warning, she would receive no protection from the thin transparent capsule.

They had been out of suspension for weeks now, drifting in a crippled vessel. The habitat still rotated, providing artificial gravity, mimicking the distant hand of Earth now over eleven lightyears — a lifetime — away.

Far out on either side of the ship, the bulky housings of the forward shield generators flanked her like an escort of squat industrial buildings, while stretching out ahead of the ship, like a needle, was the forward laser. Intended for use in prospecting operations, it could vaporize the surface of small comets and rocky asteroids so that the spectrographs on the *Starburst* could analyze their composition. From the forward laser and deflectors to the fusion drive at the rear *Starburst* was more than a kilometer long. It was built on a thin central axis with the rotating habitat in the center and the elegant, bell-shaped fusion drive trailing three hundred meters behind.

Her body was covered in sweat, and her thin white shirt clung to her breasts. The cooling systems had been destroyed in the surge that killed the crew. Even in light clothes, the temperature of the powered-up ship was stifling, the heat leakage from equipment far exceeding the gradual radiative losses through the hull.

As uncomfortable as she felt, there was beauty around her, and a welcome sense of peace. Within the observation dome, it seemed as though she was suspended alone amid all the vastness of space. Thousands of stars covered the dark blanket of the void with brilliant majesty. And one of these suns, amid the multitude, was more than a mere pin-prick, appearing instead as a small disk. Tau Ceti. It was this star and its progeny that she scrutinized through the small optical telescope, painstakingly recording astronomical data.

Somewhere close by was the source of the X-rays. She had studied nearby space for long painful weeks with manual instruments, trying to find something, *anything* that could be emitting the radiation. At first, it seemed it must be the small yellow sun, but now she knew it was not. It was something close to the sun. But how could a stellar object leaking this sort of radiation stay hidden that close to Tau Ceti?

As ship's astronomer, it was her job to find out what had caused the radiation surge, and she was determined to unravel the mystery. She had joined the *Starburst*'s crew only months before the launch, after her mentor Professor James Montague — originally selected as the *Starburst*'s astronomer — died of a heart attack. It was the opportunity of a lifetime, and Mara was determined to prove herself on her own terms. She did not want to think about the severe damage the ship had taken, their chances of survival … or Karic. She had been determined to keep everything neat and professional with the sub-commander, but she could never have anticipated the deaths, and the stresses this disaster had put them under.

All through the long year spent in training together, and the months of commissioning that followed, Karic had inspired them with a sense of purpose and energy. His brilliance and drive were compelling. She had been drawn to him, and their spontaneous affair had quickly blossomed into a passionate relationship. Mara, a hardworking academic who had little time for romance, had been swept to dizzy heights by its intensity, experiencing a depth of feeling she had not thought possible. He had seemed unstoppable, and she had stepped inside that whirlwind. She had loved his dream, loved his ambition. Loved him, desperately. At that time, she was only a post-doc researcher on the mission, a lead scientist on the team led by Professor Montague.

Then came the storm of publicity that led up to the launch of the mission. The ExploreCorp public relations gurus had gone into overdrive. With a married couple on the mission — Karic and Evelle — they had seized the opportunity to promote them as the New Age Robinsons, like the iconic pair from the 20th century classic, Lost in Space. Despite the fact that Karic's marriage was a fiction, and that he and Evelle had been estranged since before the affair, despite the fact that it made a lie of Karic and Mara's love.

Mara had laughed at the idea when she first heard it. Then she had seen the look on Karic's face. "Necessary" was the word he used. "It means nothing," he said to reassure her. Just a publicity stunt. Yet it would make their love a hidden, dirty thing in the eyes of the public who wanted a fairy tale. Something to keep hidden lest it endanger the almighty ExploreCorp machine and its quest for financial backers. Mara had believed she was the center of Karic's life. Instead she realized she was a fiction that could be moved into some hidden compartment when it suited Karic. Mara had learned the hard way that the mission was what he had really cared about. She had been nothing but a sweetener to highlight the completion of his true passion — the *Starburst*. It had made her feel worthless. A betrayal that ripped her to the core and made a wreck of her love. The long months while Karic and Evelle toured the world, feted by the high and mighty, were bitter times of isolation for her, when all the memories of their time together, revisited again and again in her loneliness, had become a torn minefield of conflicting emotions, a landscape of bittersweet pain. "It meant nothing?" *She* had meant nothing — to Karic. At first she had answered his messages and vidcalls with brief banalities, then angry outbursts. Then she had stopped responding at all. Her desire for him transformed into a hard conviction. She refused to be shunted aside when it was convenient. She had vowed never to give him a second chance, throwing herself into her work.

Once more, she adjusted the optical instrument and meticulously recorded the position of the planet she was studying, entering another set of data through a manual keypad. Damn! Why did the computer have to fail? For the thousandth time she cursed Janzen for not giving them more time to study Tau Ceti before they set off from Epsilon Eridani. Mara stabbed at the buttons of her keypad. A vital clue was missing. The problem nagged at her, but the solution remained out of reach. She was dying to run her data through her astronomical programs, but that would have to wait until Ibri and Andrai had the Shipcom up and running again.

A flash of light came from the left deflector — charged ions of interstellar gas fluorescing as they were shunted away from the bow of the ship. Behind her, the metallic bulk of the *Starburst* was impassive and silent.

Sighing, Mara bent down toward the eyepiece of the telescope.

The observation bubble was on the ship's axis, remaining still as the habitat ring rotated. It was designed as a relaxation chamber, and Mara never would have imagined she would be taking manual observations here; not with the billion-dollar sensors arrayed along the hull and the powerful computer housed at the core of the ship.

A harsh tone sounded through the bubble. The alarm on her comband. Her shift was up. She looked out into space, exhausted by the twelve-hour stint.

Mara released the straps of the seat harness and propelled herself through the tiny space. As she moved, her hair spread out from her head like a dark Medusa's mane. She tied it back with a swift, efficient movement, then pulled herself along the central accessway back toward the habitat. There were only two ways back into the rotating section — at either end of the central hold where the big seals were. She exited the accessway into the huge open space of the main docking bay, just forward of the central hold. The big hold doors — wide enough to accommodate a fully fueled landing craft — were ahead of her, the big exit doors to space on her left. She fought disorientation, and just for a moment, the vast bay with its articulated docking arms spun around her. Mara fixed her gaze on the habitat access hatch and pushed off. She sailed through the zero-g of the docking bay to the rotating bulkhead above her and her palm slapped neatly onto a grip. She steadied herself and touched a sensor to open the hatch, swung herself around and dropped into the vertical shaft that led to the habitat levels. The hatchway thudded shut behind her once she was inside, and she began her descent, the centrifugal force gripping her more with each rung.

Nothing in the biodome had survived the accident. The harsh rattle and hum of the chemical purifiers now replaced the bio-filters, and the crew were living on borrowed time. Dealing with the dead had been a tough duty, but not as hard as being trapped in the lander and watching Karic hold Evelle as she died. Not as hard as listening to her dying words …

At the bottom of the shaft, fatigue weighed on her unexpectedly as a full gee of artificial gravity took hold. When she reached the main deck, she could hear raised voices from the infirmary. Even muffled by the sealed door the tones were unmistakable. Karic and Janzen again. *Idiots!* Her weariness vanished. She clenched her jaw and closed the distance to the hatch in quick steps, triggering the sensor with a flick of her fingers and slipping inside, ready for anything.

Karic sat in one of the infirmary chairs, his uniform jacket carelessly discarded over a nearby bed. His arm was tied off with a rubber tourniquet, just above the elbow, and he was carefully injecting himself, the plunger of the syringe descending slowly. An empty vial stood on the desk beside him.

Janzen stood above him, his uniform coat sealed right to the neck despite the heat. His commander's badge glittered gold in the bright infirmary lights. The thick yellow band of his retracted odin — data-glasses used almost exclusively by the corporate world — ruined the military image. His short hair had grown unruly in the weeks out of suspension, but he was still an imposing figure.

"I am sure you are aware that I still need that analysis on the repair of the suspension equipment," said Janzen, scrolling through the display of a handheld electronic reader.

Karic's eyes fixed on Janzen. They were dilated, the black pupils grown to dominate the normal deep brown of his irises. His face was white and drawn, the wavy brown hair even more disheveled than usual. Karic, more than any of them, had been working around the clock to get the ship running.

"The sets are ruined, Janzen. We have to regain control of the drive. Then at least we can reach orbit."

"Of course, of course … I would agree that takes priority," said Janzen reasonably. "However, I still need to understand the damage. I need to know exactly how bad things are."

Janzen's insistence on detailed reports at every step was a drain on all of them, and at heart she supported Karic's focus on restoring the ship's systems. Yet to side with Karic openly against the commander would add another source of division when they could least afford it. She was furious at being put in this position. Her brief liaison with Janzen, the

ExploreCorp executive playboy, before she met Karic was another complicating factor. It had been no-strings-attached, and at the time, she had no idea they would all end up on a mission together.

Both of them were maddening.

Mara snatched up the vial and read the label. *Uppers.* "What the fuck do think this is going to solve?" said Mara, shaking the vial in front of Karic's face. "How soon before you can't even think straight?"

Janzen and Karic looked at Mara in surprise.

***

Karic put down the empty syringe and took off the tourniquet. He watched Mara carefully. *She looks exhausted.* Karic felt new clarity sweeping through his mind. The stim-tabs were no longer enough to keep the fugue at bay. How could he explain that to Mara? To any of them?

Ibri entered the room and stood just behind Janzen. His dark face was impassive, the deep-set eyes avoiding, yet his physical presence at Janzen's shoulder provided tacit support, bolstering the commander's authority. The lack of reaction from Janzen at Ibri's stance unnerved Karic, implying some sort of unspoken agreement between them.

Karic stood and rubbed his arm.

Andrai swept in through the doorway, smiling at Mara as he walked across the room to stand next to Karic. The blond tech was out of breath, and must have run through the length of the ship, no doubt hot on Ibri's heels. Karic felt the warmth of gratitude. If the lanky tech was in Janzen's corner, than Andrai was definitely in Karic's.

"Maybe you can explain to me how I can write a report on the repair of the suspension equipment when they cannot be repaired? The suspension equipment is finished," said Karic.

Andrai helped Karic assess the damage and knew how bad it was. Ibri's dark eyes met Karic's, stunned. The empty vial slipped from Mara's fingers to clatter on the floor. Her face grew ashen.

Janzen seemed unmoved. This puzzled Karic. He would have thought the news would devastate him. It meant the end of any chance for a resounding success from the mission. Their hopes for survival now rested on the Tau Ceti target planet. If it could support life, then they had a chance — but there would be no return to Earth.

Janzen scanned their faces, his penetrating blue eyes calculating, weighing. His voice was warm, resonant, pitched to fill a room twice the size of the infirmary. "We need to all pull together with a shared purpose — that's the key to our survival. There is always a way if we can all put our minds to it. Always other options."

Karic shook his head in bewilderment. "What are you talking about,

Janzen? What options?"

Janzen tilted his head back in an unconscious gesture. "We all need to do our part. If you can deliver that report by the ten o'clock meeting, Karic, we can deal with all of this as a team."

With that thought lingering in the air, Janzen left the room, Ibri behind him. Karic understood Janzen, this demand for detailed reports was his way of trying to get control of the situation. Yet, since the incident, he had seen something else in the commander. A distance. A cool calculation. Was this something unnatural? A consequence of shock? Or had the crisis stripped away an outer layer of pretense revealing what was there all along? The thought was unsettling.

Mara's face twisted into an angry frown. "There are only five of us, Karic. We have to work together, or can't that penetrate the drugs in your brain?" Mara turned and strode from the room, calling over her shoulder. "Some of us have work to do."

Andrai watched her walk away, his eyes drawn to her slim hips and the shapes of her legs in the form-fitting uniform. Sensing Karic watching him, the tech looked away quickly.

The full force of the drug hit, then. His heart hammered. His mind was full of plans. New configurations for the jury-rigged fusion control system, ways to bring the fission reactor back out of a dangerous reaction zone. Karic started pacing the infirmary.

"You OK, boss?" asked Andrai.

"Yes, Andrai." Karic smiled at the good-natured tech.

"Listen. Over the last few weeks … Thanks for your help."

Andrai shrugged his shoulders. "I can read the writing on the wall as well as anyone. Janzen has no idea how to deal with this — even if he thinks he does."

"Janzen is doing what he knows. He is a good man, but he's not the man for this, Andrai. I no longer trust his judgment."

"What do you want me to do?"

"We have to get control of the fusion drive. If we can't decelerate we will pass right through the Tau Ceti system. Then we are finished."

"OK. Right. I'll get back to the plant and pick up where we left off."

"Good. Thanks, Andrai. We'll beat it. It's only a matter of time."

Andrai sauntered out of the room, a slight smile on his face.

Karic picked up the vial and syringe and dropped them into the secure disposal. He was shocked to see how many discarded vials were inside. All were his.

"What are you trying to do, Karic?" he asked himself. He had told Andrai he was sleeping two to three hours a night. The truth was he had stopped sleeping at all. His body could not take much more of this. But with so much of the ship damaged, he could not afford to slip. He had to resist the fugue. Any sleep, even a short rest with his eyes closed, seemed to bring it on now. It was growing stranger too, the visions were increasing in complexity, clarity.

He raised a hand to his head. The pain was intense. But pain he could deal with.

Karic walked swiftly to the door, giving vent to the restless energy released by the drug. He had to get to the fusion plant to help Andrai.

He walked to the rear of the habitat section and climbed up the shaft to the axis. He sighed with relief as the pull of artificial gravity left his fatigued limbs. He pulled himself out through the top hatch and pushed off, sailing through the zero-g no-man's-land between the rear end of the cylindrical central hold and the accessway that trailed out behind the ship to the fission reactor and the fusion drive. The air was hot and stale here, and he suppressed the sense of anxiety the space always provoked in him. A truncated cone with sides that sloped down to the diameter of the rear accessway, it was a place that said: *be elsewhere*. The spatial confusion did not help either. Karic felt a moment of disorientation as his frame of reference shifted. Above him the hatch to the access shaft now rotated with the motion of the habitat, while the big doors to the dock behind him and hatch he was drifting toward became stationary. Light gray metal bulkheads arched overhead, the stark struts and beams like illicit visions of the *Starburst*'s secret heart. The high-tech anti-corrosion coatings had held well in the dry environment, yet there was always some moisture. The red-orange blooms of rust tinted the gray paintwork on some of the welds. *Time is the natural enemy of the works of man.*

He pushed through the hatch into the access tunnel. His stomach churned and his throat tightened. The burnt, rotten smell still lingered. This was where he found Ryal. There had been nothing left of the thin, energetic man he knew. Nothing but a burned corpse, tattered uniform hanging in strips, the close-cropped hair still horribly the same above a ruined face with glassy, withered eyes. Blood and fluids had surrounded him in a cloud, like some ghastly nebula.

Karic shook off the memory and pulled himself along the accessway toward the bright lights of the reactor control room, going faster and faster — as though he could leave that memory, and the images of the other dead, behind him. The dead were all together now, in one chamber off the central hold, open to vacuum, slowly cooling to ice as the last of their warmth radiated inexorably into space. Karic began to sweat with the exertion. He cried out in sudden fear as he lost his grip on the rungs, slamming his head into the side of the shaft. He lay curled into a ball, bumping down the corridor under his own momentum.

Andrai was at his side. "Boss! What is it?"

Karic could not speak. *The nausea. The pain.*

"I'm taking you back to your cabin," said Andrai.

Karic tried to protest, but nothing but a groan came from his lips.

Andrai guided him gently up the accessway, then into the lowest level of the habitat, where the sleeping quarters were located. By the time they reached the cabin door, Karic had recovered sufficiently to master his voice. His ideas flooded out in a torrent. Andrai listened intently to Karic's instructions, nodding to acknowledge each key point.

Andrai hit the door release. It slid open with a soft sigh.

"Don't worry, boss. I'll keep working on it. A few hours of sleep will do you good."

"You're right, Andrai."

He had pushed himself for long enough. His body needed rest.

Karic pushed himself gently across the room, slipping into his sleeping sheath. The shiny plastic fabric felt cool and rough on his drug-sensitized skin. Around him, the walls enclosed him in a suffocating gray embrace.

"OK. I'll come to wake you at the end of the shift," said Andrai, as he exited the tiny cabin.

Karic was alone.

For hours he lay awake, forcing himself to lay still despite the drug pumping through his system. Eventually, darkness claimed him.

Then the dream began again.

It always started with a silent scream. Karic would stand immobile, unable to move, barely awake, as Evelle slipped away from him. The radiation would appear before his mind's eye like the blaze of dawn in orbit, blinding, and beneath this heat, Evelle's body would appear burnt and smoking. A dead thing. Yet there she would be, floating above her body, hand outstretched toward him, fighting against a savage wind that tore at her, clawing at the bright substance of her being, impelling her to be away. She would scream, and he would feel it amid the silence and struggle to move toward her, his whole core longing to join with her and take flight. But slowly, she would slip away, lost eternally with each moment. Then she would be gone. The blaze would continue, peaking finally in a surge of power before fading.

Then the presence would appear, floating outside the ship, a mass of undefined energy with two hate-filled eyes. He was convinced now it had come to watch them die, hot with desire for their destruction.

Karic woke in confusion, the eyes of the watcher still upon him, lingering ghostly amid the clarion call of the ship's alarm. It sounded in deafening waves from the speaker above him. Fighting weakness, he unzipped his sleeping sheath and floated across the room to get away from the speaker. The low-g gradually took him down to the floor, but allowed him plenty of time to flip himself around and get the soft polymer surface under his feet.

Karic looked at his communicator. Four hours had passed.

He touched a small button on his comband and croaked, "What is it?"

It was Ibri who responded, his voice mocking, "Meeting in ten. Janzen and Mara already here."

The clarion stopped.

Karic settled into a chair, his hands pressed to his temples. He had a pounding headache. His body felt weak, filled with the soul-numbing lethargy that followed the uppers. Usually he would be heading for the infirmary now. But the dangerous feeling of weakness in his body — and the incident in the access tunnel — told him it was time to stop. Trying to assemble his thoughts and clear the fog in his head, it was hard not to want that white diamond of instant clarity that the drug would deliver. That wave of energy that would banish all the negative thoughts.

Thoughts that beckoned him now.

This was the end of his life's dream of space exploration. He would die without ever touching another world. He had lost Mara, Evelle ... everything. The suspension equipment was destroyed, despite triple redundancy, his best designs and the shielding. The only thing he had left was the determination to give them every edge he could before survival became impossible. Perhaps if they could stabilize the ship's systems, get control of the drive, they would still be able to achieve something, discover something remarkable before the last hours would arrive, with *Starburst* ceasing to be a starship and becoming instead their mausoleum, cooling steadily in the depths of space, even while their last transmission sped toward Earth.

Now was the most dangerous time. The time when he could slip into the fugue state so easily. But he could not afford that, not with the crew waiting for him.

His body was soaked in stale sweat, muscles stiff and taut from constant work and fatigue.

He pushed himself upright.

Karic washed his body in the stale fluids which the ship recycled and dressed in dry clothes, combing back his wavy hair, which he kept short in an attempt to control its willful nature. He looked at himself critically in the mirror for the first time in weeks and saw a stranger. Older than he remembered. Worn out. Face leaner, cheekbones even sharper.

Karic turned and left his cabin for the conference room.

As he worked his way down the shaft to the main deck, his mind worked over the familiar problem of Janzen. There was something odd about the commander's decision to make for Tau Ceti — then a mostly unknown system. Janzen was always strategic, trying to stay one step ahead of the game. He always took the time to think things through. Yet when their exploration of Epsilon Eridani had proved a disappointment

— based on a misleading analysis of their original target system — Janzen had immediately commanded the ship to divert to Tau Ceti. From what he knew of the commander, he would have expected the opposite response: a call for caution and careful planning.

Having descended to the main deck, Karic made his way through the control room to the conference room. The fatigue in his body seemed worse in the full gravity and he felt every hour of the missing sleep. He paused on the threshold of the room and took a breath. The room was compact and tastefully furnished with faux wood paneling. The white polymer-glass table gleamed in the overhead lights, and the form-fitting metal chairs would not have been out of place in an Earth-side boardroom. It was a familiar, comfortable space for Karic. He must have spent thousands of hours in here, teasing out technical problems with his team, directing operations ... those times seemed impossibly carefree now.

All five of the surviving crew assembled, and he observed them with a clear head for the first time in many days. Janzen's blond hair was immaculately styled, the blue eyes startling in his handsome face. The classic Davis looks that inspired confidence in their corporate machine and raised them to the status of celebrities. So familiar across Earth on vid-links and electronic billboards.

"Sit down, Karic," said Janzen, shifting in his seat. A smile played on his lips. It amazed Karic how Janzen managed to maintain his confidence in the face of this disaster. It made Karic question himself.

Ibri's dark, deep-set eyes were fixed on Karic. The direct stare from the lanky tech, sitting now at Janzen's left, was unusual, and Karic felt some undercurrent of contempt that had overcome his passivity. Mara fidgeted with her e-reader and adjusted her hair, strangely distracted. Andrai was slouched over the table, looking tired and bored, and nodded in greeting.

Karic sank into a chair. Janzen signaled Ibri to begin. Their situation was not good. The core processors that drove the Shipcom's artificial intelligence functions were badly damaged, with more than half the ship's sensors and all the robotic control units out of service.

"Any indications on what caused the surge, Mara?" asked Janzen.

Mara shook her head, spots of color rising on each cheek. "Nothing. I have been observing the system for days now, but haven't been able to make any sense out the figures. Tau Ceti has a family of large terrestrial planets. Only the one orbiting at 0.55 AU shows any possibility of being an Earth-analogue. It's right on the edge of the habitable zone and spectral analysis has shown indications of oxygen and water. We've known its mass for some time — over four times Earth's — but now we've managed to get an accurate size. Its radius indicates a lower density than Earth, not surprising given Tau Ceti's low metallicity, putting the surface gravity a little over 1.2 gees."

"Excellent news, Mara," said Janzen.

"But it's still impossible to say if the planet has an Earth-like atmosphere," said Mara. "It's on the hot edge of the habitable zone. It could be a super-Venus. Heavy gases like carbon dioxide would make it a hell planet."

"What about the planet at 1.35 AU?" asked Karic.

"It's right on the outside edge of the habitable zone," said Mara. "The light atmosphere has worked against it. It's a frozen planet. Despite the low density, its mass still makes its gravity just a little too high for colonization, around 1.4 gees."

"Is Tau Ceti the source of the radiation?" prompted Janzen.

"I don't think so." Mara sighed in frustration. "I need more computing power and use of the remaining ship's sensors. I will never get enough data manually."

Ibri leaned forward, looming over the table. "I need priority. I have to get the AI operating."

"I agree that the Shipcom is a priority, Ibri, but we need the astronomical programs online first to understand what danger we are in. I am sure you understand," said Janzen.

Ibri looked like he had just tasted something sour. His dark eyes fixed on Mara with a feral gleam.

Janzen turned to Karic, his eyes cold, assessing, despite his affable expression.

"Karic, perhaps you can give us your report on the state of the suspension equipment?"

The crew turned to Karic.

"All the suspension equipment is destroyed and completely beyond repair. That's my report."

The room was silent, and the crew sat unmoving, all other concerns put aside.

Janzen straightened in his chair, then smiled. There was something predatory in the commander's expression.

"This was to remain a contingency," said Janzen. "But there are eight additional sets of suspension gear in storage in the heavy lander. They were to be kept secret until every other avenue failed. The additional shielding should have protected them." He turned to Karic. "I expect you to check them out immediately."

For a brief moment, there was no sound as relief swept through the assembled crew, then the air was full of excited questions.

"Kept secret!" A wave of adrenaline rushed through Karic, banishing his headache instantly. A second set of equipment. Another chance at survival. He shook his head in amazement, wondering how ExploreCorp techs had managed to smuggle the sets on board without his knowledge.

Yet none of that mattered now. Karic had new hope. They could all look toward a future again. He could save them — save the ship — and his voyage of discovery. His dream of space exploration was alive!

Then something clicked into place in his head. The lander was very tight on storage space. The only reason sets would be hidden on the lander was if someone knew about the radiation danger — *even before the ship had left Earth orbit.* Janzen had known about it all. He had known about the oxygen-water signature of the unknown system, and the radiation. He had kept it as a secret backup plan in case Epsilon Eridani had not been all he hoped. *That* was why he had been so confident about the radiation levels — and why he had been so shocked when they spiked. He had been expecting non-lethal levels.

There was a loud rushing in Karic's ears as his thoughts tumbled on. Janzen had known about the radiation, but had put them all at risk anyway, unwilling to forgo the financial success of the mission. Evelle, Ryal, Gemma and the rest of the crew — they would all be alive now if they had kept station at Epsilon Eridani.

Karic slowly rose to his feet. The others fell silent. "You knew, didn't you?"

Janzen tilted his head back and stared at Karic from beneath his odin. There was a telling pause before his reply. The commander's piercing blue eyes flicked to the side as he thought rapidly, then he turned back to the group. "We have a fresh opportunity here. It's important that we all work together, that we all look forward. As a team, we have to focus on the future."

This is not the scenario. That's what Janzen had said when the spike had hit. At the time Karic had put it down to shock, but Janzen had already been expecting a radiation threat — just not as lethal.

"You knew about the radiation risk in the Tau Ceti system. Even before we left Earth," said Karic.

Janzen smile remained fixed, but his eyes gave him away. They darted across the room. Karic had caught him off guard. *My God. It's true.*

"Karic, I think you should wait until those drugs you have been taking leave your system before you start making accusations."

Janzen adjusted the position of his electronic notepad on the desk and looked up. He swept his gaze across the crew, then back to Karic. He straightened in his chair and tilted his head back once more, his head shaking with a kind of swagger. Karic's heart burned with anger. Instinctively, Karic knew that Janzen had been waiting for someone to make the connection — and would have all the right answers ready for them.

A cold wash of reality came across Karic. What he had seen as friendship had been nothing more than a convenient partnership — one that had benefited Janzen. This had always been about profit. The whispers of the ruthless Davis family — that he had always dismissed — now came back to him. Political opponents who were discredited and disgraced. Difficult employees who ended up in prison on fraud charges. Others who died in sudden accidents. He had hoped Janzen was different. *Believed* he was different. The sense of betrayal was acute.

Karic was shaken. He had let Janzen sway him. He had accepted his reassurances when he cancelled the revival process for the crew. He should have realized. If he had fought harder, if he had challenged Janzen right at the outset — reinstated the revival process — the crew could have been saved. Now he felt that blood on his own hands.

"Think, Karic. How could it be true?" said Mara. "Janzen would be putting himself at risk as well."

Karic nodded. "Yes, that's true. He would not have expected the amount of radiation we were hit with. But he would have based his decision on data from Earth satellites, while the radiation we have been monitoring is directional. Earth would not have detected most of it."

"But what other evidence do you have?" continued Mara.

"The spare suspension sets. They are bulky. They would have had to dismantle them to get them into the lander at all. They would need a very good reason to do that."

Mara's eyes narrowed. She was silent as she considered the implications.

"The lander is the most heavily shielded area of the ship," said Karic. "The best place to put anything if you were concerned about radiation damage."

"Come now, Karic. This speculation doesn't benefit any of us." Janzen's voice remained smooth. Reasonable. "We have to all pull together — now more than ever. As for the decision to put the sets in the lander, it was for … security."

Karic looked at the commander's perfect face, the steady smile. The lie was effortless, his piercing blue eyes as clear as a summer's day. Karic's stomach flipped as he realized he would have to reevaluate every single thing this man had ever said to him. How could he have misjudged him so badly?

"It's credible," said Mara.

"There are a thousand better places to store suspension sets on this ship, Mara, and you know it," said Karic.

"That does not justify trying to kill someone! Even if Janzen deceived us, he would not have known he was putting us in this sort of danger. Besides, you haven't proved anything," said Mara.

"Really?" said Karic. "Why don't you ask Janzen to open up his private files? He won't."

The commander smoothed back his hair. "Look. It's natural to be feeling a high degree of stress in this situation. Accusations don't help any of us. We need to put all this behind us and get on with the mission."

Mara was quiet for a moment. Then she looked directly at Janzen. "I agree with Karic. The best way to settle this is for you to open up your files, Commander. Then we can see for ourselves you had no plans to make for Tau Ceti."

"You must understand that is out of the question." Janzen gave them a patronizing smile. "It would mean compromising ExploreCorp security codes that I am honor-bound to protect."

Mara looked across to Karic. She was starting to believe him.

"What else are you holding back from us, Janzen?" asked Karic.

Janzen ignored the question.

"I want you all working on the control of the fusion drive. In the meantime, we must characterize the source of the radiation. I want Ibri and Mara to work together getting the sensors back online. Andrai, you keep working with Karic."

Ibri frowned, displeased. He clearly thought that astronomy was secondary to the restoration of the Shipcom.

"What if another X-ray surge hits us?" asked Andrai. "How will we protect ourselves? Not even the shielding on the lander might protect us if the source is in the Tau Ceti system — we are getting closer to it."

Janzen straightened in his chair and smiled, displaying a glib confidence. Karic was watching him carefully. He was back on familiar territory. All this had been worked out in advance.

"There is no better radiation shield than a planet. As soon as we have full control of the fusion drive, and the sets have been put together, we will make for the planet at 0.55 AU from Tau Ceti.

"That will be all for now."

Janzen swept from the room, his exit spoiled by the need to duck under the lintel. Ibri was hot on his heels. "The AI is crucial. Hundreds of systems …" Ibri's voice trailed off as he disappeared into the corridor.

"Whatever the truth, it does not change what we need to do." Mara pushed herself to her feet and looked Karic up and down. "For God's sake, clean yourself up," she said, walking out of the room.

"Do you think we can survive this?" asked Andrai.

Karic smiled. "With functioning suspension equipment set up inside the lander …? We have a chance."

"What next?" asked Andrai.

Karic stood. A cold conviction hardened inside him. Evelle was right. If they were to survive this, he could not let Janzen make one more operational decision. The commander had shown himself to be a cold-blooded opportunist that would weigh human life against profit like an accountant reconciling a business account. It sickened him.

What next?

"I remove Janzen from command."

Chapter 4

Karic wandered through a verdant wilderness — an endless twilight world — marveling at the absence of his pain.

Surely this is a paradise.

The leaves were broad and dripping with sweet moisture. Huge blossoms towered over the forest in a profusion of color, dwarfing the plants that gave them birth. Above, the sky was blue ebony, untroubled by the passing of time or the touch of sun or moon.

Karic could not guess how long he had wandered. He came to a deep tangle of green. Deep shadows writhed within the thicket, pulsing with change. Karic knew instinctively this change was forbidden. The hidden place needed protection if ever the crucial birth was to occur.

He drew closer, until he stood within the shadows. The darkness writhed at his feet then burst open, spraying him with the fluids of birth. Then brightness flared. Karic raised his arms to shield his eyes as something emerged, bright as a golden sun, flashing with brilliance. It flew past him, rising higher, and he was drawn into its substance as though swept heavenward on the breath of a god. He was rising, climbing higher, speeding with the joy of new life, onward toward a towering brilliance that even now stirred to receive him.

Karic.

He woke suddenly from a deep sleep, noting immediately that the pain in his head was gone. Above him the cabin lights flared into his eyes while the clarion pulsed angrily, surrounding him with confusion.

He tapped his comband. "What?"

It was Andrai, his voice excited. "We need you right away. The planet has an atmosphere, Karic. An atmosphere!"

***

Karic rushed into the conference room, his mind running in excited circles. He sought Mara out immediately.

"Is it oxygen-nitrogen? Are we close enough for a spectral analysis?"

Mara nodded, yet remained silent and aloof. Her fine-featured face was pale with tension.

Karic sat down, confused by the somber expressions of the assembled crew. The principal mission of the *Starburst* was to seek out Earth-like planets for settlement, and here — amid disaster — they may have found one. When Andrai told him they had found a planet with an atmosphere, he had dared to hope their mission would succeed, despite everything. Now he was unsure.

"How close to orbit?" asked Karic.

"Wait for your questions. There is something else ..." said Mara.

Something unpleasant judging by these long faces.

Janzen entered the room with measured poise. He was wearing a white commander's dress outfit with red trim, the bold red stripe down the arms and legs bright against the pure white fabric, giving him an authoritative, almost martial presence. He had a new red odin that matched perfectly. The comband on his wrist was a non-standard version, bright with diamonds and gold chasing. Karic knew that this was the news Janzen had been waiting for — confirmation of a habitable world.

Janzen sat down and nodded to Mara to start her presentation, totally unaware of the mood in the room.

"I finished the detailed spectral analysis an hour ago, and I have all the results, which are promising. Then, when the astronomical processors came back online, I ran my manual data and the raw data the sensors have been collecting on the system through the program."

She faltered.

Karic looked at Andrai. The usually relaxed tech was downcast and tense. Something was wrong.

Mara took a deep breath and continued.

"The planet is a super-Earth, 1.2 standard gee surface gravity, and has an oxygen-nitrogen atmosphere. The helium and argon content lighten it enough to give around one standard atmosphere of pressure on the surface. Very low greenhouse gases, hardly any carbon dioxide or methane, which is surprising. It also has a magnetosphere comparable to Earth's. But the temperature profiles —"

"Don't be so glum, Mara. That is excellent news," said Janzen. "We will be shipping back colonists in no time."

"I don't think so," said Mara.

"Why not?" asked Janzen, nonplussed. The commander looked around the room, a knot of tension appearing on his usually smooth forehead as he looked at Mara and Andrai's long faces.

"The astronomical program finished running just minutes ago. I haven't ... had time to tell you, but the program informed us of a black hole in the system. That is beyond a doubt the source of the radiation and particle surges. It must have been only recently captured by Tau Ceti, because it has not developed a large disk of gas around it. It was difficult to spot. But the computer pinned down its approximate orbit by analyzing the orbits of Tau Ceti and its planets. I still haven't found any trace of the gas ring optically, even knowing where to look. But it will be there."

"But something like that, it would have been detected from Earth, surely," protested Janzen.

"Ordinarily, yes. But this one is the size of an asteroid, and a small one at that. Without a visible gas ring, only the X-ray radiation would have given it away. The gravitational effects on Tau Ceti would be insignificant, and certainly would not be observable from the Earth system. Standard theory says a typical black hole should have a mass similar to our sun. The existence of one this small will rewrite the astronomy books."

Karic took a sharp breath. *Of course.* X-rays would jet through the system as the superheated gases first spun around the heavy nucleus of the black hole, then fell into its steep gravity well. A portion of the mass was always ejected outward, the gases squeezed so hard in the intense gravity that some acquired enough energy to escape before the rest disappeared below the event horizon.

"Is the black hole in a stable orbit?" asked Andrai.

"For now," said Mara, chewing her lower lip. "But the writing is on the wall for Tau Ceti. Eventually, the black hole will feed off the sun itself — then this system will die.

"Now that we know where to look, we should be able to predict the surges by monitoring the temperature of the gas ring."

"How close are we to entering an orbit of the planet?" asked Karic.

"Months."

"Not for us," replied Karic. "I have finished assembling the sets and they are in working order. We can be in orbit in a few weeks of live time." The time spent out of suspension was "live time" — time spent awake and physically aging — as opposed to the actual elapsed time as the ship travelled through space, during most of which the crew were held in stasis. "We should probably set up a beacon in orbit and descend to the planet itself to wait for a response from Earth. With a black hole orbiting Tau Ceti … escaping the system without major damage would take a miracle. And the ship cannot take another major surge." Karic tapped the table with his fingers as he worked steadily through the implications. Every eye was on him.

Janzen had taken off his odin and was staring at the table, his hands spread out on the white polymer glass in front of him, as though to steady himself.

"In suspension on the planet, we at least know that we are safe. We can use the planet to shield the *Starburst* while we wait to hear from Earth. If Earth cannot send a recovery vehicle, then — and only then — will we risk the return," said Karic.

Janzen was silent. News of the black hole had apparently stunned him, and Karic understood why. There was no way a planet in such an unstable and dangerous system would be accepted as a candidate for terraforming. His carefully laid plans had been dashed, in one instant.

"What else can you tell us about the planet, Mara?" asked Karic.

"It is the fourth planet from Tau Ceti. It has no moon. As I was saying before — the temperature profiles indicate that it's tidally locked. Its rotation is fixed, with one face always directed toward the sun, much like our moon-Earth system, but in this case dividing the planet into perpetual night and day."

"Tidally locked," said Janzen the harsh tension in his voice at odds with his usual smooth assurance. "But … but that's only a factor for the small M-class stars. Tau Ceti is G-class. The planet is a super-Earth—"

Karic's eyes narrowed. This was another factor Janzen had not planned for.

"I know. It is surprising, even for a small G-class star like Tau Ceti," said Mara. "This planet is an anomaly. It has no moons at all, unlike the other Tau Ceti planets. It's the only planet in the system that is tidally locked. I can only assume there were some unusual conditions in its early development. The lack of a companion satellite, a very low rate of initial spin, an unusually low dissipation function—"

"But can it be colonized? Is it habitable?" Janzen leant in toward Mara, his blue eyes betraying a naked hunger Karic had rarely seen in the commander.

"We can only read the temperatures across the upper atmosphere, but we can extrapolate. There is no doubt the day-side surface will be an arid hothouse — it would be like living inside an oven. The sensors have not been able to penetrate the dense cloud cover on the planet, so there is no way of telling if conditions on the surface of the dark side are favorable or not, but it's most likely a frozen wasteland. The biggest unknown is how geologically active the planet is. We know so little about worlds like this."

Janzen leaned back into his chair. He took a deep breath and let it out slowly. Janzen smoothed back his blond hair with a delicate touch of his right hand — an unnecessary gesture since it was still perfectly coifed — and once more the handsome Davis was back, a slight smile tugging at the corners of his mouth, blue eyes lit with something that might have been excitement and perhaps relief.

"Even if the planet is tidally locked, if the atmosphere and temperatures are right there will be colonization potential — even if it's only around the terminator — the temperate zone between the bright side and dark side. That will still be a sizable area on a planet that size. Plenty of real estate." Janzen showed a fine line of white teeth as he smiled. "In terms of protecting ourselves from the radiation, we should stay in orbit. Descending to the planet will be too risky."

"Orbit?" said Karic, amazed Janzen would even suggest it. "Janzen, any orbit would expose the ship to Tau Ceti on a regular cycle. It would be like playing Russian Roulette."

Janzen put his odin back on, straightening in his chair. The left data-screen lowered, and his lips moved silently as he quickly reviewed a file. No doubt yet another contingency plan drafted by an ExploreCorp engineer before they left Earth.

Janzen's odin contracted into a single band once more. He tilted his head back into a familiar posture of command as he addressed Karic. "We can use a synchronous orbit." He smiled as inspiration struck. "Positioned in the planet's shadow."

"Hold on," said Karic. "Mara said the planet was tidally locked. Any synchronous orbit would put us millions of kilometers out. Well outside the planet's shadow."

"This planet has a mass more than four times that of the Earth," insisted Janzen. "Surely —"

Mara cut in, her voice sharp and impatient. "A synchronous orbit is a function of both mass and rotational period. If that planet is tidally locked to Tau Ceti, its rotational period is the inverse of its orbital period around Tau Ceti. And that's damn slow."

Karic shook his head. "We have no choice. Despite the state of the ship, we will have to set the *Starburst* for station-keeping inside the shadow before we descend in the lander."

"What …?" Janzen's left data-shield lowered once more, and he waved his hands at Karic to stall him, trying to keep ahead of the argument while still reviewing more information. "But … but if we take the lander to the planet, we could lose the lander or damage the sets. It is too great a risk." Janzen's voice betrayed an edge of panic.

"I disagree," said Karic. "We will be much better protected from the radiation on the planet. Trying to take the *Starburst* out of the system and all the way to Earth is just too risky at this point. If Earth cannot send a heavily shielded recovery vehicle, then it's a call we have to make. But at least we can do it based on years of data on how the black hole behaves, and the patterns of radiation. If there is a cycle, we may be able to leave Tau Ceti during a window of low radiation. In the meantime, we need to find the best place to wait. That means descending to the planet."

Janzen gave up on the odin. The data-screen contracted with a snap. As he faced Karic, his face flushed red.

"I am still the commander, Karic!"

"You brought us all here, Janzen. Don't bother trying to deny your knowledge of this system, or the radiation risk. But you didn't plan for a black hole, did you? Or a tidally locked planet?" said Karic, evenly.

"Groundless accusations. I warn you, if you go too far, I'll have you up on charges," said Janzen, but his voice lacked its usual bombast.

Karic looked quickly around the room, judging the mood. *Now was the time.*

"You have shown yourself unfit to lead this crew, Janzen. I am relieving you of command."

The room went quiet.

Janzen forced a laugh, then looked around at the crew. His eyes grew wild as he took in the silent resolve forming around the table.

"You can't!" said Janzen. "ExploreCorp put me in charge of this mission, and I intend to see it through."

Karic looked around at the crew, "Who is with me on this?"

"I am," said Andrai.

Mara nodded reluctantly. "So am I," she said, meeting Janzen's gaze squarely.

"I want no part of it," said Ibri, scowling at Karic.

"It is not unanimous! It *cannot* carry!" said Janzen.

"It doesn't have to be, Janzen. As sub-Commander, I only need the support of the majority of officers, which I have."

"I own this vessel!" said Janzen, pulling himself up and glaring at the crew. "The Davises were the ones who funded this mission, and, by God, I intend to keep control!" His posture was confident, but the tremor in his hands betrayed him. "Oppose me in this and you won't see a cent of your fee. Not a cent! *Do you hear me?*"

Karic smiled grimly. Janzen was showing his true colors at last.

"None of that matters now," said Karic. "First, we have to stay alive. I *am* taking command, Janzen. I should have at Epsilon Eridani. I can't believe I let it go this far."

"I won't stand for this, Karic. I have the codes that activate the suspension sets, and I will not give them to you if you proceed with this."

Karic's heart raced. It would have been so easy to give in to his anger at that moment, but he kept it under a tight rein. He would not give Janzen a single edge over him. Not now.

"So you would condemn us all to a slow death rather than admit you are responsible for crippling the *Starburst* and killing thirty-three people?"

"You are out of order, Karic!" said Janzen. His control had finally cracked. He seemed pathetic as he shouted back at Karic. "I am the legally appointed head of this mission."

"Really? Well, not anymore. Remember, Janzen, I designed that suspension equipment. Don't you think I could bypass a simple lockout?"

Karic pulled eight IC chips from his pocket and threw them on the table in front of Janzen. The former commander swallowed and looked up from them to Karic.

"I've already replaced the coded chips, Janzen — and you have played your last card. ExploreCorp is not in charge here anymore."

Janzen blinked rapidly, his eyes glassy as he returned Karic's gaze. His mouth worked soundlessly as he struggled to rally his thoughts, but nothing emerged. His face pale with shock, Janzen seemed to shrink into himself, now looking ridiculous and out of place in his immaculate uniform.

Karic stood. "I am now commander of this mission." He swept his gaze across the room. "I intend to get us all back to Earth, *alive.*

"We are undermanned and have a huge, complex ship that is damaged. We have wasted way too much time on ridiculous exercises like cost-benefit calculations and damage reports."

Karic sighed and pointed at Janzen. "I want you to help Andrai and Ibri get the systems back up and running. You aren't a technician, but you know enough about the ship to be useful."

The former commander looked back at Karic, his jaw slack, face set in a rare expression of incomprehension, as though he could not believe this was really happening. But Janzen was never thrown for long. He blinked again and cleared his throat. "We still cannot send down the lander without knowing what the conditions on the surface are like. We have to stay in orbit."

He saw the fear in Janzen's eyes. But he was a member of the crew. Karic's crew.

"That's true. We need to know what the conditions are like. If we still have insufficient data when we reach the planet, we will try an unmanned probe."

"And if your unmanned probe fails, Karic? What then?"

"One of us will make the descent in a pod."

Mara's eyes widened. "But the pods have only minimal shielding! They are designed for descent only; and only if the conditions are perfect." She looked around the group for support. "We should use the heavy lander for planetary descents."

"No. We cannot risk the lander. Janzen is right about that. Not with our only suspension equipment hardwired into it." Karic looked around at the crew. "Mara. Tell them."

She closed her eyes for a moment and nodded, as though in defeat. When she opened her eyes again, she spoke with a heavy resignation. "The heat pumping into the planet's day side from Tau Ceti might be having drastic effects. It could be driving tectonic activity across the whole planet — earthquakes, tidal waves, super-volcanoes, seas of lava that appear without warning from beneath the crust, dissolving vast areas of land—"

"So, if the planet's environment is hostile, we have to know, before we take the lander down," said Karic.

"Yes, but the ... pod could be lost," said Mara. Everyone in the room knew what her momentary hesitation meant. It was not the pod's destruction that concerned her — the *Starburst* was equipped with seven — it was the pilot's.

"So let us be clear, then. You are asking one of us to carry out a suicide mission, Karic," said Janzen.

Karic smiled ruefully. "That's why, if it has to be done, I'll be taking the pod down."

It was an agonizing decision for Karic. After taking control of the *Starburst*, the last thing he wanted to do was to leave Janzen free to work mischief, but he could see little choice. He himself was the best pilot left alive. Hopefully, the unmanned probe would do the job.

Janzen fidgeted with his data-glasses and remained silent.

"You all have your tasks cut out for you," said Karic. "As soon as we have control of the fusion drive, we will enter suspension. We will drop into a close orbit around the fourth planet and drop the probe. Then, if we have to, I'll pilot a pod into the planet's atmosphere and reassess our situation based on the data we receive.

"Either way, *Starburst* will then break orbit and move further out into the planet's shadow."

Karic stared at Janzen. "I expect you to get that uniform off. You can wear a plain officer's uniform without insignia for now. Bolan was about your height."

"How dare you!" snapped Janzen.

Karic held out his hand. "I'll take the badge now."

Janzen's hands shook as he pulled the gold diamond off his left epaulette and handed it to Karic. His eyes never left the badge as it disappeared into Karic's fist.

Janzen stood up, struggling to keep his face impassive. He turned and left the room quickly, followed by Ibri.

"You know what to do, Andrai," said Karic. "Just make sure that Janzen pulls his weight. If you have any trouble with him, let me know."

Andrai shook his head and smiled. Then he left the room.

Karic and Mara remained behind.

"I should have seen it," said Mara, face twisted into an angry frown. The astronomer had struggled for weeks with inadequate equipment and found nothing. Even more, she had missed observing a powerful sun that was a danger to all of them: a black hole.

"Don't be too hard on yourself, Mara. This was a tough one on all of us. Now we just have to survive."

"I don't need any sympathy from you, Karic." Her face softened. "I am worried about this descent. The manual states all planetary work should be undertaken in the heavy lander unless there is absolutely no option." She searched his face, then took a deep breath, letting it out slowly. "The pods do not have enough propulsion to regain orbit, Karic. You know that."

Karic felt energized. At last he was in control of his own destiny, his own dream. The *Starburst* would complete her mission on his terms, not Janzen's. "I know the risks are pretty high, Mara, but all of us are in danger. We may all die in a second radiation surge before we even reach the planet. Transporting to the planet's surface is the only way to ensure we survive until a rescue ship can reach us.

"Have you thought of names for the black hole, or the planets?"

Mara smiled weakly. "I haven't even thought about it."

"You are the astronomer. You should be the one to name them."

Mara's brow creased in concentration for an instant. "How about planet Oasis? After all, it's a stop on our way home. A place to rest. Besides, I think 'New Earth' would be a bit premature, don't you?"

Karic laughed.

"I wouldn't count on any palm trees," said Mara.

The words had a strange effect on Karic. Whether the planet sustained life or not remained a mystery, yet one thing was for certain — no sun or moon had traveled the sky of the dark side for many millions of years.

His dream returned, bringing with it visions of an empty ebony sky.

Chapter 5

The explosive bolts fired away, loosing the pod from the body of the mother-ship. The small craft trembled and started to tip as it dropped away from the *Starburst*. Karic quickly stabilized its fall using maneuvering jets and swept his gaze across the console. He checked and rechecked his position. He shuffled against the harness straps, uncomfortable in the bulky spacesuit. Almost ten months had passed since the surge that took so many lives. Most of that time had passed while they were secure in stasis — with around two months of "live time" that had been a blur of furious activity in preparation for their arrival at Oasis.

His eyes wide with intense focus, he felt fiercely aware. The interior of the pod brightened, every display and polished surface brought to an unreal brilliance by the adrenaline that flooded his brain. After all the planning, all the analysis and decision-making, he was *here*, hurtling toward the planet's surface.

He had volunteered for the descent in the pod if the unmanned probe failed — and it had. They had waited anxiously as the little probe dropped through the upper atmosphere, finally shedding its outer heat-shield and deploying parachutes. The signal had lasted only a few minutes. Whether it had even reached the planet's surface was a mystery. The intense storms in the atmosphere below must have given the little probe a rough ride, yet even so, it should not have been destroyed so quickly. It had vanished without a trace below the seething atmosphere of Oasis.

Karic looked through the viewport, catching his last view from the relative calm of space before the thick, cloud-strewn atmosphere claimed him. They had positioned the drop just inside the line of the terminator. He could see its bright line in the distance, held in place for time immemorial. The glare of the yellow sun was hidden by the bulk of the planet. Soon he would lose sight of the terminator as well.

The planet loomed. A dark, featureless orb slowly swelling to fill his vision. Oasis. It looked anything but a haven. Above him, the bulk of the *Starburst* vanished into darkness as she shifted from her temporary low orbit and began a series of station-keeping maneuvers deeper in the planet's shadow.

And he was alone, racing toward an alien world. Perhaps the first human in history to visit a planet outside Earth's solar system.

"This one's for you, Grandad." Of all people, his grandfather, Lein, would understand what this meant to him. Lein and a small group of elite astronauts had been selected for the first interstellar mission to Alpha Centauri, almost sixty years before *Starburst* set out. Their ship, the *Starsurfer*, had never left the Lagrange docks. It was left abandoned and half-built as the nuclear strife of the late 21st century raged on the planet

61

below, his grandfather's dreams of space exploration unrealized.

He fell toward the planet for long minutes, using the small maneuvering rockets on the outside of the craft to adjust his angle and position of entry. It was critical not to use too much fuel in the initial phase of descent. The pod was designed to use its heat shield for the bulk of entry breaking. The external tanks for the descent — fitted to the top section of the pod — completed the classic, tapered upper section of a cone-shaped entry capsule that would have been recognized by the Apollo astronauts. Except for size. It was bigger by far than its 1960s counterpart, and could accommodate up to four personnel in an emergency, although the weight of the additional crew would make post-descent flight problematic.

In its atmospheric entry configuration, the pod would use fuel only for course correction. As it approached the ground the fuel in the external tanks would be used in a sustained burn to halt its descent. Then the pod would jettison both the external tanks and the lower heat shield, revealing a sleek, aerodynamic shape — a flattened lozenge of a central cabin with short, stubby wings and a short flaring tail, the maneuvering jets extending like stubby landing legs from its undercarriage. Its heavy shielding gone, the pod would become a miracle of lightweight materials that could use its onboard fuel and maneuvering jets for short-range atmospheric flights. At that final stage, it would be planetbound for good. There was no return to orbit for the strange little aircraft it would become. Or its pilot.

The target landing zone was some one hundred kilometers inside the dark side of the terminator and it was Karic's mission to put the pod down as close as possible to that point. If all went well, his beacon — indicating the surface was safe — would then guide the lander down from *Starburst* with the rest of the crew. He sighed, watching as the planet drew slowly closer. The pods were notoriously difficult to pilot, and it was going to be a rough ride.

An image of his grandfather came back to Karic. The aging astronaut stood on his front porch, looking up at the stars. On this particular night, Karic had been working late, trying to finish an assignment for his undergrad degree. He had taken a break and wandered up the street from his parents' house to visit his grandparents, as he had a hundred times before. The soft, fall air of Boston carried the earthy scent of a nearby stand of oaks and the sweetness of a late-flowering vine.

Karic's grandfather and the other *Starsurfer* astronauts had been genetically modified so they could achieve a partial hibernation state. The gene-splicers had assured Lein the altered DNA would not carry to the next generation, but they were wrong. Karic's father had been spared, but his whole life, Karic had struggled against unpredictable fugue states. His brain would switch to a hibernation mode even though his body and his senses remained at full alertness.

Lein could often be found out the front of his house, looking up. Sometimes he would be lost in fugue, and Karic would wait silently. Other times, he would just be watching the night sky.

Karic climbed the steps and stood beside his grandfather on the porch. He followed Lein's gaze across the familiar constellations.

"Never forget they're real, Karic," Lein said, without turning. "Some people go their whole lives and never really think of them as anything more than points of light."

The darkness had softened Lein's gaunt face into youth, the gray wavy hair a dark blur in the night.

"They are suns, Karic. Real suns. People know it, but how often do they look up and understand it? Really feel the truth of it?"

A warning tone filled the pod's small cabin. He had entered the upper atmosphere. Karic lowered the heat shield over the outer viewport, blocking the view. It was built to withstand great pressures, but the clear polymer would quickly lose structural integrity, and eventually rupture, if subjected to the intense heat of atmospheric entry. Darkness enveloped the pod. He activated the external cameras he would use to make the descent.

"Good luck, Karic," said Mara, over the com. "We'll be coming to pick you up soon."

Karic smiled at Mara's optimism.

"Don't wait too long."

As acting first lieutenant, Mara was the most senior crewmember after Karic. In his absence, she was acting commander. He hoped she could deal with Janzen.

After having taken command from Janzen, he had unlocked the restricted news that had reached them at Epsilon Eridani. What he found troubled him. The absolute control that United Earth maintained over the off-world colonies and space stations had been shattered. Only thirty-three years after *Starburst* left on its mission, a coalition of colonies inside Earth's solar system — comprising Mars, the Moon, and settlements on the Jovian moons — calling itself the Free Colonies, had put an embargo on trade with Earth. It was a stranglehold. Earth relied on its off-world facilities for almost all its raw materials, fuels and high-tech goods. Well planned and executed, it had taken Earth completely by surprise. All their attempts to launch fleets were blocked by orbiting weapons. It was the perfect, bloodless coup.

The first act of the Free Colonies had been to seize all off-world assets. The Davis Industries Platform in the Lagrange point between the Earth and Moon — notorious for its poor living conditions and safety record —

had been shut down and disassembled, the modules distributed across all the Free Colonies. For DavisCorp, it was a killer blow. The huge mega-corporation, once in the top ten on the World Exchange — privy to the decisions of the United Earth itself — was finished. It had dropped out of the top ten only three years after they left Earth system, suffering an endless series of contractions. Only two months after the embargo, it collapsed completely. Janzen's legacy was just a memory.

Yet ExploreCorp remained, a highly speculative stock on the fringes of the market. Although they were the first to send out a ship, nine others had left between 2157 and 2190, when the embargo had ended the interstellar program. All of them were faster and better targeted, the last capable of cruising at over $0.34c$ — almost fifty percent faster than *Starburst*. Although, Karic noted with a feeling of pride, all still used his suspension technology.

The success of the *Starburst's* mission was the only thing that could restore Janzen's fortune. He had already proved himself ruthless, willing to risk lives. So far the deaths had been accidental, the result of bad errors in judgment. How far would he really go, now that everything was riding on the outcome of this mission?

Karic adjusted the image of Oasis on his console. It was as black as the void. A jolt of fear sent his heart racing. He could be killed in entry or landing. And if he found the surface was unsuitable for the lander, he would slowly asphyxiate as the pod's supply of oxygen ran out.

Karic and Andrai completed a series of radio checks. The transmission began to break up under the influence of the planet's intense magnetic field and increasing cloud cover.

"Just keep listening for my beacon!" shouted Karic through the link.

The reply was garbled, lost in static, and Karic switched off the radio. Communications would be useless now.

His small craft dropped through the atmosphere, buffeted by turbulence as it sliced through the thick cloud. So far the craft's orientation was still good — allowing the big heat shield to perform its task of entry braking without endangering the pod.

The magnetic field of Oasis was unusually strong. The associated magnetosphere would act to deflect the charged particles of Tau Ceti's solar wind and other high-energy particles, even more effectively than Earth's own magnetosphere protected it from the Sun's similar effects. Without it, Oasis's atmosphere would be vastly different, water and oxygen literally be pushed out into space by the solar wind, much like Mars and Venus, which both lacked a strong magnetosphere. Together with Oasis's thick atmosphere, the *Starburst's* crew would be well protected from harmful radiation on the surface, yet those same factors made his mission perilous. Once having attained the surface, he would attempt to assemble a directional transmitter and send a signal to those who waited above. If the beacon did not reach the ship, they would have to assume he had failed. He would be abandoned on the surface; cut off from the *Starburst* and all those he had left behind.

Karic entered the lower atmosphere. Life — awareness — contracted to a tiny shell of exotic alloys, heat-resistant ceramic, and plastic. A capsule of life, rushing downward. The pod was designed as a robust reentry vehicle, yet within the alien atmosphere, it seemed as fragile as an egg.

Karic was dropping faster than the speed of sound and still accelerating. The exterior heated rapidly. The pod shook and spun. He fought to stabilize it, using the pod's small rockets to adjust his attitude. He worked frantically, sweating as the interior heated. The instruments monitoring the temperature of the heat shield climbed to max then abruptly dropped to zero. *The sensors are fried.*

A high-pitched warning tone cut through the stuffy air in the cabin, a light on the console blinking red in time with the alarm.

"Damn!"

The exterior temperature of the pod's shielded upper section — containing the fuel needed for its deceleration — was over its safety limit and still climbing. They had known that the planet's gravity, slightly greater than Earth's, might cause complications, but they had hoped the safety factors used in the design of the pod would compensate. Apparently not. If the shielded fuel tanks that formed the pod's tapered upper section ruptured — the explosion would shred him and the pod into a thousand fragments of metal, plastic and flesh.

Karic fought down panic. His eyes swam as he tried to watch every inch of the console at once. He could not fail now. Not now.

A shimmering began at the edges of his vision. An all too familiar echo of the changes starting in his brain.

"No! *No!*"

It was too soon, but Karic had no choice.

He engaged the entry burn. The main thruster ignited with a thump that shook the whole pod. Its distant, low growl powered against Oasis's gravity, slowing the craft's acceleration. He watched his instruments anxiously, eyes flicking between readings of downward velocity, altitude and dwindling fuel stocks. The pod was slowing, *but too damn slowly.*

His mouth dry, he tried to swallow past a sudden constriction that had grown in his throat.

The fuel in the external tank was burning fast. The minutes crawled. Time stretched and still Karic pushed against its flow, as though he could fight his own fate through sheer strength of will. Even so, the moment arrived.

The muffled roar of the main thruster cut to eerie silence.

I'm too high.

His mind dull with shock, his body took over, hands moving quickly across the console in a sequence he had practiced — and executed — hundreds of times.

The core section of the pod trembled as explosive bolts fired beneath it and above it. Outside — amid the dense clouds of Oasis — he knew the heat shield would be tumbling away beneath him, the heavy main thruster with it. The empty external tanks had been ejected from the pod's upper section, launched to either side of him by tiny rockets on the tanks. Now, only the insubstantial hull of the inner framework was left.

Karic engaged the wing and tail, listening anxiously to the sound of the motors as they labored to extend and lengthen the exterior surface, creating the additional surface area that would give the pod an aerodynamic profile.

Waves rose from his mind. Surging, sighing. Falling. Drawing him down. He felt his mind expand, quivering as it filled the pod's tiny space. His heart slowed.

"No!"

Karic hit the console in desperation, smashing his fist into the hard metal until he was bleeding; until his hand was a mass of pain. He could not let the fugue take him now.

His mind expanded. It stretched, then filled like a balloon. He was both inside and outside the pod. The surging rhythms of his mind flickered rapidly, sweeping the space around him with tendrils of sentience.

He tasted the cold, bitter scent of the cloud. Saw into its dirty red depths. Felt its fury. His skin was searing with heat, at one with the pod. A hurricane washed over him, but did not cool him. He heard the ticking clockwork of silicon circuits, watched the roar of chemical ignition as his mind swept through the rocket nozzles. *The combustion is not in balance.* Lein was outside in the storm, riding the turbulence that surrounded the pod, his eyes far away, staring at a distant point of light. Evelle was gone.

This *was* the fugue state, yet unlike Karic had ever experienced it. Time had not dilated! He saw the console, the meters and readings, the tiny viewscreen, yet his mind was also expanded. At his wrist, the display on his comband ticked off the seconds with mundane regularity.

He turned.

A huge storm front was approaching from the east. It filled some part of his mind, churning with a mindless fury, moaning with a desire for his destruction. *If something like that had hit the probe, no wonder it didn't survive entry.*

Amidst the vast vista of his enhanced senses, the pod's console gave no hint of its approach. It was far away, yet approaching rapidly.

His hands were sure on the controls as he turned the pod into a soaring dive that would take him below the storm.

The warning tones sharpened. The exterior temperatures increased to critical. He was burning. Dying. The ceramic surface was now failing across the entire leading edge of the lower wing. The pod began to destabilize and spin in the intense turbulence.

Karic worked at the console frantically.

The clouds vanished.

His mind was a blur of green. He tasted sweet moisture.

The lower hull was melting, and the cabin filled with choking smoke.

Karic gripped his chair with desperate strength as the pod shook in the hostile atmosphere. If he did not slow soon he was finished. Below, he could sense the surface of the planet rushing up to meet him.

His throat burned, and the fugue state fled.

The cameras on the console showed a wall of green. *They must have been damaged in the descent.*

Karic diverted the small chemical rockets downward and increased the thrust to maximum — then waited. His breathing was ragged, his hands shaking. But he was alive. And he was beneath the cloud. Below the storms.

The craft continued to hurtle downward, yet the deceleration was mounting. He watched the meters on the console with a grim finality, strapping himself into the pilot's chair. He was falling, the deceleration increasing; one gee, two gees, three gees …

Karic regained consciousness slowly, choking on fumes from burning plastic. He thumbed the release stud on his harness and fell forward onto the console, his eyes blurring. The pod was now making a controlled descent, the maneuvering rockets easily pacing the gravity of the planet.

He had survived!

Coughing, he slapped the console, attempting to clear the external image, which was still a mass of blurred green. He checked the speed of the craft and opened the front viewport, hungry for his first glimpse of the planet's surface. The screen drew back — revealing a verdant landscape flooded with ambient light.

"Mother of God."

He took control of the craft, spinning it in a full circle. It was a jungle wilderness, filled with life.

"It should be in darkness," he said. "This is the night side."

The filters had now removed most of the smoke from the cabin air.

He sped over the endless canopy, searching for a place to set down the pod and assemble the transmitter.

How could this be happening? It was a paradise. A new Earth!

Karic checked the outside atmosphere. The humidity was high — mists shrouded the tops of the forest — and it had an abundance of oxygen. He carefully trimmed back the feed to the rockets, switching to a partly air-breathing mode that made use of the local oxidizer, saving his stored oxygen. The pod was flying well, despite the heat damage to the outer shell.

Karic spotted a clearing near a small lake. He angled the pod toward it.

He could see a mountain range in the distance ... but it was no normal landform. It glowed, emitting a warm, soft light. This was what lit the surrounding area of the dark side. But how could anything like this possibly develop naturally? It was huge. Crystalline. Transparent. It glittered, shedding light like a jewel, making shadows in the lee of the hills and deep within the forest canopy.

Karic hovered over the clearing, spellbound by the soft white light, the stillness of the wide lake beneath him and the tall, unearthly vegetation that crowded around it.

He gradually cut the power to the pod's rockets and lowered the craft to the thick grasses of the lake shore. He watched in amazement as bizarre, fleet-footed animals with segmented legs and huge multicolored insects with wingspans of up to a meter sped away from the pod into the plush growth.

He waited, impatient, as the small analytical devices within the ship analyzed the trace elements and gases in the atmosphere, searching for toxic components.

Clear.

Karic's heart beat wildly against the wall of his chest as he shrugged off his spacesuit. In place of the suit, he donned a small mask, designed to filter out hostile bacteria and viruses. He broke the seal on the hatch. With a hiss of inrushing air, the pod's door swung wide. The ceramic tiles on the stubby wings and the leading edge of the hull glowed with a red heat. They hissed as a light, misting rain blew in off the lake.

He felt the cool touch of air on his skin.

Karic exited the pod, moving awkwardly in the planet's gravity, which was twenty percent above Earth's. At eighty kilos, that meant he was carrying an extra sixteen kilos with every step he took. He carefully regulated his breathing, wary of the high oxygen content. He did not want to hyperventilate.

Karic looked around him in awe. He stood in another world — filled with alien life. He had dreamt of this, and now he was here. This was real!

Bending down, Karic ran his hands through the thick, luxuriant grass. It felt coarse beneath his fingers. The thick blades of grass were bluish green on the underside. He looked up to the thick wall of vegetation nearby. Everything was familiar, and yet ... odd. The shapes were different. Some trees too thick, others impossibly thin. Leaves were broad and slick with moisture, dropping like green sheets to the ground.

Three big, green insects, reminiscent of dragonflies, but with heads like birds, glided from the canopy nearby, sweeping down to drink from the lake on the wing.

Two multi-faceted eyes watched him from a tree. An enormous yellow insect with six legs moved out slowly from cover. It was close to a grasshopper in shape, yet almost a meter and half long, with strong, well-developed mandibles. Its abdomen pulsated in a quick rhythm, hinting at speed.

The rain grew more intense, but it was warm. Karic hardly noticed as it sheeted off the high-tech fabric of his uniform, leaving him dry beneath.

How could all this life survive here on the night side? And what was producing the light that emanated from the crystal range?

There was a quick movement. A rustle of leaves.

The big yellow insect and the flyers vanished back into the trees.

The lakeshore was wrapped in silence. Not a breath of wind stirred the forest.

Above, the sky was empty.

Karic retrieved the beacon transmitter from the cabin, carrying the sleek metallic cylinder outside, where he pulled down three legs folded flush with its sides and extended them until they formed a tripod base. He set it upright then flipped open the access panel to begin programming it.

Around him, the silence seemed unnatural.

He found himself stopping without warning to scan the undergrowth, or peer into the queer reeds that grew thickly around the edge of the lake.

There was nothing, and yet ... his unease grew.

Here he was, in this fantastic world, yet beneath his excitement, he knew he was alone — and far from Earth. This world, so green and lush, was strange to his human senses. The sooner the others could join him the better.

As the alien sounds of the jungle gradually returned, Karic found himself watching the sky, looking for any sign of change in the seamless dark blue.

But there was nothing.

Chapter 6

It was dark in the lander's cabin.

The high-pitched roar of the lander's six rockets filled the space as it descended smoothly toward the upper atmosphere of Oasis, using a delicately balanced combination of aerobraking and thrust to make its controlled descent. Yet one sound was missing. Every moment without the reassuring tone of Karic's beacon signal ratcheted the coiled tension inside Mara up another notch.

Starburst had received the beacon transmission less than two hours after Karic's drop, signaling Karic was alive and that the planet was safe for the descent of the main lander. With only a limited supply of oxygen in the pod, Karic needed immediate rescue. They had begun the descent within an hour of receiving the signal. The lander's less sensitive radio receiver could not match the *Starburst'*s high-gain dish antenna and amplifier, so they now waited to pick up the beacon again. So far it had been blocked by the thick cloud cover.

Mara was in command, and she felt the responsibility keenly. Analyzing the display, she checked the rate of descent and fuel use against her projections, then the lander's attitude. The lander's external tanks nested around each other and could be jettisoned in series during the descent as each emptied, reducing weight, yet preserving the vehicle's overall aerodynamics. Two of the biggest external tanks had already been discarded and the heavy craft was handling well.

She turned to her right, eyes narrowed. The crew were strapped into four of the six chairs along the console, which ran around three walls of the roughly square cabin. The lights were dimmed for flight. Mara tried not to think about who might have been sitting in the empty seats if things had gone differently. Mara had positioned Janzen along the right-hand wall at a non-critical workstation, an empty seat beside him, leaving her and Andrai free to work the center or "front" console where the flight controls were. Ibri sat at one of the two stations along the left-hand wall, opposite Janzen. The soft white light of their display terminals lit their faces, while their field gear was outlined in an irregular patchwork of green, red and yellow by the console lights. The two chairs that had been positioned along the remaining wall — on either side of the airlock — and the two emergency chairs that had folded up from the floor in the center of the cabin had all been removed to give them room to set up the suspension equipment.

Andrai was piloting, his hands white on the controls. He gave her a quick smile, wiped the sweat from his palms, brushed his chaotic blond hair back from his face, then returned his attention to the lander.

Ibri worked methodically to monitor the lander's systems. He was relaxed, leaning forward over his workstation, a slight smile on his lips, as though amused at a private joke. The console lights etched the contours of his long, dark face into sharp lines of shadow.

Janzen's gaze flicked between Andrai and Mara. He could not keep his left leg still, and his knee jigged rapidly. He put his odin on, then a moment later took it off again, the left data-shield still lowered.

Mara's fingers tapped out an impatient rhythm on the gleaming console, giving vent to the internal pressure. *"Come on,* where's the signal?"

She had expected this. They should easily receive the beacon once the lander had descended into the lower atmosphere. But how far into the lower atmosphere would the turbulent storm activity extend?

"Andrai, don't descend too rapidly. Keep control," said Janzen.

"That means more fuel, Janzen," said Mara. "We are working to optimize it. We will be on the surface soon enough, don't worry."

Janzen went to speak, then stopped, returning the odin to his face, his mouth tight with restrained anger.

Mara smiled to herself. Even after the last few months, Janzen was not used to being rebuffed, or taking orders. He still ordered Ibri around as though he was commander and challenged Mara on every second decision. He had found some obscure reference in the ExploreCorp rules of command that allowed major shareholders a voice on commercial decisions. Since then, *everything* was a commercial decision according to him.

Old habits died hard. Without Karic around, even Andrai would sometimes unthinkingly follow Janzen's orders. During the preparations for launching the lander, there had been too much to think about to follow Janzen around countermanding every minor order he gave to the crew.

"Andrai, recheck the frequency," asked Mara.

Andrai checked the frequency for the seventh time. "We are on channel." But there was nothing but static.

Then the beacon tone rang out.

"Yeehaa!" cheered Andrai. Mara reached over and hugged Andrai, tears of relief falling down her cheeks. She found the solid warmth of his shoulders comforting and melted into him. He was always there for her, yet demanded nothing. She looked across to see Janzen watching her critically. The former commander's brows drew together with unspoken disapproval. She broke away from Andrai on reflex, wiping away her tears. Ibri shook his head, no doubt wondering what all the fuss was about.

Janzen shifted in his seat. He was dressed in a gold, body-hugging jacket of shimmering synthetic material with an ExploreCorp logo on the shirt-breast and sleeve, with matching pants and boots. With his chiseled features and stark blue eyes, he looked as though he had stepped out of an ExploreCorp vid-link advertisement. In contrast, the rest of the crew were in standard field gear, plain khaki uniforms, their badges of rank the only adornment.

"We should be concentrating on the descent," said Janzen, the tone of his haughty comment barely concealing the barbed taunt beneath it, implying her conduct was unprofessional.

Mara tensed, and bit back a sharp retort. The blond tech gave her a smile and she relaxed. She was in charge here, not Janzen. Mara refused to dignify his commentary with a reply.

Mara turned her mind back to the mission. She looked over at Ibri, who was working steadily at his console, monitoring the operation of the thrusters. Typically, he had ignored the whole exchange.

The beacon's low, regular tone sounded strongly through the cabin. Based on a series of readings on the incoming signal, Mara calculated Karic's approximate position. It was way too far inside the terminator. It had to be wrong. She decided not change their course. Perhaps the cloud was affecting the instruments. She would get a more precise fix when they were below the cloud.

Above them, the *Starburst* was far back in the shadow of Oasis, protected from both the harsh emanations of Tau Ceti and the lethal radiation emitted by the black hole's ejecta — the tortured portion of gases that escaped its steep gravity well as it slaked its endless thirst for matter.

The last eight hours had been a frenzy of activity as they shut down non-critical systems and prepared the ship for the long wait. They were confident they would be able to keep contact with her for the many long years ahead before their rescue. The Shipcom was fully functional, and should have no trouble controlling the ship's drive and keeping station above Oasis. And over the last few weeks, Ibri had also assembled and programmed a pilot robot that would give them arms, legs and eyes in the control room. They all felt more secure knowing they had command of some mobile artificial intelligence on the ship, should any problems arise.

All's well. I just need to keep following Karic's beacon to the source, reunite the crew and get everyone into stasis.

It was hard not to consider the possibilities for scientific exploration on Oasis, but the environment was likely to be hostile and dangerous. The dark side would be frozen, locked away from the touch of the planet's sun, swept by violent storm activity. They did not have the gear, or the resources. They would need to stay in stasis simply to survive.

The plan was to take very short shifts out of stasis each year for the next twenty-three and a half years; little more than a few weeks of personal time. Hopefully by then *Starburst* would have received a reply from Earth. They would find out if there was to be a rescue mission ... or not. Like all the interstellar exploration companies, ExploreCorp would be keeping a fleet of colony ships ready for flight, poised to reap the enormous profits of claiming a new world. Should the news arrive, they would be the first to respond. Yet Earth was so far away. Would ExploreCorp still exist when their news arrived? Would they respond with a rescue mission without the lure of profit? Or would the jury-rigged *Starburst* have to risk the journey home?

The lander trembled.

Mara took a deep breath, then looked down, to check her display. She laid her palms flat on the cool silver metal of the console to either side, comforted by the smoothness, the familiar technology at her command. At heart, she was a space-rat — born and bred on a station — and this was the world she knew.

"OK, we are starting to enter the lower atmosphere. It's all yours, Andrai," she said.

They checked their padded harnesses to make sure they were firmly strapped in. Janzen carefully folded his odin and zipped it into a pocket on his shirt. He pulled the straps tight across his broad chest.

"Hold on folks, we should be through this in a few minutes," said Andrai.

The lander was a solid craft, built for just this sort of descent. It represented centuries of incremental design improvements. It was no mean task to descend to a planet's surface with enough fuel to regain orbit. Mara leant back against the padded headrest and tightened the harness straps again, heart beating fast with excitement. "I can't wait to see the surface."

She was burning with curiosity. Despite their efforts, the heavy cloud had defeated all but the most rudimentary attempts at gathering data on the surface below. Radar scans had given them a very crude relief map, with the spectrographic analyses and drone-gathered samples of the upper atmosphere showing more water vapor than Earth and intriguing traces of light hydrocarbon molecules.

The lander shook, then lurched sideways, taking Mara's breath away.

The ride was about to begin.

"I hope I get my money's worth," yelled Mara to Andrai over the roar of the thrusters.

The buffeting on the exterior of the craft increased. The lander lurched and careened out of control, spinning wildly.

Mara yelped. Her hands flew to the harness straps, gripping them tightly. She looked across the small central cabin toward Andrai. His face was calm, his concentration total, as he stilled the lander and brought it back on course. He continued to monitor the exterior composition of the clouds and atmosphere as though nothing had happened. The turbulence continued, yet Andrai kept tight control. They soon grew used to the constant shaking.

There was so much they did not know about this system. After months of intensive study, there was still not a shred of direct evidence of the black hole, even after the Shipcom reactivated, giving them the full power of its computing systems. Yet she *knew* it was there — orbiting within 0.1 AU of Tau Ceti. Yet there was no detectable gas ring. Even the orbit of the thing seemed to change, which was impossible. *Impossible.* How could something like this hide from them? How could a black hole that small even exist?

The lander spun once more. Stale water and food rations — a hasty meal before the descent — swept up her throat, but she swallowed it back down.

They had launched a probe from *Starburst* six days ago that would slowly orbit Oasis, swinging through the shadow and back across the bright side. It should get an excellent view of Tau Ceti. It would download its data to the *Starburst* on each transit. Hopefully the programs they had set up for the Shipcom would be able to pull something useful from the data. If they had to make it back to Earth themselves, it could make all the difference.

The buffeting on the lander eased. It was warm inside the cabin, the air heated by their bodies, the instruments and the waste heat from the engines. Mara forced herself to let go of the harness straps — one finger at a time. She looked across to Janzen. His face was paper-white. His hands shook as he fumbled with the zipper on his shirt. Ibri's head was bowed over his terminal, lost in his work once more. He had already loosened his harness straps.

The roar of the heavy lander's thrusters increased as Andrai halted the rate of descent. The rocket engines were still using only a fraction of their power.

"Standby for tank ejection on my mark," said Andrai.

Mara checked her console, watching the last of the fuel drain from next external tank to be ejected in the entry sequence. The fuel valves switched simultaneously, the thrusters now supplied from the new tank.

"Three, two, one." Andrai flipped the cover from the number three tank ejection button, his finger poised. "Mark." Andrai's finger stabbed down. The craft jolted as the seals were disengaged and the tank tumbled away.

Outside, unknown gases swept around them, whipping the hull with moisture and savage winds.

Inside, there was a haven.

The beacon drew them down to the dark side — towards safety. Mara found herself focusing on its regular beat as the craft shook, as though willing them closer to Karic, alone on the surface below.

Finally, the turbulence stopped. Andrai worked with quick, sure movements, adjusting dials, fingers tapping and sliding across the surface of his monitor's active screen. The craft tilted into its atmospheric flight posture. The roar of the braking thrusters dropped away, leaving only the faint whine of the flight engines. A light tone sounded as he switched the craft to automatic pilot. The lander was now cruising as smoothly as a big passenger jet.

Andrai released his harness, stood up smoothly, then stretched. "We are underneath the cloud."

"Already?" Mara checked the altimeter and looked back at Andrai. All their modeling predicted that the storm activity would extend all the way to the surface.

Janzen swallowed and released his harness. "I think it is time we discovered what sort of a planet this is."

"Leave the orders to me, Janzen," snapped Mara. Janzen was getting under her skin. "OK. Let's get to work."

Andrai continued to assess the atmosphere, working with the many analytical instruments that the lander was equipped with. Ibri monitored the lander itself, ensuring all critical flight systems continued to function properly. Behind them, Janzen sat back in his chair and lowered the left screen of his odin. A dissonant hum filled the air as he activated the full immersion mode and began dictating notes to the AI, his mouth moving rapidly, his blue eyes lit with excitement. Again and again his eyes flicked to the main viewport, which appeared like a dark wall above the center console, its shield still in place to protect the polymer-glass from the heat of entry. His left leg tapped out a rapid rhythm.

Mara looked back at her own console. It was her task to assemble and interpret all the incoming data, piecing together a picture of the strange world outside the heavy steel of the hull. She soon became absorbed in her work. The first thing that surprised her was the temperature of the atmosphere. The dark side should have been frigid and set with ice, and yet the ambient temperatures were well above freezing point, climbing as they descended toward the surface. They soon entered the typical range experienced in the tropics on Earth.

"Just above one standard atmosphere, just like you predicted, Mara," said Andrai. "Looks like the lighter molecules like water and oxygen balance out all the gravitational effects, giving about the same weight of atmosphere on the surface as Earth. Interesting."

"Send all that over," said Mara.

"Coming your way, boss." Andrai made a flicking motion on his screen and a link to his data appeared on hers.

Mara ran an atmospheric model, incorporating all the new data. On

Oasis, water vapor seemed to sweep from the light side to the dark side, where its energy was released with violent intensity as it cooled. This caused not only permanent cloud cover, but continuous storm activity in the upper atmosphere. Yet their data indicated that below this maelstrom lay a calm, mist-shrouded expanse.

As they descended, Mara found that the temperature varied constantly with position. This puzzled her until she realized the distribution would be consistent with numerous sources of radiant heat, all located on the surface of the planet. Could they be volcanic vents?

"Any further sign of storm activity, Andrai?"

"No. The radar is showing nothing but low-lying cloud in the distance. Nothing near us, and nothing as violent as the upper atmosphere."

Her heart raced. It was time.

"OK. Let's have a look at the dark side of Oasis."

Andrai flicked a switch, and the low drone of electric motors sounded over the whine of the engines.

They crowded around the center console as the heavy steel plates that covered the polymer glass viewport drew back.

Bright light flooded through the gap, stinging their eyes.

And they saw Oasis for the first time.

Lush. Green. How can it be?

Andrai sat forward, his eyes full of wonder. "It's a paradise."

"How ...?" muttered Ibri.

Janzen took off his odin, the little AI automatically snapping out of full immersion mode. His eyes were alive. He drew himself up, his head tilted back as he took in every detail.

"Yes! Yes! *Yes!*" shouted Janzen, pumping a fist in the air.

He returned his odin to his face and started pacing the short deck.

For a long moment, Mara could not speak. It was beautiful. A vast world of vibrant life — untouched — vegetation stretching to the horizon. More than an oasis, this world made Earth, with its huge interconnected cities and fenced wildlife reserves, look like a desert of steel and concrete.

"Get another fix on that beacon, Andrai," said Mara.

Andrai worked rapidly, but he could not stop his gaze from drifting back to viewport.

Janzen paced behind them.

Andrai found Karic's position and paused, perplexed. "Karic is deep inside the dark side, thousands of kilometers from the terminator."

So she had been right.

"Plot a course," said Mara, turning to watch Janzen, who was dictating rapidly into his odin. He had forgotten to reactivate the full-immersion mode, and although he was speaking in a low voice, Mara could hear the odd word over the roar of the engines.

"... life ... certain that colonists will risk ... Downplay black hole ... scientific error ... experts to refute ..."

He was behind her chair.

"No terraforming is required. An Earth-like *living* planet! Easy marketing. Premiums. Notify the mining conglomerates as a priority. Drilling and exploration to start immediately."

Janzen looked down at her. His eyes glowed with triumph.

"Back to your seat, Janzen. Strap in." She could not keep the tremor out of her voice.

She turned back to the viewport, captured by the vast panorama. Never in their wildest dreams could they have imagined this. Not after the death and misery that they had suffered. Soon, they would meet Karic and walk the surface of this strange new world. The first of mankind to find life, *alien* life, amid the sprawling expanse of the cosmos. But how? How could it be here?

"Where is the light coming from?" asked Andrai, his eyes fixed on the view.

Her head pounded.

There should be no light.

"We are below the cloud now. Deploy the sensors, Andrai," ordered Mara.

Andrai nodded then retracted the heat shields over the sensors. The delicate instruments extended beyond the hull, then unfurled.

"Sensors, active."

They slowed the lander, then circled, allowing the delicate sensors to sweep the area.

Mara flipped through the data coming in, her heart beating wildly. No. Not possible.

"Mara?" said Janzen.

She shook her head.

On the descent, she had theorized multiple sources of heat. These could have been natural. Volcanic vents, for example, emerging from a vast area with high activity in the mantle. *But this?* There were multiple sources, but not just emitting heat. There was a broad band of electromagnetic radiation; strongest in the infrared and visible spectrums, but with narrow bands of radio and microwave. It was distinct, like a signature.

"Mara?"

"I'm not sure. There seems to be many sources, and they ... they can't be natural."

"Cannot be natural?" Janzen was indignant. "First you cannot find a black hole — which you claim is such a threat to us. Now this?"

"Do you have any conception of the amount of power it would take to heat and light half a planet!" shot back Mara.

Janzen looked down at her and snorted dismissively. "Do you have any proof? Any data that proves these ... *sources* are constructed?"

"Well no, but ..."

"Then you have no idea if they are natural or not. After all the trouble we went to at selection, instead of scientists, we have overblown technicians that run on conjecture. You are as bad as Karic."

Mara took a deep breath. "Thank God you are no longer in command. You are fucking clueless, Davis. Now sit down before I have Andrai and Ibri secure you to that chair."

Janzen's eyes widened, and his face flushed red.

"Oh, and by the way — data-glasses snap out of full-immersion mode when you take them off."

She watched Janzen as the realization hit home. Now he was truly disturbed. Even so, he regained his composure quickly. He was about to speak when the beacon abruptly ceased.

For hours it had been part of the atmosphere in the cabin — now it was gone. For tense minutes, no one spoke.

Janzen walked over to Andrai. "Why have we lost the signal? Is anything blocking it?"

Andrai worked frantically for long minutes then stopped, turning to Mara. His face creased with tension. "It's just *gone*."

"Is there any way to locate him without the beacon?" asked Janzen. His voice was neutral, his eyes calculating.

Mara ignored him. "Andrai, is there anything you can think of that would affect the beacon?"

The tension in Andrai's face eased as he thought it through out loud. "There are no atmospheric phenomena that could have caused this, no geological features anywhere near the horizon. The beacon was either switched off ... or it failed."

"We have already laid in a course based on the approximate position of the beacon, so take us there. Better tuck away the sensors," said Mara.

"OK. Everyone strap yourselves in," said Andrai.

Once they were secure in their harnesses, Andrai applied full thrust.

The acceleration pushed them deep into their seats. Their speed climbed into the supersonic, then hypersonic zones, the blunt wings and struts on the exterior of the squat craft now coming into their own.

Please, God. Let Karic be alright.

Chapter 7

Within an hour they decelerated.

Below them, a lake spread out majestically. It glittered in the light of a vast crystal mountain range. Mara shivered with excitement. She knew without a doubt that what she was observing was one of the many sources of light and heat on the dark side of Oasis. In shape, the mountain range looked like any other geological feature, driven up from the mantle by volcanic forces in the planet's history, yet it was as clear as glass — completely transparent — its crags and curves containing myriad internal facets. And it was lit from within by a warm radiance. She looked away from it to her viewscreen, blinking away a stark afterimage of the mountain's jagged shape, imprinted on her retina.

"Andrai, redeploy the sensors," said Mara.

Her readings confirmed the unique EM signature. This was one of the sources she had first detected. It did not *look* constructed. It was as irregular, eroded and worn as any natural mountain would be — although devoid of vegetation. And how could something so monolithic be manufactured?

The clear light gave the scene a dreamlike quality. Below the mountain, the lake and the nearby thick walls of vegetation were still and tranquil.

"It's so beautiful," said Mara.

"There's the pod," said Andrai, banking the lander into a wide turn that showed a clearing on the right below them. There was no sign of Karic.

"I can see the beacon. It's in position. It must have malfunctioned," said Andrai.

Mara tried the radio link. "Karic, do you read me?"

Silence.

"Karic, this is Mara, do you read me?"

She hailed him for another five minutes as Andrai slowly circled above, but got no reply. Mara took a slow breath.

"Activate the landing sequence, Andrai," said Mara.

"We should wait," said Janzen. "Observe." His leg was tapping out a rapid rhythm on the deck once more.

Mara spun in her chair. "Janzen! If you contradict one more of my orders, I really will have you gagged."

Janzen turned away without comment and slipped on his odin, lowering the data-shield.

Andrai leveled out the lander. Maneuvering rockets slowed their forward speed, then the braking thrusters engaged with a sudden roar, bringing the big craft down for a vertical landing. As they descended, Mara strained against the glass of the viewport, hoping to catch a glimpse of Karic. Beside her Andrai did the same.

"Where is he?" whispered Mara.

At last the lander touched the solid surface of the planet. The engines gave a final roar and cut, leaving them in abrupt silence.

The pod lay askew on the thick grass of the lake shore, the door wide open, the panels discolored with the heat of atmospheric entry. Even from the lander, they could see it was empty. Beside it, the transmitter array had toppled to the ground. It was blackened and inert, the paint peeling from the metal casing like dead skin on a corpse.

"Lightning strike," said Ibri, venturing a rare comment.

They released their harness straps, fumbling with clasps and tripping in the cluttered space as they moved slowly through the cabin.

Mara moved her limbs experimentally in the planet's heavier gravity. After the initial elation of finding life here, she was fatigued and uncertain. The surface gravity had added ten kilos to her weight, at least.

"How's the air, Andrai?"

"The atmosphere is safe, and breathable. High in oxygen, but within safe limits. We should wear the particle filter masks just in case there are some airborne nasties."

"OK. Janzen, you and Ibri go and check out the pod. Take one hour. Examine the pod then scout the area and see if you can find Karic. Stay in radio contact. Andrai and I will take the lander up and do an aerial survey, then scout for a camp nearby."

"I can't do that, Mara," said Janzen.

"What did you say?" said Mara, rounding on Janzen.

Andrai and Ibri froze.

Janzen smiled. "Section thirty-five, part eight of the code. 'Only ExploreCorp officers and crew can take part in advance planetary landings or scouting missions of a dangerous nature.' Since I have been removed from command, Mara, I am a civilian. Nothing more than a shareholder. I cannot be part of this expeditionary force."

Mara locked eyes with Janzen. He returned her gaze with a smug smile. She knew immediately he had planned this in advance. And while they argued, Karic was in danger on a strange planet. Perhaps dying while they talked and did nothing. It seemed inconceivable she had ever let Janzen near her. Beneath his cheerful friendliness, he was a self-serving egotist. A Davis to the core.

You are going to pay for this, Janzen.

She knew that for Janzen, this was just another move in an elaborate chess game. At least she was able to separate the former commander from Ibri, for the lanky, taciturn computer specialist had made his allegiance to Janzen clear from the outset. God knows what Janzen had offered to persuade him to his side. She could trust Andrai to follow her commands and keep Janzen on a leash until she could rendezvous at the base camp.

"OK. Ibri. You come with me. Andrai, you and Janzen take the lander up. Stay in radio contact, understand me?" Andrai nodded. "If you find a good site for a base camp, put down the lander, secure the site then send out a probe. I don't want us too near that glowing mountain, or too near the jungle. At least not until we understand more about this planet."

Mara was anxious to get the lander away from the lake. Whatever had threatened Karic and the pod could also be a threat to the bigger craft. They could not risk the lander. Protecting it meant their survival. Once they found Karic, they would be able to fly him to the base camp in the pod.

"But under no circumstances do anything without my orders. Understand?"

Andrai nodded.

Janzen turned and walked to the console. He sat down in Mara's seat, his back turned to her. *More fucking games.*

Gritting her teeth, Mara walked to the storage compartments. She entered the security code and opened the arms cabinet, removing a Davis XR32, a small handgun equipped with small, rocket-propelled, high-explosive rounds. She strapped it to her waist, then took out another XR32. She secured the arms cabinet and took out two masks from storage.

Mara stared at the XR32 in her hands. Having grown up on the space platforms at L1, Mara was uncomfortable with any kind of projectile weapon. There were absolute taboo in space — the risk of hull rupture was too great. Janzen had been insistent that they bring them from the beginning, and Mara had to admit, for a planet-bound expedition, they were reassuring. Still, somehow the weapons seemed out of place.

"Here, Ibri," said Mara, handing him a weapon and mask. He took the XR32 with wry amusement, buckling the weapon's black synthetic holster around his narrow waist, then slipped the filter mask over his face.

"OK, I want everyone's attention," she said.

Andrai and Janzen swiveled their chairs to face her.

"Andrai. I am leaving you in charge of the lander. Give yourselves an hour. If you do find a good site, radio in coordinates before you land. If you don't find a good site, return here. It's 11:28," said Mara checking the time on her comband. "Let's check in every ten minutes. I'll either hear from you or see you back here by 12:38."

She took a deep breath and turned to Ibri. "Let's go."

Already wearing his mask, Ibri nodded in acknowledgement.

Mara and Ibri crowded into the lander's airlock. The tall tech frowned in annoyance as he hunched beneath the low ceiling. She suppressed a smile. Ibri seemed to take any obstacle to his progress — whether human or inanimate — as a personal affront. The inner door sealed shut automatically behind them. Janzen followed them to the lock. He watched them through the glass window of the inner airlock door, his clear blue eyes as unreadable as chips of painted tile.

Mara adjusted her mask. She was uncomfortable with the bulk of the XR32 pressed into her side. Beside her, Ibri entered the sequence into the keypad beside the outer door. A low tone sounded and the seal broke.

Air rushed in around them, warm, and oddly scented.

Her head spun. Her legs felt suddenly weak. *I am hyperventilating.* Remembering the high oxygen content of Oasis' air, Mara deliberately held her breath until the lightheadedness passed. They were about to step onto an alien world. It seemed so unreal. Karic may be already dead. She drew the XR32.

The outer lock swung open, and Mara followed Ibri onto the lush green grass of the lake shore.

"We are prepping for liftoff." Andrai's voice issued from her comband like a wraith's whisper.

"Acknowledged," she replied into the communicator, her voice muffled by the filter mask.

Mara and Ibri walked quickly to the edge of the clearing, giving Andrai plenty of space to take up the lander. The thrusters ignited with a deafening *thump*. The sound hit her in the chest with physical force. She pressed the heels of her hands to the sides of her head to block her ears. Beside her Ibri did the same, his dark eyes narrowed critically as he watched the liftoff. Outside the lander, they got a firsthand experience of how much power those thrusters had. Every bit of that thrust was needed to get the massive craft airborne. Most of its weight was fuel in the remaining external tanks, all needed to eventually regain orbit. Mara gained a new appreciation for the lander's clever design as it lifted into the sky, the nested fuel tanks fitted so snugly around its fuselage that they formed part of its aerodynamics: sections of them doing dual service as extensions to the stubby wings or as aerobraking surfaces. It climbed steadily, then the thrusters cut and the flight engines took over. It shot toward the horizon, banked right, then spiraled out from their position in a search pattern. Less than a minute later, the big craft was gone.

Silence.

First they investigated the pod. They circled around it. There did not appear to be any damage to the tail or wings, although the scorched undercarriage and the leading edge of the wings told their own story of the tiny craft's dramatic descent. As they approached, Mara held out a tentative hand to the skin of the pod to gauge its heat, but the ceramics and alloys had already cooled to ambient temperature. The pod was too small for an airlock, and its single hatch was wide open, exposing the interior to Oasis' atmosphere. As they saw from the lander, the tiny cabin with its four cramped seats was empty. There was no sign of Karic.

Mara stepped over the threshold of the hatch into the darkened interior. She sheathed her weapon and tapped on a viewscreen. *Dead.* "The system is down. Ibri, why don't you see what you can do with the pod while I scout the area."

"OK," said Ibri, clearly looking forward to the challenge. The specialist was always happiest when engaged in his work.

Mara knew that recovery of the pod was important, but what she was really concerned about was Karic. Where was he? Why had he left the pod? And the beacon transmitter. How could lightning have struck it from a clear sky? The storms of the upper atmosphere were kilometers above them, but here, there was only a light, misting rain. It was hard to believe there was an electrical storm here only hours ago, when they lost the beacon signal. Still, conditions here were unknown. The data from the pod would tell them — once they restored power.

Mara walked around the pod in ever-increasing circles. The grass had been trampled in a wide path leading away from the pod. She knelt low and examined the grass. It looked as though a group of large animals had moved through here. She stood and followed the path as it led toward the lake shore. There, caught in the reeds, and now blowing in the wind, was Karic's filter mask.

It took her a few seconds to absorb the shock. Horror images of him being torn to shreds by a pack of predators filled her mind. No. She was jumping to conclusions. Maybe he lost his mask and left the lake before the animals appeared. Her stomach tied itself in knots as she followed the trail from the lake shore to the jungle, expecting at any moment to see blood ... or worse.

The forest understory was broad-leaved, and grew thickly and tall trees reminiscent of palms, but topped with huge flat leaves, soared from the canopy. All the bark was brightly colored with ragged patches of clinging fungi. Huge blossoms adorned the forest, spilling powerful scents into the humid air. The floor was littered with a mad jumble of rotting detritus and huge leaves. An elephant could pass through it and leave no sign. She had lost the trail.

Mara looked into the thick wall of vegetation, caught between the impulse to search for Karic and her duty to pursue the logical course of action — a return to the clearing and the methodical search for answers. Reluctantly, she turned back to the pod. Every step took deliberate effort. The warmth was thick and oppressive, heavy like the tug of the planet beneath her. Her legs were already aching in odd places, little-used muscles complaining at each movement.

The light of the crystal mountain was bright and harsh, yet under it everything was so beautiful, surreal. It was as though she walked across the ocean floor, beneath a clear sea. Dreaming.

Sweat made the grip of the XR32 slippery.

Suddenly, the bushes behind her and to her left parted. The animal gave a shrill screech as it came at her, moving in a blur of yellow.

Mara turned on her heel, her XR32 following the sweep of her gaze. She pointed and fired, screaming as the tiny projectile shot from the weapon. The recoil sent the gun tumbling from her grasp. Then she was knocked from her feet by a thudding concussion. A thicket of broad-leafed palms lay charred and blackened. A dozen small animals struggled within the flames. Beside her, an enormous insect like a grasshopper lay stunned, its glazed eyes perplexed as it searched for the nest and its young amid the smoking ruin. One leg had been shattered by the blast. It righted itself and hopped awkwardly back into the jungle, disappearing from sight.

She scrambled across the grass to the XR32. She swept it up and swiveled around her, expecting the animals she had tracked to come bursting out of the jungle next, looking for a human meal. But there was no sign of movement. Just a lone animal defending its nest.

The lake was deathly quiet.

Shaking, Mara pushed herself up off the ground. She had not expected the recoil, and had been way too close to the detonation point. Why had Janzen stocked *Starburst* with these damn things, she thought, looking at the deceptively small handgun. Did Janzen expect to fight a war?

Ibri had not even stirred from inside the pod, and Mara cursed the insular man under her breath as she wiped heavy beads of sweat from her forehead.

She clicked on the safety and sheathed the gun with a feeling of nausea. Then she scanned the area. Nothing.

It was time to check in with Andrai. She raised her comband to her mouth.

"Andrai, can you hear me?"

There was a slight delay.

"Yes, Mara. We have covered more than two thousand square kilometers, but there is no sign of Karic. There is a noticeable pattern in the vegetation though. It thins out rapidly away from the light sources. There are a number of sites in the more open forest that would be ideal for a landing site."

Mara considered telling Andrai what she had learned, but she wanted more information first.

"Take the lander down. There's no point wasting fuel. Let the probe do the survey work."

"Understood. Andrai out."

A chorus of animal noises began to rise from the jungle and lakeshore. Small animals and larger flying insects in a glittering array of colors darted from cover to drink at the lake, then flashed back into the safety of the concealing foliage.

Mara walked back to the pod. Inside, she saw Ibri at work under the console. An access hatch was open, wires trailing across the metal floor.

He looked up at her. "What was that noise?"

"I had to fire on an animal," said Mara. "What have you found?"

"Power's on. Systems still down. Can't find anything wrong with the hardware. Puzzling."

"Can you access the central memory of the computer?"

"Yes."

"Can we get at the video footage?"

"Yeah. Visuals only. Audio's out."

"After the pod's landing, the external camera would have continued to function. Call up the memory. I need to see it."

Ibri gave Mara a puzzled frown, then maneuvered himself out from under the console.

Mara climbed into the cramped cabin of the pod, sitting next to Ibri as he replayed the visual sequence shot during the descent of the craft; it was dramatic and yet told them nothing.

"Rough ride," said Ibri.

Mara tapped the tiny viewscreen impatiently.

Finally, the footage showed the craft landing. The figure of Karic came into view. He methodically set up and activated the transmitter.

"Take it forward to when the beacon stopped."

Karic's hours passed in fast motion. They watched as he rested, then scouted the area, finally stopping to eat rations.

Huge beings, larger than bears, thrust out from the lush growth in unison.

Ibri took his finger off the button and the images slowed to real time.

They were hairless, bipedal, their thick pudgy arms ending in a three-fingered hand with an opposable thumb. Their rough skin was a pale, creamy color, mottled with random blooms of yellow, red, green and purple, and hung in huge flabby folds from their stocky frames. Along the torso, running from under each arm down to their hips, were two long columns of raised points on the skin, like pale nipples.

It seemed they were moving slowly, awkwardly, but watching them close on Karic revealed this to be an illusion created by their size.

Mara held her breath.

Karic ran for the pod, but was easily subdued, held immobile in those thick, doughy hands.

Mara could see Karic's eyes widen as he stared up at them.

Their faces were fleshy and smooth, like a panda's in shape, but strangely uniform, as though someone had crafted a mould then melted it until it ran together. Their mouths were wide, filled with large, flat teeth and a tongue the size of a dinner plate. The mottled colors of their bodies concentrated on the head, forming a solid band across the crown that spilled over onto the thick, rounded shoulders. Their two round eyes were huge and black, without eyelid or noticeable iris or cornea; more like raised nodules. The two stubby ears were set wide apart on the side of the huge head. There were no visible genitalia, but anything could have been concealed in the folds of flesh that hung down off the big thighs and rubbed together beneath their legs as they moved.

It was a coordinated attack. One of the aliens stood back, directing the others. His body and head were decorated with sticks and leaves and skins, woven into bizarre shapes. A head taller than the others, the mottled colors on his bald dome were dominated by a vibrant gold and green that contrasted sharply with the more prosaic skin-shades on his underlings. At his side, he held a primitive scepter covered with bright strips of animal skin and insect wings of all shapes and sizes. He looked like a shaman, and clearly held power over the others. The scepter was a clear sign of rank.

They had no weapons and no clothing, relying only on physical strength to subdue Karic. They had acted in unison, and with restraint, which demonstrated intelligence. Karic was dragged from the field of vision, then there was nothing but grass, and the tranquil lake scene.

Suddenly, everything fitted together. This planet *had* been engineered. And the locals were still here.

Mara had seen enough. "Turn it off."

Ibri tapped the console, freezing the image. He stared at the viewscreen for a long moment, his deep-set eyes unreadable; he blinked once, then returned to his work.

Mara chewed a knuckle on her right hand, deep in thought. She was missing something. Something in the recording …

Adrenalin was pumping through her. *She had to act.* But a wrong, hasty decision now would be disastrous for them all.

Mara lifted herself over Ibri and out of the pod.

She started pacing the thick grass, trying to burn off her anxiety. The beings looked primitive. But that did not make sense. A race that could construct those crystal mountains would have vast resources. What were they dealing with, then? Two races? A fallen culture? A dark age?

"Damn it!"

It did not matter. All that mattered was surviving. Finding and rescuing Karic. Protecting themselves and getting back to Earth. It was significant that the natives captured, rather than simply attacked Karic. But what that meant, what their intentions were, she had no way of knowing.

"Mara, are you there?"

Mara started at the sound of Andrai's voice, weirdly thin and out of place as it sounded from the tiny speakers of her comband. Her hand dropped to the hilt of her gun, and her heart beat double-time with a sourceless panic. *Damn, I'm jumpy.* She took a deep breath, noticed the safety of the gun was on and flicked it off.

"Mara, do you read me?"

"Yes, Andrai, I read you."

"We have found a site. Three point six kilometers from your current position, bearing one hundred and three degrees."

"Copy that," said Mara.

"Any sign of Karic?"

She took a breath and let it out slowly. "There are intelligent natives here, Andrai. Some sort of tribal-level bipedal beings. They have taken Karic." Even as she said it, her mind spun with a sense of unreality. "The whole thing was captured on the pod's camera."

"Understood," said Andrai, after a long moment. "We are about to descend and send out a probe. Once we go down, your comband won't be able to reach us."

"I know, Andrai."

"Is the pod functional?"

"Not yet."

"If you can't get the pod operational, Mara, I'll use the probe to relay a signal in two hours." Airborne, the probe could bounce a signal over the horizon from her to base camp and back.

"OK, Andrai. When you set up the base camp, make sure you deploy the defensive shield."

"Copy, that. Anything else, Mara?"

"No. Just stay put. I'll brief you when we take the pod over."

"Copy that. Andrai, out."

Mara watched the lander appear over the horizon, then drop down out of sight below a line of low hills. It was good to know they were so close.

A few minutes later she heard a distant roar, then the high-pitched whine of small chemical rockets as the probe shot skyward from the lander and disappeared from view.

Mara realized how tense she was, standing rigid, hands clenched by her sides. She opened her fists, shook her arms and rolled some of the tension out of her neck. All was going according to plan. No need to worry. One strand of dark hair had come away from her tight braid, and she worked it back in with quick, practiced movements of her fingers. The probe was equipped with the best survey sensors money could buy. The images and readings it relayed back to the lander would be continuously analyzed by its computer. They *would* find Karic, wherever he had been

87

taken.

Ibri worked tirelessly with the onboard systems to restore the pod's functions, while Mara stood guard, her eyes swimming with fatigue as she scanned the tree line.

They attempted one lift, quickly aborting the attempt after losing control only meters from the ground. There was something seriously wrong with all the systems. It was baffling. With the pod in this state it could not fly twenty meters without destabilizing, and nothing would respond to the controls. The analyzers, the cameras, the wing, the radio, all were inert. Karic could never have made the descent with the pod in this condition.

Mara held the XR32 nervously, staring into the broad canopy that surrounded the lake. The hours drew on, and once more she looked to the sky, willing dusk to come so that the day could end; yet no sun was to be found in the deep blue expanse above her, and no comfort. Time had no meaning here on the planet's dark side. This half-day that surrounded them was endless. The raucous noises of the jungle continued in all their alien vitality.

Fatigue drew her down like a weightstone.

The probe shot by overhead on its preprogrammed flight path. She completed a radio check with Andrai. The lander was down and safe, the defensive shield deployed.

The link died as the probe disappeared over the horizon. Her heart sank as she watched it go. It would not return to the area for another ten hours. She was effectively out of contact with the base camp.

She shook her head to clear it, then circled the pod once more, coming to rest near the ruined beacon transmitter. Bored, she examined the central shaft and dish. The paint fell away at a touch, charred to powder. Intrigued, she sheathed her XR32 and prized open the inspection plate. The transmitter had not only been toppled and broken, the interior wiring and circuitry was literally *melted*. It lay fused in a single mass, still warm to touch. *This was hit by an energy weapon.*

Mara sprinted to the pod, clambering through the cramped internals to sit before the main console. Ibri lay across the floor of the craft, inspecting the rocket's control mechanisms, which lay under access panels in the floor. He gave her a dark look, no doubt annoyed at the interruption, and returned to work.

The blank image was still frozen on the console, as it was left by them hours ago. On the margins of the picture, the beacon transmitter lay upright — and untouched.

"God! I'm an idiot!"

She activated the recording. The scene was brought to sudden, silent, life. One of the aliens reentered the view. He touched the transmitter gingerly, then turned and spoke to someone behind him. The alien left the frame, yet scarcely had he moved out of view than another took his place. It was the shaman, unmistakable in his bright decorations. It would have been easy to dismiss him as primitive, and yet his self-assurance — the menace in his slow, deliberate approach — raised goosebumps across the skin of her arms and neck.

The shaman stood before the transmitter, regarding it for a long moment, then suddenly he turned — facing the camera. The raised black nodules of his eyes began to glow yellow, then pulse. Even though it was an image, Mara was transfixed by his gaze, held by the reality of his presence. Finally, he turned back to face the beacon. He lifted the decorated scepter at his side. As the short staff rose, the ragged skins that covered it fell away, revealing the bright metal beneath. A dazzling bolt of blue leapt from the end of the weapon. The electrical corona of the discharge wrapped around the beacon, lifting it from its tripod and turning it into a smoking ruin. He turned to the pod. Once more he raised his weapon. There was a flash of blinding light.

Mara screamed involuntarily, pulling back from the screen.

When she looked back, there was nothing but static.

"Ibri. *Ibri*."

"What is it?" snapped Ibri.

"The beacon and the pod were hit by a weapon. Those aliens have energy weapons!"

At once, she had Ibri's interest. He stood up, suddenly excited, hunched beneath the low roof of the pod as he focused on the grayed-out viewscreen. "Of course. An energy discharge of the right voltage would scramble the software, but leave the hardware intact. That's it! We need a full diagnostic. Reboot the software."

Mara paled. "Before we attempt a second lift?" A full diagnostic took hours. Wasn't he listening to her! *They were in danger from aliens with energy weapons!*

Ibri nodded.

Mara had a sick feeling in her stomach. "We are all in much greater danger than we thought." Could the lander's defensive shield stand up to advanced alien weapons? She had to warn Andrai and Janzen. "We must contact the lander as soon as we can. We have to set out on foot for the new base camp. It's the only way."

Ibri's deep-set eyes fixed on hers. "Through unknown jungle? Abandon the pod? No. We can fly there once I finish."

"That's an order, Ibri. We set out on foot. Now." Mara held his gaze, trying to enforce her orders through sheer force of will. Having to look up at him didn't help, but she held firm. She watched the contemptuous light drain away from his dark eyes, to be replaced with something else.

"I have to finish this," said Ibri, his usually soft, tenor voice raised to a high-pitch of agitation. Mara realized with a shock what she now saw in his eyes. *Fear.* Ibri's need to continue the repair was obsessive. The prospect of being taken away from the task once a solution was in sight provoked a kind of terror in him. On *Starburst,* that trait was an asset. Here it meant putting others in danger. That brief flash of fear was quickly replaced by a contemptuous defiance.

"The pod will be worth nothing to us if we are dead," said Mara.

Ibri turned his back to her. After a pause, he knelt down, sliding the access panels back into place with quick, almost fevered movements. "I'll have this flying in half an hour," he said.

She gritted her teeth. Ibri was hard enough to deal with at the best of times. *Damn Janzen.* His continual efforts to balk her had eroded her authority. Yet, it would be better to return to base camp in the pod.

"That's all the time you've got," said Mara, injecting as much authority as she could into her voice.

The world around her continued. The same noises, the same light. She paced the thick grass in frustration. They had to be warned. But for her to set off alone? That was too risky.

She looked at the display on her comband. There was still more than nine and a half hours before she could reestablish contact with Andrai. The aliens knew where the pod was. It was only a matter of time before they returned.

Three point six kilometers. She could jog that in less than thirty minutes, surely — despite the extra kilos the planet's gravity would add to her slight frame. Ibri could lock himself in the pod, fly it to the new location once the systems were responding. No. *No.* Don't be an idiot, she told herself. Anything could happen to her in that jungle, and they would never find her. She and Ibri had to stay together. They had to stick with the plan.

A painful throb began behind her eyes. Karic was in danger. They were all in danger. She had to do something!

"Janzen. Andrai. Can you read me?"

Static.

The damn things were not designed for this.

She balled her hands into fists and screamed.

Beside her, the lake glittered in perfection.

Chapter 8

It was a surreal trek for Karic. His early attempt to break free had seen him tackled by two of the creatures and slammed into the forest floor under a crushing weight of hairless flesh. He remained disoriented for some time after that. The huge natives also took precautions. One of the aliens flanked him on either side, each gripping one of his wrists in their big three-fingered hands, while the others loomed in front and behind. They walked for a long time, the skin-clad shaman leading, scepter by his side, the others following behind.

They had been silent at first, yet now they spoke to each other in a strange musical fluting. He could sense a new purpose driving them, and guessed they were drawing close to some destination. His heart thumped double-time, driving him to a sharp alertness. The verdant green of the forest, the heavy air — redolent with sweet resin and spicy scents — came into sharp relief.

Karic looked up into the doughy too-smooth faces of the creatures and tried to read some intent or emotion in their big, black eyes. He had a sudden sense of how alien they were. He swallowed against a reaction of nausea, as though something had tried to crawl up his throat, something with hooked beetle legs and barbed flesh. The aliens were even larger up close. At least three meters in height, yet as bulky as polar bears — but without the hair. The two that held him were slightly different from the others, taller and thinner, with a predominance of red color on their head and shoulders. There was no way he could hope to overpower them; yet, for all their strength, they seemed to lack an instinctive coordination that was second-nature to a human. Maybe he could outdistance them. Outmaneuver them with his primate-derived agility. He just needed a chance.

The slope steepened as they climbed toward a ridge. The aliens began to speak at once, their voices sliding over each other from note to note until they harmonized together in a weird musical scale. The vocal gymnastics appeared to be natural to them, and it was in their voices, rather than their faces or bodies, that Karic could read a rising excitement. The forest, which had initially thinned out, now grew thick. The path became constricted as trees and vines, grown rampant in the waxing radiance of another crystal mountain, pressed in from either side. Just for a moment, one of his alien wardens released his grip on Karic's right hand in order to negotiate a bend in the path.

Now.

Karic twisted his left hand out of the grip of the second alien warden and fled off the path.

He pushed through the thick growth, desperately looking for any escape. The forest became a blurred capsule of green as he sprinted away. His lungs were raw with the effort, his limbs burning in the heavy gravity.

He spotted a huge wall of vine, weaving around two fallen forest giants. The whole tangled mass blocked a steep gully that led down into a narrow valley far below him. If he could force his way through this wall of vine, the bulky aliens would waste hours finding another way around.

He ran for the vines.

They filled his vision. Huge purple leaves, shaped like teardrops. Strings of small white flowers. A pungent, sickly scent.

Almost there.

Karic felt a pressure behind him and leapt to his right. A bright flash seared his vision as something struck him on the arm. A surge of electricity shot through him. The chain around his neck burned into his skin with sudden heat. His body twisted and he tripped into the vines. His head hit one of the gigantic, fallen trees and he collapsed onto the thick grass, stunned. The leaves and flowers above him shriveled instantly to black as the last of the discharge swept through them. The scent of the vine was overpowered by that of burning vegetation and the smell of ozone.

A hot wave of agony flared across his left forearm, bathing his mind in fire. He opened the seam of his jacket with his other hand. His chain fell to pieces in his hand, the links melted. The blackened St. Christopher medal tumbled from his shaking fingers to the leaf-strewn ground. He clawed at the soil, desperate to find it.

But his vision blurred, and darkness took him.

***

Karic groaned in pain. He hovered in dark, suffocating molasses, a grim shadow world lit by distant flames. His limbs were impossibly heavy. He could hear voices around him, conversing in high melodious tones. Fear filled him, yet desperation gave him will. He swam to consciousness.

A flood of color stung his eyes.

He sucked desperately at the humid air, looking around him with wide eyes. His head swam, and he forced himself to slow his breathing.

Karic was no longer in the forest. He was on his knees, his arms held firmly by two towering, red-crowned aliens. Other aliens crowded the space, speaking slowly in their mellifluous language.

He looked up at them, and immediately they grew silent.

Karic pushed himself to his feet. His head throbbed, yet this pain was nothing compared to the agony in his left arm, which had been burnt by the discharge of the energy weapon. The long, ragged burn was bleeding, the damaged skin torn by the rough grip of the alien's huge hand. Up close, he could see their skin was roughly textured, patterned like a reptile's — it felt like sandpaper.

He was inside some sort of circular structure. A raised dais was set before him, bathed with warm amber light. Seated there was one of the aliens, huge even compared to those he had seen. His skin was stretched tight in places, the bloated belly and torso dwarfing the round face. His huge eyes glowed faintly in the dim light with yellow phosphorescence. The colors across the skin were faded almost to black.

The shaman was at the base of the dais. Karic recognized him immediately in his distinctive regalia of sticks, leaves and skins. The shaman's henchmen he knew from his trek through the forest, recognizing them by the distinctive colors on their heads, shoulders and torsos. Behind Karic, a score of the creatures were gathered in ranks, solemn and attentive to the events beneath the dais. Assembled, they presented a maze of colors that dazzled his eyes. Beyond the strangeness, his heart quailed at the sheer size of them, the weight and power beneath their mottled skins.

In the gathered creatures, he could see a variety of postures and facial expressions, yet had no way of knowing what they meant. Their eyes were multi-faceted, like an insect's, and scattered the light across their surface like expertly cut gemstones. In the dim light he could see that all the aliens' eyes possessed the same quality of bioluminescence. These subtle variations of light and color brought them to life. Despite being only raised nodules, they were capable of being extremely expressive.

Karic turned back to the dais. The leader's eyes — for this was unquestionably their leader — seemed to slumber with suppressed power, and Karic had the sense of great age.

Karic looked across to the shaman, staring deep into the alien eyes trying to judge his intelligence. The shaman stared back with unconcealed malice. The emotion was unmistakable, and strangely human. This dark dislike, the first real communication between human and alien — albeit on an emotional level — made his stomach squirm with fear.

Karic's limbs trembled with fatigue and he sank to his knees. A wave of dizziness threatened to drag him down, but he fought back to consciousness. The effect of the heavy gravity was not just added weight. His knees and lower back throbbed, and he felt the strain in every joint and muscle as they struggled to adapt and function.

The shaman raised his scepter and pointed it at Karic. Turning to the great figure on the dais, he began to speak once more, gesticulating wildly with the skin-covered instrument.

Karic had seen what destruction the scepter was capable of, and watched it with great anxiety. In the torchlight it gleamed with the bright finish of burnished steel, undulled and perfect. The end was tapered and set with a faceted lens unlike any Karic had seen. It delivered a pulse of energy far beyond anything a device of its size should be able to command, and was out of place amid these primitive surrounds. It spoke of a technology far beyond anything he had seen on this world. Far beyond anything humankind had yet devised. What was he dealing with here? A fallen culture? Two races, one advanced, another primitive, yet sharing technology?

The shaman turned back to him. The alien's eyes grew brighter, becoming twin orbs, filled with hate. A desire for his destruction.

Those eyes ...

Karic had a sense of recognition. A distant voice of realization was calling for his attention amid the clamor of the *Starburst's* alarms and the smell of burned flesh ...

The thought was lost below the edge of consciousness.

This time, he felt, rather than saw, the shimmering, surging patterns that preceded the fugue. He had spent so much of his life fighting it, developing an arsenal of tricks and drugs that would keep his mind in the here and now. Yet now his instincts urged him to surrender. The voice of reason urged him to fight, to keep his wits, but exhaustion and pain dulled that voice.

The fugue's usual effect was lost time — he would experience strange visions while time dilated. What would seem moments to him would be hours where he was lost, immobile, staring into some unknown space. It was frightening for those who witnessed it. He would appear like a man trapped in a catatonic episode, unresponsive to outside stimuli. Thankfully, his family recognized his first fugue state, having seen his grandfather experience the same condition, and helped him both conceal and manage it.

Yet the fugue had changed.

When he was overtaken by the fugue state during the pod descent, amid the turbulent fury of Oasis' storm-wracked upper atmosphere, there had been no dilation. No lost time. His mind had grown outward, meshing with the storm and the matter of the pod, but he had remained acutely aware of his surroundings and the normal passage of time. He had experienced the fugue as a state of heightened awareness, with his senses enhanced in new, unexpected ways.

After that episode in the pod — that strange, focused state — a secret, reckless hope he had always held close to his heart, that he would one day learn to control the fugue, emerged with new strength, urging him to leap into the unknown. For a brief moment, Karic hovered on the edge of fear.

Then he let the fugue take him.

His vision expanded. Karic reached out, desperate to anchor himself, to prevent the time dilation.

His mind swept around him, insubstantial tendrils whipping and surging with his dreaming mind. Rhythms brought into his conscious mind through genetic manipulation and chance. His nervous system, somehow, had expanded beyond his body. And he was connecting …

The walls were alive. A vast living dome of thickly interwoven branches lit with primitive torches. A pungent, oily smoke filled the expanse with an aromatic odor. Hundreds of the beings were behind him, arranged in a circle. They were silent, their heads bowed.

He focused on the shaman, on penetrating the mind behind those huge, glowing eyes.

His heart raced.

In his heightened awareness, the realization came with the shock of a blow to the head, emerging like a bullet from the depths of his subconscious where the knowledge had already coalesced.

He knew those eyes. The eyes of the watcher outside the *Starburst*. The twin orbs of malice that he had first seen during the fugue in the biodome. The hate-filled hunter that had haunted him before the surge of radiation that had killed thirty-three men and women and crippled their starship. He was sure of it. But if this being was real, did that mean the shaman had some hand in causing that damage to the *Starburst?* Or the death of Evelle? He had managed to contain his grief and his anger at the tragedy by rationalizing it; telling himself it had been an act of God. The thought that this being attacked them … No. It was not possible. How could this primitive shaman direct such an intense burst of EM radiation? And why target them? It did not fit. But nothing about this world seemed to make sense. The dark side should be frozen. Lifeless.

He pushed through those eyes.

It was fire in his mind. Power. Flooding him. Light and motion. A swarm of tiny blue and white flames surrounded him. Some were buried deep, some linked together, others seeming to float on the surface of his consciousness.

But one sped into his right eye, expanding with blinding pain.

He was suspended in space, filled with power and purpose.

This was a memory, but not his. *The shaman's.*

Before him, a vast device. A superstructure that would dwarf every station in the Earth system. Huge curved beams enclosed an ovoid space, the materials of construction virtually transparent, visible only through reflection.

The light — blinding. A yellow sun — filling nearby space. The device — in orbit. Slowly, he drew closer to the massive bulk. Within it a core of darkness, the size of a small moon. Waves of energy radiated, then were absorbed across a shimmering field that stretched between the supports of the ovoid superstructure. The dark core constantly spinning, trying to shift its position, but held confined.

Closer still.

His mind was filled with a confusion of colors, geometrical shapes and readings — a flood of information he did not understand.

The complex visual tapestry shattered in a blast of outrage. He was abruptly thrust out of the alien's mind.

The shaman's eyes were beacons of fury. Around the alien's head was a maelstrom of dancing, swirling lights. Intuitively, Karic realized he was seeing a depiction of the alien's mind, as interpreted by his own overdriven brain. A new, hot light grew amid that cognitive aurora, then shot toward him.

Defiler! I am Utar of the Imbirri! I suffer no such outrages.

Karic fell into a depth of swirling color. His last thought before he surrendered to unconsciousness was that he had not only read the shaman's mind, he had just communicated with him telepathically.

If only Lein could see him now.

***

Utar trembled with fury as he watched the human collapse. He gripped the scepter with all his strength, turning it on the intruder. His thick thumb hovered over the stud.

"No, Utar. This is not the time for killing," said the Awakener from his dais.

With a supreme effort of will, Utar took his finger away from the activating stud. Torn with frustration, he spun to face the Awakener. "I am the Deepwatch. It is my responsibility to protect us. You must understand the danger to the Imbirri! These intruders must *all* die."

Ten seasons ago, Utar had seen the greatest danger yet to their way of life. In Farsleep he could travel paths he alone knew. While his body remained in a comatose state, his mind could travel time and space. It was during such a journey that he came to know them, these humans. Then again, he had risked the longest Farsleep yet to sow the seeds of their destruction. Had left their craft crippled — and the humans who remained helpless to avoid their own deaths — or so he thought. He had risen dangerously weak from that last, long Farsleep; his stores of fat depleted, his body drained, and his mind haunted by the scenes of destruction he had wrought. But for all that, he was satisfied. Yet ... yet barely seventeen sleep cycles had passed before he saw his worst fears confirmed.

Not only had he failed to destroy all the humans, the survivors had violated the sanctity of the planet Cru. Five of them were on the planet. Utar could feel the feeble pulse of their mortality, and sense the danger they represented.

The thirty-eight First were silent. Expectant. They were the most senior of the Imbirri — brought to consciousness by the Awakener and Utar at the very dawn of time — yet their thousands of years of life had not prepared them for this scene: the abhorrent sight of the alien intruder, or the conflict its appearance had provoked between their two leaders.

Reth and Ember, the two reds who held the human, looked at Utar then the Awakener. As Utar's acolytes, they owed allegiance to him. Yet all of the Imbirri, including Deepwatch Utar, were ultimately bound to the Awakener's will.

The Awakener shifted his great bulk forward on his throne and favored Utar with an indulgent smile. "How long have we presided together over the Imbirri, Utar?" His voice was soft and sweet with melody.

Utar lowered the scepter. "Almost nine thousand seasons."

Otla, the most senior of Utar's seven acolytes, stepped forward respectfully from the ranks of the First, the vibrant green of his crown and shoulders shining with reflected torchlight. "It is the 8771st season of redwings, Awakener." Otla had always had a head for numbers, and never failed to note the time of the annual Redwing Swarm — when the fat grubs that infested the lush forests near the crystal mountains hatched into vibrant red-winged butterflies. The acolyte bowed and rejoined the First.

Green Patch gently touched Otla on the shoulder as he took his place. Although a gold, and an avid player of the Pod Game, Green Patch was named for the odd splash of emerald on his forehead, like the mark of hand stained with bright green sap. Green Patch and Otla often sang together and shared their choicest foods. The bond was a gentler, softer echo of that between Utar and the Awakener.

Utar ground his teeth together in frustration. In the last few centuries the Awakener's vast and powerful mind had turned in on itself, becoming lost in a blurred sea of memories and emotion. How could he make him see the immediacy of the threat?

Utar regarded the pitiful human, now given in to his weakness. The alien shared some of the inherent powers that made Utar a Deepwatch — senses that extended beyond his physical form, allowing both mental communication and a vision of future potentials. Utar sensed that the human recognized Utar from his Farsleep travels. He cared not. Better he should know his executioner.

"Awakener," said Utar in a level voice. "The influence of these humans must be eliminated before it is too late. "

The Awakener was silent. Worse, he seemed to be drifting back into dream.

Utar's lips compressed into a grim line. "Awakener, hear me! They must be destroyed, as are the forbidden ones. If they live only days more, the Imbirri are in great danger."

The Awakener smiled and shifted his great bulk, his dark eyes meeting Utar's with loving benevolence. He turned and looked around at the assembled Imbirri. The First were silent, waiting for the wisdom of their leader.

Utar also turned to watch them, his eyes narrowed. Only thirty-eight First remained. Once there had been forty-six. Over those thousands of seasons, some had succumbed to the Changes despite his best efforts and regular doses of the Elixir, which prevented them. They had ... were *becoming* abominations. Transforming to twisted creatures with no place in the forest. All had been destroyed by his own hand before they could emerge as horrors that would bring terror to the peaceful Imbirri. He remembered all the missing faces, and their silent voices, now absent from the harmonies. Even now, the nipples on either side of his bulky torso grew moist with sadness at the memories. Yet sacrifices had to be made. It was their blissful, changeless existence that he was protecting.

The First stood in lines, ranked in the order of their awakening. Here, as for the Imbirri as a whole, the greens like Otla dominated. The golds — like Utar himself — were rarer, perhaps one-tenth of the population. There were others too, smaller groups like the purples and reds. All Imbirri were marked with various colors across their bodies, but it was the predominant color on the crown of their heads that distinguished them. The Awakener himself had been an undiluted green — a rarity — before his color began to fade.

The First watched the Awakener in hushed expectation. Unlike Utar, they saw the same leader they had always known. Their trust, their love, was undiminished. None of them saw the changes in the Awakener that Utar saw. Not surprising, since none of them had the deep relationship with their leader that the Deepwatch had. He and the Awakener were the first of the changeless Imbirri. The first to share their voices in the verdant innocence of Cru's ancient forests.

"In truth, you are all my children," said the Awakener. "But you, Utar, you were the first of the First. I rose you up, here beneath the branches of the Tree. So long ago ... long ago. Yet you remember, do you not, my friend?"

Those memories were vivid to Utar. The Tree had been young then, open below its high canopy. Over long eons they and the First had lovingly pruned and woven its branches together to form a great, living dome, its only entrance an arch of living boughs cunningly concealed by overlapping branches. A sacred space of fellowship and union. Endless seasons filled with love and joy, marred only by the violations of the few among them.

The Awakener smiled at Utar.

They regarded each other for a long moment. Utar's heart lifted at the sight of that big, familiar face, the powerful glowing eyes. He felt the first note of a melody swelling in his chest, and drew in a sharp breath. A flush of heat ran to the nipples down the sides of his torso, and he longed for an intimacy between them that was impossible with the First here. He fought to clear his mind, to escape the welling emotion, but the Awakener's presence was overpowering.

"It is as I taught you," said the Awakener. His huge chest rose with an indrawn breath and his voice wrapped the silent First in tones as deep as forest shadow. "The Elixir is the breath of life! Without life, there is no love, and love is eternal."

The Awakener rose from his primitive seat of boughs and the First fell to the ground, faces raised in adoration.

The Awakener looked at the First, his face filled with delight.

"You serve me well. Yes. Well," he said, sweeping his gaze across the prostrate First.

"But you, my friend," he said, returning his gaze to Utar. "You are the greatest of my servants."

The Awakener stepped down off the dais, walking to the Deepwatch, taking Utar's hands in a soft grip of friendship. The tips of Utar's nipples grew hot at the contact.

"Utar. You were beside me to share the beginning of time. You know the joy of life — unending life. Why should any existence, even that of these strange beings, be ended?"

Utar stepped away from the touch of the Awakener, his emotions in turmoil. Never would the Awakener understand the peril in which the Imbirri lay. Time was endless on Cru, unmarked and unchecked by the hands of fate. His friend and master, the Awakener, had become lost within his teachings, having sheltered too long beneath the warmth and strength of years. He was trapped by his visions, as surely as the Tree encircled them.

Utar bowed his head, defeated, and raised the scepter high, surrendering his authority to his master.

The Awakener took the scepter. He untied the skins and decorations that covered it, letting them drop to the ground. He held up the naked, gleaming cylinder and turned to the First.

"Go my children! Go forth and raise others as you have been raised high!"

Utar straightened, his eyes solemn. It had been more than a thousand years since the last of the Imbirri were raised to sentience. The Awakener was lost, sadly, within the immensities that gave them birth; yet Utar could still not defy him. "What of the human?"

The Awakener looked at the alien and laughed. "Place him in the punishment pit until I decide."

Utar bowed, then gave curt orders to Otla and Munch — the latter, a short, plump purple who was another of his senior acolytes, and who had earned his name from a long-standing habit of noisy eating.

As he watched his followers drag the human to the punishment pit, Utar trembled with a desire for the being's destruction. He could wait. He would bide his time until the vile beings that had violated Cru made their presence felt in more insidious ways. He would wait until the cancer of destruction within them rose and smote the Imbirri as he knew it would. Then the Awakener's consciousness would fully return to the present. *A great reckoning will follow, even if I must die to bring it down upon them.*

The Imbirri will be preserved.

Chapter 9

The minutes passed in agonizing slowness.

Mara checked her chrono and — for the thousandth time — searched the sky for the position of the sun. It was a hard habit to break, even for a space-rat who had spent less than a decade on-planet.

Fuck this.

She started pacing again, seeking an outlet for her nervous energy. The XR32 felt heavy, inert, in her hand, but she would not sheath it.

She studied the lakeshore and the jungle, alert for any movement that would indicate a threat.

The dull throbbing behind her eyes had developed into an intense headache, sharp edges of pain working at her temples and neck.

The pod's systems were still laboriously running through the diagnostic, Ibri checking hardware manually with the limited tools he had. Fatigue weighed down on her, and her body craved darkness and sleep. Her concern for Karic and the rest of the crew had grown steadily, fed by the silence and the frustration, until it was overpowering.

Mara made for the pod, hardly pausing as she straddled the hatch and entered the cramped cabin. Ibri ignored her, his attention focused on a circuit board that he was investigating with a small probe, wires trailing across the floor to a meter.

"Ibri."

When Ibri did not respond Mara snatched the circuit board from his grasp and tossed it out of the pod, watching with satisfaction as it sailed through the air and speared into the grass.

Ibri glared at Mara in mute anger.

"It's been more than two hours. This is taking too long. We have to get a message to Janzen and Andrai. These aliens are dangerous. They and the lander could be in danger."

Ibri snorted in contempt. "We can't walk to the lander with the aliens out there. We've got to get this pod operational. Fly it to base camp."

Mara shook with rage. "We have to get back to the base camp now — *with or without the pod*. We have its position. We could reach it in less than half an hour. They are just on the other side of that ridge, damn it!"

"Safer to fly the pod," said Ibri obstinately.

Mara was afraid of the jungle, and of the aliens. They were big, intelligent and equipped with weapons, but Janzen and Andrai had to be warned. She and Ibri had to attempt the walk. She now realized how optimistic Ibri's initial estimate was. The pod could be inert for up to a day, depending on how badly the software had been affected; and during that time more lives could be lost. Together, they would have a good chance in the jungle. Alone, she could perish quickly if threatened or injured.

"Finish up, Ibri. We are walking to the lander. We will put the damaged transmitter inside the pod."

Ibri turned away and continued working.

"Did you hear me? I just gave you an order."

Ibri simply looked at her.

She should not have shouted. The pain in her head was bringing tears to her eyes.

"You are coming with me, Ibri. Now."

"I'm not going anywhere, *Commander*. Janzen can handle things at the lander until we are finished."

"Janzen ..." *But I left Andrai in charge.*

Mara met Ibri's eyes, sudden comprehension banishing her headache in a flood of adrenalin. Ibri had never stopped supporting Janzen. And the longer Janzen was left alone with Andrai, the more chance he would have to manipulate events. *God!* Here she was, obsessed with the aliens, when it was Janzen she should have been worrying about. She knew Ibri would never attempt the walk, not when he had a reason to keep her here — and give Janzen more time to sway Andrai.

Mara was suddenly aware of the weight of the XR32 in her hand. She briefly considered threatening Ibri, but put aside the idea as untenable. Ibri was just arrogant enough to call her bluff — and she knew she would never deliver on the threat. She sheathed the weapon.

"Still Janzen's lapdog, hey Ibri?"

She had the satisfaction of watching sudden doubt bloom in his dark, surly eyes. She had hit the mark. He turned quickly away from her and busied himself at the panel beneath the console.

"Secure the pod. Take no chances. I am walking to the lander. Fly it over to base camp when you are done."

"Sure."

She slammed the hatch with every ounce of her strength and stood there fuming. This was turning into a nightmare.

Mara walked to the edge of the jungle without a backward glance.

Up close the vegetation towered above her, cutting off any view of the ridge that hid the lander. From the lakeshore, it had seemed so simple. The lander was close by — less than four kilometers. She had seen it land.

Behind her, she heard Ibri leave the pod to retrieve the circuit board, then slam the hatch once more as he secured himself inside.

Mara took a bearing and set off. The combands had a built-in compass. Thanks to the strong magnetic field of the planet, she could not lose her way.

Within minutes she was surrounded by lush green growth. Inside the forest, chittering, screeching and hooting calls came from everywhere. She saw few of the bizarre insectoid animals, but could hear them moving all around her, some small … and some large. She had not forgotten that huge insect that had surprised her at the lake, and she walked now with one hand on her sheathed weapon. The muscles around her shoulders soon grew stiff with tension, the pain in her head throbbing in time with her steps.

She took another bearing and turned to look behind her. The pod, the lake, and the crystal mountain were out of sight.

Her head swam. Her breath came faster.

She was surrounded on all sides by green, with only the merest depression of the thick humus beneath her feet to mark her passage.

"Get a grip, Mara," she muttered to herself.

She tried to slow her breathing. Her legs quivered with strain.

Swallowing, she set off once more. Away from the lake, the vegetation was becoming thick and tangled. She had to push through it, and stumbled repeatedly on vines and the uneven surface. The ground began to slope upward.

"I must be at the base of the ridge." Her voice sounded odd, muffled by the thick growth.

She wove between the living walls around her. Her thighs and the muscles in her hips and rear burned. She was breathing raggedly, taking in too much oxygen. She felt faint and missed her footing. She tripped, crying out as she threw her arms out to break her fall, tumbling back down the slope. Faster and faster.

She slammed into a tree, winded.

Her face was bleeding where the sharp spikes of a vine had slashed her, and her mask had been ripped off. She had wrenched her right wrist, but nothing was broken.

"OK. OK."

She forced herself to her feet and found her mask. The straps were snapped. She tucked it into her belt. "Hated that damn thing anyway," she muttered.

Mara took a deep breath and started climbing again, pausing every ten steps to regulate her breathing and let her muscles recover. Soon she had found her rhythm and had crested the ridge. She had been expecting a view of the lander but was disappointed. The growth was still too thick. She pushed on, moving down the hill, stepping carefully over the fallen stands of wood and tangled vines.

After a time, the thickness of the vegetation decreased and she made good time, passing into open woodland.

She stopped, exhausted, and took a bearing.

She was heading in the right direction, but there was still no sign of the lander. The terrain was tough, foreign to her station-bred senses. *This is the longest four kilometers I have ever walked.*

So much had happened. The deaths, the fear of the radiation. And now this strange alien world. Her limbs were so heavy. She sat back against a tree, replaying in her mind the recent events that had led them here.

She checked the chrono on the comband.

"Just three minutes rest. Three minutes."

A warmth crept over her, and before she could resist, sleep took her.

Mara woke slowly, conscious of the stiffness in her body, and hovered on the edge of waking. A rhythmic crunching sound was coming from very close by. She opened her eyes.

A big, hairless head filled her vision, the huge eyes like dark reflective pools.

Mara screamed.

She scrambled back against the tree trunk and drew her XR32, flicking off the safety. Her heart raced, her mouth suddenly dry.

Up close the bulk of the creature was frightening. Before now, the closest Mara had ever come to wildlife had been historical vid-casts. She could see the patterned texture of the pale skin with awful clarity, a pattern that continued beneath the colored blooms that swarmed across its body, culminating in a vibrant green crown. She recognized it immediately as a member of the same race as those that took Karic.

The alien continued to regard her with absent interest, munching on a branch of succulent leaves it held in its right hand. It sat like a panda, the fleshy bulk of the body flowing over its frame in rolls of folded skin, rows of pale nipples down either side of its torso. The rounded ears moved sensually as it ate, like cats' tails, each a mirror image of the other.

Mara aimed the XR32 right between its strange eyes. Her hand shook with the weight of the gun, and she heard herself whimpering as her finger hovered over the trigger. She was all too aware of the power in the being's giant frame. It could crush her like an insect if it chose to.

But something did not make sense. Where were the others? Where was the shaman with his energy weapon that she had seen in the pod's recording?

Mara looked around, jerking her head from left to right. She was alone with it.

The being made a soft, cooing sound. It stopped eating and held the branch of leaves out before it in a simply parody of her posture.

The shaking in her hand increased, and sensing she was in no danger, Mara lowered the gun. The fatigue and fear were suddenly overwhelming. She could not stop herself crying as the alien dropped the branch gently at her feet, as though in offering.

Slowly, the alien pushed itself upright and padded off into the jungle, moving swiftly along the base of the ridge and out of sight.

"God," she said, wiping away the tears. She had to get to the lander.

She stood and sheathed the gun. Checking the chrono, she could see she had been asleep for less than ten minutes.

Mara took a bearing and set off at a run. Her muscles screamed, but she ignored the pain, focusing instead on her breathing. That was the key. She had to move fast. She could not afford to get caught alone again, not with so many of the aliens around her.

The light was dimming now, fading with the distance from the crystal mountain. After a few minutes, she crested a small rise that had been hidden by the lay of the land, and below her, set under a sparse yet towering canopy, was the lander.

Elated, she ran down the gentle slope.

Closer to the craft, she could see it was surrounded by the shimmering blue of the defensive shield, slicing through the air between the tall repeater posts. The powerful magnetic fields that stretched between the posts contained a layer of super-hot plasma. Each containment section could not maintain its critical integrity over more than three meters, hence the repeater posts. The main unit, the source of the shield's energy, was a tall rectangular obelisk. The defensive shield was one of the greatest technological refinements to emerge from the nuclear strife of the late 21st century, proof against physical attack, fast-moving metal projectiles, pulse lasers and energy weapons. Contained within the separately shielded structure of the main unit were the powerful nuclear battery, resupply cylinders for the plasma gas, and the processors that controlled the system. The repeater posts and the conductive framework that joined each of them at the base and tip — and transmitted both control signals and electrical energy — were crafted from a high-tech memory metal that could bend to any shape. Now they were standing as straight as posts, forcing the shield into a shape of a circular fence, open at the top.

Mara walked to the main unit and gave a verbal command. A small section of the shield dimmed to full transparency as the plasma inside was magnetically shunted away, exposing the control panel. A green light flashed, indicating it was safe to touch. She entered a security code then waited as the shield section between the main unit and the repeater post to her right first dimmed, then deactivated, repeating the same process of plasma-removal on a larger scale. Once more a green light flashed, and she stepped through. She reactivated the shield from inside the perimeter, then made for the lander.

She cleared the lock in record time, sighing with relief as she swept into the cabin.

"Andrai …"

Her heart skipped a beat.

Both Andrai and Janzen were gone.

Mara sped across the cabin to the main console, searching the log for any sign of what had happened. Janzen had left a message, curt and to the point.

"I released the atmospheric drone, Mara, and have reviewed the initial survey results." He was wearing his odin, the left screen down over his eye. Looking back at her with a familiar expression of superiority. Her stomach twisted. "The aerial photography showed us the village where the aliens took Karic. It's nearby. I will lead a mission to intercept and retrieve him." He smiled, tilting back his head. "Remain and station the lander until we return."

Mara felt her blood boil. An unbearable pressure filled her head.

"Fuckingfuckingfuck! Damnit, Andrai! I told you to do nothing!" She loved Andrai's warmth and undemanding stability, but any romantic leanings she might develop toward him — and there had been some — were continually scuttled by his lack of toughness. She was drawn to strong men, often disastrously, but there it was. Andrai should have stood up to Janzen.

She checked the time on the message. She had missed them by less than twenty minutes. And Janzen had left her the message, not Andrai. That meant that somehow Janzen had reasserted his command.

"So you can't take part in field missions, hey Janzen? You fucking, lying, prick.

"Fuck!" Janzen had completely manipulated her.

Her legs began to tremble. She sank into one of the plush, off-white console chairs. The soft, familiar comfort was bliss to her tortured muscles and frame.

This is a mess.

Mara's worse fears had been confirmed. Now Janzen, Andrai and Karic were all in serious danger — and she had left Ibri alone and vulnerable. She had to get control of the situation.

First, see if Ibri was safe.

She checked the location of the probe. It was still over the horizon but closing fast. Andrai had reprogrammed it to take station between the village and the pod. No doubt to allow communication. She changed its flight plan so she could relay a message to Ibri. She waited anxiously for it to return to local airspace.

She and the *Starburst*'s crew had been expecting a frigid wasteland. A long wait in suspension, with only short trips outside to check the condition of the lander. They never imagined they would be carrying out expeditions like this, otherwise they would have brought proper field radios. As it was, space in the lander was severely limited and provisions — and the suspension gear — were top priority.

A soft tone sounded, a green indicator lighting up on the console.

"Ibri, can you read me?"

"Yes, Mara. I have a good signal."

"How is the condition of the pod? Is it ready for a lift?"

"Negative, Mara. The diagnostic has hours to run. I am still checking the hardware."

"Stay secure inside the pod, then fly it to base camp when it's operational." Then what?

She chewed her knuckle, considering her options.

"Is that it, Mara? I am busy here."

Mara gritted her teeth. "I'll give you further orders when you return to the lander. If I am not here, check the log. Mara, out."

"Understood. Ibri out."

Now was the hard part. She examined the photo-records of the survey and quickly identified the village and the enlarged shots that showed Karic being dragged and secured inside a pit.

He was alive.

"Thank God."

From the photographs, a rescue looked easy, but Janzen and Andrai did not know about that weapon — or what it could do. So far, the aliens had not killed. But how easily provoked would they be?

"What the hell are you playing at, Janzen?"

She directed the probe on a short search pattern between the lander and the village, hailing Janzen and Andrai on the radio, hoping that she would be able to make contact. After three transects, and with the probe almost out of fuel, she reluctantly gave the command for it to return to base. The jungle was too thick, the ground terrain too difficult to interpret under the thick canopy. They could be anywhere, forced to take a wide path away from the direct line by any number of obstructions.

By the time the little probe had touched down outside the lander, she had made up her mind. There was nothing else she could do. She had to warn Janzen and Andrai before they got themselves killed.

She left a brief message log for Ibri, ordering him to man the lander, then retrieved the data on the position of the village. She filled a small backpack with provisions and downloaded a copy of an aerial photograph onto a reader. Mara knew how tough that jungle was to get through, so she planned a longer route through the open forest that grew in the dimmer areas behind the ridges. Longer but faster. She was going to run it.

Beyond the defensive shield, she paused to check the site's security, before taking a bearing and setting off into the woodlands.

***

Janzen lay observing the alien's village through high-powered field glasses. Andrai was stretched out beside him, also watching. They were at the top of a forested ridge above the camp, taking cover behind a low hill.

A small, clear stream ran along the edge of the settlement, which was in a large, circular clearing. All the aliens were fully grown, without any sign of progeny or a visible distinction between the sexes. They were big: between two and a half and three meters tall. None wore clothing.

Karic was in a pit on the edge of the clearing. Janzen drew his XR32 and examined the weapon. It had been one of DavisCorp's biggest sellers, with military contracts in twenty-three countries and plenty of civilian sales; some through the front door ... some through the back. They were notoriously difficult to handle, but very effective, operating just as reliably in a vacuum as in normal atmospheres. He sheathed the weapon and forced a tight smile.

A light misting rain started to fall, glistening on the forest foliage. Precipitation was frequent on Oasis, alternating between drizzle and heavy, wind-blown bursts of tropical intensity. Exposed as they were, it was miserable to be out in it, and Janzen longed for the luxurious, controlled atmosphere of the DavisCorp complex back on Earth. With a sharp twist of mental pain, he remembered that his former life of privilege was just a memory. An echo of a long-dead past.

Just before they made the descent in the lander, the new satellite they had launched into orbit around Oasis had intercepted a transmission from Earth, bringing news dated current up to 2236. The others had all been in the lander prepping for the drop when the news came in.

So only he knew.

Earth, damaged by the 2190 Embargo, had gone to war with the Free Colonies — the Mars, Moon, Jovian-moons coalition — and lost. *Lost.* All hope of controlling off-world facilities within Earth's solar system was now gone, and with it the last chance to restore the prior Davis empire. And there was worse. News arrived in 2229 from the *Sheffield* of a habitable world around a dwarf star 12.7 lightyears from Earth, which had been named Kestrel. A huge colonization fleet with new ships capable of 0.41c set out the following year. With a confirmed new world available for colonization, the ExploreCorp stock plummeted. His own family, virtually ruined now, had siphoned off all the funds he had left in trust with them to offset their losses. In a complex legal maneuver worthy of the Davises, they had "sold" him their ExploreCorp stock for the exact value of Janzen's remaining fortune, leaving him penniless. Sole owner of a worthless corporation.

Through his seat on the United Earth Enforcement Council, Janzen's father had commanded armies with a word. Ordered the downfall of regimes over a snifter of Armagnac. *That* was real power.

And no one was going to deny him his birthright.

This world ... it was his last chance.

The profits of the colonial trade would be enormous. Enough to put ExploreCorp back in the top ten. Enough to restore the Davis seat on the United Earth Enforcement Council.

The ExploreCorp colonization fleet was safe — pulled back into a defended low Earth orbit before the start of the war. He would show everyone just how *worthless* ExploreCorp was. News of another habitable world would create a sensation. The ExploreCorp fleet would launch for Oasis, packed with high-paying colonists. He would return to Earth immensely wealthy, ready to take control of a newly expanding empire.

Janzen gritted his teeth and mentally stepped through the elements of his plan.

First. Surveillance.

Below him, he saw scores of simple huts, each built on a wooden frame, with reed roofs and woven grass walls. Scores of outdoor hearths dotted the valley, plumes of white smoke trailing lazily into the still, humid air. The air was filled with song. Hundreds of voices that would have shamed an operatic superstar, every single one of them woven into a complex framework of harmony and melody as casually and instinctively as birds singing at dawn.

The vocal gymnastics did not slow them down. The creatures were as busy as bees. Some would vanish into the surrounding forest, ambling away in a quick, ungainly trot, while others would emerge with equal haste, their woven nets and baskets filled to the brim. The produce was poured into neat piles of glistening leaves, brown nuts and ripe berries, then the process would start all over again. Others delivered large golden pods that looked like big, twisted melons with pointed ends and laid them carefully beside the other raw foods.

All this activity, perhaps even the singing, would be typical of any other native culture in Earth's history — but that was where any kind of explicable behavior ended.

As he suspected, their technology was very rudimentary. The outcome of his plan would hinge on their initial reaction to his first attack. So far he had seen no indication of overtly aggressive or warlike behavior. There did not appear to be any sort of warrior class, so typical in primitive human societies. He had seen nothing remotely resembling a weapon — not even a sharp stick. That was encouraging.

One group was playing a contact sport, though. These he watched closely. Most of those involved had bright gold markings on their crowns. One team would stand in a loose circle around the big tree in the center of the clearing, while the others would approach them carefully, each carrying one of the large golden seedpods. The pod-carriers would try to dart and weave toward the tree, and if they made it past the ring of guardians still carrying their prize, they would hold it up in triumph and sing a long, high note. Those that were made to drop their pods had to surrender them to their intercepting opponent, who slunk toward the tree clutching the pod with — what looked like — a smug expression on their strange, fleshy faces. It was anything goes, with body-slamming, wrestling and what could only be described as dirty tricks like jabbing, pinching and gouging to win through. Then when the last player approached the tree, the winners would crack open the pods with powerful blows from their doughy fists and scoop out the dark, rich meat inside with their fingers, licking every last morsel from their pudgy digits with their big, flexible tongues. Then the teams would switch places. The pod-runners would select new seedpods from the piles around the camp and it would all start again. The pod game seemed all very innocent, and more importantly, not in the least bit militant.

In terms of colonization, the natives would present no threat to his plans. A small team equipped with modern weapons could deal with them when the time came. The problem was that any casual inspection of the field data by United Earth inspectors would reveal that the beings were intelligent — that information would have to be kept strictly confidential.

Janzen had come here determined to implement a desperate, lethal strategy. Karic had given him no choice. The engineer had failed to respond to reasoning, financial motivation or any of the levers of ambition that had shifted his stubborn mind before. Ibri and Andrai were easy to sway, and even Mara, despite her whiplash temper and her drive for independence, could be easily manipulated by his array of tactics. Yet despite Janzen's determination to do what was necessary to defend his family and his fortune — and do it without delay — he could not help but pause and watch the aliens' bizarre activities.

Food seemed to be the central focus of their world.

Three other groups were busy creating artworks from the piles of gathered foods — nothing else was used. Two of the groups were large, almost a hundred in each, the gathered creatures marked with iridescent green on their crowns. Their raw-food sculptures grew rapidly, each of the aliens working in a seamless team to produce weird shapes with a clear pattern of tessellation, but no discernible analogue to anything he could recognize. They used a sticky green sap from one of the fruits to glue their materials together, licking the stuff from their fingers when they were done. They sang as they moved, each group's choral efforts forming a distinct element in the overall tapestry of song. A smaller group, with dark purple markings, was at work on a third shape. These sang in a brash bass, and here Janzen did recognize their work. The hairs on his arms stood on end as a wave of goose pimples flushed across his skin. They were producing an exact replica of Karic's pod, each aerodynamic feature, turret and jet nozzle replicated with exact precision. Was this some sort of cargo cult? Like the natives of New Guinea after World War Two, who produced exact replicas of landing strips, air control towers and hangars from bamboo and palm-leaf thatch in the hope of attracting the "great birds" that brought them gifts from the gods?

One of the green-crowned groups, well ahead of their competitors, stood back from their completed sculpture and formed a ring. They sang a single chord of stunning power, then raced in toward the artwork, attacking it in a frenzy. Each ripped off the nearest piece and began stuffing the food into their huge mouths. They sat back, grinding the stuff to multicolored paste between their big, flat teeth. Then, swallowing, they would go back for more, not in the least concerned they were destroying hours of work. No doubt a similar fate awaited the other two uncompleted sculptures.

Other smaller, mixed groups were gathered around the open hearths, undertaking complex cooking procedures with hundreds of steps. In addition to the raw foods, these native chefs used other ingredients that had been gathered or prepared earlier. Some of them were roasting foods, while others used cooking pots of woven bark, the fluid inside bubbling and steaming above the flames. The exercise consumed their full attention, their focus almost manic in its intensity. They would take a pinch of this, or a small handful of something else from containers crafted from seed pods or woven grasses or reeds, and use these carefully in their preparations.

Some were more solitary. A scattered few of a taller, less bulky type of alien with a stark red crown stalked restlessly around the camp's outskirts, always on their own, yet still munching on food as they went. Perhaps they were ostracized by the others. Some sort of color-based discrimination?

Not all the creatures were active. Some lay on the thick green turf of the village clearing, lost in torpor, the remnants of their meals scattered around them in piles of abandoned husks and shredded vegetable matter.

Second. Select a target.

He looked closer at the towering tree in the center of the settlement. Janzen had ignored it earlier, but now he could see that its branches had been deliberately interwoven into a continuous dome. So it was clearly important to the natives, and was the focus of the pod-running game. Perhaps it even had some sort of religious meaning — so much the better.

The rain stopped and he stared down at the pit.

His mouth was dry as he lifted the field glasses. He scanned the camp and wondered how much the natives' skins might be worth on the black markets of Earth. ExploreCorp would probably even fund an archaeological expedition — once they were all dead.

It had been an easy matter to delete Andrai's message log to Mara and replace it with his own while Andrai was completing the installation of the defensive shield. There was nothing like sowing a little dissention.

Janzen lowered his field glasses.

He licked his cracked lips. A flush of fury heated his skin as he remembered, yet again, how Karic removed him from command. A Davis. An executive of ExploreCorp!

Janzen swallowed down his anger like the poisonous bile it was. Victory could only come from a clear head. Strategy. Planning. And cold-blooded execution.

Third. Initiate distraction as required.

He shifted his field-glasses from hand to hand, wiping away a sudden sheen of sweat.

Fourth. Feign rescue attempt.

He clenched his jaw. He was a Davis. A cut above the sweating, swarming masses of humanity that served his family's empire. After two hundred years, he refused to let the dynasty fall.

Fifth. Kill Karic.

Janzen swiveled his field-glasses toward the pit. From his elevated position, he could just see Karic waiting motionless inside the hole, watching the camp. The pit was covered with a tight grid of heavy stalks, similar to bamboo, and was not guarded.

Janzen's breathing was ragged. His heart thumped in his chest.

He signaled to Andrai.

They backed away into the jungle, circling lower down the hill toward the camp, XR32s held ready. They paused on the edge of the forest clearing.

He released the safety catch on his XR32 and looked at Andrai. The tech was cautious as usual, pausing to watch the camp. Well, this was one time he was not going to wait.

Janzen stepped forward eagerly.

He felt Andrai's hand on his arm.

"Hold on, Janzen. Not yet," said Andrai.

Janzen shook off the hand. "What?"

Karic had infected them all with his little mutiny. He could not believe this was the same lowly tech who would never question an order.

Andrai looked at him suspiciously. "Why are you so eager to get in there, Janzen?"

Janzen dripped with perspiration, his knuckles white on the grip of his XR32. He forced himself to relax.

"Look. Karic is in that pit, and we have to rescue him. *Now.* Who knows what they will do to him if we wait?" It was the same draw card he used earlier to get Andrai to break Mara's orders. He watched with satisfaction as doubt and concern filled the tech's eyes.

"That's why we had to get here quickly," said Andrai. "But now that we have him under observation, we should wait until we have a link to Mara and Ibri at the pod. Besides, the longer we wait, the more prepared we are. We can get their exact numbers, get some idea of their weapons. We can't just run straight in. Not if Karic is not threatened."

"We *have* watched them. They have no weapons. One blast from this will send them running," said Janzen holding up the XR32. "They are savages, Andrai. Can you give me one good reason to wait?" He had to get this over with. It was distasteful, lowly work for a Davis, but it had to be done.

"Well? Can you give me one good reason and back it up?" said Janzen, his chest heaving.

"The linkup is more than thirty minutes away," said Andrai. He looked into the alien camp, and the pit where Karic was imprisoned. His face creased in frustration, Andrai tapped his comband. "Mara? Are you reading me? Mara? Acknowledge!"

There was a hiss of static, broken twice by a garbled squeal. Janzen's stomach clenched as — just for a moment — he thought he heard Mara's voice. But that was impossible. Without the link, she would have to be within a kilometer of their position. *Christ!* Of course. She had followed them. *Damn her.* Now his timeline was more compressed than ever. He probably had less than ten minutes.

Janzen forced a carefully neutral expression on his face. "See. Nothing. It is up to us, Andrai. We cannot falter now. We have to act while we can."

Andrai turned off the link with a tap and gave a slight nod. "OK, Janzen. You've convinced me. We go together. A quick thrust in, rescue Karic and out again. We can link to Mara after the rescue and let her know he's safe."

"Good. Come on," said Janzen, marching forward.

***

Karic looked up through the bars. He had bruises all over his body from the rough handling of the natives — the *Imbirri*, Utar had called them. The burn on his arm throbbed angrily. Despite the pain, he smiled with relief when he saw Janzen advance from the overhanging branches.

"My God, Janzen. I didn't think you had it in you." Karic never thought he would be happy to see Janzen, but he was. Andrai followed behind Janzen, moving more cautiously.

Janzen held his XR32 at the ready, scanning the camp. His movements were awkward in the heavy gravity. His face was set with a grim determination so at odds with his usual charismatic nonchalance it took Karic back a moment. This was a side of Janzen he had never seen before — this attempted rescue showed he was willing to set aside their differences when it really mattered.

The aliens, busy on their food sculptures, did not see the two intruders at first, intent on their work. The third group was still busily pulling apart their artwork in a frenzy of noisy eating.

The Imbirri playing the pod game stopped immediately. Their singing ceased and they became completely motionless. They swiftly arranged themselves in a long line, starting at the tree and radiating out into the camp. They shuffled in place, some swapping positions until they settled on an order. Then the alien closest to the tree — the first in line — pushed through its low-hanging branches and disappeared inside its leaf-shrouded dome.

Movement drew Karic's eye. One of the aliens lying motionless on the turf, with a bright green crown, sat up suddenly. It studied Janzen and Andrai for the space of a breath then sang a low, tremulous note. Immediately, the beings at work on the sculptures froze. Those eating dropped their food to the turf. A moment later, all of them surged into a flurry of motion, arranging themselves into a large semicircle on the far side of the tree. Once again, they changed positions until satisfied with the order, then they began to sing together, their black, bulbous eyes fixed on the approaching humans. The aliens that remained asleep on the grass grew alert at the sound of this new song, pushing themselves to their feet. Some joined the chorus, others stood in tense stillness, eyes fixed on the intruders.

A high note sounded from inside the tree. Then a second. Another voice sang in response, followed by a chorus of joined voices that was stunning in its beauty and complexity. Those singing outside immediately changed their weaving songs to harmonize with the new chorus. Karic had little time for the music. He just wanted to get out. He lost sight of Janzen and Andrai as they came down the hill into the camp.

Karic lifted himself up to get a better view of the camp.

"Over here!"

Janzen saw him, but did not respond.

Andrai and Janzen talked quickly, then Janzen moved toward the pit while Andrai watched the large group of aliens around the tree, his XR32 pointed straight at them.

Janzen was soon at the side of the pit. He looked back to Andrai, whose back was turned, then back to Karic. His eyes were set like chips of blue ice.

"Janzen. Call Andrai back. You'll need help with the lattice cover. It

114

weighs a ton," said Karic.

Janzen took aim at Karic.

Karic quickly ducked back inside the cage. "Janzen, *you bastard!*" His heart leapt into a sprint. His head spun with a sense of unreality. *Janzen was here to kill him.*

He looked desperately around the pit. He was trapped!

"Keep still!" Janzen's voice was thick with tension.

Inside the pit, Karic could hear Janzen as he worked his way around the edge, trying to get him back into his sights. Crouched back against the wall, Karic thought rapidly. He had only seconds. What the hell was going on? Janzen would never have convinced Andrai to help him with murder. Of course. *Andrai.*

"Andrai! Over here!" yelled Karic. "Over here! Andrai! We need help with the cover! *We need help with the cover!*" Karic knew his shouting might provoke the aliens, but it was that or die.

Karic saw one of Janzen's booted feet on the bamboo lattice, then Janzen came into view. Looming over the top of the pit, he started to raise his XR32, but then hastily lowered it again.

"What is it?" It was Andrai, calling to him as he ran up to the pit.

Janzen swiftly holstered his gun and made a show of trying to lift the heavy lid.

So I was right. Janzen is acting alone.

Karic watched Janzen through the bars, trying to understand what would drive the self-serving elitist to murder. "What was it? Taking your command?"

Janzen's eyes flicked to meet Karic's, then back to Andrai. They were cold. Calculating.

"No. It's not that, is it?" said Karic. "It's money. It's always about money. I should have taken command at Epsilon Eridani. Then I should have flushed you out of an airlock."

Karic leapt at Janzen, reaching up through the bars to try and snatch the XR32 from his holster.

Janzen leapt back from the pit, just as Andrai came into view.

Andrai looked at Janzen suspiciously. "I heard Karic shouting. What's going on?"

"Andrai! Help with the cover!" shouted Karic.

Janzen's face was devoid of expression. "Everything is going fine," he called across to Andrai. "We just need a diversion before we work on freeing Karic." Janzen aimed his XR32 at something back in the village and fired.

"Andrai!" called Karic. "Janzen is trying to kill me!" The sound of the concussion swallowed Karic's words.

The singing faltered and died.

Karic desperately leapt for the bars, pulling himself up to get a view. Janzen had fired on the big dome-shaped tree in the middle of the clearing. The aliens who had gathered around the outside of the tree scattered. Most fled in panic, racing for the forest verge. Those creatures standing motionless on the long grass turned and ran with the others. Strangely, the aliens with purple crowns gathered into a tight group and sat to watch, eyes intent. Others, taller, and with red crowns, arranged themselves around the edges of the camp at equidistant points. There they turned, bodies poised, eyes flaring a deep red, as though standing guard while the others fled. The reds began a low, ominous drone, their voices weaving around each other in bass dissonance.

Janzen's eyes flicked from the pit to Andrai. The technician was watching the destruction at the tree. Janzen raised his gun, this time pointing it at Andrai's back.

***

Ibri examined the circuit board with focused intensity. In this tiny world he was truly at home, here within the paths of silver and gold, the capacitors, resistors and black silicon processors, all playing court to the elegant domes of the molecular modules, rising like silver queens from the board. Everything had its function, everything in its place. No mysteries — just logic. He moved the probes swiftly over the board, pausing only to read the diagnostics on the meter, itself a powerful, portable computer. In each of the minute pathways within the molecular modules, millions of switches and connections were assessed and corrected in the fraction of a second.

Satisfied, Ibri carefully slipped the circuit board back into its slot beneath the pod's console and sat back. Every piece of hardware in the pod had been checked, repaired then rechecked. *It had hardly been a challenge.* Ibri smiled briefly. He was the best of the best and knew it. At least Janzen could recognize his brilliance. He had taken Ibri aside before the lander's descent.

"You are the only one with the true talent, Ibri. I've already doubled your bonus. Once we get the surface, I have a few plans I would like your help with, if you agree. Of course, elite technicians such are yourself deserve the rewards, you and I know that." Janzen had flashed him a smile and Ibri's heart had glowed at the praise. "Help me on the surface. Help me to break this strange hold Karic has on the others, and I will see your bonus *tripled*. There will be opportunities to split them up. That will give me time to bring Andrai and Mara to their senses." Janzen had gripped Ibri's arm in a gesture of solidarity. "You and I, Ibri. We are the true leaders on this team."

Janzen was the commander. The true leader of the mission. He knew how to get things done, and knew enough to reward those with the talent. Andrai and Mara had always thought they were better than him, and their dismissive treatment had fueled his contempt. And Karic … the engineer was a sentimental fool. A dangerous fool, with the ability to blind the others. He did not fool Ibri.

The computer specialist leant forward to the simple console. The screen now showed a schematic of the pod and its systems, highlighted in red and yellow. Most of the software systems were still in the process of being rebuilt, the symbols flashing steadily … slowly. The pod's radio was still out.

He knew precisely where the lander was. He was sure Mara would have reached it by now. The tempestuous astronomer irritated Ibri. The opportunity afforded by Karic's disappearance had been a godsend. Delaying her so that Janzen could reassert his authority over Andrai, simplicity itself. When *Starburst* reached Earth, Ibri would be rich beyond his dreams, at last rewarded for his talent by someone with the intelligence to recognize it.

He turned his thoughts to the mass of data that still remained unprocessed on board the lander. It was waiting for him there. He could be working on an analysis with the full power of the lander's computers at his command, rather than wasting time here. Ibri frowned. As for the pod, he could judge for himself the reboot would run for at least another fourteen hours — one factor he had underestimated.

He waited for twenty minutes, cramped within the confines of the pod, and that was all the time it took him to make up his mind. He could already anticipate the feel of the lander's console beneath his fingers. Needing little rest and only four hours of sleep a night, boredom was a constant problem for Ibri.

Easily shaking off his fatigue, he strapped the XR32 to his waist and sealed the pod. He set off toward the jungle at a solid pace, following dead reckoning.

He gave the pod a last fleeting look as he left the clearing. There would be plenty of opportunities to retrieve the pod. Once the diagnostic was complete, it could be piloted on remote by the lander's computer if necessary. Ibri smiled, thinking of Mara's impetuous behavior.

Janzen's plan had worked perfectly.

***

The boughs of the Tree arched majestically overhead. Beneath the tightly woven canopy, the First — the select group of Imbirri who were first raised to sentience by the Awakener — assembled in reverent silence.

Sconces flickered along the walls, the lamps within burning an aromatic oil specially distilled from forest plants, which filled the dome with a redolent fragrance. The Awakener sat upon his throne, and Deepwatch Utar, first of the First, stood below the dais.

Light flashed through the dimness. Utar turned to see Swith run through the Tree's opening, eyes dark with tension. He was the most senior gold of the Gathered — those Imbirri who had been raised to sentience by the First over the last few thousand seasons. Swith outstripped all the Gathered gold in years of sentience. He knelt at Utar's feet and waited, not daring to interrupt the ceremony. Outside, the song of the greens and purples stopped abruptly, only to begin again soon after in a chorus of warning and entreaty. Something had disrupted the Gathered at their play.

The mental bond that had been building for hours between the First and their leaders now rose to a critical threshold in Utar's mind. Whatever had disturbed Swith would have to wait.

A great expectation arose among the First. They could sense without knowing the first notes of song begin to swell within the minds of their leaders. The Awakener's eyes filled with emotion as he surged to his feet, drawing breath from the scented air. Then he sang. The note was pure and long, resounding with familiar nuance. The Awakener came forward from the dais, toward the First, toward Utar. There he uttered the second, perfect note.

Utar trembled as the notes of the response gathered within him like an irrepressible tide. His eyes met those of the Awakener and the years swam around them like a bursting flood. Utar burst into song, his eyes fixed on those of the Awakener. Immediately, the First followed him, and the canopy above trembled with the voiced harmonies. The Imbirri were empathic, and each could feel the emotions of the others through their song.

The Awakener was filled with sheer joy.

Utar could not keep a note of sadness from his voice — he feared for his people — and his senses told him it was already too late to protect them. Even so, he wanted desperately to join with the Awakener — to consummate their love.

Utar increased the power and emotion of his song, striving to harmonize with the being who had raised him from the dim world of pre-sentience, yet he could not match the Awakener's joy. Hot yellow tears of sorrow ran from Utar's nipples, streaked the sides of his torso. He ceased his song and turned from the assembly, torn with grief. He needed the comfort of union, however incomplete it always seemed, and yet he could not join in their joy knowing their days were soon to end.

The song was reaching a crescendo of passion when a thunderous concussion shook the Tree, its crown engulfed in a fireball. The flames filled the space with an intense burst of light before fading. Ambient light now flooded in through the ragged hole in the canopy. The First cried out in shock and dismay, and the song faltered to silence.

Utar turned, possessed with sudden anger. His awareness expanded like a titan, swelling beyond the confines of the enclosure. Outside, through his spirit-eyes, he could see two of the alien beings, standing near the punishment pit with weapons of destruction.

"*Violators!*" howled Utar. The outburst stunned the First. Swith tumbled to the ground, driven unconscious by the vehement psychic force that accompanied the curse.

The Awakener strode toward Utar, his face set with fury. A second concussion ripped through the encampment. Through his inner vision, Utar could see the aliens were using their weapons to drive the Imbirri away like animals. A hut of dried reed and wood vanished in an instant, the explosion bursting with a violent power that left nothing in its wake.

"What is it, Utar?" asked the Awakener, his eyes terrible in their focus.

Utar withdrew from his spirit-sight and spun toward the Awakener.

"Humans! They are here! Ready to reclaim their companion and spread their destruction!"

The Awakener stood silently for a moment, his vision clearing, the sense of purpose within him strengthening.

Utar stepped forward and grabbed at the Awakener's arms.

"Give me the scepter! Let me destroy them! There may still be a chance to save us."

The Awakener shook off Utar and moved his immense bulk toward the overlapping branches that concealed the entrance. "Long have I sheltered here, my friend."

Utar nodded. The redwings — the vibrant red-winged butterflies of Cru's forest the Imbirri used to mark the start of a new year — had spawned many hundreds of times since his leader had even stirred from his dais. How the years pass.

"I would see these beings for myself. Then I will judge them."

***

"*Andrai!*" shouted Karic.

The technician turned. His eyes widening as he saw Janzen with his XR32.

Janzen quickly changed his aim and fired, his face a twisted mask of frustration. One of the primitive huts exploded with a thudding concussion. Many of the golds, who had hovered at the edge of the clearing, now vanished into the foliage.

"That's enough, Janzen! Let's get Karic and get out of here!" yelled Andrai.

The leaves of the tree parted and around forty of the bulky beings filed out. Janzen raised his weapon, but hesitated, perhaps sensing something different about this particular group of aliens. He was right. Karic recognized the tall, gold-crowned form of the shaman, Utar, and the imposing bulk of the Imbirri leader behind him, the dark, faded colors of his swollen body strangely ominous.

Janzen lifted his aim and fired another rocket at the tree, blasting the upper branches. The rocket flared briefly, leaving another small hole in the canopy. Unlike the huts, the living tree did not burn.

The new group of aliens was spellbound by the sudden impact, but they did not run like the others. Instead, they simply looked up to examine the destruction, then back to Janzen and Andrai. Their huge heads turned in a slow, synchronized movement, their huge dark eyes glowing with outrage as they fixed on the humans.

Utar sang a high note. The red-crowned aliens around the verge of the clearing ceased their eerie song and moved forward to join the group from inside the tree.

The group of purple-crowned aliens stood and began to walk down the hill toward them, their steps precisely matched, as though they were a single organism. Their concentration was total. Their lack of fear was a startling contrast to the other Imbirri who had run from the camp, and Karic guessed the purple coloration was more than just pigmentation, it must denote some specific caste within Imbirri society.

All the Imbirri grew closer, inexorably closer, moving across the thick grass in menacing silence. Their sheer size, the power in those frames ...

"Goddamn it!" yelled Karic. "Just get me out of here! There is still time. *Get the cover off!*"

But Janzen was frozen, his eyes grown wide and white with fear.

"We have to stop them!" muttered Janzen. "Stop them! *Stop them!*"

Andrai fired, targeting a nearby hut. The explosion snapped Janzen out of his rigid terror, but did nothing to slow the aliens. Clearly, this new group were not going to be scared off by warning shots.

The physical presence of the enormous beings triggered some primal response in Karic. He could feel it, squirming in his guts. The sense of confinement in the pit was overwhelming. He was desperate to be free.

"*Target them!*" yelled Janzen.

Janzen and Andrai fired together. The tiny rockets sped through the intervening space. Janzen's missile struck an Imbirri in front of Utar. One moment the hulking creature with its vivid green crown and multicolored body was standing with the others, the next it had disappeared in a violent explosion, splattering dark yellow blood and red tissue across the green grass. Andrai's rocket failed to explode, piercing a gold-crowned alien with an odd green mark on its golden forehead and continuing through its bulky body to strike a green-crowned Imbirri in the shoulder. The projectile flew on to detonate in the surrounding jungle. With a dissonant howl, the second alien fell to the earth, mortally wounded, clutching a gaping chest wound. Its screams of pain were quickly echoed by the third Imbirri, who ran for the jungle. An Imbirri with vivid green across its crown and torso ran forward and knelt by the fallen alien, wailing in a high-pitched screech as he tried to stem the flow of bright yellow ichor from the ragged hole in the fallen Imbirri's torso.

The tall red-crowned aliens closed ranks. They began to issue their strange, dissonant drone, eyes pulsing red.

The purple-crowned aliens rushed forward to examine the remains of the dead Imbirri and the mortally wounded one. Then they cooed softly to each other and spoke in a short, rapid tones as they shared their observations, leaning forward to take in every conceivable detail from various angles with their protuberant, multi-faceted eyes. They drew back to a respectful distance as the leader of the aliens and the shaman, Utar — distinctive with his skins and decorations — came forward to stand over the fallen.

At first both Utar and the Imbirri's colossal leader stood in loose-limbed silence, their lidless eyes focused on the carnage, as though trying to make sense of it. Then the leader began to tremble, the great folds of loose skin shuffling against each other. He spoke rapidly with Utar in alternating tones so close to each other the overall effect was a harsh dissonance that made the skin rise on the back of Karic's neck. The leader made savage motions with this thick arms. When he turned back toward Janzen and Andrai, his eyes were alive with a rapidly pulsing luminescence that invoked the same instinctive alarm in Karic as a brightly colored viper.

Karic watched as the leader raised his arm. Now he could see the sleek, metallic scepter clutched in his hand. One thick finger made an adjustment to the weapon while another moved toward the activating stud on the shaft.

Then Mara burst through the trees above the camp.

"Janzen! Andrai! Look out, it's an energy weapon!" she shouted.

Her XR32 was sheathed at her side.

"No, Mara! Run!" called Karic. "All of you, *run!*"

Janzen barely had time to turn before the discharge of the weapon caught them. Blue tendrils whipped across the space. The alien leader had aimed directly for Janzen and Andrai, yet had been distracted by the appearance of Mara. The main force of the discharge struck between them, sweeping past like a sudden wind into the surrounding jungle; yet the blue corona that surrounded the discharge trapped all three of them.

Mara screamed then fell. Janzen and Andrai were thrown to the ground, the weapons flying from their grasp.

"No! *No!*"

Janzen struggled up from the ground.

"Janzen! Help them!" yelled Karic.

Janzen snatched up his XR32 and ran for the jungle, leaving the others behind. Andrai was stunned for a moment, but also struggled to his feet. Mara's limp form was unmoving, sprawled on the grass. Andrai ran toward her, leaving his weapon behind. Karic knew there was no way Andrai could escape burdened by her unconscious body — especially in this heavy gravity.

"*No, Andrai! Run!*" yelled Karic.

Andrai froze, motionless for a long moment of agonizing indecision, then ran after Janzen.

The second blast of the scepter scorched the grass where Andrai had stood only moments before. Karic watched them as they ran for their lives, their limbs pumping as they sprinted for the forest. On the verges of the camp, the edge of the beam swept past them again, sending Janzen flying to the ground. Andrai paused to help him up, and with his help, Janzen once more found his feet and raced into the safety of the surrounding forest. The tall red-crowned Imbirri ambled after them, but at a high tone from Utar they broke off their pursuit and returned to camp.

"Damn you, Janzen. *Damn you!*" Karic pounded his fist on the solid bars of the cage. First Evelle, now Mara. If she died … nothing could save Janzen.

The Imbirri swarmed around Mara. "*No!*" He feared the pressing weight of their bodies, the terrible damage their physical retribution could deliver to her fragile frame. His breathing stopped, trapped in the rigid cage of his chest. He did not want to see, yet could not look away. The aliens boiled around her, bodies in motion, limbs moving. He heard their soft melodic speech and blinked as two of the big aliens straightened, bearing the limp body of Mara between them. Utar reached to her wrist and stripped off her comband. He had also taken Karic's before he was imprisoned. For a simple people they were very thorough where technology was concerned.

Karic started to breathe again.

Under the direction of Utar, the two aliens carried Mara toward the cage. Four others ran to the pit ahead of them and bent to grip the cage in their big, fleshy hands. The lattice cover lifted away from the pit. Then Mara was dumped roughly into the mud.

Karic ran to her. There were no burns, but she was not breathing. He checked her pulse. *Nothing.*

The scepter. Its discharge was electrical. Of course. *It stopped her heart.*

Karic's anxiety vanished as his training took over. He quickly checked her airway was free, then started on cardiopulmonary resuscitation and mouth-to-mouth, he pumped fast, counting compressions. *Thirty. Now two breaths.* He watched her chest rise and fall with each breath, then continued the compressions. One minute stretched into two, then three. His breathing was ragged. Sweat stung his eyes, but he had no time to wipe it away. At eight minutes, his arms and back were burning from the effort, but he refused to give up. The memory of trying to revive Evelle in the lander rose into his mind as sharp as shattered glass. He pushed it away. He refused to accept that Mara would die here in the mud after everything they had been through. As he entered the tenth minute, he realized he was reaching the limits of his endurance. He could not keep up this pace much longer. The CPR routine was punishing for a single person.

Then, miraculously, she gasped in a breath. Her back arched, then she slumped back onto the ground.

"Mara. *Mara!*"

Karic shook her, but got no response. She was breathing, her pulse weak, but steady. He sank back onto his heels. Mara had lapsed into a coma, but she was alive. *For now.* She needed medical attention. The drugs and diagnostic equipment on the lander. He might as well wish for a magic carpet to take him back to the *Starburst's* medical bay.

"Please God, let her live."

Chapter 10

Karic looked up at the bars of the cage for the hundredth time, the pale wooden poles — thicker than his arm — weathered and discolored by age, yet rock-hard. Trapped. He had been so unprepared for this. How could he have expected intelligent aliens? They had not even expected life here! The dark side was supposed to be a frigid ice-desert. The thought of Janzen free on the surface while he was forced to sit here in the mud was almost more than he could stand.

Karic looked over to the other side of the pit, where Mara still lay unconscious. He clenched his jaw in frustration, unable to do more than watch her until she woke — if she woke.

He should be the one on the outside, leading these people. Janzen was going to get them all killed. *At least I have finally seen his true colors, the treacherous bastard.*

Karic had been imprisoned for over a day now, although time was difficult to judge. The aliens had given Karic and Mara water and a variety of nuts, berries and shoots. He dared not touch the food, but he had risked the water, which was cool and clear. The heavy gravity, the lack of food, and the burn on his arm, were beginning to take their toll on him.

The cage stank with mud and excrement and the air was infested with thousands of insects. Mites, biting flies and bizarre multi-jointed insects of every color, most of which had a penchant for crawling into bodily orifices, swarmed through the pit.

Karic stood. He shook the bars and shouted. The aliens ignored him.

"Conserve your strength, Karic," he told himself. *You will get out of here.*

He walked over to where Mara lay prostrate along one wall of the pit. He had stripped off his jacket and bundled it under her head as a makeshift pillow. He knelt beside her and gently brushed a bright yellow beetle off her cheek. The humidity was intense and she was drenched in sweat. Karic picked up a bowl of water and a cloth, torn from the lower hem of his uniform shirt, and began to bathe her face and arms.

Here he was, trapped in an alien cesspit with a woman who hated him. He had nothing more to look forward to than death at the hands of vengeful aliens, while Janzen — that self-serving incompetent — was free on the surface busily destroying any chance they had to survive.

Mara gasped softly and opened her eyes. She raised her hand to touch the cloth. "Cool. Nice," she muttered dreamily. For the briefest of moments, she accepted his tenderness and his heart melted.

When her eyes fully focused on him her brow creased and she batted his hand away. Karic felt a dark gulf open up between them.

"Mara. Are you alright? Can you hear me?"

She nodded. "Water."

Karic lifted the bowl to her lips.

"I feel like I have been beaten. What ...?"

Karic was relieved she had regained consciousness without any sign of brain damage. "Just rest now."

Mara pushed herself into a sitting position.

"No. Lie down and rest," said Karic, reaching to stop her.

She ignored him, pushing herself back against the rough earth wall. She had little strength, and with his help, took small mouthfuls of water.

Mara brushed her dark hair back from her face. "Janzen? Andrai? What happened?"

Karic sat back and sighed. "They escaped. But these aliens now have two of our XR32s. Janzen and Andrai could have had me out of here before they even knew I was gone if Janzen hadn't started shooting at everything in sight."

He looked at Mara, wondering how she would react to the news that Janzen had tried to kill him. Would she even believe him? Worse. Would she take Janzen's side? Accuse him of being paranoid?

He had left her in charge of the lander and the small crew. It had all seemed simple enough, but then, nothing was simple where Janzen was concerned. He had to restrain himself from interrogating Mara. He was furious with her. How did Janzen get his hands on an XR32 and end up here trying to kill him?

And where the hell was the lander?

He looked over at her, burning with questions. But this was not the right time. She had almost died, and was still weak and disoriented.

Mara looked up through the thick wooden struts of the cage. The bowl started to shake in her hands, and Karic took it off her, placing it carefully on the rough floor.

"Maybe I will lie down." Mara slid back into a lying position. Her eyelids fluttered as she struggled to stay awake. "It's my fault. I should have left for the damn lander straight away ..." Her words were slurred.

"Just rest, Mara."

A light misting rain started to fall and Mara fell into a fitful sleep. Karic watched as her breathing grew deeper, slower. At least she was alright. So far no one had been killed. All they had to do was get out of here.

The hours crawled by.

Karic's mind gnawed over the events, going in circles. There was nothing he could do. Not until he was free.

A small black cocoon hung from one of the struts of the cage. The tiny capsule began to rock violently, finally splitting to reveal a splash of color within. Karic watched in silent wonder as the butterfly gradually drew itself out from the confines of the chrysalis to stand upside-down on the thick bough. Its wings were large and oddly shaped, swept with intricate designs and vibrant with delicate hues of violet and blue. The butterfly slowly moved its wings in the clear light, while outside the sounds of the jungle filled the air.

Mara stirred, and the butterfly started, flying awkwardly up through the cage. Then it was gone.

Mara looked at Karic then sat up. She looked stronger.

"Why isn't it dark yet?" she muttered. "Oh … there is no dark."

Karic smiled in sympathy. He had gone through the same thought process scores of times. He offered her more water, which she drank greedily.

"Are you ready to talk?"

She glared at him, then took a deep breath. "Yes."

"Where's the lander?"

"Safe. We have set up a base camp in the shadowed areas behind the lake ridge. Everything protected by the barrier shield."

"The pod?"

"It was badly damaged by the energy weapon. Ibri is still there trying to get it up and running."

"How did you know about the energy weapon?" asked Karic, settling himself as comfortably as he could against the rudely fashioned walls of the pit.

"The pod's camera was still recording when they took you."

"Ahh." Karic watched Mara in silence. He could not put this off any longer.

"Mara … What the hell happened? How did Janzen get control?"

Mara pressed her fingers into her brow. When she spoke, her voice was tight with tension.

"Communications were difficult. We had to split up. Andrai and Janzen went to set up the base camp." She looked at Karic, meeting his eyes defiantly. "I left Andrai in charge. He had strict orders not to do anything until Ibri and I returned with the pod. But when I got to base camp Janzen had left a message log saying the aerial probe had found your location and they were going to get you.

"Arghh! I don't know how he did it, but he managed to get to Andrai somehow. I thought he would have taken a tougher line with Janzen."

Hot accusations leapt to his tongue, driven by his pain and frustration, but he clenched his jaw and remained silent.

Mara shook her head. "I should have left for the base camp sooner. I should have left Janzen with Ibri and gone with the lander myself. But damn it! I didn't want to leave Janzen with Ibri. You know how much influence he has over him."

Karic felt the pressure build in his head. So much *should* have happened. He should have anticipated Janzen. "Mara, you cannot control what's been and gone. Focus on the here and now." It cost him to say that.

She grimaced and sat back against the wall of the pit without a comment. She looked defeated.

They could not give up now. Now more than ever they needed to be positive.

"Look, Mara. Ever since you failed to find the black hole in this system you have been blaming yourself for everything that has happened. You have done your best. More than most. If you had not warned Andrai and Janzen at that precise moment, they would have both been dead. The power of that weapon is … immense."

Mara smiled cynically. "If only they had waited. *Christ!* I was hoping they would observe the camp for at least an hour before they attempted a rescue. Damn those combands! They are frigging useless on the surface."

"We didn't expect to be going more than a few hundred meters from the lander, Mara. But you're right. It's not what they are designed for."

Mara chewed her lower lip. "So, how're we gettin' outta here?"

"I hate to say it, but the only thing we can do is wait for Janzen and Andrai. I have tried lifting these bars, but the cover must weigh hundreds of kilos."

Mara nodded, leaning forward to take some of the water from the bowl and splash it over her face.

A shadow fell over them.

Karic looked up. It was Utar, the shaman. So was this it? Had they come for them at last?

Mara clasped her hands together in her lap to stop them shaking.

Karic met Utar's gaze with defiance.

The garments of skin and leaves were gone, but he was unmistakable. His eyes were huge and golden, glowing with rage and power. He stared at each of them in turn, the message clear: they were now under his power, and their fate had been sealed — they were to die.

Utar turned and left.

It will not be long now.

"Can you stand?" asked Karic. "Step up onto my shoulders. I want to know what is going on out there."

Karic squatted down and Mara climbed unsteadily onto his shoulders, careful to avoid the burn on his arm. His muscles quivered as he took the weight. He stood and her head was thrust through a space in the heavy frame above. This way she could get a view of the whole camp. She gripped the bars and shook, testing their strength.

"Forget it, Mara. We have no hope of escaping the pit without a tool or a weapon." It had been constructed to hold the aliens, and they were big and strong. Each joint was set with a resin that set like stone.

"What can you see?"

Mara turned her attention to the camp. "The shaman has just entered a small hut on the edge of the village."

"Can you see anything else?"

"There is another of those crystal formations in the distance. Less than a kilometer away. This one is not as large as the range near the lake. It's a single structure.

"The camp had been cleaned up. All the huts have been repaired and cleaned, the charred debris removed. The remains of the native who got hit with the first rocket is gone, but … hmmm. That's strange."

"What?"

"Let me down."

Karic knelt and she sprang free, laying back against the wall of the pit with relief. "Everything has been cleaned up. Everything *except* the body of the fallen alien."

"They have left it?"

Mara nodded. "They aren't going anywhere near it. They seem spooked by it. Like it's diseased or something."

"Has it begun to rot?"

"It's discolored, and bloated. I think so."

"What do you think about those crystal formations?" asked Karic.

Mara took a breath of the heavy air. "There is no way they could be naturally formed. They must cover the whole of the dark side in a regular pattern. Each one emits exactly the same spectrum of light, like a characteristic signature. The readings I took on the lander confirm it."

"You think they were constructed?" asked Karic, astounded.

"Yes. I think the whole dark side has been engineered to support life."

"But the resources and technology required to do that … These beings are primitive."

Mara looked up through the bars above. "Another race must have existed here once. A powerful one." She shivered.

Karic stood and tested his strength against the bars, as he had uncountable times. He looked wistfully at the broad sky above. Finally, he returned to sit near Mara.

"A race that existed once — or still does," he said.

"Then what are these aliens?" she said, rising to her feet to peer up through the bars. "Apart from the color markings they are almost identical. Most are playful, almost innocent. And I haven't seen any little ones."

"Of course! That's what is so strange about this village. It's been nagging at me ever since I was brought here. No progeny. There don't seem to be any sexes either, and no obvious pairing."

Mara's eyes brightened and she grabbed Karic's arm.

"That's it, Karic. There is no death here. The way they move around

128

that body, it's like they have never seen this before."

"Never seen—"

"Karic, they don't die."

***

Utar stood before a small brazier. Within it were hot coals, fanned and nurtured to the exact heat he required. Fire was one of the essential components required for the Elixir and the Ritual of Life. Imbirri cooking fires burned at a low heat. Natural retardants in the vegetation used for fuel and the high moisture content kept the temperature down. There were only one or two kinds of bark and a few particular nuts from the forest that would sustain the sort of fire he needed, and the nature of these materials — and the design of the stone-built fire pit with its ingenious bellows of wood and woven plant-fiber sealed with resin — were as carefully guarded a secret as the Elixir's formulation itself.

Time passed without leaving a visible mark on the Imbirri planet Cru, yet each of them knew when the power of the Elixir began to lose its hold on them; their bodies cried out for it. The destruction and terror that had been visited on them lately had increased the rate at which it was consumed, hastening their need.

Utar continued the preparations, allowing himself to become absorbed in the ritual. He was attended by Otla and Munch, his most trusted acolytes. Otla's memory was astounding, better even than Utar's own, while Munch's quick mind and capacity for creative insight were equally impressive. Otla worked the bellows with practiced, rhythmic movements, singing softly to himself to keep time. The green's grief over the death of Green Patch had faded to a mournful sadness that darkened his song with painful nuances, yet Utar did not have the heart to end his only expression of anguish. Munch was silent as he passed Utar each of the ingredients of the ancient formula in turn, the luminescent patterns rippling across the purple's eyes showing he was lost in thought, his mind meandering through some unknown mental territory.

Utar and the Awakener had been the first. For years beyond counting, they had wandered together, sharing the fountain of awareness, drinking in the joy of life. They had aged during this time, changing and growing as were all the Imbirri during the Dawn. In time they came to discover fire and marveled over its properties, heating upon it all manner of leaves, fruits, roots, nuts, barks and saps garnered from the forest around them. Experimenting, always experimenting, much as the younger Imbirri did now on their outside hearths.

It had happened by accident. A freak combination of ingredients, a precise order, the exact heat. The Elixir was born: giving them changeless life. For the Elixir prevented the horrific Changes, preserving the Imbirri in their beatific perfection.

As he dropped a precise measure of the final ingredient into the mixture, Otla ceased his aeration of the red-hot heating bed, and his sung melody faded away. The fluid churned and bubbled with evolved gases, then dramatically changed from a grayish green to a clear yellow. There was a poignant silence as they shared the moment of inexplicable transformation.

Utar sat silently before the bowl, waiting for the heat of the coals to fade, breathing deeply of the aroma he knew so well. At last, he grasped the bowl and held it high in silent reverence. Otla and Munch bowed forward, heads touching the soft woven mat on the floor of the enclosure. He lowered the bowl, staring sadly into the golden solution there, for Utar knew their doom was upon them. The humans had yet to visit a fraction of the destruction they would bring; and beyond this lay an ending of the life the Imbirri had known.

With determination, Utar raised the bowl to his lips and drank deeply. This was the pure concentrate. A thousand times more powerful than the diluted potion that would be given to the rest.

It had many properties and triggered many changes in them, but it was also a strong narcotic. He carefully replaced the bowl and waited for the drug to take effect. Despite the grim promise of his prior visions, he refused to give in to these beings without a fight. Those humans within his grasp would die now and those who would come after would also pay for their crimes. Perhaps ... perhaps there was some way to avoid the future these human invaders would bring to Cru.

Utar fell back onto the floor of his hut, the drug within the Elixir now taking full effect. His soul hummed like a vibrating string in the currents of the spirit-wind as he embraced the Farsleep. His mind expanded and the familiar paths spread out before him. The potentials of all life and matter on Cru and nearby space extended into a vast matrix of causality and chance, where probability, will and consciousness collided. There was no single future, only the many, the myriad likely and unlikely. Yet sometimes this vast array of possibilities coalesced into a single future.

As always, it was the path of the Imbirri that he watched. Despite the elation of his state, he could see that the terrible events he had foreseen if the humans came to Cru were upon them. Every Imbirri future was the same. Destruction. Ending. Not a single one of them would escape. Utar kept despair from his heart as he sped along the spirit-path of his people. It grew darker, like the night of the void, until it unraveled and was lost within a nebulous cloud of black. Nothing: nothing remained.

Utar paused, suspended in non-space, aghast, yet determined to see it all. He sped further along the path of his people, fighting through the dark cloud of the unknown. The thick, sticky substance of it clung to him, blinding him. He pushed on, plumbing the depths of his power to extend the breadth of his vision. At last the cloud was gone and what he saw beyond stunned him more than anything he had ever encountered. For an eternity he lingered, drinking in the vision, at last knowing new hope for his people. Then he sped back toward his body.

Never would he have guessed …

Utar rose to see his acolytes beside him, waiting in silence. The enclosure was dark and the coals spent. The effects of the Elixir were still strong. His vision swirled and shifted, his mind surging, but he forced himself to focus. He had to be *here*. In the Now.

"Attend me." The notes of his voice echoed strangely in his ears, making multiple harmonies that extended into the far distance like a chorus of singers with his own voice. He ignored the effect.

Otla and Munch rose and helped him to his unsteady feet. With the swift movements of long practice, they hid the fire pit and all the tools and ingredients associated with the Elixir's preparation. With everything cleared away, they cast back the walls of the enclosure. Then they began to prepare for the procession, a ritual that recounted in symbolic form the discovery of the Elixir and its deliverance to the Awakener.

Utar was steadier now, his powerful mind focused fully on the moment. He stopped his acolytes with a signal. "Listen to me." His voice was raw, redolent with deep, husky tones, yet resounded with the power of his vision. A voice of prophecy.

"Soon I will die."

Otla and Munch both froze, and their eyes grew dark with fear. Utar laid a hand on each of them to reassure them, touching them deeply with emotion. "Do not fear for me."

Utar stood back, determined. "This is what must be done with my body."

***

Utar made his way across the open ground with measured steps, his awareness held within the confines of the moment. He knew that his own time was drawing to a close, and he drank in the sights around him with the thirst of a dying man, savoring and cherishing the life he saw. Behind him followed his two acolytes, carrying a huge bowl between them.

He watched the Imbirri at play. So innocent. Changeless. They had already forgotten the great desecration visited on them by the frail aliens, their minds lost in the present, focused fully on the rituals and habits learned and reinforced during their vast history of unchanging years. These simple creatures would soon be gone forever, yet now they were alive and vital. Utar smiled, an unfamiliar sadness touching him, driving hot tears from the nipples along his torso. *How much longer will I see through these ancient eyes of mine?*

His small procession moved forward at a slow, measured pace. As they drew closer to the Tree, Utar reluctantly drew his eyes away from the scene and regarded the huge living dome above him. Its crown lay blackened and skeletal. This destruction no longer disturbed Utar as it had, for it was symbolic of the plight of the Imbirri. New growth would come, and the darkness, the charred fragments, would fall away under the hand of time.

Without pause, Utar entered the great living dome, breathing deeply of the incense that filled the expanse. The great bulk of the Awakener filled the ragged throne. Above them, the rough tear in the crown admitted the constant light of the dark side of Cru, breaking the perfect gloom in which they had worshipped for so long. These changes now excited Utar, for they were heralds of a new age. He approached the dais, moving through the ranks of the First who had assembled here.

The Awakener accepted the Elixir grimly. His hands still shook with grief and rage. Utar and his two acolytes bowed and withdrew to the ranks of the First.

As the Deepwatch straightened he met the gaze of his beloved Awakener and saw the pain there. How he longed to reveal his vision to the Awakener, to fill him with the same hope that softened his knowledge of their inevitable end, but he could not. Walking the paths of the future had stretched his spirit through the years and it was the future that silenced him. All now balanced on a knife-edge.

The shaman turned away from the pain-filled gaze of the Awakener.

He could speak no longer.

A low humming began to fill the air as the Awakener took a draught of the precious liquid, passing it on to the ranks of the faithful who surrounded him. Gradually the melody rose, flaring suddenly into impassioned voice like a rising cloud of frenzied redwings. The huge steel bowl that contained the Elixir was passed from hand to hand, a taste enough to reaffirm its powers.

When the last of them were sated, Utar signaled for his acolytes to begin the ceremony and they led the First from within the embrace of the Tree. As the last of them pushed through the low-hanging branches that covered the entrance, Utar remained within the Tree.

The Awakener rose from his dais and came toward him, his great face etched with pain. He searched out Utar's gaze as though seeking shelter, laying a hand on his friend's shoulder.

"Why should this have happened? For so long we had peace. It seemed it would last forever." The Awakener glanced up toward the broken canopy. His smooth face twisted by rage. "They have destroyed that which we loved!"

It was a long moment before the Awakener could collect himself. "You warned me, my good friend, but I did not listen. Destroy them, you said, before they are our doom! I should have listened, Utar. Yours was the wise council."

Utar watched his dear friend in silence, as though he was already a spectral being, divorced from the living.

The silence stretched.

"I implore you! What should be done? Tell me, Utar, that it is not too late. That if we destroy them now, utterly, we will still have a chance to save this rapturous piece of eternity."

Utar felt the Awakener's grief, his awareness focused fully on the present as though through a powerful lens. The overlapping boughs and branches of the Tree, as tightly woven as a basket, every leaf and piece of bark, the soft hiss of the torches, the pungent odor; each sensation was sharpened to clear reality, and Utar knew he would take these last moments with him to his funeral bier.

"Why are you silent? Is this your cruel punishment? Here! Take the scepter, destroy them!" The Awakener thrust the scepter toward Utar, but the shaman pushed it away.

"I can no longer act," said Utar, opening his heart. "And I can no longer speak."

The Deepwatch turned away from him and left the Tree's sanctuary. Behind him, he could feel the Awakener's grief turn to despair.

"Utar!" The Awakener pushed through the entrance to watch him walk away, his mind and heart now closed to him.

"*Utar!*"

Chapter 11

It was like the fugue, yet unlike it. Once more, Karic's senses had expanded beyond himself, yet now he was connecting to something at the very limits of his consciousness, at the boundaries of this new world itself.

In this strange, lucid dream, Karic had been drawn across the surface of the planet by the power of another sleeping mind, trapped like him in a cage of silent flesh. Through the checkerboard pattern of light and shadow created by the crystal mountains of the night side, across the terminator to the blinding brilliance and heat of the day side, glimpses of vast, glittering structures flashed past him until, at last, all motion ceased and he was there.

This torpid Other was encased by technology, encircled by the power of his own mind, held like a precious jewel amid the lucent, golden torrent of Tau Ceti's undiluted light.

As he had with Utar, Karic tried for connection. "Who are you?"

The Other stirred. Karic sensed that the alien's sleep was like a numbing drug that weighed him down. The merest fragment of the being's consciousness swam to the surface, enough for the briefest of answers, dredged from an alien dream. *I await the call.* The thoughts formed in Karic's mind like a string of amber jewels. That outreaching tendril of the alien's consciousness sank back into sleep. Then, as though from a great distance, one more chain of thought reached Karic before the Other was gone. *For so long I have slept now, waiting for my children to come.*

He could no longer maintain the bond over such a distance. Karic's mind fled back across the planet's surface to verdant forests of the night side.

Karic!

Someone else called him now.

Karic!

His strange, lucid state snapped like an overstretched cable.

Karic turned to see the bars of the cage above, bent dreamlike in the lens of sleep. *I am a prisoner.*

"Karic, wake up!"

He felt himself being shaken violently. He opened his eyes to see Mara above him.

"Mara. What ... ?"

In response, she turned her gaze upward, toward the huge figure who stood at the edge of the pit. It was the shaman. *Utar.* A jolt of fear sent his heart racing.

"Have they come for us?" Karic sat up. His burned arm throbbed painfully.

Mara shook her head. "No, I don't think so. It's something else."

His head still swimming from the lucid dream, Karic stood up.

Above him, the shaman waited patiently for him to stir. The savage gleam was gone from Utar's eyes, instead they were filled with a softly flickering glow. Karic sensed resignation.

As Karic watched, the bulky being bent forward to kneel beside the cage. He held up a comband, which was dwarfed by the size of his hand. He dangled the device just above the bars of the cage and with deliberate motions turned one of the tiny switches on and off, repeating the motion as though to ensure they understood.

"What is he doing?" said Mara, drawing closer to Karic.

The engineer nodded, finally understanding. "He's switching the comband's emergency beacon on and off."

"What is he telling us?"

Karic raised his eyes to meet those of Utar. They regarded each other without emotion, recognizing each other as human and Imbirri.

The light within Utar's eyes began to build.

Karic felt the hairs on his arms stand up as a delicate field of energy wrapped around him.

There was a tingling, aching sensation in his mind. A longing. His heart took a leap as he realized what it was. It was the fugue state in its most embryonic form, asking to be given birth. He had spent his life resisting the fugue. It had represented everything that could destroy him: lack of control, the brand of dysfunction in the eyes of others — all intolerable for a man of his intellect. Yet now he knew it for what it truly was. *A gift.*

And he hungered to see the alien's mind.

As he had before, the first time he communicated with Utar beneath the tree, Karic surrendered to the fugue. His mind expanded, reaching out to connect with the world around him. The rough walls of the pit. The intense vitality of the jungle. Mara's fear and desperation. But it was Utar who was the focus. The alien's mind was a glowing thing, spinning off thought — like steam rising from a geothermal spring. A little gem shot toward him from Utar's mind, tumbling like a miniature crystal, silvered glass panes set with irregular, irresistible genius across its outer surface. As he focused, it expanded in a flash of white light. Utar's thought blossomed in his mind.

The small spark of Vision within you is growing rapidly, human. I am relieved, because time is short.

Karic could feel Utar's surprise at his abilities.

My name is Karic, the leader of this crew. I am from a planet called Earth. I did not sanction the attack on your people. We mean you no harm.

His thoughts were easily read by Utar, who sang a short, bittersweet melody.

I am Utar, Deepwatch of the Imbirri. My people have suffered, Karic, since you set foot on our sacred planet of Cru. What you meant, or did not mean, is now of no consequence. The future will be served. Karic could feel Utar's determination strengthen. *Will you help the Imbirri?*

Karic was unsure what the price of helping the Imbirri would be, or if he would be endangering the survivors of the *Starburst*. But if there was a chance he could win his freedom, he would take it.

Will you free us? Karic asked, across the link.

Karic could feel Utar's sorrow as the Deepwatch replied. *The future demands it. Each of us — human and Imbirri — has our part to play before the future finally becomes manifest. You will be freed, I will see to it.*

He could see a resonating field of thought that Utar was holding close to his mind. Secrets he was not to know ... yet.

Your task, Karic, is to follow the song of this device. Utar lifted up the personal beacon, his eyes shining with increasing brilliance. *Use it to find me, Karic. Do not fail. All depends on you. Beware the Awakener.* An image of the huge alien who led the Imbirri filled Karic's mind.

Karic was filled with questions, but the mental link with Utar broke as the big Imbirri turned away, striding rapidly from the pit. With an effort of will, he shifted his awareness away from the fugue state. Once more, he was confronted with the rough walls and the rancid smells of the pit.

He was confused, but the important thing was what he had learned. They were going to be freed! So far, none of the crew had been killed. If he could get back to the lander, take charge, he could salvage all of this.

"What was that all about?"

In the intensity of the exchange he had forgotten about Mara.

Karic looked across at her, his mind still filled with the strange excitement engendered by the communication. A sense of unreality hit him. Here he was, standing on an alien planet, communicating telepathically with the natives. He would have laughed if the situation had not been so dangerous. As it was, his unexpected gift — the altered fugue state — had enabled him to strike some sort of deal with Utar.

"What the frigging hell did you think you were doing? Having a ten-minute staring match with that shaman? Do you *want* him to kill us?"

What could he say to her?

"Mara, his name is Utar. He is a Deepwatch — some sort of protector — for his people, the Imbirri. He spoke to me, Mara. Mind to mind."

Mara shook her head. "No ..."

Karic ploughed on, pushing through her skepticism. If he did not tell her now, he would lose his nerve. It had always been one of his greatest fears that others would think him mentally imbalanced, or unstable, because of the fugue. "This planet, Mara. We called it Oasis, but the Imbirri have a name for it. Cru. It is sacred to them, Mara. No wonder they reacted to us like they did."

"Damn you, Karic. Why are you carrying on like this?" Mara's fists were clenched, her face screwed up in anger. She did not believe him.

"Utar was against us from the start, Mara. I knew that. But something has changed. He is some sort of shaman, and he has seen something. He would not let me see it, but something has changed his mind."

"Ahhhh. Shit!" Mara covered her face with her hands and paced around the pit like a trapped animal. "This is a frigging nightmare! What is this planet doing to us? First Janzen, now you, Karic. I can't trust either of you assholes anymore."

Karic grabbed Mara's arms and forced her to look at him. "Everything I am telling you is true! Utar is going to free us."

Mara pulled out of his grip.

How could he explain the fugue state to her? His altered genes? The transformation he had experienced?

Mara sat at the far end of the pit, her back turned to him.

He slumped down, defeated in his attempt to win her over.

What did Utar mean? *Follow the song of your device.* Of course! It was the personal beacon on the comband. Somehow Utar had figured out how to activate the beacon, and had identified its low-powered radio signal as the "song" of the device. It seemed impossible that he could have known this without equipment, but Karic was sure. At some point after they were freed, Utar wanted him to locate the wrist-worn communicator by following the beacon. But why? What would Utar demand of them once they located him? Why the elaborate scheme? What was he planning?

He rubbed his face, weary of his circling thoughts. "Once he frees us, we have to find him, following the personal beacon," said Karic. "That's what he told me."

"Shut your frigging mouth!" Mara turned to face him. "Just stop it. *Stop it.* I need you sane." Her face was red and wet with tears.

Karic jumped as a wall of harmony filled the air. It was as though all of the Imbirri had given voice at the very same moment.

He waved Mara toward him. "We need to see what's going on. This gives us the best view."

Mara looked at Karic, confused by his apparent lucidity.

After a brief hesitation, she climbed onto his back once more. He straightened and her head emerged through the thick bars of the cage, giving her a good view of the camp.

"What's happening up there?"

"It's some sort of ceremony," said Mara. "They are all gathered in a circle, passing a bowl between them."

"Can you support your own weight?"

"I think so," said Mara.

He sprang from the floor of the pit to grip the bars and hang beside her. Thousands of Imbirri had gathered in the center of the camp, and more were emerging from the surrounding jungle. They stood together in what appeared at first to be concentric circles, yet as he studied the camp, Karic realized they were not a series of circles, but one great spiral. Along the arm of this spiral, which now encompassed the whole campsite, bowls were being passed from hand to hand. A single sip was taken by each of the Imbirri and the bowls passed on. Karic saw the empty bowls being refilled by the acolytes of Utar from a huge metal urn.

The vision of the camp was spectacular, yet it was not the scene that captured Karic, it was the song. It swelled — filling the air — turning the valley into a vast cathedral. Thousands of voices, each pure and true, a score of melodies threaded together like a tapestry. The sheer power of the music was overwhelming, swirling about them like a tempest.

His arms burned as he struggled to keep his head above the bars, but he soon forgot his aching muscles.

"It's wonderful," she said.

The music had a purity Karic had never experienced before. The Imbirri, now having all tasted their sacred potion — Karic guessed some sort of naturally derived drug — began to sway as they sang. The great spiral geometrically perfect.

Karic heard distant thunder. No, not thunder. It was too continuous, more like a muffled roar. It grew rapidly, becoming a deafening sound.

Thrusters.

"It's the lander!" yelled Karic.

The huge, bulky shape of the lander swept across the village. Simultaneously, Andrai and Ibri ran from the forest verge, XR32s held at the ready.

"What is Janzen doing?"

Only one of the lander's sensors was deployed, a long, unfamiliar aerial, projecting from the front. Karic had never seen it before — and he knew the lander's specifications backwards.

"What the ...?"

The scene was lit with a bright flash as a pulse of laser-fire swept through the Imbirri. Six of the beings were cut down, twice as many screaming as their skins charred to black at the merest touch of the beam.

The lander fired again. That was no aerial! *It was a laser turret!*

"Did you know the lander was equipped with a pulse laser?" said Karic, furious.

"No," said Mara.

"I should have left him in stasis on *Starburst*." *What else had that bastard kept from them?*

The song ceased immediately, replaced by screams of outrage and panic, voiced together from a thousand throats. The perfectly choreographed spiral dissolved into a surging mob of alien flesh. Most of the Imbirri made for the forest verge, but not all. The purple-crowned Imbirri gathered into a single group and loped across the turf toward the lander. The giant Awakener — towering over all the Imbirri — emerged from the chaos, followed by his inner circle. The Imbirri leader sang a series of notes, then the tall reds ran forward. The taller Imbirri grabbed the purples and dragged them back to the safety of the trees.

Only the Awakener and his entourage, a group of about thirty Imbirri, stood their ground. They turned as one to face the new threat. The laser bursts were coming quickly now — a trail of fire sweeping in an arc toward them.

Andrai and Ibri advanced quickly, taking advantage of the confusion, then paused on the edge of the village. They were not coming to the pit. Instead they seemed to be waiting for something.

"Andrai! What the hell is going on!" yelled Karic, but Andrai was too far away to hear.

Janzen took the lander down, turning his weapon. Even from this distance Karic could see what he was doing. He was targeting the big laser on the Awakener — and the energy weapon. "He's trying to take out the leaders and the scepter in one go."

It was bloodthirsty overkill, but he had to give Janzen credit. It was a solid plan. If he succeeded, no one on Cru would challenge them in firepower. Yet ... if he had not been so hell-bent on destruction in the first place, they would all be safely back at the base camp. Even now, there would have been ample time for Andrai and Ibri to remove the pit-cover and free himself and Mara. Instead, Janzen had them doing something else.

The Awakener drew himself up. He shook his scepter at the lander, screaming in outrage. His eyes glowed with hot light as he turned to Andrai and Ibri, waiting nearby on the grassed hill.

"Hurry, Janzen," said Karic.

The lander was hovering barely three meters off the ground. Janzen adjusted its position, taking his time to target the Awakener.

Karic's eyes were drawn to Utar. The Deepwatch was taking in the scene calmly. Against the outrage of the Awakener, and the panic of the other Imbirri, his calmness was eerie. Karic let his mind drift into the fugue state. He could sense Utar's consciousness. It was buoyant — floating on a soundless sea.

Then Utar stepped in front of the Awakener — a split second before Janzen fired the lander's pulse laser.

The beam effortlessly punched a hole through Utar's heart, searing the grass behind him. Thick yellow gore pumped from the ragged hole, splattering across the burnt skin of his torso. He sank to his knees, his eyes growing a startling silver color as he turned one last time toward the Awakener.

For a time, all stood frozen. The Awakener met the gaze of Utar and each knew the heart of the other before the vital energies of the being called Utar finally fled. The Deepwatch's eyes faded to black, and he fell heavily to the ground: dead.

"No!" screamed Karic. His heart went cold. With Utar dead, they no longer had a friend in the Imbirri. Their last chance of freedom now depended on Janzen's success.

The Awakener screamed in rage. His huge frame swelled with power. Long before Janzen could even sight his laser a second time, the enormous energies of the scepter were lancing across the field in an arc of blue-white fire. Karic had never seen this much energy flow through the device.

The wave struck the lander. The laser turret melted in moments, then a jagged line of red-hot metal began to snake across the surface of the craft. The thrusters began to destabilize. The lander shook, slamming into the ground before rising once more.

Karic took a sharp breath. *"Get out of there, Janzen!"*

The discharge of the energy weapon ceased and the spluttering flow of fuel to the thrusters was restored with a sudden roar of flame. The lander flew straight up, then shot toward the horizon. It was soon out of sight.

The discordant moans of wounded Imbirri filled the air.

The Awakener turned on Andrai and Ibri. A front of white-hot energy swept Andrai and Ibri before it like a storm-front. Each of the humans was lifted by the force of the corona and their screams were terrible as the electrical energy surged to earth through their bodies. Each fell unconsciousness to the ground, their clothes sputtering with flame.

"Damn you, Janzen!" said Karic. *"All you had to do was walk in and lift off this damn cage."*

Mara was stunned to silence.

There was no way Janzen would come back for them now. He would stay inside the magnetically confined plasma of the lander's defensive shield and enter stasis, leaving them to die.

And Utar — the Imbirri who had promised them freedom — was dead.

Catching sight of Karic and Mara as they peered over the rim of the cage, the Awakener swept an arc of energy across the pit. The humans fell back into the hole and pressed themselves flat against the earthen wall of the rough enclosure to escape the power of the weapon.

Silence.

Then the cage door opened above them. The two prisoners looked up expecting only death, yet instead, Utar's followers stood above them, bearing the bodies of Andrai and Ibri. They dumped the limp forms into the cage and closed the lid.

Feverishly, Karic and Mara checked Andrai and Ibri for some sign of life. Neither had a pulse, and they tried to revive them. As the minutes crawled by, they were losing hope, then at last Andrai's heart — stopped like Mara's by the discharge — began to beat once more. He was soon conscious.

Ibri's heart remained still. Judging by the savage burns to his torso, he had been saved a painful death. Had they managed to revive him, he would have been in agony until shock, infection, and pain killed him hours, or perhaps days later. Unlike Andrai, the fires started by the weapon had continued to burn into Ibri's frame as he lay unconscious, fed by the enriched oxygen in the ambient air.

Andrai had been lucky, escaping with only a few minor burns.

The three prisoners laid Ibri at rest along one wall of the pit and covered his face with a charred square of cloth. For a long time, they sat in silence, too exhausted to speak.

Karic looked around the primitive cage, listening to the soft Imbirri melodies that had started outside their prison. In the face of death, the alien music made his hands tighten in rage.

How on Earth did they end up like this? Imprisoned. Abandoned on an alien world. This should have been the time of their greatest triumph. Instead, they waited for execution. They were at the mercy of the Imbirri and — thanks to the insane actions of Janzen — the aliens had every reason to want them dead.

Yet Karic did not give up hope. Remarkable things had happened. Unexpected things.

The trauma, the pain. The loss. The accelerating power of his mind, culminating during the descent in the pod to the surface of the planet. All had given him something he had never, ever thought to gain: control over the fugue.

It had turned from a curse into a remarkable and unexpected gift. A way of connecting with the world around him and the sentient minds of others that he would never have believed possible. Thought, like light, was now within his spectrum. He could see it, the tangled mass of it as it sped around the consciousness of others.

He remembered the eyes of the Deepwatch, and the promise offered there. Utar had turned, at the last moment, from their enemy to their only ally on Cru. His death should have crippled his hope, but it did not.

Why?

Then he remembered the terrible resignation he felt within Utar, the thoughts that were locked away from him, and the pieces fit into place. Utar knew he himself would die.

Just as he knew they would escape.

Chapter 12

The Awakener stood vigil over the body of Utar.

He had drawn his mind above the swiftly moving streams of the moment to a stiller place, and the clouds and misting rains seemed to come and go across the grassy sward like silent, flickering light-shows.

Yet even in this state, his grief remained.

There was so much to grieve for — and so little left of the life that had once seemed so endless. Once they had thought to live forever. The end of that hope, of that arrogance, was bitter.

Around the Awakener lay an assembled host. Nearest to him were the First, and behind these the Imbirri who had returned from the jungle after fleeing from the ceremony of the Elixir. The reds prowled around the perimeter, hands clenched in silent fury, while the purples ran in excited groups between all the evidence of carnage, lost in their wonder.

As the hours passed, others emerged from the concealing safety of the jungle and rejoined their people. They instinctively arranged themselves in the order of their awakening. Each knew from long experience who preceded them, and who followed. All sang together in subdued melodies, drinking from the same well of grief. But there was no song for this.

The body of Utar was swollen with the Changes and encased in a sweet-smelling ichor of gray-purple that had already hardened. Only paces from Utar's body lay the remains of Green Patch, one of the First killed in the alien's initial attack. The ichor surrounding the body of Green Patch had become a seamless, green shell, his original form barely recognizable in the opaque contours of the casing.

With trembling hands, the Awakener raised the scepter. Around him the people of the Imbirri waited for the Ceremony of Ending with the patience of a people who barely marked the passage of time.

Above, the sky was unblemished — the clouds buoyant – as if suspended. In the distance he could see the slender, twisted shape of the nearby crystal monolith, glowing brightly.

A simple adjustment extended the capacity of the scepter to maximum. The power within the instrument now built steadily, until the energy cell hummed with impatience.

The Awakener brought the staff down, releasing a mere fraction of the staff's power in an intense burst of heat. The body of Green Patch, wrapped within a shell of organic resin, was swallowed by a sheath of flame. In seconds, the huge casing had blackened, then it began to melt and burn. Briefly, a golden form was visible within, then the whole was swept to darkness. The beam of power ceased, and a sudden gust of wind swept the ashes across the verdant field where they had all shared so much joy.

Each of the Imbirri stood in silent contemplation, lamenting the passing of another of their race.

The Awakener opened his eyes. The power remaining in the staff sought release like a violent child, reaching out to turn his thoughts from peace to rage.

His gaze fixed on the still form of Utar's corpse.

He knew what must come to pass. His mind screamed for him to raise the scepter, to unleash the energies of destruction onto the remnants of Utar's physical form, yet he could not. It was too soon. With a cry of pain, he raised the weapon skyward and unleashed the energy until the scepter lay cooling in his hand.

Above them, the low clouds swirled with the heat of the beam's passing.

Below, all was still.

The Awakener turned from the body of Utar. The Ending would have to wait until his grief had passed from him, when his mind was clear. Then he could reduce Utar's remains to ashes with the proper poise. *I will follow with the destruction of the aliens and their strange craft.* His desire for revenge burnt within him like a dying sun aching for nova.

"Find the craft of the aliens," he said to Reth, a red-crowned First, as he made his way back toward the Tree. "Take Ember and together lead all the Imbirri reds in the search." The ninety-four reds were the most single-minded and tenacious of the Imbirri, too aggressive even for the Pod Game, from which they had been banned more than a thousand seasons ago, after an incident in which a red had been almost crippled in a pod-fight. Led by Reth and Ember — the only two First reds — they would soon ferret out the hiding place of the human defilers.

"We will destroy every last trace of them." The Awakener's face was set like stone. "But first, I have to rest. Go."

***

Otla had waited patiently throughout the ceremony. The Awakener's presence, usually bright like the never-ending light of the crystal mountains, was now dimmed with clouds of pain and indecision. It was painful for all the First to see that change in him. For so long, his vast mind and spirit had been the indomitable foundation of the Imbirri culture, the everlasting font of wisdom, enlightenment, and guidance.

Now Otla's multi-faceted eyes followed Reth and Ember as they trotted around the camp to gather the reds, their deep voices chanting in unison. Reds ran from every corner of the clearing, adding their voices to the bass chorus. Time was running fast now.

Otla watched as his leader disappeared through the living walls of the Tree, imposing even in his agony. Most of the First followed, but the seven acolytes of Utar — Otla, Munch and five others — remained by the Deepwatch's encased body. Some of the First always kept watch on a slain Imbirri until its remains could be destroyed, to keep the others away and insulate them from the danger of the Changes, which were often triggered by the pungent odors of the transforming body. As acolytes of Utar, this duty had fallen to them.

Otla knew that the First who had entered the Tree with the Awakener would follow their leader to the end, no matter where his grief and anger would lead him, or how clouded his mind became. The seven acolytes had an allegiance that went beyond even that — to Utar and his last commands.

Munch and Otla touched minds briefly. It was they who must carry out the next phase of the plan. Alone, and in secret.

Otla hummed a soft series of notes as he considered the five other acolytes. They also had their part to play. Briefly, he considered telling them everything. If all went according to Utar's plan, it would be the last time they saw each other — as Imbirri. The four greens were loyal, yet greens were always easier to sway when the songs began, and the Awakener's power was unquestioned. Too much depended on secrecy. The gold, New Bough, could be trusted to remain silent, but even so would be subject to the Awakener's control. No. The full details of Utar's audacious plan must remain a secret, even from them.

"Go. Rejoin the First," sang Otla.

New Bough turned in silence and stalked off. Otla could tell the gold was uneasy at being dismissed so curtly by a green, but Otla was not only ahead of New Bough in the order of Awakening, he was the most senior of Utar's followers. The greens sang a soft harmony of departure as they followed New Bough toward the Tree, walking in a tightly knit group. Their lighthearted innocence tore at him. This world they had known for so long was soon to end. The knowledge of that, and of what he and Munch must do, burned in his mind.

Otla and Munch were soon alone beside Utar's body. The casing that surrounded it was now hard and stiff, the shape of the Deepwatch's form barely recognizable inside the resin. It was rare that the Changes were allowed to progress as far as this strange, chrysalis stage. What came after ... not even Utar would tell him.

With a heave, they lifted the body to their broad shoulders. The Imbirri around the camp watched them curiously, but did not interfere.

The two acolytes bore their burden toward the forest, disappearing into the thick growth. They marched steadily toward a place that lay in darkness, beyond the lush green they knew. Many hours later, they reached the dark valley. A place hidden from the great spans of light that swept out from the jagged crystal towers.

Here they labored, building a bier from the stout trunks of forest trees they had stockpiled earlier. At length, they set the body onto the raised platform. Beneath the body of Utar they set the alien artifact, given to them only moments before his death by Utar himself. With a delicate series of touches on the tiny human device, Otla activated the beacon. He shifted his consciousness briefly, as Utar had taught him, and confirmed that its strange monotonous voice was active, singing in the unseen registers of light.

Otla and Munch lowered their heads and stood motionless, waiting in fear. The dull, pulsing power within Utar's inert form reached out to them and at last they fell.

To be consumed by the Change.

***

For hours Karic watched the thick wooden bars of their cell, beyond sleep. Both Mara and Andrai were lost in a deep coma of exhaustion, heedless of the stink of death or the bright light that flooded into the pit. A cloud of alien insects buzzed and crawled around the corpse of Ibri, and the engineer had long since recognized the futility of waving them away.

The burn on his left forearm was beginning to heal, the skin torn open by the rough grip of his Imbirri captors now scabbed over with no sign of infection. There were no blisters, thankfully, just angry red flesh. He had dressed it with torn strips from his shirt and learned to ignore the constant pain, and the lingering numbness.

Karic jumped up to grasp the thick beams of the cage and maneuver himself into a position where he could peer outward at the camp. By hooking one arm over a bamboo strut, he could push his head past the bars and watch the village for long minutes before the ache in his shoulder and neck drove him back to the pit floor. For now, all seemed quiet.

Some hours before the Awakener had emerged from the living dome of the Tree with a score of his followers. He had stalked around the camp, enraged, pointing toward the grassed verge where Utar's body had lain. Although he did not see it happen, Karic could deduce from the Awakener's tirade and the sheepish reactions of the other Imbirri that some of the aliens had taken the body of Utar, in defiance of both custom and the will of the Awakener. Utar's remains had escaped the sure destruction meted out by the power of the staff.

Karic had watched the incineration of the first encased corpse and intuitively knew Utar's was to follow. These beings feared death and the strange transformation that seemed to accompany it.

145

After a long and heated oration, the Awakener had led his followers out of the camp, leaving the simpler Imbirri in his wake, bewildered. Karic knew this was the time to escape, yet how was he to shift the massive weight of the cage door? He had tried to chip at the resin that glued the bars together, but without success. Even with the proper tools, it would be like chiseling granite.

Karic let himself fall to the floor of the pit, inadvertently awakening Andrai. The tech sat up against the earth wall, his eyes taking in the stiffening corpse of Ibri in a moment of sickening disorientation.

"How are you feeling, Andrai?" asked Karic.

Andrai touched the burns on his chest and arms gingerly. "I've been better, boss, but I'm alive and still in one piece. Any idea how we can get out of here?"

Karic gave the tech a wry grin. "I'm sure Janzen will be here any moment."

Andrai grimaced. "You know he won't be back again."

Both knew that Janzen would stay in the base camp, safe behind the defensive shield. There he would use the stasis sets to wait out the decades required for a signal to reach Earth from Tau Ceti, and for the reply to be received.

"How come Janzen was at the controls?" asked Karic. He tried to keep his voice even, but it was hard. Janzen was an amateur pilot compared to Andrai and he should not have been at the controls on an expedition like that. The former commander's ability to manipulate every single one of them was aggravating in the extreme. With the benefit of hindsight, Karic could see that simply removing him from command had not been enough. Not nearly enough.

"Janzen activated some sort of lockout on the controls. None of us could do anything without his voice activation." Andrai smiled bitterly. "I'm sorry, Karic. The plan seemed like a good one, even with Janzen at the controls. None of us suspected what that alien weapon was capable of."

Karic sighed. Recriminations were useless.

He turned sharply as a shadow fell across them. The cage door above them opened, falling back onto the ground surrounding the pit with a heavy thud.

Mara woke suddenly, leaping to her feet with a gasp of fright. Her dark hair cascaded around her face and shoulders. Her wide, dark eyes took in them, the pit, then the open sky above them in a series of quick, feverish movements. "What's going on?"

"We're not sure," said Karic.

Karic, Mara, and Andrai unconsciously moved closer together, the three of them looking up expectantly at the five towering Imbirri who appeared above the pit. Each of them instinctively searched for some means of escape, but they would be caught easily if they tried to climb the sides. The Imbirri reached down into the pit and seized them. The three humans struggled, but were powerless to prevent the Imbirri from taking them.

The group of five Imbirri, who Karic recognized as followers of Utar, took them to the forest verge. There they released them.

The three humans stood confused for a brief moment, but one of the Imbirri spoke quickly to them in their melodic native language, waving them into the forest and away from the camp.

At last they had their chance.

"Come on!" Karic led them into the forest at a run.

Soon the village was lost from sight. More familiar with the area around the alien's camp, Andrai and Mara took over the navigation. After a few frustrating hours inside the confusing morass of the jungle, they succeeded in identifying enough key landmarks to strike out toward the base camp. They were exhausted from lack of food and fatigue, yet not one of them entertained thoughts of stopping. The promise of safety in the lander's shielded encampment drew them on.

Karic was personally looking forward to wringing Janzen's neck.

After three hours they finally crested the last rise.

"Look! There's the lander!" Mara pointed toward the gray metal shape of the craft through the trees. They could just make out the rippling blue curtain of the shield enclosure that surrounded it.

Hooting in triumph, they ran down the hill, safety in sight at last. Yet as they approached, Karic began to notice signs around them that a large group had passed this way.

Karic's elation fled. "Stop!" He pulled Mara and Andrai to the ground. They began to protest, but noting his urgency, they responded without question. He waved them into hiding.

The lander was now only hundreds of meters away. From their place of concealment they could see the gray turrets and sculptured metal of the hull. Solid, seemingly impenetrable.

As they watched, Karic's worst fears were confirmed.

The Awakener's cohorts, at first hidden by the terrain, could be seen surrounding the craft. Red-crowned Imbirri circled the shield constantly, like tigers around a wounded elephant, testing its defenses, looking for a weak spot. They darted in with quick, vicious movements, showing an aggression Karic had not seen in the natives so far. The aliens attacked in twos and threes, thrusting branches and logs at the screen, or beating at the relay posts in an attempt to disable them. They backed away swiftly when the wood erupted into flame, but they continued their relentless assault with new weapons snatched up from the forest floor. Behind them, the Awakener watched in silence, his huge, multifaceted eyes as dark as obsidian, yet alive with a chilling intelligence. He was surrounded by another group of mixed Imbirri, who watched the attack unfold with the same detachment as their leader. Karic guessed these were the same group who had emerged from the Tree with the Awakener during Janzen's ill-fated attacks on the Imbirri encampment. They seemed higher in status — and intelligence — than the other Imbirri. The Awakener towered over them all, standing almost four meters tall.

"Like bringing a knife to a gunfight. No way they can damage our shield with sticks and logs," said Andrai, forcing a smile.

Karic's gaze was drawn to the Awakener, and the metallic sheen of the energy weapon he carried in his right hand. "It's not stick and logs I'm worried about."

The Awakener sang a quick series of notes and the red-crowned Imbirri withdrew into the surrounding jungle. The Imbirri leader made a quick adjustment to the weapon then unleashed its power. Twin streamers of jagged lightning shot across the clearing and struck the shield with a sizzling crack and a discharge of ozone.

A worm of fear slithered in the pit of Karic's stomach. Not even he could guess at the shield's limits when confronted with this powerful alien technology.

The blue fields rippled and stretched. Inside the magnetic containment, where the attack met the shield, the charged plasma glowed an intense yellow. Even from hundreds of meters away, Karic felt the heat on the side of his face. The swirling yellow expanded as the shield's processor spread the absorbed heat and energy across its whole plasma storage. The Awakener howled with fury, moving closer to the shield as the power issuing from the alien weapon ramped up another notch. His mouth dry, Karic tried to swallow past the sudden lump in his throat. All three of them had their gaze locked to the shield.

The heat spread through the shield until the whole enclosed mass of plasma glowed an effulgent gold. The containment area expanded as stored gas was ionized and injected into the plasma containment to absorb more of the energy. Soon, even the powerful magnetics would reach their limit.

Mara gripped Andrai's arm, her dark eyes wide in fear. Her hair was still loose, crowding around her thin face. It made her look younger, more vulnerable.

The Awakener was only paces away from the shield now. Karic squatted down lower, instinctively going deeper into cover to conceal himself from the huge being and the awesome power he wielded.

Then, with a blinding flash, the shield vented plasma. All three of them cried out and dove to the ground as the super-hot plasma, ejected from the magnetic containment as it reached its programmed limit, expanded overhead. Leaves in the overhead canopy flashed and burned to carbon in an instant, then the plasma was gone. Dissipated.

Karic leapt to his feet in time to see the Awakener disappear into the jungle.

Of course. Having reached the limits of its expanded containment, the shield shed the energy by releasing the plasma instead. The shield was designed to defeat energy weapons after all. It would continue to absorb energy and vent plasma as long as the stock of replacement plasma gas remained. The AI in the shield would now work to radiate away its heat, gradually extracting and storing the excess gas until it returned to its initial state.

The lander was safe.

The three of them exchanged smiles of relief. They ducked back into cover as the red-crowned Imbirri returned, more incensed than ever. Despite their lack of success before, they continued to attack the shield, prodding at the shimmering containment over the posts and the main unit, still looking for a way in. Their methodical determination — and their aggression — was disturbing.

There was a low thud of metal against metal from the lander. Karic scanned the hull for a long moment before he noticed one of the probe launch doors was open. A detonation echoed through the valley as the probe's tiny rockets ignited, then the familiar high-pitched whine reached them as it shot skyward from the lander.

"Why is Janzen launching a probe?" said Andrai, his wide forehead creased in a frown. "Maybe he's going to survey the village. To check on us."

"No. He's written us off." Karic watched as the probe lifted then cast off its outer casing, deploying wings and small laser turrets. The tiny rockets swiveled in place and the probe hovered, turning slowly. It was locking targets.

"Damn. What now?" said Mara, unconsciously pushing her hair back from her face.

"That's a Davis XV78 attack probe," said Karic. "Better take cover. That thing will kill anything that moves."

It seemed that suspension sets were not the only things that Janzen had snuck aboard the lander. It made him wonder what else was hiding on board. But so much armament? Had Janzen been expecting to fight a war?

The XV78 started firing.

It shot small focused bursts of laser fire, faster than the eye could track. Suddenly, the Imbirri were falling by the dozens, some howling in pain, others in ominous silence, smoking holes drilled through their heads and torsos.

"It's a massacre," said Mara.

Karic felt sick. Beside him, Andrai had his head in his hands.

He turned back toward the lander, but now his attention was drawn to a lone figure standing some distance above them on a small rise. It was the Awakener, the slim metallic shaft of the energy weapon in his hand.

A long, blue-white tendril of cracking power whipped across the top of the clearing.

The XV78 took evasive action, jetting skyward away from the burst, but the edge of the corona, which had broadened as the wave approached, caught the tiny probe. Its systems failed, and the tiny rockets cut out. It immediately fell — straight into the main part of the beam.

It exploded with a sharp *crack* that echoed across the valley.

Andrai looked up, his eyes wide.

Mara followed the beam back to its source and her face paled. "*Fucking Christ!* The weapon is higher than the shield!"

Karic's head spun with a sudden sense of unreality. Mara was right. The sickening realization hit him with stunning force. The shield was a powerful means of defense, but it had been deployed as a high-tech fence, rather than an enclosing dome. From above, the big lander was exposed and vulnerable.

The Awakener raised the staff once more and a surge of power leapt across the top of the barrier toward the lander, enveloping it within a radiant landscape of energy. The three of them could feel the heat from where they lay, growing more intense by the second.

"No!" howled Karic.

He watched in despair as the hull of the lander heated rapidly to red, then white. All its leading surfaces — the lower hull and the edges of the struts and wings that made first contact with the rushing atmosphere during flight — were designed to withstand these temperatures and more, yet other surfaces were never meant to take this kind of treatment. They began to melt. The biggest of the remaining external fuel tanks ruptured. The boiling fuel instantly expanded into a huge cloud, then the lander was lost in a massive fireball. It exploded skyward in a cascade of sheet metal and shattered components. Three explosions followed, each heralding the destruction of the craft's remaining external fuel tanks and the main propulsion systems. The air was filled with the roar of combustion as the enriched fuels, scattered to the winds, heated, flashed and ignited in hundreds of brilliant, burning spheres, then dropped fire onto the forest.

As the smoke cleared, they could see that the energy barrier was still intact, but the space within it was charred and blackened; littered with twisted alloy. The sky was filled with burning metal, plastic and ceramic, and for long minutes they lay face down; jumping at every impact, waiting for the deadly fragment of debris that would end their lives, as surely as the fireball had ended Janzen's.

Finally, the maelstrom ended.

The air was filled with the terrified screams of the Imbirri.

Not a single section of the lander remained intact inside the barrier. They were cut off from the *Starburst*. Trapped on Cru.

"The suspension equipment ..." The words were torn from Karic, and there was little he could do to disguise his utter despair. Their last hope of ever reaching Earth was gone, reduced to hot shards of useless metal.

Karic sank to his knees.

Beside him, Andrai and Mara were stunned. Motionless. He took a deep breath. They needed him. He had to lead them.

"The pod," said Karic. "Was the pod still functioning?"

"Ibri checked it from the ground up and started the diagnostic. It must be completed by now," said Mara, gasping for breath.

"Slow your breathing, Mara." She glared at him, but a new look of determination replaced the dullness in her eyes.

"That being knows where it is," said Karic. "We have to reach it before him." *We have to get out of here.* Their last hope was to run for it. It was a promise of hope — on the shores of the lake where they had first touched the soil of Cru.

"This way!" Mara pushed herself to her feet and ran up the slope. Her dark hair bounced on her shoulders as she ran. Small and lithe, she seemed to be more agile in the heavy gravity than any of them. They raced after her through the sparse growth of the forest, driven by fear, tree limbs and leaves flashing by them in a blur. They crested the ridge and ran down. The light ahead of them grew as a towering crystal range rose ahead. The growth around them grew thicker, the air more heavily scented. Eventually, they broke through a thick stand of vegetation and waded into the long grasses of the lake shore.

The pod was gone.

Cursing, Karic raced toward the area where he had set the pod down. As he neared, he could see the blackened depression caused by the small rockets, at first concealed by the long grasses of the lake shore. They followed a wide track in the grass that led away from the lake. The track led them to the edge of the forest. Here they heard a jumble of dulcet voices.

It was a group of squat, purple-crowned Imbirri, now alarmed at their approach. The aliens had dragged the pod from the lake, and were attempting to take it further into the concealing growth.

As the humans approached, they hooted in fear and ran.

With relief Karic realized the chieftain must have sent another group to the pod to conceal it while he dealt with the lander. For the moment they were safe.

Karic raced to the hatch. After releasing the door mechanism, he climbed through the opening into the pilot's seat. Andrai and Mara looked into the cabin uncertainly from outside the craft.

"Come on!" yelled Karic. "It'll be cramped, but the pod can lift four of us if need be."

Andrai and Mara turned to check for pursuit, then squeezed into the craft. Once inside, they lay breathing heavily, nursing cuts, bruises and strained muscles from the long run.

"Damn this heavy gravity," said Andrai, massaging his ankle.

Karic's hands flew over the console. With a whirr, devices and cooling fans sprang to life within the compact craft. The computer's viewscreen flashed to brilliance, all systems running rapidly through a quick start-up sequence. Everything was in perfect running order. Within minutes the tones that accompanied the sequence had completed their familiar melody, and the screen displayed the simple message — *Ready For Flight*.

The three survivors of the *Starburst's* crew exchanged glances, and without a word, paused for a moment of reverent silence, like an unspoken prayer for the dead. It was Ibri's work that would save them now.

With a low roar, the small, yet powerful chemical rockets lifted them above the lake shore. Once airborne, Karic pivoted the ship around in a full circle, scanning the terrain, searching for any sign of the Awakener.

"There he is!" yelled Andrai.

A large group of Imbirri appeared over the ridge, the unmistakable bulk of the Awakener in the lead. Just for a moment the pure white light of the crystal range glistened on the haft of the scepter.

"It's the Awakener," said Karic.

Mara looked at him sharply.

Karic was only too aware of what that weapon could do. He turned the craft toward the massive crystal range and applied full forward thrust, the pod climbing slightly as it flew.

Where to now? He had to forget about the loss of the lander, and their ultimate future on Cru.

Now they just needed to survive.

Then he remembered Utar — switching the personal beacon on and off. The small communicators had proved ineffective on the ground, but from the air he would be able to pick up a signal.

Karic began to sweep the airwaves. The automated scan locked onto the beacon's frequency. The tone repeated insistently in the cabin. He felt a flood of relief. A small voice of doubt had been at work in his mind, questioning everything he had experienced. But there could be absolutely no doubt now. Utar's acolytes had freed them so they could follow this beacon's signal to its source. He had to trust them. They had nowhere else to turn.

"That's it," said Karic. "Remember, Mara? When Utar came to the pit. That's the personal beacon from my comband — the one he showed us. We need to track the signal and find his followers."

"Karic, there is no way we can know what Utar meant," said Mara, her patience frayed by fatigue and fear. Her fingers worked quickly in her hair, trying it back from her face in a series of braids, as though restoring her battle armor.

"Trust me."

Mara glared at him, angry and uncertain, but a fierce intellect was at work in her dark eyes.

Andrai watched the interaction between them, mystified, but remained silent. The tech calmly returned his attention to the console, absently smoothing down his blond hair as he worked the interface. "We can find out what sort of signal it is by analyzing the signature."

Mara smiled thinly. She reached across Karic to operate the console as he piloted the pod. "Let's see if you're right, Karic."

"Could it be some automatic signal from the *Starburst?*" asked Andrai.

Mara shook her head and continued working. After a few minutes she stopped. She stared at the console in disbelief, shaking her head. She checked her results again, working furiously, then held her head in her hands as though to clear her thoughts. She turned to Andrai and Karic. "It's a personal beacon."

"A personal beacon?" said Andrai. "All the rest of us are dead. Maybe one of those aliens was playing with a comband and set it off by accident?"

"Or the leader is luring us into a trap," said Mara, glaring at Karic. "So he can destroy us and the fucking pod!"

Karic could understand Mara's doubts. She was a scientist and had spent her life working with concrete facts. She was used to things she could see, touch and control. But Mara had not experienced the mind of Utar firsthand. If the Imbirri had intended to destroy them, Karic would have sensed it.

"Mara, where is the beacon coming from?" asked Karic.

"Around twenty kilometers away, in the shadow of the mountains," she said reluctantly. "On the other side of the alien's camp."

"That is nowhere near the leader or his people, so it's unlikely to be a trap," said Karic.

"You don't know that! There could be another group with another one of those weapons waiting for us!"

"I am going to follow the beacon," said Karic. "We're stranded here. If some of the Imbirri are inclined to help us, it could be our only chance to survive. We have to take the risk and check this out. What other choice do we have?"

Mara turned away, refusing to respond.

"Who is Utar? And who are the Imbirri?" asked Andrai, unable to hold his questions back.

"Those aliens are called the Imbirri. Utar was their Deepwatch, a sort of shaman. Hold on." Karic set the autopilot to execute a line-of-sight course toward the source of the beacon and turned to face Andrai and Mara.

"So you're saying that one of these *Imbirri* wants to help us and is using the beacon to help guide us to safety? It does seem a little far-fetched, Karic," said Andrai. "And how do you know all this?"

"I know it seems crazy, but you must trust me. Utar is trying to help us," said Karic.

"One of the Imbirri is trying to help us?" asked Andrai.

"That shaman is dead, Karic," said Mara.

Andrai shook his head, confused by the whole exchange.

The pod jolted violently.

Karic swung back to the controls and cursed. The automatic pilot had set a course straight to the beacon — taking them directly over the path of the Awakener's group, now in the forest between the ridge and lake.

"Damn it! I should have checked the course," said Karic.

Turning in his chair, Karic sighted the distant group of Imbirri, massed together amidst the growth of the forest, and applied full thrust in the opposite direction, banking the craft steeply to avoid the weapon's powerful beam.

A jagged bolt of lightning swept past them, sending alarms ringing.

The pod shook.

"We've got high temperature alarms, Karic!" yelled Mara.

Karic wove the craft madly. It seemed they were in the middle of a lightning storm, the sky flashing around them — but finally they exited the range the Awakener's weapon, and the deadly light show stopped.

He kept them running at full power until the Imbirri were lost below the horizon, then he backed off the thrust and dropped down, flying meters above the forest canopy. He reset the autopilot, the pod nosing its way forward by radar toward the source of the beacon. The level of liquid rocket fuel in the pod's tanks was alarmingly low. The tiny craft had been stretched to the limit propelling three people at full thrust through the thick atmosphere — and heavy gravity.

***

Two hours later all three of them looked out the viewport, waiting anxiously to see who — or what — awaited them at the beacon's source.

The darkness had deepened. It was an empty dark, a featureless landscape of night that drew the spirit from them. As the light faded, the vegetation around them had grown huge and frail. They passed massive stands of pale fungi, twisted into fantastic shapes — some painted with bizarre, dream-like colors, others glowing with luminescence. It seemed they had slipped into a netherworld untouched by time.

A tone sounded through the cabin.

"We have reached the source of the beacon." Karic slowed the pod, switching on the outside lamps. The three crowded forward.

"My God. Utar's body," said Karic.

Anxious not to waste any more of the pod's fuel, he gently lowered the craft to the bare earth. The craft shook with a soft impact, then the muffled whine of the engines cut to silence.

Releasing the pod's door, they stepped out onto the clearing.

Hesitantly, they approached the bier. On the center lay the raised body of Utar, a solid, formless lump in the dim light. On either side of the raised platform were the prostrate figures of two acolytes of Utar, their features only just discernible as the sticky resin oozing from their skin began to encase them.

"They are all dead," said Mara, picking up the comband from the ground in front of the bier. She turned off the beacon.

Andrai tapped on the casing around Utar's body. It was as solid as concrete. "This was Utar?"

"Yes," whispered Karic. "Their bodies seem to undergo this transformation when they die."

"Well, whoever he was, there is no doubt he wanted you to follow the beacon to this spot," said Andrai.

Mara's mouth tightened, but she said nothing in reply to Andrai's matter-of-fact observation.

Karic looked at the bodies. Why did Utar want him here?

A feeling of excitement and danger flooded him as he considered triggering the fugue. It seemed insane, but he was determined. He let the state develop in his mind, then reached out to the prone figures, at first touching the lifeless shell, then pressing deeper. *They shone like suns!* Filled with warmth and life. He was so shocked the connection vanished.

"They're alive," said Karic in whispered awe, scarcely believing it himself.

Mara shook her head in disgust and stalked to the edge of camp.

"Look!" cried Mara a moment later.

The two men turned to follow her outstretched arm. Deep in the pale growth, glistening in the pod's lights, stood a metal structure. The thrill of seeing it was indescribable.

"That has to be a remnant of same culture that constructed the Imbirri weapon," said Karic.

They approached it cautiously.

It was constructed in curving lines. The sides, at first appearing straight, were a series of intricate, interlinking arches, giving a sense of strength and union. As they drew closer, they could see it was not an isolated structure, but an entrance. Steps of the same metallic material stretched out below them, and they descended together, eventually entering a vast underground enclosure. Strips of crystalline material ran across the floor, each emitting a clear white light that was barely enough to drive back the gloom. The walls and roof were lost in shadow.

Ranks of machines filled the space, hulking shapes of metal with unknowable functions. As they walked deeper, the white light reflected from the strange angles and curves of the stored machines as though caressing their alien, silvered surfaces with a desperate, immortal avarice.

"They look brand new." Without thinking, Karic reached out to touch a strut extending from the side of a bulky machine the size of a truck. He snatched back his fingers at a sudden, numbing shock.

"I don't believe it." Karic leant closer to the machine, massaging life back into his numbed fingers. He had come into contact with enough stasis fields in his work to recognize the effects on naked flesh. What astounded him was the similarity with his own invention, in use here on this distant, alien world.

Now that Karic was looking for it, he could see it. Each machine was surrounded by a ghostly energy field that gave off a faint whitish glow. "Stasis fields."

They wandered for hours through the ranks of alien equipment, spellbound. Each becoming separated from the others. The cavern was huge and stretched for kilometers. Scores of machines, some smaller than a personal vehicle, others as large as the lander, filled the expanse in irregular rows. As intriguing as they were, they remained untouchable, like exhibits trapped behind the glass of an alien museum. The frustration was unbearable. Karic had hoped that perhaps there was some central control unit that he could access to cut the protective fields, but whatever controlled the stasis fields was inside each machine. He could not begin to guess at how he might disable them. Reluctantly, he accepted that these preserved remnants of Cru's ancient technology would continue on through the centuries, unreachable, until whatever powered the stasis fields failed.

"Karic!" *Mara.*

The engineer looked up from a huge tractor-shaped machine in alarm. He ran toward the sound of her voice. He and Andrai arrived together, both out of breath, but ready for anything.

Mara turned to show them a rack of glistening, cylindrical objects, hefting one from its mountings.

156

"Careful," said Karic, wary of the ubiquitous stasis fields, but then realized there was no field here. A power failure? Or had these strange artifacts never been encased by a stasis field?

Mara smiled as she handed it to Karic. He took the heavy object in his hands, feeling the cool metal, unsure of its precise shape in the gloom. He moved it into the white light from a floor strip and drew in a sharp breath.

It was a twin of the Awakener's weapon.

Chapter 13

The Awakener sat alone, slumped on his throne.

Even the First had been sent from his presence. The torches had been extinguished, and the ragged rent in the top of the Tree sealed with woven mats. Only the dull red glow of incense bowls could be seen in the darkness.

The Awakener's life with the Imbirri had revolved around Union, the fulfilling joining of spirit the Imbirri could achieve through their telepathic abilities, most fully developed in the First. It seemed as though he drifted further from that life with each passing hour, each act of revenge.

The Imbirri who had survived the attack on the human's camp, those who could walk, had returned with the Awakener from the site of destruction. So many had not returned …

He had sought to obliterate the craft of the aliens with fire, and so heal them all, but the attack on the human artifact had taken a terrible toll. How many Imbirri now lay dead? How many First? He did not have the will to count. Over half of those that had returned with him had fallen, consumed by the onset of the Changes. The milling groups of the Imbirri, those who had remained in the encampment, watched with strange fascination, drawn toward the bodies. The Awakener had not waited as before. He had incinerated each as they fell and scattered those who gathered to watch, knowing they were in danger of succumbing to the Changes.

The scarred and bleeding faces of the First he had burned crowded into his mind.

"*Why?*" he cried in discordant anguish.

They had all tasted the Elixir. Never before had this act failed to banish the specter of the Changes. Yet now, it was as though an avalanche had begun.

After he had dealt with the fallen First, he had rushed to the punishment pit, only to find it empty. He stood there — covered with the ashy remains of Imbirri — consumed with impotent rage. How he had longed to kill the humans, as though by destroying them the loss of the First would be lessened. Instead, he had been cheated. He guessed immediately the humans had been released by the same agents who had stolen the body of Utar, and that the small alien craft he had failed to destroy had carried them to safety.

To think he had them in his power for so long, yet failed to act!

He had remained above the empty pit for hours, the other Imbirri too frightened to approach. Eventually, even the rage had seeped away. A dark miasma of hate settled on him, like a caustic shadow beneath the shroud of dark ash smeared on his skin.

Time passed beneath the Tree. The images of destruction faded, leaving him empty of pain, yet incapable of joy.

He would never allow the Changes to take the Imbirri. He was determined to rebuild the life they had known. He would appoint a new Deepwatch to replace his beloved Utar and let the scars heal.

A sharp wedge of light cut through the dark as one of the First entered the Tree's living dome.

"Awakener ...?"

He lifted his head. "Speak."

Hesitantly, the Imbirri messenger stepped forward through the gloom. "The scouting party has returned from the place of destruction. Part of the alien's craft survived the fire and lays near the strange barrier, concealed in the forest. We have tried to enter it but it will not yield to us."

His attack on the main craft had not been complete. In the massive convulsion that followed the initial burst of heat, it had been difficult to be sure. His first instinct was to vaporize the fragment, then swiftly seek out the remaining aliens on the planet and reduce them to ashes as well. He rose to his feet, but then paused. The Awakener had lived countless years. For most of that time he had been lost in a dream. Not so now. His vast sentience was focused solely on the destruction of the humans, who had taken so much ... But no, there would be no swift action this time. The Awakener turned back to his throne and sat down.

"We will use this to our advantage." The messenger backed away, frightened by the cold light that shone from the Awakener's eyes. "Gather those who remain. We will conceal ourselves near the artifact and await the intruders."

The messenger fled.

The humans *would* return. Now that they had the smaller craft at their disposal they would seek out everything that remained of the larger vessel. When they did that, he would finish them, and end this dark chapter of Imbirri history.

Only then would he find peace.

***

Deep in the thicket, a black cocoon stirred. The walls were like wet leather, and they bulged and rippled as the occupant writhed within. A sudden split disgorged a spurt of sticky fluid. A single, golden limb slipped through the gap, its edges razor sharp. It paused, then it flashed against the black, working in a frenzy to widen the fissure and reduce the imprisoning sheath to ragged strips.

A figure of glistening gold emerged from the discarded cocoon.

The dark green juices of birth clung to her skin. She flexed her slender limbs then stood motionless in the small clearing. Although roughly humanoid in shape, her body was lean, thorax and abdomen elegantly tapered, head elongated, her eyes multifaceted. She took a breath, savoring the moment. The green of the deep forest filled her mind.

She cleaned the stuff of birth from her limbs with small, graceful movements, then she tensed the huge muscles across her upper back and extended her powerful wings. They quivered, held in check like a new breath. Slowly, she moved them, gradually drying them in the humid air. They beast faster, until the copse stirred in a gale of wind.

Then she lifted into the misted sky.

Higher she climbed, reveling in the freedom of flight. She longed to soar and dive within the currents, to taste and test this new form, yet she did not: she was driven onward by an aching desire. The need pulsed within her, and the absence was as stifling as suffocation. She spurned the cool air that swirled around her, seeking heat. Fire. She sped to the crystal range. Soon she was above the massive monolith, yet its white light was not enough to satisfy her. Frustration fueled her passion.

She rose above the glowing mountain and extended her senses. They flowed out across the surface of the planet. With excitement, she sensed warmer air and swam into it. She felt the air heat and knew her course. She folded her legs, streamlining herself for rushing speed.

Time fled. Lost in rising warmth, she was alone with the winds, the open sky, the heavy clouds. She drank in sight, sound, sensation, her mind hungry for it all. There was no memory within her, only thought. Only an intense sense of being — and rising slowly from this core of sentience like the first note of a song — her name. *Asthel.*

At last, the golden face of the planet lay before her. She sped toward the terminator with a burst of speed, driven forward by instinct.

For the first time, Asthel gave voice.

To the wind she sang. To the many who must follow, she burst fully, into voice exultant. Yet there was none to hear, and no song answered her. Undeterred she sped on into the flashing brilliance of the bright side.

Calling.

Chapter 14

Mara looked past the harsh glare of the pod's lamps into the still, empty darkness. It was such a strange planet. The presence of life, yet the absence of any natural rhythm. Always the same sky, bereft of sun and moon. No dawn. No dusk.

On the dark side of Cru light came only from the crystal mountains, which were positioned across the dark hemisphere in a pattern so regular it could only be the result of terraforming on a vast scale, created by a culture with technology so advanced she could hardly conceive it. The climate churned against these artificial confines, driven by the resulting patterns of heat and cold. Everywhere around her was a sense of ... tension. Life held in abeyance. Mara longed for the familiar beauty of distant, turning Earth, so often glimpsed by her through the oil-streaked viewports of the Davis Industries Platform. Throughout a childhood spent in dank, artificial environments, Earth was always there. Day and night, winter and summer, flood and drought, each following the other like an unspoken promise. Here, on Cru, there was something fundamentally unsettling about the *lack of change*. And her feeling of unease was growing.

Karic, Mara and Andrai sat together in silence on dark, moist soil with a patchy cover of grass-like fungi. Light from the pod's external lamps flooded the small clearing. Around them, faint noises announced the presence of tiny creatures, evolved over time to live within the shadowed regions of the planet's night side. Above, the sky was a deep, deep blue, lit occasionally by the flashes of faraway storms.

They had worked for hours trying to operate the energy weapon. No matter what they tried, the alien artifact remained an inert, lifeless cylinder of metal. Along the haft were a score of dials and gauges, but no manipulation of these controls had any effect. They reluctantly drew the simple conclusion that the weapon had no power — it was uncharged — and it was useless to them. After running in fear, it had seemed as though they would at last have some way of defending themselves. It was not to be. The staff lay on the ground beside Karic, who was lost in the strange, distracted mood that had infected him since their arrival on Cru. *God knows where his mind is.* Yet they still needed him, and his brilliance. Needed his leadership.

Andrai caught her eye and gave her a warm smile, his unshaven cheeks now bristling with the beginnings of a ginger-blond beard. *He looks cuter than ever.* Her heart flipped and she returned the smile. Andrai had told her about Janzen's cunning deception — deleting the video log Andrai had recorded before they left the lander to rescue Karic, then substituting his own. All done to throw her off her game and get them at each other's throats. *Janzen, the fucking snake.* She felt ashamed now at having judged

Andrai so quickly. That was her — always shooting from the hip — and most of the bastards out there deserved what they got. But not Andrai. He really was different. Her heart was only now opening up to that strange possibility, that he was someone she really could trust. And where her heart led, her body followed ...

She felt her cheeks flush hot and looked away. This was not the time or place for romance, but she could not deny the new desire for intimacy with Andrai that was building inside her. Mara knew he was interested — and always had been — but he had always been the overlooked nice guy waiting in the wings while she obsessed over the alpha males. That too, she had begun to question. Life on the industrial space platforms had been harsh. Gangs. Rapes. Violence. A packed mass of humanity left to fend for themselves in a cage of metal bulkheads where only production quotas mattered. She had carried a knife from the age of nine — and used it too. You had to be strong. It was the soft, the weak, they were the victims waiting to happen. Even then she had sought out the pack leaders. She had let them use her, abuse her, as long as they could protect her. When she went Earth-side to study for her undergrad degree in astronomy, she had thought she was free. But now she could see she was just following the same old pattern. Her knife had been replaced by a viper's tongue, and she had gone after the same men — influential professors, Janzen himself, then Karic. Men with power. Narcissists obsessed with themselves and their own self-serving visions. As though she needed their strength to be safe. Well, she didn't.

She was no longer that scared girl walking home through the dank, greasy access tunnels of the Davis Industries Platform. She was the astronomer of the first Terran starship. Mara had proven herself again and again, with nothing more than guts and talent. She would be her own strength now, and she wanted a man who was there for *her*. A man she could trust.

Mara sidled closer to Andrai and hesitantly touched his hand. The contact set her heart racing. His hand enfolded hers gently, blissfully warm against her cold skin. She looked across at Karic, but he had not even noticed. The new commander was looking into the shadowed world around them, lost in his own thoughts.

***

Karic's thoughts swirled around him like a pack of startled birds with no place to land, crying out in vain for the island-rookery that had just slipped below the surface of the ocean below them. He knew he had to lead his crew. To find some way out of danger, and off Cru, yet there seemed to be no way out. They were trapped here, and the best they could

162

hope for was to buy themselves time before death found them. Losing the lander had been a bitter, bitter blow.

The body of Utar lay on the raised bier. The two unnamed Imbirri beside him were also encased in dark shells. Finding the strangely transformed bodies of Utar and his acolytes had fueled Karic's hope. He had felt certain the answer to their survival was right here, along with the prone form of the Deepwatch. But he was out of answers. They had already used up all the meager rations of food and water from the pod, and he had no plan.

Karic turned to see Andrai and Mara sitting close together, hands touching. A jagged blade of jealously twisted inside him. He suppressed it. He knew it was only to be expected that they would turn to each other for comfort. Even so, seeing them together sharpened his sense of isolation. With an iron control, he forced himself to be objective.

Andrai's face was drawn, his shoulders slumped with fatigue. The pod lights reflected in miniature in his light gray eyes. Mara sat pensively, dark eyes fixed on Karic's as though expecting censure, and he knew the highly-strung woman was close to exhaustion herself − and ready to snap.

There were more important things to consider than the strange love triangle that had developed here. Having escaped death at the hands of the Imbirri, they now faced the question of survival. That was what they needed to focus on. Maybe together, they could do just that.

Karic cleared his throat. "Utar must have led us here for a reason."

Andrai gave a mocking smile. "Yeah, boss. To give him a good Christian burial."

Mara shifted. A curl of dark hair had escaped her braids, and lay against her pale cheek like a bruise. "We don't know, and we can't even guess. Maybe he still plans to destroy us."

Karic looked at Mara critically, wondering if she really believed that or was just opposing him out of reflex.

Andrai's eyes brightened. "What about the stasis fields in the cavern? Maybe we can use them to stay alive down here until a rescue probe can arrive from Earth."

Karic shook his head. "Preserving machinery is one thing. The complexity required to preserve living tissue is another."

The stasis fields they used on *Starburst* were specially configured not only for living tissue, but for living *human* tissue. Using the alien fields would not work, and it would be dangerous to try. The process was a function of cellular biology on an *atomic* level. But as he looked at their hopeful expressions, he could not bear to tell them. "Perhaps one could be modified. I'll look into it."

"We have to do something!" Mara glared at him. "We have no food, no water, only enough fuel for a short trip, and no foreseeable way of ever reaching Earth again. And the Imbirri are still hunting us. We are going to die, Karic! Here on this miserable, unchanging world."

Karic could see that Mara was on the verge of emotional collapse — they all were. This was a critical time. He was the commander of the mission and had to give them a focus if they were to carry on. Even if they were to die in this strange world, old and alone, forgotten by a world lightyears away, they would have to live with purpose. They needed to sustain their spirit. For that, they needed a hope, however faint, that they may one day feel the familiar embrace of Earth again.

Andrai leaned into Mara, as though for support. She touched his thigh in unconscious rapport. The intimacy tore at Karic.

"We have to find out what can be salvaged from the wreck of the lander. The energy screen was intact, remember? With that, we need not fear the Imbirri, or that weapon. Maybe one of the fuel tanks escaped the explosion un-ruptured."

Andrai stirred, his expression wistful. Hopeful. "Is there a chance?"

Mara frowned as she considered the question. "The lander was destroyed. We heard the explosions and saw the wreckage. How could there be anything more than frigging scraps left?"

Karic swallowed, forcing himself to smile in encouragement. He did not believe that anything could have survived the destruction of the lander — the maelstrom that had shaken the forest thicket had been too complete — yet he needed to make his two crew believe him. They had to be distracted from their dangerous lethargy.

"We don't know for sure," reasoned Karic. "None of us were observing the explosions carefully; it was minutes before we could even look at the landing site and assess the damage. The screen was still intact. Perhaps other valuable sections of machinery were thrown clear. The initial explosion would have been massive enough to throw part of the main section kilometers from the landing site. The sound of the concussions could have masked anything."

To Karic the words sounded contrived, yet he could see he was convincing them. Andrai sat straighter.

"How should we start?" asked Mara. She let go of Andrai's hand and got to her feet. Andrai raised himself from the ground with a perfect economy of effort and stood beside her quietly. *Always ready to follow.*

Karic summoned all the confidence he could muster. "Try to connect with the lander's computers — it's a long shot, but it could be worth it. Then try to set up a link with the *Starburst*; if the atmospheric conditions are right, we may be able to use the ship's radar array to map the distribution of the wreckage. It's time we reestablished contact with the ship to check the onboard systems anyway.

"I will scout around the perimeter of the clearing for a water source and collect samples for testing. I'll also look around for other structures or anything left by Utar."

Mara and Andrai set off for the pod with a renewed sense of determination. As he watched them go, he felt something break inside him. The terrible responsibility of command, and the new intimacy building between Mara and Andrai, both created a gulf in him. A distance from human contact.

Karic walked into the darkness with a small flashlight. Tiny creatures fled across his path. He knew the learned response of flight indicated a predator stalked these small creatures, yet he felt no fear. After a time, the clearing was lost from sight behind him and the light of the tiny torch seemed feeble against the blackness.

On impulse, he climbed to the top of a sheer outcrop, the rock as smooth as glass under his fingers. Finding a perch, he sat down and leaned back against the unyielding surface. He switched off the torch and waited for his eyes to adjust.

They had set the pod down in a broad valley, sunk into permanent twilight. The world around him was alien to his senses, but he pushed this aside and tried to think. After he had touched the mind of Utar, he had felt so sure they would escape this planet. Now that hope seemed a delusion.

The initial excitement of finding the alien structure had been replaced by a dull resignation. The cavern had proved to be nothing more than a storage area — the cryptic devices inaccessible inside their stasis fields. The enigmatic culture that had fashioned those works of high technology had vanished from Cru, or perhaps had regressed to the point of primitivism, the tribal Imbirri their last remnant. Either way, there seemed no help for the last remaining crew of the *Starburst*.

He had been so confident. So sure space could hold nothing but glory and wonder.

Against his will, Karic relived his wife's death. The loss. Then the guilt. Watching the purple of the darkened sky, Karic wished he could cry, but tears were beyond him. Instead, he felt a heavy knot in his chest that would not ease.

His feelings of guilt were amplified by the physical desire and love he felt for Mara. His initial affection for her had grown quickly into love. He had been a fool to risk that. But he had been so concerned with failure, so worried about the future. He had feared the reaction of ExploreCorp if he refused the publicity tour with Evelle. Feared that he would be taken off the crew and then lose his only chance to explore space. Now he had lost Mara, Evelle was dead, and he himself was struggling to survive. But for the first time he was starting to get angry with Mara. He had made the wrong call, but she had never once tried to forgive him.

He shifted his weight, trying to find a more comfortable position. Sitting within the alien darkness, Karic's mind slowly cleared. For a long moment he thought of nothing — felt nothing. Then a single thought leapt into this mind. *The future cannot be controlled.* So simple. And yet now he understood this in a way he never had before. Man only has power over the present, he realized. He can be true to his beliefs, and strive to make the best decisions, but no more than that. He had made mistakes, but Mara had also made her choices. She had chosen pride over forgiveness. Would she ever forgive him? There was no way he could know. For now, he had to focus on their survival.

An old memory filled his mind. Like all the days leading to his departure from Earth, his schedule had been ridiculously full. He was up at four in the morning to make the flight to L1, the long drive to the spaceport making the day even longer. They needed him in the spacedock to oversee the early tests of the Shipcom. Problems with integration of the complex network of the AI's submodules. The more scientists and engineers tried to duplicate true consciousness, the more complex and inexplicable it appeared. Neither sheer processing power, nor increased memory, nor quantum computing, had solved the conundrum.

He was on transit to the spaceport when he got the call.

"Call for you, Karic," said his driver from the front.

Karic sighed, absorbed as usual in some problem on his portable computer. "Divert it to message bank."

His driver pulled the limousine over to the curb.

"Hey Lenny, what are you doing? We'll miss the flight."

With the car stationary, his driver turned to face him over the thick leather of the driver's seat. "It's an emergency. I think you should take this one."

Karic groaned. He had at least two weeks' worth of messages to catch up on. He just did not have time. The *Starburst* was launching in less than a month.

He took the call.

"Karic, is that you?" It was his grandmother, Rosa, her face pale and drawn over the link. "Lein is dying, Karic. He is asking for you."

"How could this happen so fast! Why hasn't someone been in touch with me?" He was furious that this could come at him out of nowhere.

There was a moment of silence on the line. "We have been trying to reach you. For weeks, Karic." Her voice was rough from grief and tears.

"Should I turn the car around, Karic?" asked Lenny.

He nodded dumbly.

Later, at Lein's side, Karic found the old astronaut focused as always. He was filled with questions about *Starburst* and the progress of the fitting out.

"You're finally doing what I could only dream of, Karic," said Lein, taking a small sip of water through a straw and reaching to set the cup on the shelf beside his bed. His hand shook with the effort. Karic was horrified to see how weak Lein was. He helped his grandfather set down the cup.

Lein sat back with a sigh and looked at Karic with a penetrating intelligence that belied his extreme weakness. "You will do it, Karic. And bring them home again."

They shared a moment then, both dreaming of space. It was only when his grandmother reentered the room, and Karic snapped back to reality, that he realized both he and Lein had been lost in fugue.

Rosa helped Lein sit up straighter on the bed, fussing with his pillows.

Lein began to tremble then, his eyes squeezed shut as he fought against a sudden pain.

"What is it?" asked Karic.

"It's the medication. The same dosage is having less and less of an effect," said Rosa in a low voice.

"What can I do?"

Lein was whimpering in pain. To see his strong-willed, brilliant grandfather like this ripped the core out of him, leaving him sad and overwhelmed.

Rosa looked at Karic blankly. To someone else, it might seem she was emotionless, but he knew her too well. She was trying to hold herself together. To be strong for Lein. "You better leave. You can come back and see him later, at dinner time."

There was no dinner time. Not for Lein. He died two hours later, attended only by his wife and two medical staff.

Karic was on a satellite hook-up at the time — in the hospital waiting room — trying to deal with the Shipcom issues across the crackling link, fretting with every time-lag delay. It was during one of those frustrating spaces in transmission that he drifted back into the fugue again, fatigue creeping up to overwhelm his tired mind. For a long moment, it seemed he was back in the room with Lein, sitting quietly by his grandfather's side.

"Never forget. You are not going alone. You are part of humanity, Karic. Don't forget it. Don't forget," said Lein.

"I wish you were coming with me, Grandpa," said Karic, his voice sounding oddly young in his mind.

Lein smiled. "Oh, but I am, Karic. I am."

The satellite link had buzzed static in his ear, snapping him out of the fugue. "Karic, are you there?" It was Andrai on the line from the spacedock at L1.

"I'll call you back!"

A sudden intuition gripped Karic and he rushed to Lein's bed to find the sheet across his grandfather's face. Rosa had collapsed forward onto the bed, at last giving vent to months of sadness and grief.

His driver, Lenny, had appeared at the door.

"Take the limo back to Boston, Lenny," said Karic. The man smiled sadly and left.

Karic silently took a seat by Rosa's side.

Even back then, his grandfather was able to see the forces in Karic's life better than he could.

Above Karic, the sky of the darkened valley remained unchanged. The sun did not rise, and there was no promise of morning. Cru was silent. Inexplicable. Hunger gnawed at him, and his head and arm throbbed with pain. He had no time for either. He had to focus on survival.

He stood up atop the outcrop, fighting a brief wave of dizziness, and contemplated the climb down. He could not afford a broken leg. Not here.

Karic had communicated with Utar telepathically. But even before this, he had known the Deepwatch. It had been his eyes that had hovered in the void, watching them through time. There had been other images since he arrived here — dreams of golden beings — what did they mean? He would get no answers from Utar now.

He switched on the torch to aid his descent. Beneath him, the surface of the rock appeared dark and smooth, unmarred by vegetation. A flash from within the depths of the hill startled Karic. Instinctively, he shone the torch toward the source. Images of the small lamp stretched to infinity beneath him, held suspended within a transparent matrix. Karic shone the torch around him at the substance of the hill, suddenly transfixed. *He was standing on one of the crystal light-towers.* Unlike the others, this small, jagged outcrop had grown dark centuries ago, leaving the valley in night.

Karic left the hill and scouted around the camp, identifying two small streams that ran with clear, icy water. He collected water samples in two small vials and packed them away carefully. He would check these for bacterial count and heavy metals. Game proved harder to catch, however, and nothing vaguely resembling a fruit or a berry grew in the dark valley. His gnawing hunger now made him regret every morsel he had refused to eat while imprisoned by the Imbirri for fear of poisoning or alien infection.

Karic returned to the campsite. Twin beams of white light cut through the gloom, casting the funereal stillness of Utar's resting place into weird relief. The metal of the alien structure glistened as though wet, shimmering and catching the light like a cut diamond, a teasing will-o-wisp luring them down to the unusable artifacts stored below, as though daring them to enter that alien labyrinth of false hope. The pod itself dominated the space, glowing with artificial light. Through the door, he glimpsed Mara and Andrai at work, the colored lights of the console playing across their intent faces.

As he broke from the shadowed cover of the twilight forest into the clearing, Karic forced himself on with a grim resolve. He prepared, then discarded encouraging words — incentives to carry on searching for anything in the remains of the lander. He was determined to help these people, to bring them all safely to some haven where they could at least live unhindered by the vengeful Awakener.

As he approached, he noted Andrai and Mara had set up an antenna in order to communicate with the mother-ship keeping station above the dark side of the planet.

Mara emerged from the cabin. She leapt through the small doorway and raced toward him. "We have made contact with the mother-ship. The *Starburst* has been in communication with the lander! It survived!"

Karic was astounded. "The lander's core *survived?*"

"Yes." Mara's smile was dazzling.

It all fell into place. "Of course! The lander's core section was ejected skyward by the concussion of the main fuel tanks and fell back to the ground before the explosions died. It was designed to survive a planetary impact." Karic took Mara by the shoulders, wanting to hug her.

"The computer on the lander cannot give us any details on the location, but we think we can locate it using the *Starburst's* radar array. Andrai is coordinating it now," said Mara.

"Janzen?"

"I'm not sure. We have not been able to raise any response. But one of the suspension sets is in use."

"In use?" That meant not only had Janzen survived, but that the sets were intact. He felt dizzy with relief. "Thank God!"

"The computer indicates some loss of function, but we will not know what systems have failed until we can check them out by hand." Mara turned out of Karic's grip and raced back to the pod.

He stood in the pod doorway, watching the furious activity of the two scientists. His mind sang with the news. The suspension equipment was intact! Plans and schemes filled his head in an excited rush. *Now we have a chance!*

So Janzen had survived. Good. He was going all the way back to Earth to pay for all the blood on his hands. He could not wait to see the look on his face when he came out of stasis to see Karic standing over him. No doubt he would be expecting a rescue team.

"We have to reach the lander's core section, redeploy the screen around the core, and this time ensure the camp is fully enclosed. Not even the energy weapon of these aliens could touch us then. With enough power we could wait a thousand years for help to arrive," said Karic.

Andrai looked up through the pod door and smiled, his face etched in yellow and red by the shifting lights of the console.

"The mother-ship is conducting a scan of the local area now. With the decreased grid size, we should get fairly good resolution. We'll have the location pinpointed in minutes."

"We will head there as soon as we have the location. That is where we have to locate our base camp," said Karic.

"What about the body of Utar?" said Mara. "We still haven't discovered his purpose for leading us here."

Karic looked around the dark clearing, full of shades and swelling shadows. Despite the tantalizing presence of the vast alien chamber beneath them, he would be glad to leave it. "We will return. First we have to get to the lander core and set up the screen. Only then will we really be safe."

***

Asthel flew across the surface of the bright side, drinking in the golden light. The warmth, the heat, was delicious, and so *right*. She soared between the bright sky and the thin yellow clouds, suspended in amber.

The sun rose from the horizon toward the center of the sky as she flew onwards, the heat growing to a luscious warmth. Great jeweled cities fled past beneath her, the towers and buildings, arching bridges and slender walkways shimmering through the powerful haze of stasis fields. The cities were enticing, but she sped on. She knew her goal lay ahead.

At last the sun stood in the exact center of the sky. Below lay the greatest of the cities, beautiful in its austere complexity, yet as still as a sculpture. Nothing moved in the city. Asthel felt herself relax in the intense heat. Streamers of radiation glowed like rainbows in her vision. Higher she floated, riding on the powerful thermals rising from the vitrified surface of the planet. For a time she drifted, content, then slowly a desire rose within her.

Asthel sang.

The sensuous tones formed a melody that was ancient when the Earth was nothing more than spinning gas. Again and again she voiced the song. The intensity grew with each breath.

Beneath her, a sleeper woke.

The Fountain had dreamt for an age, waiting for the notes of this song to wake him and the children of his race to come. He rested in the gable of the highest tower, which extended beyond the reach of the immense stasis field that enclosed the empty city. He rose from a slumber akin to death. His brittle, ancient body stirred to life as devices injected precious fluids into his skeletal frame.

As vast as the other cities were, they were empty of his race and now remained in stasis from cycle to cycle — a sign of the decay of his ancient race, the Fintil. Only this city, Zenith, was now used.

The Fountain was the only Fintil who remained of the prior generation. He lived on here in a deathlike slumber for the next generation of Fintil to emerge from Cru's dark side. Once there would have been many Old Ones to greet the newborn, yet now he alone remained as guardian and keeper of the Fintil race — the fountain of their knowledge and history. He had abandoned his own name, his own identity for the privilege of carrying their culture into the future. Not that there had been any choice. Of the Fintil Old Ones of his generation, he alone had possessed the strength and power for the task. The other three had long faded to dust, their ability to rebirth finally exhausted.

He rose from the stone altar that had been his resting place, overcome with a heavy fatigue. The muscles in his legs and arms protested at the movement. Despite the weakness, he flexed his wings and leapt from the tower, rising high on thermals, casting his eye across the golden space, searching for his children. The Fountain's narrow, tapered abdomen and rear legs folded together forming a sleek, aerodynamic surface. He beat slowly, maintaining height, and the powerful wing muscles on his thorax — almost a third of his bodyweight — soon warmed with the effort. He turned in wide circles, confused at the emptiness, seeking the single song that rose where thousands should have echoed. He scanned the skies with superbly adapted eyes that could see in the merest light — and even in the infrared spectrum — but now effortlessly filtered out the harsh glare of Tau Ceti.

He saw the young female and called to her. She sang her name in response. *Asthel.* Overwhelmed with joy, she flew to him, and together they descended to the platform atop the tower. Asthel was beautiful: full of strength and brimming with energy and fertility — yet she was alone. Swarms of the young Fintil, newly hatched, should have reached the bright side together. Why had the other newborn not reached the bright side?

Asthel skipped across the platform, alighting briefly to land before the machines that had monitored his ancient body during his hibernating sleep. She touched each with newly-hatched curiosity, her nascent mind humming with suppressed power. Already she was reaching out to bridge to them, and their artificial interfaces. The green flaring along the sides of her graceful thorax, and the leading edges of her gossamer wings was vibrant and vivid, signaling her fertility. Asthel could not be the last of the Fintil. She was too vital. Too *alive*. Too beautiful.

Marshalling his energies, the Fountain formed a mental bond with the system that controlled the city of Zenith, a coherent array of fields that operated in a dimension outside normal space. With vast processing power and almost limitless memory, it was sustained by a steady influx of energy from the fusion generators below the city. Its sensory fields left normal space at thousands of locations across Zenith, streaming data to its core, while discreet electromagnetic signals were returned at others, controlling vital equipment and automatons.

His mind was sluggish as he entered the control landscape. He flew through the virtual space with effort, searching his memory for the key thought sequence that would open the portals of its innermost workings. Hovering above the kaleidoscopic interface, he summoned the history of his sleep. The colors swirled around him, rising and rising. In a moment of sickening disorientation, he thought his mind had slowed beyond saving, but then realized the system simply required more time than usual to compile the record. Much more time.

High in the Zenith tower, his wings quivered with tension.

He heard Asthel singing sweetly, softly, blissfully unaware of the crisis he faced.

Within the virtual landscape of the system interface, the record opened around him. He cast his mind through it with ever more frantic mental commands. The cycle of the Fintil took barely a century. He had lain asleep for almost ten thousand years! Fear began to overwhelm him. Was this young female to be the last of them? Had the weakening seed of the Fintil finally failed them at last?

The Fountain's mind withdrew from the system. He refocused on the bright interior of the tower room, the empty altar and its attendant array of machinery.

And Asthel.

If she was truly the last, there was no future for the Fintil. The Old Ones — those Fintil like himself who had the rare ability to rebirth themselves as newborn Fintil, with their memories intact, and so extend their lifetimes — were infertile after their second rebirth, and he had lived through dozens.

Fintil were born as adults, their minds fully formed. Although they possessed formidable capabilities, the typical Fintil adult lived only a few decades. While the feeding stage of their hatched eggs, the mindless quadrupedal Fin, took almost a century before they matured and entered their chrysalis. Because of the Fintil's unique physiology, no stasis field could be used to preserve them between generations — the stasis was interpreted on a cellular level as death and triggered a regenerative transformation that in most cases was abortive, killing the Fintil. Some of their more radical scientists persisted in trying to solve the problem, yet there was little support. The drive to follow their ancient ways was deep in their genetic coding. So, despite all their advanced technology, the cycle of rebirth had remained virtually unchanged for all their history. That was why the Old Ones were so vital. They were the only living link to the last generation.

Casting aside his fear, the Fountain turned to Asthel, and despite himself felt new hope. She sang to him and the years fell away.

"Asthel. I am the Fountain." He spoke in the language of the Fintil, yet also touched her mind with the thoughts. This was the way the newborns learned the Fintil speech, and the proper mode of thought. Formally, he gently touched his wingtips to hers.

"Fountain. I am Asthel." He hummed with delight. Her recall was perfect.

The Fountain remembered his own birth-flight so vividly. He had also been the first to reach Zenith, racing from the dark side, full of passion and desire. Many young Fintil had followed him, yet most were weak and sterile, others had lingered on the dark side, disoriented and malformed. There had been so few like him — then a fertile male. So few.

The Fountain turned toward the dark side. His ancient eyes betraying no emotion as they glittered in the intense heat.

The answers would lay there.

***

The Awakener checked the position of his followers, which were concealed in the jungle nearby, then settled himself to wait. He could see the blackened form of the alien craft clearly from his vantage. *The bait in the trap.*

He chewed on a succulent fern, thoughtful. The scepter lay on the ground, close at hand. The First surrounded him, yet increasingly kept their distance. He could no longer deny what he heard in their voices, read in the empty darkness of their eyes. *Fear.* He had become something strange and fearsome in their eyes. That saddened him, but there was no swerving from this course. He was sick with grief, and poisoned by the destruction, yet running faster and faster on the path to his final solution. There had to be an end to this. He had to make an end to it.

He ate the last of the fern, jaw working idly as he ground it to a tasty pulp. Then he reached for the scepter. His big hand stopped short of touching the cool, familiar metal. His stomach churned with nausea as memories of all those he had destroyed flooded his inner vision — so many, destroyed before the Changes could take them too far …

The Awakener felt a sudden urge to throw the scepter away, to run alone into the jungle and leave all the pain and grief behind, to return to the mindless existence he had known before his awakening, almost ten thousand years ago. His deepest heart cried out for an end to this. For an ending of it all.

The Awakener swallowed and forced himself to grip the scepter. There was no swerving now. He had to finish this. He had to destroy the last of these humans. He had to be strong for all the Imbirri and do what they could not.

He fixed his gaze on the human artifact with renewed determination. All he had to do was wait. And if there was one thing any Imbirri could do, it was to bide their time.

Chapter 15

Karic flew low over the sparse canopy. Inside the pod's cabin, he reached past Mara to adjust the forward thrust, anxiously watching the pod's dwindling fuel supply on the viewscreen display. She leant away from him as far as the cramped cabin and harness restraints would allow. He gritted his teeth and focused on the problem. The tiny craft was burning through the remaining onboard fuel at a prodigious rate, struggling to keep all of them in the air against Cru's heavy gravity. He had used an array of tricks to conserve fuel, but none were working as well as he had hoped. As he calculated the remaining flight distance, he realized he had grossly underestimated how far the pod could travel.

Below, the dull gray of the forest slowly changed to green as the pod rose from the shadows into the light of the crystal mountains. Andrai and Mara worked at the console beside him, using the distant computers of the mother-ship to navigate to the lander. So far, the signal strength of the uplink — relayed through the ground-based transmitter and antenna they had set up in the darkened clearing — was holding.

Andrai and Mara both reached across for the same switch, their hands colliding with a thud.

"Ow!" said Mara, rubbing her fingers.

The corners of Andrai's mouth twitched up into an amused smile. "You go," he said, waving her forward.

"OK." Mara gave Andrai a quick, almost shy smile, then reached forward to adjust the gain on the signal from the *Starburst*, leaning her body across him with a familiarity that only emphasized their increasing intimacy. Karic managed to shunt aside the sharp twinge of jealousy, but could not suppress the resentment that followed on its heels so easily.

The pod entered a thick wall of mist. Karic slowed the craft, edging forward under instruments.

"How far to the lander, Andrai?" Karic banked the pod around a tall palm that appeared ghost-like from the mist.

"Just over twelve kilometers," said Andrai, rubbing his hands together in excitement. "I wonder what condition the core section is in."

"The fact that the lander's computer survived at all is a pretty good sign," said Mara.

Twelve kilometers — damn, we're not going to make it. "Bad news, guys. I'll have to put the pod down here."

Andrai's smile fled. Mara gripped the edge of her seat, as though willing the pod to stay in the air. Karic understood their reaction. None of them was eager to leave the cabin. For hours it had been their haven, a place of safety on a hostile world.

"Andrai, take a bearing on the position of the barrier fence and the lander's core section." Karic powered down the pod. It sank swiftly through the tangled green canopy, settling toward the thick organic skin of the planet. The craft settled with a thud and Karic switched off the small rockets.

Mara flicked through the fuel display, and Karic knew she was checking his calculations.

"We have to conserve enough fuel to retrieve the uplink equipment from the valley," said Karic, preempting her question. "We'll have to make it the rest of the way on foot."

"What about the salvage operations at the lander site?" asked Andrai, his forehead creasing with tension.

Karic nodded. "It will make it difficult, but the screen will have to be carried to the core section. Any equipment we can't move by hand will have to wait until we have more fuel or another pod."

Mara's eyes lit with comprehension. "A robotic drop."

Karic smiled. "That's right. Now that we have established communication with the mother-ship, we can initiate a launch sequence for one of the six remaining pods. It can even be piloted remotely. But all that can wait until we have reestablished the base-camp."

Mara released her belt clasp with a decisive movement. "We can drop more rations, portable computers, more fuel …"

"And more weapons," finished Karic.

They locked the pod securely and covered the small craft with cut tree limbs and large leaves from the forest understory. This time they took no chances.

"Fix the position of the pod in your minds," said Karic. "That ridge," said Karic, pointing up through the misty forest, "and those tall palms should stand out from any high ground."

Andrai and Mara paused to take their bearings, then the three earthlings set off through the dark-side forest of Cru. Despite the lack of power in the cylindrical weapon from the alien storage cavern in the darkened valley — the twin of the Awakener's scepter — Karic took it with him.

The light from the crystal mountains grew to its full intensity. The mist disappeared and the air became hot and humid. It was tough going, and they were breathing heavily. Their clothes were soon soaked with sweat.

Karic slipped in the soft earth as the rod snagged on a rubbery vine, pulling him off balance. He yanked the gleaming artifact free and pushed on. The vine snapped and swung backwards, slapping Mara across the face. Her dark eyes fixed on him accusingly.

"Oh, sorry," said Karic.

"Why are you carrying that damned thing?" snapped Mara. "It must weigh almost twenty kilos in this gravity, and it's dead."

Karic paused to catch his breath. "It may be useful," he said to Mara and Andrai as they clambered over a fallen log. "Maybe we can bluff the natives if it comes to a confrontation."

"It's not going to bluff the leader. He has one that works, remember," said Mara.

"Yes, but it should work against the other Imbirri."

"We'll have the barrier fence. We won't need it," said Mara, reaching to accept Andrai's hand as she stepped down from the huge log.

Karic was exhausted. For days he had been putting on a show of confidence for Andrai and Mara, while he had borne the brunt of Mara's aggression and anxiety.

"I am in charge of this mission, Mara. It's my decision to take this damn thing," said Karic, slapping the haft of the inert weapon, "and we will damn well carry it with us!

"As for the Awakener, we will deal with him when and if we meet him again."

Mara stopped mid-stride. He had never shouted at her before, even during their painful estrangement.

"It's your turn to carry it," said Karic, handing her the cylinder.

Mara grimaced, but did not reply as she took the heavy rod.

They walked in silence for another half-hour. Each took their turn carrying the heavy metal rod. Progress was slow as Karic led them toward the lander's core section. The jungle was thick, and no landmarks were visible through the green. They were relying solely on manual compass readings and the bearings they had taken from the pod. Also, they had to stop repeatedly as they came to clinging vines and rotting deadfalls that blocked their path. Karic carefully led them around these obstacles, setting a new bearing toward the lander's core section at each change of course. Behind him, Andrai and Mara drew closer together, whispering in low tones.

As the hours crawled by, the tension rose and they walked in silence, haunted by the same thoughts. Everything depended on the condition of the lander and of the stasis equipment. The suspension fields were their only link to Earth — allowing them to wait in stasis during the decade-long communication delays.

Despite their fatigue, they increased their pace.

They had to reach the lander.

***

Mara was desperate to see Earth again.

Images flooded her mind. The lashing fury of the tempest and the beautiful calm of morning. The sand and sea, always changing. Sunsets. It

177

seemed ironic she had to propel herself so many lightyears from Earth before she truly grew to love it. And it was love. An intense ache for Earth's embrace; the familiar sights and smells, the simple things they had always taken for granted. Mara craved the enveloping touch of the stasis field, and the welcome oblivion that followed. In her mind, she had already dismantled and rebuilt a score of critical devices damaged in the disaster. Anything to get that equipment working. To get home.

It was only now she could look back over her childhood on the space-based Davis Industries Platform and identify the emptiness that lay within every memory. Her isolation amid the cheerless gray of metal walls and access ladders, while her Brazilian parents devoted their waking life to running the station's AI for DavisCorp.

She had never seen Brazil. Born on-station, her first glimpse of Earth was the DavisCorp space complex outside Boston when she was accepted at university there. Her parents had transferred Earth-side with her. She was seventeen. Earth seemed an alien, frightening place, both dangerous and enticing with its lack of boundaries. Even then, her world had been dominated by her parents and their work ethic. Both electronic engineers, they had climbed their way from the slums of Brasilia to corporate-driven wealth. She had worked hard to emulate their success. When she had been picked up by DavisCorp and offered a scholarship to study astronomy in the newly formed ExploreCorp subsidiary, it had been a dream come true. Professor Montague, lead space science researcher for the *Starburst* mission, had taken her on as an intern, and later as a researcher on the mission, when she completed her doctorate.

Then Janzen, the heir to the Davis fortune, had courted her. Everything that had ever driven her — the quest for position and advancement, the need to make something of herself — was suddenly offered on a plate. In her early twenties, it had been easy to drift into fantasies of becoming a Davis, moving by marriage into the heart of power. But no matter how much she loved that dream, she could not ignore reality. She soon found Janzen had a string of women, all questing like her for a taste of power and wealth. It was over. She had buried it, and had buried herself in her work.

It was on the *Starburst* project that she met Karic for the first time. She found herself drawn to a different kind of power. The power of passion and intellect. She thought he loved her, and perhaps he did in a way. But it was not the love born of respect. When he left on the tour with Evelle, she felt like she was nothing more than the sweet young icing on the cake of his ambition.

In the end they had both disappointed her. When Professor Montague died just before the *Starburst's* departure, it was Mara who was selected to take his place on the mission. At last she had a chance to show her own mettle. She had mourned the passing of her mentor, but truth be told was not sorry to see an end to the increasing tensions between Janzen and Professor Montague.

Yet after all her achievements, in her heart she was still the neglected child, crying alone in a meter-square metal cell, longing for someone to take her away from that grim isolation and give her power over her own life.

It was time she stood up and opened that door herself.

Mara looked around her into the alien growth. They were all so lost here on this strange world. She caught a flicker of movement in the corner of her eye and turned toward it. Mara saw the hulking form of an Imbirri against the green wall of the forest. It was only meters away.

"Karic!"

Andrai and Karic ran toward her, but they were too late.

The huge Imbirri advanced. It reached out and grabbed Mara's arm. She struggled, but the alien's grip was too strong to break. Six more mottled forms pushed through the jungle toward them, cutting off any hope of escape.

The circle of Imbirri closed around them.

***

Karic wasted no time trying to free Mara from the huge, green-crowned Imbirri. He knew from personal experience just how strong the creatures were. Instead, he lifted the cylinder and shouted. The Imbirri who held Mara let out a discordant shriek. The alien let go of her and backed away, the dark nodules of its eyes fixed on the gleaming haft. The Imbirri sang a rapid series of notes to its companions. A warning? In the space of a breath, all the aliens had turned and fled, leaving only swaying vegetation in their wake.

Mara trembled in shock.

Karic ran to Mara, his eyes filled with concern. "Are you alright?" he said touching her arm.

"Yes! Stop crowding me, damn you." She shook his hand off her arm.

"What now, Karic?" asked Andrai.

"We must be less than two hundred meters from the core section. Damn! If the Awakener is waiting to ambush us we will have no hope of doing anything there except getting captured." He lifted the inert weapon. "If only this cursed thing worked!"

Karic thought rapidly. "How close are we to the defensive screen?"

Mara had recovered her composure and looked around them at the lay of the land. "I recognize that ridge," she said, pointing upslope. "Not far, but through this jungle? I would say about two hours."

"We'll never make it," said Andrai, shaking his head. "The Awakener must be close by. He'll be on us in seconds if we try to run. We have to hide."

Karic looked at Andrai. The technician was exhausted. The physical extremes of the planet had worn away his endurance. He had always admired Andrai's enthusiasm and energy, but realized now that like many naturally energetic people, the tech had never had to dig deep to push through the extremes of fatigue. Now there was no choice. They had to run. "We can't hide from the Imbirri. They know the forest too well."

"Let's make for the pod, then," said Mara.

"No. The pod is our only link to the *Starburst*. We can't risk it," replied Karic. If the main force of Imbirri were waiting at the core section to ambush them, there was a chance that making for the screen at the old base camp would take them off-guard. At least they risked nothing by trying. They could always circle back to the pod later.

"We'll make for the screen. If we can reach it, we will have some defense against that weapon. We have to move quickly. Come on!"

Already exhausted by their trek through the jungle, they turned toward the ridge and ran. They kept to cover as much as possible, dodging branches and slipping in the thick organic mulch as the slope grew steeper.

Above them, the ridge rose like a knife-edge from the canopy of the forest. It was crowned by a towering column of gray basalt, which had a sparse growth of gnarled trees clinging to its sides.

At the top of the ridge they collapsed to the ground, gasping for breath. Sweat soaked their uniforms, dripping down their faces and into their eyes. Mara swept back her sodden hair from her face. The sheer basalt peak rose above the ridge behind them. For long minutes they struggled to control their breathing, trying to limit their intake of the thick, oxygen-rich air.

Below them, they could see the former base-camp, in which the Awakener had unleashed the power of his weapon. In the center of the ragged, blackened area, the roughly circular shape of the screen shone a clear blue, a sharp contrast to the destruction that surrounded it.

"We've made good time," said Karic, smoothing back his sweat-slick hair. "In little more than an hour, we will reach the screen. We will carry the control module and the repeater posts back to the pod — you know how compact they are in storage mode. If we are attacked we'll deploy the screen around us. This time we will set it up properly, as a dome-shaped field." If Janzen had done his job right the first time, the lander would still be intact.

Mara looked up wearily from the ground, where she was sprawled beside Andrai. She looked at the screen, far below them, then at the thick jungle in between and back to Karic. "Then what? The Awakener will follow us for sure, and we will be trapped if he catches us."

Karic shrugged. "I hope we can reach the pod before then. But if we are trapped, at least we'll have some means of defending ourselves," he said, meeting Mara's gaze.

Mara turned away.

Perhaps the Awakener will be too cautious to follow us knowing we have one of the energy weapons. Karic shook his head. He did not think it was likely. He remembered back to those brief moments before the attack on the lander, when he watched the Awakener raise his weapon, preparing to strike. Karic knew the leader of the Imbirri was intent on their death. And they had no way to defend themselves. All their weapons had been taken by the Imbirri. If only he knew how to activate the cylinder!

Karic stood and the two others climbed to their feet. They all felt safer now that they could see the screen below them, inviting them on.

"At least it's downhill from here," said Karic.

Lighting flashed across the sky, striking the peak above them. The afterimage dazzled Karic. He watched the dull basalt lighten from gray to yellow for a long moment before his vision cleared. Then the gnarled trees that clung to the slope began to buckle and char, finally bursting into intense flame. *"That's no lightning strike!"*

Karic spun around.

Below them, hundreds of Imbirri emerged from the jungle. The Awakener loomed over them. In his hands he held the energy weapon — and it was aimed directly at them.

"Give me the cylinder," shouted Karic to Andrai, who had been carrying the inert metal rod, but the tech did not move. His face was slack with shock.

A bolt of blue-white swept past them, as jagged as lightning. The distance was working against the Awakener, the weapon losing its accuracy across the length of the treeless slope that led to the ridge. Even so, it was only a matter of time before he got lucky.

Karic snatched the weapon from Andrai and pointed the cylinder at the distant figures of the Awakener and the other Imbirri, trying to scare them off. Sweat streamed from his brow and his arm shook with the weight of the rod. The aliens stood firm.

"It's not working!" screamed Mara.

Karic watched helplessly as the Awakener lowered his weapon, made an adjustment and raised it once more. A blue-white arc of energy lanced toward them. It struck the sheer face of the peak above them with a deafening concussion, blasting tons of rock away from the slope. Mara screamed, then was struck by a jagged piece of flying rock that sent her spinning to the ground.

"He's started an avalanche!" yelled Andrai.

Karic looked upslope. Huge pieces of rock began to shear off the mountain. His fingers grew slack and the scepter fell to the ground at his feet. The wall of rubble gathered pace, hurtling toward them. By some miracle, the shattered rock, dislodged boulders and flying scree passed them by and disappeared over the ridge, leaving them inside a choking cloud of dust.

Karic shielded his eyes, desperate to find a way out.

Swirling patterns began to form in the cloud, echoing the rhythms of his mind. The fugue! He embraced it. Immediately, his senses expanded, and he quested ahead through the thick cloud. He had more control of the strange, enhanced state than ever before. His abilities were evolving.

Here was their chance. They had to get out of sight before the dust cleared.

Karic hauled Mara to her feet and gripped Andrai by the arm.

"Andrai, grab the cylinder."

He led them both toward the peak. Guided by his enhanced vision, he navigated through the choking cloud of dust, stepping around piles of hidden debris.

"This way!" yelled Karic.

There was another explosion. Blue-white light flashed nearby, diffused by the dust.

More rocks tumbled down the slope. Karic could see them through the clouds, darker knots within the darkness, tumbling toward them, bouncing unpredictably. A random promise of death. He led them through the danger and up to the base of the peak, then around it to the other side of the ridge.

On the other side, the winds had cleared the dust. Here, he found what he was looking for.

"There!" he yelled. "A cave. If we reach it before the dust settles, he will think he has killed us. Andrai, did you get the weapon?"

Andrai held up the inert cylinder.

"Karic, how did you ...?" asked Mara.

"That doesn't matter now. Let's go." Karic led them to the cave, an elongated fissure at the base of the peak that broadened rapidly into a dark, empty cavern. The air was cool and free from the heavy dust. The three eagerly squeezed through the entrance to safety.

"How did you do it? How did you see through that dust?" pressed Mara.

Andrai watched Karic with a curious gaze.

Even now, Karic could not admit the fugue state to anyone. Call it habit. Call it caution.

"I just ... knew. That doesn't matter now. Without advanced sensors, there is no way they will find us here. With luck they will think we are dead."

"Luck? I think we're out of luck," said Mara.

***

The Fountain hovered above the bright, crystalline mass of a transmission node, one of an extensive network that provided heat and light on Cru's dark side, supporting a thriving ecosystem here. The nodes had all been engineered to resemble natural features, appearing as glowing mountains to the untrained eye.

Used to the bright side of the planet, even the turbulent thermals rising from the glowing node below him felt cool to him, chilling the delicate skin between the segments of his exoskeleton and the exposed flesh of his wing muscles where they exited his thorax.

The Fountain used a small, yet powerful instrument to examine the spectrum of radiant energy the artificial mountain was emitting, comparing it against the raw feed to the network from the fusion reactors buried below it. The loss was minimal. Even after all these thousands of years, the transmission network that distributed the carefully designed spectrum of radiant energy across Cru's dark side was functioning well. A tribute to the caste of Fintil scientists who once designed and maintained it, now long vanished.

He had at first hoped to find more of the newborn, like the Fintil female who reached the bright side, but perhaps incapable of flight, who had lingered overlong at their hatching site. He had found none.

Although he feared the worst after such a vast period of elapsed time, the Fountain had searched all the hatching areas, and the nearby forests where the growing Fin feeders — the Fintil young — should have been. He found trace remains of the hatched eggs, yet there had been no sign of the innocent, lumbering quadrupeds. There should have been. The Fin were dumb animals who never wandered far from food. He examined marker animals — those whose physiology was similar to the Fin feeders — for diseases, but their populations were as he expected, with no sign of a plague that may have affected the Fin. He deployed aerial probes that surveyed the biosystem, fearing the evolution of a new predator in the carefully designed environment, yet there was no sign of a threat. The whole dark side had been crafted to nurture the Fin feeders for the long decades as they grew, matured, and at last began the Change to adult Fintil.

A sharp concussion sounded in the distance, followed by a deeper rumble that echoed across the valley. Perhaps a landslide? If so, it was a major one. He lowered the spectral analyzer and turned away from the brightness of the crystalline mountain. His senses expanded, flowing south toward the concussion. For a brief moment, he felt the presence of an alien mind.

His wings beat faster, and he felt himself rising up, the analyzer forgotten in his hands.

Aliens!

This is why his beloved children had not reached him. Cru had been invaded. He had been a fool not to consider it. The Fintil had been alone too long. His mind grew dark as he saw how vulnerable the growing progeny of the Fintil would be to spacefaring aliens — new races who had no conception of the ancient laws that preserved peace in this quadrant. He reviewed the weapons at his disposal. Weapons of awesome power. To the Fintil, the dark side was sacrosanct. The eons-old races that formed the confederation of which they were a member all understood this. That an alien would even dare to disturb the Fintil mid-cycle was crime enough. To enter the dark side … if they had destroyed the precious progeny of his race, they and their home worlds would suffer a terrible retribution.

With a burst of speed, he swept toward the fading rumble, checking his shielding devices. All of the instruments registered at full power, as they should. The devices used on the dark side were activated and powered by part of the spectrum emitted by the transmission network.

First, he must seek out the invaders. These aliens who had dared to threaten his children.

Then he must destroy them.

Chapter 16

Karic sat watching the cave entrance. The rumble of the falling rocks had long ago subsided, the billowing clouds of dust settling across the higher slopes or swallowed by the damp mists of the jungle below.

Mara raised a hand to her temple, gingerly touching the small wound there. Andrai had left an hour ago to explore the depths of the cave. "What now?"

"We need the lander. The suspension sets in the lander core are the key to our survival. I had hoped we could do that without outright conflict with the Imbirri — using the defensive shield to protect the new base camp around the lander — but the Awakener is too prepared for us. Too intent on seeing us dead … and he has an army." Karic let out a long breath. There would be no bloodless victory now. "We are going to have to fight our way to the screen, then to the lander. For that we will need weapons. Equipment."

Mara gathered the long strands of her dark hair, which had become loose in their flight from the Awakener. Her fingers moved quickly to bind it into two tight braids. The whole time her eyes never left him.

"We cannot outrun them on the ground," continued Karic. "With a second, fully fueled pod, we could land, disassemble the screen and fly it to the core section. This time we'll survey the site in detail before we approach. I'm not getting surprised again."

"So it's back to that damn valley. A robotic drop, then back here again. This whole trip was a waste of time," said Mara.

Karic ignored the comment. "We should wait here for a while, then backtrack to the pod."

"Wait here?" Mara tied the two braids into a bun behind her head, then laid her hands on her thighs, fists clenched. "What if the Awakener discovers us in this cavern? He could make it our tomb with a single burst of that energy weapon. What's to stop him destroying the lander? We have to get that shield around it now."

"The core section withstood that weapon once before." Karic swallowed, trying to rid his mouth of the taste of bitter dust. In truth, he had no idea if the core section could withstand a determined assault from the Awakener's energy weapon.

"You really believe he won't destroy it?"

Karic knew that the Awakener would not be satisfied until he had destroyed them and every last trace of them. Until he had turned their bodies to ash like the fallen Imbirri. He also knew that reaching the lander or the shield was impossible right now. "We have no choice." Wearily, he lifted up the heavy shaft of the inert weapon and examined it. If only they could fight the Awakener with a weapon that rivaled his. The tragedy was there had never been any need for violence. All the *Starburst* survivors had wanted to do was to find a quiet corner of the landscape in which to wait out the centuries while a rescue probe could reach them from Earth. *All the survivors except for Janzen.*

He walked to the small cave entrance, searching the verges of the jungle outside for any sign of movement.

Janzen, who had caused all this, was now the safest of all of them, in stasis in the lander's core section. He may be the only one to survive. If so, it would be his story that would become history. Karic would be branded an incompetent traitor. He seethed with anger and frustration.

The situation had conspired against them from the beginning. Why did their presence here have to precipitate such violence, such catastrophic change? Why did so many have to die?

"We have to leave here," said Mara, standing. "If we are found inside this cave, we are trapped."

Karic nodded, deep in thought. He tapped the heavy shaft of the scepter into his left palm as he paced. "I know, Mara. And yet what happens if he gets us in the open?"

"Then perhaps we should recover the shield and bring it here."

"The Awakener will be watching the lander and the screen, waiting to see if we'll return."

They stood silently beneath the oppressive mass of the mountain peak.

When they had left the darkened valley in the pod only hours ago, it seemed as though nothing could stop them. The technology that had brought them to Cru was once more at their command. The lander's core section and the intact stasis gear was right in their grasp. The prize — survival and ultimate return to Earth — had been so glittering, so enticing, that it had blinded them. Karic blamed himself. He should have foreseen the Awakener's trap. It was only determination and luck that had enabled them to elude him. If the fuel in the pod had not been critical, they would have flown directly to the lander and a final destruction at the hands of the Awakener. Karic's anger rose to fury. Yet there was nothing they could do except run for the darkened valley and hope they made it.

"Karic. Mara." Andrai emerged from the rear of the cave, grinning, his blond hair and face streaked with dirt.

"Andrai, did you find anything useful?" asked Karic.

"No. The fissure ends in solid rock about a kilometer inside the mountain."

"God. You're a sight." Mara wiped at Andrai's face with the sleeve of her uniform, which was only marginally cleaner.

Karic's stomach twisted, but he forced himself to focus. "Let's try to make it back to the pod."

"At least we'd be getting out of this damn deathtrap," said Mara.

The three of them left the cave, taking care to move quietly. In the distance, Karic could see the lake where he had first set down the pod. The waters glistened with the captured image of the crystal range beyond it, and for an instant it seemed to be the reflection of some impossibly gibbous moon.

They emerged onto the treeless slope below the peak, now strewn with sharp-edged stone blasted away from the cliffs above them. As they wove between the rubble, heading for the tree line below them, Karic felt uneasy. He looked behind them, and above at the peak, then scanned the wall of green below. There was no movement, yet he could not shake the feeling of exposure. Of being watched.

Mara and Andrai slowed too, instinctively sensing something odd.

"Boss. There are no insects," said Andrai, his voice lowered to a harsh whisper.

Andrai was right. There was no sound at all. The bizarre calls of the local forest — the insect ecosystem — were completely absent.

"Stop," hissed Karic.

He was just about to trigger the fugue, to reach out with his new, enhanced senses and check the path ahead, when a score of Imbirri emerged from the jungle. Karic's heart sank as they fanned out across the tree line and up the slope to either side of them.

"*Karic.*" Mara shrank back toward him. Andrai instinctively followed.

They were trapped. Following behind the Imbirri, his head raised in triumph, was the Awakener. After all they had endured, this was it. There was no way out.

The Awakener pointed the scepter at them.

"*Damn you to Hell!*" screamed Karic.

***

The Fountain circled the peak. The vegetation that remained on it was charred and twisted. One side of its sheer face had been blasted away, the slope around the peak littered with debris. This was the source of the sound that had drawn him, he was sure of it. The alien intruders would be close. He could almost feel them ...

There!

When he first sensed the aliens, he had feared his children were lost. Not just laid waste by time, but the victim of atrocity. But he could see them! Almost a hundred, each twice the size of the normal Fin feeders, and bipedal! Their rough skin was mottled with color, the main band across their crown hinting at the mature Fintil they would become — greens and golds destined to be males and females, reds and purples the mixed-gender castes of warrior and scientist.

Spellbound, the Fountain glided down toward them. He was amazed at the changes, at this miracle of survival after so many millennia. His mind flowed down to touch them, caressing them lightly, as though they were too precious to be held. His excitement doubled. Not only were they alive, they were strong.

How was this possible? How could they have survived like this for thousands of years without closing the cycle from Fin to Fintil?

His senses wrapped the Fin like protective wings, and he savored their essence, yet there was an odd dissonance in their midst. As he drew closer, he saw why. Three aliens were with them, dwarfed by the feeders that surrounded them. One of these must be the alien he sensed from the transmission node.

The Fountain dove down toward them, determined to protect the innocent Fin from the intruders. As he approached, he could see a wide swath of destruction carved through the nearby jungle, littered with debris. An alien shielding device squatted like an insult inside the blackened scar, a crude construction that relied on magnetically confined plasma.

Rage welled within him. Not once, in many millions of years of Fintil civilization, had an alien dared to disturb the sanctity of Cru during this delicate part of their cycle.

The Fountain drew a weapon from his belt and steepened his dive. Deceptively small, the little device could channel enough power from the transmission network to reduce the whole peak to rubble. He reached out expertly with his mind, communicating, adjusting the targeting so that none of the Fin would be harmed.

Justice would be swift.

He was closing fast. The blackened ground reflected in his multi-faceted eyes as he swept down toward the aliens.

The Fountain was ready for anything — except the scene unfolding below him.

Many of the Fin clutched crude weapons, the normal padded forepaws of the feeders evolved into a three-fingered hand. He saw the faint glow in their dark eyes, the intent way they moved.

All the signs coalesced into a single stunning realization.

Intelligence.

He pulled out of the dive and hovered. Thoughts flashed rapidly through the chambers of his ancient mind as he struggled to bring this new development into context.

Once, many millions of years ago, the planet of Cru knew true night and day. It knew dawn and dusk, and its skies two moons. Although living in the hottest regions, the Fintil females would lay their tiny, leathery eggs in the cool, dark places: jungles, caves near fertile valleys,

188

beneath the thick humus of the jungle floor. Here, the hatched spawn — the quadrupedal Fin feeders — would roam free, foraging and growing until the time of their Change.

The Fintil civilization grew and prospered. Their scientists unlocked the secrets of interstellar travel, and both moons were collapsed into a singularity — contained within a vast machine — which was further grown until its mass rivaled a planet. The singularity could then be harnessed for instantaneous space travel. Such devices were needed for moving any physical mass in Timespace. In their hubris and lust for exploration, the Fintil kept the device, the Translocator, positioned in orbit around Cru. Over the millennia, its gravitational field clawed at the planet. The planet's rotation decreased. The scientists gave dire warnings. The Fintil factions argued, and the massive cost and effort required to shift the Translocator, and the vast time period required to execute the project — over multiple Fintil lifecycles — led to an impasse. As the planet slowed, the cooler forests shrank and finally died under the hot, ceaseless sun, or withered in the long, cold dark. Hatcheries were devised, but the Fin were dying in their thousands. Some natural element was missing.

The decrease in Cru's rotation accelerated, driven by increased travel through the Translocator. Before the Fintil could reach consensus or act, Cru became tidally locked to Tau Ceti, a single face presented to the hot sun for eternity, another to the depths of space.

The crisis finally spurred the Fintil to action. The Translocator, which had caused the planet's reduced rotation, was shifted to an orbit around Tau Ceti. The dark side of Cru was altered to become a garden nursery, the night-shrouded half of the planet transformed by an extensive network of transmission towers that provided heat and light. The bright side remained home to the heat-loving adult Fintil, where they constructed the new cities of their revitalized civilization. Once more, they grew and prospered. Then eons passed. Despite all their technology, some flaw in their makeup led to a decreased fertility rate, and despite the best efforts of their scientists, they once more declined. Now another change had appeared in the Fintil genetics. Another point of crisis in their long history.

The Fin he had known, little better than animals, had vanished from Cru, and evolved into a new form.

Below him, the Fin feeders milled in a single group, standing on two legs. They arrayed themselves in order. He saw them speak with each other. Communicate in their own language. Close now, their individual minds sang to him the thrilling, frightening song of sentience.

Here, under him, surrounded by the Fin, stood the three alien beings. Their type was unfamiliar to him. He examined them closer. *One held a power rod!*

He turned into a dive once more, readying his weapon.

Despite the impossible changes in the Fin — their transformation from unintelligent quadruped to bipedal sentient — all that really mattered was their protection.

So intent was the Fountain on the aliens he failed to notice that the leader of the Fin also carried one of the power rods and was now preparing to use it.

He landed in a blur of gold. A tall, magnificent being. Wings outstretched, translucent. Standing between Karic and the nearest of the Imbirri, he was now blocking the path of the Awakener's weapon.

The Fountain kept his wings fully open, as though to shelter his children. He activated a shield that would protect him and the Fin from the force of any blast. He was waiting for it, ready to answer any attack from the alien intruders with devastating power. Yet there was no attack.

The Fountain touched the mind of the alien holding the power rod. He could sense the alien's intent, and knew with sudden certainty he had never intended to destroy his children. This ... *human* ... felt only fear. Yet of what?

***

To Karic, it seemed as though the golden being emerged out of nowhere. He looked up in astonishment. *It was the golden figure from his dreams.*

The Imbirri broke ranks, some running in fear, others captured by the Fintil's beauty. Most of those that remained waited for the Awakener to pass judgment on the newcomer, but their leader was as stunned as the rest. The huge Imbirri stood frozen, his eyes dark with shock.

Karic approached the Fintil.

"*Karic! What are you doing?*" Mara's narrow face was white with fear.

"Mara. Don't you realize what this means? The Imbirri aren't what's left of the high-tech culture. There are two races on this planet. *Two races.* This is the advanced one. It has to be. We have to establish contact. Only they can get us out of this mess." Karic spoke without turning, as though if he took his eyes off this startling, winged apparition it would vanish. "Stay quiet. I'm going to try and communicate."

"But ..." Mara choked back her words, her face a mixture of fear and anger as she looked up at the tall alien.

Andrai stepped closer to her, drawing her back protectively. "Let him try, Mara. He must have done it before, with the other one — the Deepwatch. How else could we have found the bier?"

"Coincidence," she spat, but she let Andrai draw her back toward the cave entrance, leaving Karic alone with the aliens. The remaining Imbirri

190

ignored them, all their attention on the newcomer.

Karic stepped forward. The golden, winged alien stood more than three meters tall. Insectoid, and without a doubt sentient. Every single ecological niche was filled with insects, from the lowest to the highest forms of life. He should have guessed the beings at the biological apex would be the same.

He felt a tremendous sense of peace and tranquility surround him. The cylinder hung loosely in his hands.

Karic reached for the fugue state. Felt his mind shimmer and expand, reaching out, hovering on the point of contact.

Suddenly, he glimpsed movement behind the Fintil.

The Awakener swung the scepter toward the Fountain, his face twisted with fear and rage. The Imbirri's hands trembled, his eyes glowing with a pale, uncertain light.

Karic's reaction was instinctive. He raised the inert weapon as though to ward off a blow. The scepter slipped in his grip, his finger sliding by chance over a large stud on the haft of the weapon. Instantly, the power within the weapon built. A lashing tendril of blue-white lightning swept toward the Awakener with a crack like thunder.

The smell of ozone filled Karic's nostrils.

I thought the cylinder was inert!

The strike missed the Awakener, yet it sent him and the other Imbirri who remained near the cave fleeing in fear. Karic watched the Awakener run into the forest below and thought he had never seen a finer sight.

The Fountain turned to watch the Fin run into the forest. For the first time he noticed the power rod in the leader's hands. Grief filled the Fountain as he finally understood. These sentient Fin were not the innocents he had assumed.

The Fountain turned toward Karic, placing a slender hand on his shoulder. This small being had saved his life. His hastily erected shield would not have protected him from rearward attack.

Without hesitation, the Fintil sent a tendril of spirit toward the human, seeking to merge with his mind. Within the matrix of this merger, like an egg taking root on the fertile wall of the womb, their minds became one. The Fintil could now understand Karic's thoughts, and sensed his confusion regarding the scepter. He received images of a darkened valley and smiled.

"The power rods receive their power from the transmission network," sent the Fountain across the link. Karic received an image of a crystalline transmission node, a glowing mountain like those that covered the dark side and fueled its artificial ecosystem and so much else. "All of our devices are inert within the darkened valley. That is why we left them there."

Karic looked toward the being with astonishment, hearing the distinctly male voice clearly in his head as each thought flashed into existence before his mind's eye. He replied to the being mentally, across the bridge of minds. Karic's first two attempts resulted in a garbled mess of conflicting thoughts. Then he discovered that if he spoke aloud, his mental message was clearer.

"So, during the time we fled from the Awakener and the Imbirri, we could have used the weapon?" asked Karic, recalling the agonizing, fear-filled flight across the ridge, the confrontation on the peak ...

"I am glad you did not. But yes, once within range of a transmission node, power would have been available to the rod. But, my friend," said the alien mind-to-mind, taking the rod from Karic's hands, "this is not a weapon. It is an antenna, a conduit for receiving energy. We use them to power our machinery."

The ancient Fintil's wings quivered. "I have so many questions. How did the Fin feeders — you called them the Imbirri — come to be in possession of a power rod? How did they come to perceive its capabilities? Why would they choose to use it in such a way?"

"They call *themselves* the Imbirri," said Karic. "I think initially they feared us. They took us prisoners." Images of Karic's imprisonment fled across the gap between their minds. The Deepwatch Utar. The Awakener. "Why do you call them feeders?"

Karic gasped as a wave of agonizing sadness struck him across the link. The big, glittering eyes of the Fountain turned toward him. He could sense the Fintil's gaze, although the eyes themselves and their many facets remained a hypnotic kaleidoscope of refracted and reflected color.

"I apologize for burdening you with my remorse," said the Fountain, abruptly shielding the emotions from Karic before he continued. "The Fin are the children of the Fintil, before their rebirth as winged, sexual beings."

"They are asexual?" asked Karic, realizing how much this explained: the lack of children, the strange uniformity among them.

"Yes. It is only when they emerge from the chrysalis that they take on their sexuality and become fully sentient beings ... or at least that is how it was."

Karic struggled to maintain some control over the telepathic link, to shield his process of cognition, yet he had no idea how. Each of his conscious thoughts tumbled out onto the shoreline of his mind to gleam like bleached shells. This did not concern Karic, though, because there was a similar openness in the alien's mind.

Karic sensed curiosity from the Fintil.

"Which planet of the Har Confederation are you from, human? You must be a new admission, because I have never encountered your species before. I ask because I have been asleep for so long; otherwise, as Fountain of the Fintil, I would know of your people."

Karic was genuinely perplexed. "My two companions and I traveled here from Earth," said Karic, his mind clouded by homesick images of the blue planet. "What is the Har Confederation?"

The Fountain was ominously silent. Although they were still connected mind-to-mind, the being had withdrawn his surface thoughts to another, inaccessible part of his mind.

The Fintil's wings contracted with a snap, his tall golden body growing rigid with tension. Karic's eyes were drawn to the long limbs, and the row of short, razor-edged ridges above the delicate hands; like knives designed to rip and slice. The Fountain's powerful mandibles ground together, the sound setting Karic's teeth on edge. They could take an arm — or a head — off with a single bite.

Karic had no idea how the Fountain had hidden his thoughts, but he felt alarmed. As though he had woken from a dream, he suddenly realized the enormity of what he was doing. Their negotiations with this powerful being would determine their fate on the planet — and whether they ultimately reached Earth again. He was communicating telepathically with a highly advanced alien — one who was more skilled at hiding his thoughts than he was. Could he trust a being this adept at hiding his true intent?

He had to think fast, while the Fountain's attention was elsewhere. There was no way he could emulate the disciplined techniques of the Fountain. That was a skill he could not begin to understand. He could try to limit his thoughts, focus as hard as he could on one thing, but how long could he keep that up? Or … he could fill his thoughts with a bevy of confusing, distracting images. Yes, that would work — and it would be much easier to achieve.

The Fintil turned back to Karic.

"By what means did you reach the planet Cru?" demanded the Fintil. The Fintil's concentration was total, and Karic felt his own mind exposed beneath the scrutiny.

Karic was intimidated by the sudden change in the Fintil, but carefully collected his thoughts. One false move would cost them dearly.

"We traveled here by starship from Earth," said Karic aloud, images of the *Starburst*, its computer-driven nervous system and fusion heart, filled the space between them. He concentrated on the image of *Starburst*, determined not to let his thoughts stray.

The Fountain was puzzled. He saw the mother-ship of the humans through Karic's eyes, and knew it to be cleverly constructed, yet even so the technology was unbelievably crude. There was no conceivable way a ship like this could master the intricacies of Transition.

"How does your ship operate?" asked the Fountain. "How did it bring you from Earth to Cru?"

The Fountain listened in disbelief as the human explained their method of traveling, going to great lengths to explain how their bodies were placed into animated suspension for the journey. *The human physiology gives them that advantage, at least.*

With abrupt clarity, the Fountain realized who these creatures were. The images of their spinning world and its single sun, so unlike all the ancient, still planets of the Har Confederation; their method of travel, the primitive technology, all of these facts shifted into focus.

"You actually traveled through space to reach this system?" asked the Fountain, in a state of disbelief.

Karic was unsure what to think. Linked as they were, there was no chance he had mistaken the other's thoughts. "How else would we have arrived here?"

The golden being broke contact. Karic watched him carefully as he sat on the dull, sparse ground cover. The Fintil's body began to shake. Tentatively, Karic approached him. As he drew closer the convulsions became more pronounced, and with an elegant motion, the ancient being threw back his head and began to bellow, howling into the darkness in a rhythmic staccato. With a shock, Karic realized he was laughing at them, laughing uncontrollably.

Karic grew angry, and his thoughts spilled out into the space between them.

Sensing the human's anger, the Fountain sobered and joined with him again. "I have to apologize. For a transformed sentient to travel in such a manner is … unheard of. Have you not begun to study the rhythms of your planet as its structure fluctuates in Timespace? The dimensions that exist beyond it?"

Karic merely shook his head, but his thoughts conveyed volumes. He was thinking of Earth again; the American continent, dominated by the authoritarian dictates of the Federated States of America. Old Europe, united now and becoming more closed to the rest of the world every decade. Asia, highly developed and chokingly populous: the myriad tiny nations all playing court to the Dragon, China. And surrounding all of them the choking hold of the United Earth, the successor to the United Nations, which coveted the last of Earth's wilderness areas with an iron hand, its uniformed officers monitoring every aspect of the environment, its leadership commanding the armies of Earth through its powerful Enforcement Council.

Had it been arrogance to fling themselves into the darkness of space leaving such division behind? Thousands of cultures and differing languages, billions of people, all vying for space on the crowded surface and the harsh stations of the Free Colonies. All separated in mind, spirit and purpose.

Karic could not speak for all of humanity, only himself. And for him the exploration of space had been his greatest dream — a longing that had driven him since he was a boy, defining each of the major turning points of his life.

Allowing himself to become immersed in Karic's thoughts, the Fountain became grave. Any humor he may have felt a moment before was being fast dispelled, and alarm filled him; for he realized he had unwittingly broken one of the most fundamental rules of the Har Confederation. The winds had grown cold and dangerous, and he must fly carefully, testing them with every stroke. The human's thoughts were disturbing, although they had given him something to use. Karic had an unquenchable longing for space. He could make him an offer that he would find impossible to refuse, and remove him from the realm of the Fintil for evermore.

Realizing that he lost control of his thoughts, Karic stilled his mind.

"Do you communicate telepathically in your home world?" asked the Fountain across the link.

"No. We have dreamt about it for centuries, but our science has never grasped it."

"But what of yourself? Your mind was ready for contact before our first meeting."

The Fintil's mind was still closed to him.

"I am not ... typical," replied Karic.

The Fountain chittered to himself gravely. As he had suspected, these humans were not only primitive sentients, they were a pre-transformation species! They had yet to make the crucial step in evolution that enabled mind-to-mind communication, a vital prerequisite for interspecies contact, and the hallmark of all truly civilized spacefaring cultures. If he had known this, never would he have attempted contact with them.

The golden being looked at Karic with new respect. This human had experienced a frightening birth within his mind and yet had accepted it. Despite the primitive savagery of the race, as glimpsed in Karic's thoughts, he now had a new respect for humanity. They were a brave and clever people. Yet any admiration he felt did not alter the gravity of the transgression.

"I should not be communicating with you, Karic."

"Why?" asked Karic. He could sense a drastic change in the being's attitude toward him.

"You are a young people, too young to have contact with such an ancient species as my own. Since you have been so injured by my children in their misguided attempts to protect themselves, I will not destroy you, as our laws dictate. Instead, I can offer you life — conditionally."

Karic's heart raced. The Fountain will *allow* them to live?

"What condition?" asked Karic.

"You will be transported out of this galaxy, to another world, much like your own. I will give you a ship — much more advanced than yours — with which you can explore space."

"Why?"

"I cannot allow you to carry knowledge of the Fintil back to your world. The ship I will give you will allow you to survive — even prosper. But it will not be capable of returning you to this galaxy. You will never see your home world again.

"Your people should not be venturing into space," finished the Fintil.

"But exploring space is one of our greatest dreams! My people will never accept that!" replied Karic, angrily.

"It is your people's choice of course. I can only advise you that it is ... a little soon."

Karic thought desperately. Despite never seeing Earth again, the idea of having a technologically advanced ship at his disposal was compelling. With one thought he could ensure survival for himself, Mara and Andrai — and fulfill his lifetime ambition of exploring space. But what of Mara and Andrai? What right did he have to choose for them? It had always seemed his dream, to cast himself into the depths of space and explore its mysteries. In his pride, he had always felt that it was his work alone that had taken him so far. His designs, his passion. But the reality was different. Always there had been someone at his side, supporting him, yet never recognized. First Lein, then Evelle, then in the heady days before the *Starburst*'s departure, Mara. Always there. His experiences here had forced him to reassess his true connection to humanity in ways he had never considered before.

Lein had tried to tell him. His grandfather's dying words came back to him now with even greater meaning. He had forgotten about anyone who stood with him.

He could not forget about Andrai and Mara. Not now.

Karic also had a responsibility to Earth. Despite the dictates of the Fintil, Earth had a right to know of this powerful race living right on their celestial doorstep.

But how could Karic convince the Fountain to let them return to Earth? What single thing could he offer the Fintil? And then there was the voice of doubt. Did he really want to reject this offer? If he did, by some miracle, convince the Fountain to let them go — would he regret it? Karic dismissed the thought. He could not think only of himself anymore. He had to do the right thing for all of them, and he had to act now.

Karic thoughts raced. Then, in a flash of inspiration, he had it. Carefully, he focused his thoughts, trying to keep his mind blank. He could not let this slip. This secret was the only card they could play.

"You said that these Imbirri transform into Fintil?"

"Yes," replied the Fountain warily.

"I know where three of the Imbirri have started the change. One of them was a leader of the Imbirri." He had just realized that Utar and his two followers, now encased in a chrysalis, were not just still alive, *they were in the process of transforming into Fintil*. If he had gleaned anything from the Fountain's mind, it was his powerful urge to protect his children, the next generation of Fintil. His race was on the verge of a crisis. Their very survival hinged on this next generation, on the Fintil that the Imbirri would become.

"Where?" demanded the Fountain. The Fountain's focus on Karic intensified until it was a physical pressure on his mind. His temples began to pulse with pain, red-hot wires snaking into his head. But he was ready.

Karic thought back to the repairs on the ship, the long, long list of pending work and all the resources they lacked. Mentally projecting himself back on the *Starburst*, he began to work his way through the list, losing himself in the massive amount of detail. Circuits to be repaired, components replaced, modules and computing systems to be cannibalized and jury-rigged together. It took little effort. For months, this was all that had filled his mind and it all came back, in all its mind-staggering detail.

The Fountain ceased his attack. The Fintil shrieked in surprise and backed away a step. Karic's thoughts had become like a mass of insistent parasites, tearing at his focus. He recovered quickly and considered the problem. The Fountain was unfamiliar with the human species and feared he would destroy Karic's mind if he pressed the man any further. Yet it was imperative that he find these transforming Imbirri before the Awakener. He could not allow one of his new children to die.

"Very well," sent the Fintil reluctantly. "Tell me what you want in return for the location."

Karic was wary. He stilled his thoughts and focused himself once more.

"Your help in returning us to our ship," sent Karic. "And your help in exiting this system so we can return to Earth. We also need to know when it will be safest to pass the black hole near your sun."

"Black hole? There is no ... Ahh. I see."

Fintil was silent for long minutes, his mind closed.

"Very well," replied the Fountain. "I know your ship is damaged, and I have no idea how to repair your technology. But I have the means to take you to orbit. As for the danger — we know our system well, and I can guarantee you that you will be safe from the ... black hole ... as you pass Tau Ceti."

"And you will not threaten our lives in any way?" insisted Karic.

The Fintil buzzed with irritation then descended into brooding concentration. For long minutes, the silence stretched out between them like a funeral procession. Finally, he gave his answer. "No. Your lives will not be threatened by myself or my race."

Karic was filled with relief. He had not expected the alien to be so reasonable, but just like that, he had won freedom for himself, Andrai and Mara.

He also felt a heavy disappointment. The chance of a lifetime had been dangled in front of him — to explore the universe in an advanced alien ship — and he had rejected it. With a grim feeling of certainty, he felt this voyage home to Earth would be his last. *But I do not know that for sure. I have to let the future take care of itself.*

The Fountain was impatient for the details of the location, and annoyed at himself for allowing these aliens so much latitude. He would return them alive to their planet — however, the secret of the Fintil's existence would still be protected. He allowed himself some small measure of satisfaction. These humans were terrible negotiators. Karic would not find all to be as he expects on his return to *Earth*. Best to move quickly before the human thinks to question him more thoroughly.

"Now tell me where the changed Imbirri are located," asked the Fintil.

Karic now understood the Imbirri and their place on this world. They were the "larval" stage of the Fintil's lifecycle, like the caterpillar of the butterfly on Earth. The hardened shells that had engulfed Utar and his followers were the Fintil chrysalis. Once, these "Fin" had been non-sentient during this early phase, yet something had occurred that altered this. They had become sentient beings and had succeeded in resisting the biological programming that would start their transformation to pupa and ultimately adult Fintil. They had staved it off long enough to create their own culture, their own society. The Change that so terrified the Imbirri would see that idyllic life destroyed forever.

"Utar's body and the bodies of two of his acolytes are in the same dark valley where we found the power rod," thought Karic to the Fintil.

Images of the bier that held Utar's body filled the Fountain's mind. He saw the encased bodies of Utar and his two attendants and through Karic sensed the power within the Deepwatch. The Fountain realized immediately that Utar would be the key to winning the trust of his children.

"You must take me to the bier at once," demanded the Fintil.

"Of course," replied Karic, but his head was immediately filled with other concerns. The recovery of the screen, the lander and the pod.

"Do not concern yourselves for your machines. We will take them with us."

The Fountain broke contact. He extended himself to full height and turned his gaze to a small device in his belt. Karic's senses were still keenly tuned, and he could sense the Fountain using his mind to activate the device. It began to hum, then grew silent.

The Fountain turned to Karic, the towering golden figure fixing him with his gaze. His wings unfurled slightly, the folded layers of golden, translucent material fluttering in the breeze.

Isolated now from the alien's mind, Karic felt anxiety build. Could he really trust the Fountain? One thing was certain, without the strange twist of genetics and fate that gave him his gift, the gulf between the Fintil and humanity would have been too great to bridge. The new gifts that had grown out of the shameful dysfunction of the fugue had saved their lives.

The Fintil made brief mental contact.

It will not be long.

The Fintil turned away, walking slowly across the slope. There, he stopped to look out at the green landscape. He remained so motionless, Karic thought he could be a statue, carved from golden resin.

He had to remain focused. With deliberate effort, he pushed the fugue state away. It was best now that the Fintil could not read his thoughts. He had been fortunate so far. Had the Fountain been less restrained, less honorable … He did not want to contemplate the outcome.

A large spinning platform appeared, flying rapidly from one of the dark zones beyond the crystal mountains. It was circular, and constructed of three disks, the top stationary, while the bottom two spun at extraordinary speeds in opposite directions.

As it approached, Karic took an involuntary step backwards — the platform was almost half a kilometer wide. His eyes narrowed, searching instinctively for its mode of operation, yet he could see nothing. No engines, no fuel tanks, no wings … yet it flew.

Mara and Andrai wandered down the hill to Karic, their eyes fixed on the extraordinary craft approaching them.

"I think it's going to be OK. I've managed to communicate with him," said Karic.

"Who is this alien, Karic? What is he doing?" asked Mara.

"His name is the Fountain. He is one of the Fintil, the race that built the transmission network — the crystal mountains that bring heat and light to the dark side of Cru."

Mara frowned.

There was so much to tell them, Karic scarcely knew where to start.

The Fintil used the device at his belt once more, and the platform lowered to the hillside.

"Here it comes!" yelled Andrai.

The strange craft dropped smoothly toward them. In the center of the circular platform was a big robot, its articulated body folded back into itself. It resembled a squat metallic spider. Its cylindrical eyepieces glittered in the white light.

The Fintil walked slowly to Karic, sending him a quick mental instruction. *Please step onto the platform.*

Karic gave a nervous glance back to Andrai and Mara and waved them on. As soon as they stepped onto the top platform, the force of the planet's gravity was dulled. They found themselves surrounded by a field of shimmering green. Within it, they seemed to glow, like particles trapped in a beam of sunshine.

The Fountain once more communicated with the device at his belt. The field around them strengthened, holding them securely in place, as though they were surrounded by a form-fitting sheath of foam.

They lifted skyward.

Alongside them, the Fountain also launched himself into the air, his great, golden wings driven by the thick bands of muscle in his broad shoulders, his gleaming carapace and tapered abdomen shining with the reflected light of the crystal mountain below. The platform adjusted its flight to match the Fintil's speed, effortlessly taking them along in his wake.

The wind rushed around them, and the engineer had to shout to be heard over the torrent. "He is taking us and all our equipment back to the darkened valley. He is going to return us to *Starburst!*"

Mara's eyes widened, and she shouted more questions back to Karic, but the air snatched them away.

They glided toward their former base camp, where the lander had come under attack from the Awakener. The Fountain soared down, landing lightly. A few seconds later the platform also touched down. The green light faded, and they were released from the field that had kept them secure atop the platform.

The Fintil waited patiently while the humans deactivated the shield and moved it onto the platform, stacking it neatly. The lander's core section, ejected skyward when the external tanks exploded, was now some distance away. Only the wreckage of the tanks and the shattered engines and their housings remained.

Once they were done, the field around them strengthened once more and they lifted into the air.

They watched the charred earth where the lander had stood in silence as they flew away, the twisted and blackened metal, the melted earth.

The group drifted higher, rising far above the jungle. Mara and Andrai looked around them with wide eyes.

The Fountain, having first risen to a height well above the volcanic peak, now dove directly toward the forest canopy on the other side of the ridge: his keen eyes searching the jungle below for the lander's core section. Gradually, the rapid descent slowed, and they hovered above the jungle.

Then abruptly they dove again, the tips of the forest canopy rising toward them like a wall. Mara screamed as they came within meters of the canopy, then suddenly stopped.

The field around them dropped away once more.

The Fountain flew to the side of the platform. As he drew close, the robot stirred to life. Its body rose, towering above them on legs more than five meters long. One by one, its six articulated arms uncurled. It was huge, and Karic found it hard to believe it could have risen from such a compact shape.

The robot stepped off the platform into the jungle below, disappearing from sight for a few moments. Then, with the breaking of boughs and the cracking of branches, the lander's core section rose above the jungle, carried effortlessly in the arms of the robot, which stepped back onto the platform, lowering the entire lander onto it.

The base of the core section was ragged and torn, but the cabin was intact. Luckily, the shield had been in place over the viewport, protecting it. The external struts and fittings had melted together, forming weird, twisted shapes. Soon, it too was surrounded by the same green field generated by the Fintil's devices.

The Fountain lifted into the air once more, striking out directly for the position of the concealed pod as shown to him in Karic's mind.

A few minutes later the platform lowered once more, the robot stepping easily through the jungle to retrieve the pod and place it beside the lander's blackened core section.

The Fountain climbed, wings beating faster as he fixed his mind on the goal ahead. He knew of the darkened valley. This was one of the places where the Fintil stored their machinery during the period of the Fins' growth. The whole dark side had been made safe for them, with the transmission node adjacent to the storage area dulled as an added precaution. Although sheathed within self-sustaining stasis fields, none of the machinery there would operate until the fusion reactor buried in the heart of the node was activated, transmitting the energy required to bring it to life.

The Fintil's wings beat faster, and together, the small group sped toward the shadowed valley where Utar's chrysalis lay.

As he flew, the Fountain used powerful instruments on the bright side to remotely check the orbit of the Fintils' Translocator. Its orbit had not decayed, and yet, the records showed that the period of Shedding — when the singularity took on mass from Tau Ceti to maintain its integrity and some of these gases were ejected or "shed" into space in the process — had been altered. He could scarcely believe it possible, but the conclusion was inescapable. One of the Imbirri had accessed the interface of their most powerful machine — and used it to send directed radiation at the humans' ship. It had been a brutal act, and yet, he could not help but feel a sense of pride. To have come so far ... It was a shame that all the Imbirri must perish to give the Fintil life. They must all be induced to enter their own chrysalises and leave this phase of their existence behind.

It would be a simple matter to delay the Shedding until the humans' ship was far distant. A few adjustments of spin, field strength ... yes, it could be done. There was easily enough mass in the kernel — the black hole's core — for it to maintain its integrity. But a seed of fear remained in his heart. What other devices of the Fintil had these *innocents* used? He could not underestimate them again.

***

Far below the Fountain, concealed within the lush growth of the forest, the Awakener watched the golden interloper sweep south, drawing the aliens and their litter with him.

The mere sight of the Fintil triggered an ancient instinct inside him, and he could feel the Changes stir. This golden being represented the death of all he and Utar had labored so long to preserve. He struggled to push aside the lassitude that this golden being evoked in him, the terrifying urge to surrender to his own body, and view him as just another alien. Another intruder.

He had to protect the Imbirri. He sensed that time was running out. Events were drawing close to some crisis and he knew he had to resolve this before that time came.

The Changed Imbirri he had destroyed still haunted him. Their faces, their vanished voices, would not leave him in peace. The violence had stained him, and he feared what he had become. Feared what his friend Utar would say of him now.

But Utar was no more.

Committed to his course, he allowed himself to feel the same hot rage he felt after Utar's death. He used this to sharpen his focus, to drive himself forward. As he watched the aliens move through the sky, he longed to give vent to that fury. To end the existence of all these strangers with one sizzling bolt of power from the scepter; but he knew it would be foolish to attack them now. That winged creature possessed devices of power and he knew he must be careful. He had to wait, plan, then strike hard.

As the Fountain finally disappeared over the horizon, the Awakener signaled to his faithful. They rose from their places of concealment and dutifully followed in his determined wake as he made his way back to the village. He would gather every one of the Imbirri left alive and follow this golden being.

The Awakener had observed much in his many years of the ways of nature, and knew that winged creatures typically flew in a direct line toward their goal. He knew what lay in that direction. He and Utar had been there before, in the long years of their exploration of Cru, before they raised the First. It was there they had found the scepter, one of the inexplicable artifacts scattered across their world, left by the enigmatic ancients, a powerful race of builders that he and Utar believed must have once inhabited Cru.

He would lead all the Imbirri to the distant encampment of these aliens and watch them until he knew the time of their weakness. He owed it to the Imbirri that sheltered beneath his protection to continue the fight. He could not let them ... change. No matter how scarred he became, how damaged by his actions, there was no choice but to continue, otherwise the pressure of the Changes would overwhelm them all, sweeping them up in an unstoppable wave that would lead to the ultimate end of all Imbirri culture. The Awakener pushed his mind away from thoughts of the Changes, away from the glimpsed memories of the golden abominations they birthed ... He walled off that part of his mind, sensing a realization brewing inside him that he was not prepared to face.

The Awakener examined the metal haft of the scepter. For long years it had been nothing but a mystical artifact. A symbol of the never-ending life of the Imbirri. No longer.

Now it was a weapon.

A symbol of their ultimate victory.

Chapter 17

Karic and his crew entered the darkened valley together, still part of the winged alien's weird convoy. He had managed to answer most of Andrai and Mara's questions as they traveled, but had long since given up trying to shout across the rushing wind as they flew south across the dark side. The three of them were content to be silent, held aloft by the Fountain's devices and enthralled by the darkening landscape that fled by beneath them. They and all their equipment were shrouded by glistening green. The field nullified not only the hold of gravity, but the effects of inertia as well. It was hard not to covet such technology.

Soon they were surrounded by deep twilight. Far in front of them, the Fountain's powerful shoulders flexed in an even rhythm, his slim, elegant body held into the wind with perfect poise. He flew effortlessly, maintaining their course as much through instinct as through design. The golden, flashing wings were now darkened silhouettes, gleaming only when the waning radiance of some distant transmission node reached briefly over the rim of the valley. Now, beneath them, outlined in dull green by the field that held them in place, they could just make out the eerie shape of Utar's funeral bier as the Fountain began his descent.

The Fintil landed with a careful economy of motion, folding his wings as he touched the ground. The platform followed a few moments later, the spinning lower plate hovering a few inches off the bare earth.

The robot unfurled once more, methodically carrying the bulky pod and lander core section off the platform and placing them gently on the ground. The lander and pod settled under their own weight, the planet drawing them covetously to its heart. The humans helped the robot carry the many barrier fence components. It made a strange companion.

Finally, the robot clambered back into position, lowering itself into place and retracting methodically into its compact form. Then the platform disappeared over the horizon. Karic watched it go, wondering how many other storage caches were dotted across the dark side, filled with Fintil technology.

Released from the spell of the strange journey, they went directly to their crafts to assess the condition of each. Karic gave rapid orders, and within minutes the pod and the antenna linking them to the *Starburst* had been repositioned beside the lander's core section. The three crew then carefully redeployed the defensive shield around their encampment, this time ensuring that the generated field formed an enclosing dome. Karic was adamant they take no more chances, despite the apparent benevolence of the Fountain.

At last they were secure within the defensive field.

Karic stood outside the lander's outer airlock, Andrai and Mara behind him. The lander's impact must have been catastrophic. There was no way Janzen could have escaped unscathed, and he dreaded what he would find inside the cabin.

He could not put it off any longer.

They had to work their way into the shattered door mechanism, using pry bars from the pod's toolkit to lever open the maintenance plate. Inside, the servos were still intact, but the power conduit had been severed in the crash. They ran an electrical lead from the pod and fed power to the servos, which whirred into life. The hatch door retracted, the seal breaking with a hiss. It stopped immediately, leaving a gap a handspan wide. The impact had twisted the hatch frame — only by millimeters — but that was enough to stop it opening. Karic peered through the gap. He could see nothing in the darkened interior. "Use the pry bar."

For a frustrating hour, they worked to restore enough clearance for the servos to fully open the hatch. They were soaked with sweat. Exhausted. The whole time Karic could hear the tiny motors straining against the obstruction. Just when it seemed they would never succeed, the hatch snapped open and they had their first view of the interior.

Janzen had activated a suspension set. He was lying prone on one of the thickly padded support frames, his body surrounded by the ghostly field. He had a wound to his head, and one of his arms was in a sling, but apart from this, he appeared in good health.

"I don't believe it," said Andrai.

"He must have been strapped into one of the console chairs," said Mara. "Otherwise, he would have been minced-meat after that fall."

"OK," said Karic. "Let's forget about Janzen for now. He is going nowhere. Let's find out how badly damaged the lander is."

Andrai went straight to the console and activated the controls, which had automatically gone into standby. Lights came on inside the cabin.

Immediately, an image of Janzen came to life on the main display.

"What is it, Andrai?" asked Karic.

Andrai tapped the keyboard, scrolling through a few screens.

"It's a record of a transmission log. It looks like Janzen set up his own link to the ship and made a transmission back to Earth via *Starburst*."

To Earth?

"Do you want me to play it?" asked Andrai.

Karic nodded, his heart thundering in his chest.

First came the flat feminine voice of the lander AI. "Log of transmission from Commander Janzen Davis to ExploreCorp command."

At the mention of Janzen as commander, Karic's foreboding grew.

The screen flickered and the log jumped back to the beginning of the transmission. Janzen stood upright before the console camera, his poise faultless as he played the part of the wounded hero.

"It is with regret that I have to report the death of the remaining officers of *Starburst*. Karic, who led an unlawful mutiny against me, died tragically on the surface of Oasis, bitten by a poisonous animal. After I confronted him, he chose to run and hide on the surface of the planet, stealing a pod from *Starburst*. Unfortunately, his cowardly act killed him. I led a rescue attempt to the surface, but the remaining officers, Ibri, Andrai, and the astronomer Mara were all killed in a tragic accident. A fault in the lander ignition system resulted in an explosion of the external fuel tanks. All were killed while taking samples outside the lander. I was inside the lander when it happened ... and am the only survivor."

Janzen lowered his head, halting, as though overcome by grief. The executive quickly glanced at his comband, which puzzled Karic until he realized Janzen was actually timing the pause. With another surreptitious glance at his comband, Janzen continued. It was exactly a count of ten seconds. The whole "moment" of emotion had been staged for effect.

"But I have the pleasure to report the mission to Tau Ceti a success! Karic's report — after his mutiny — of an X-ray source in the vicinity and a black hole were the delusions of a disturbed mind. The deaths of the crew did not result from radiation, but from a failure in the stasis equipment. Ibri, before his tragic death, confirmed it was human error, an unfortunate side-effect of Karic's deteriorating mental state. I take full responsibility for this terrible breakdown in command." Janzen paused, his face grim. Then he brightened, giving a perfect, white-toothed smile.

"But triumph can arise from tragedy. The planet of Oasis is a paradise ... Not only does it have near-earth gravity with an oxygen-nitrogen atmosphere, it already supports life! A thriving ecosystem easily adapted to intensive agriculture. Although the planet is tidally locked, a local geothermal anomaly on the dark side has created ample heat and light. Perfect conditions to support human life.

"More importantly, it is *terra nullius* — unoccupied — with no sentient life forms."

Janzen beamed triumphantly at the camera. Karic could imagine the audience of ExploreCorp executives neatly outlined before his mind's eye.

"As Chief Executive Officer of ExploreCorp, I direct the immediate dispatch of the ExploreCorp colonization fleet. A fully armed Defender ship should be arranged to arrive two months prior. I have a separate set of instructions for this ship, including my location for rescue, that has been sent earlier under encryption."

Janzen looked at the camera, his smile seemingly genuine.

"Gentlemen and ladies of the board, this is a new era for mankind, and it is ExploreCorp that will lead the way.

"Commander Janzen Davis, ExploreCorp. Signing off."

Karic savagely stabbed at the console to shut off the recording. His head thumped with sudden pressure. His ears rang as the blood surged through them.

"Andrai, can you get at the other encoded transmissions?"

Andrai worked long, silent minutes.

Karic's eyes were locked on the still form of Janzen, his head filled with dark thoughts of revenge. The bastard had never expected them to survive. But now …. now Janzen was at their mercy. It would be all too easy to abort the suspension sequence. He would be dead in minutes. But Karic would never do that. It would be cold-blooded murder. No. Janzen must answer for his crimes.

Andrai looked up and grimly shook his head. "No go, boss. I will never crack that code."

"Damn him! God knows what instructions he has sent back to Earth via *Starburst*. If a Defender class ship arrives here — it will start a damn interstellar war."

Karic thought quickly. He needed to send another transmission back to Earth to refute Janzen's slanderous lies, but before he did so, he needed to know exactly what commands Janzen had sent back to the Earth system. That idiot had no idea of the power of the Fintil. The very survival of Earth was at stake. He would need to revive Janzen and interrogate him. Damn! He did not have time for this. Karic knew he needed to get them all off this planet and on their way back to Earth before anything else went wrong.

He forced himself to think it through. It took months to prep a ship for an interstellar voyage. So he had plenty of time to deal with Janzen and organize a second transmission. Ideally it would be Janzen himself who would send it, admitting to everything and canceling his orders; then Karic could send a followup message, fully confident of its reception by ExploreCorp and Earth.

"Forget him, Karic. We are still here," said Mara. "We know the true story and we will make sure it is told when we reach Earth again."

Karic glared at Janzen. Some day he would get exactly what he deserved.

"We need to get operational," insisted Mara.

With a supreme effort, Karic tore his eyes away from the still figure. "OK. Let's get to it."

Karic and his crew inspected the lander's core section. Although the structure was intact, the damage to the hardware and controlling systems had been severe. This Karic was willing to accept — it was the suspension gear that really mattered. They would need it on their return to Earth. The engineer carefully tested the other portable sets, each locked securely behind thick doors of shielding metal designed to protect them from radiation.

They are serviceable.

Karic's heart raced with new fire. He had devoted years of his life to developing this technology. He had been willing to risk everything to be part of this first journey of mankind into space. To find these sets intact was like finding a part of himself, a part that he had lost. Replacing the equipment carefully into its protective casings, Karic gave instructions for Mara and Andrai to bring any system they could back online. The more diagnostic computer power they could muster, the better. They would be in suspension for centuries before they could be rescued. It was imperative that they could rely on the systems that would keep them alive. The uplink was also crucial. Karic would need this to send his messages back to Earth.

He started to pace around the cramped cabin, getting in Mara and Andrai's way. After a few annoyed looks in his direction, he left the cramped space and walked around the inside of the defensive shield. When would the Fountain release them? It was crucial to their plans. They had to know. Finding out meant approaching the aloof Fintil once more.

His mind made up, Karic left the protective enclosure and went looking for the Fountain. He saw his silhouette against the crude structure of the bier, and walked slowly across the darkened clearing toward him. Karic had taken for granted the illumination the pod's light had provided before. Not even the metal structure that marked the entrance to the underground cavern was visible, although it lay close by. Karic made a mental note to set up a better lighting system.

He stopped at a respectful distance, not wanting to disrupt the being from his thoughts. Moments later, the Fountain stirred. Although Karic could not see them, he knew the big, faceted eyes had turned toward him. Like a cloud of breath, the mind of the Fintil washed over him. Karic's mind swelled to meet the Fountain's, and in an instant they were joined.

"I trust the transport I offered did not alarm you?" sent the alien.

"No," said Karic aloud, although his inner fears contradicted him.

"I see your race has no fondness for heights," replied the Fountain and let the matter rest.

"I need to ask when you plan to return us to our ship. We wish to leave Cru as soon as possible."

The Fintil's thoughts were unreadable. The pressure on Karic's mind grew. It was unmistakable. Once more, the Fountain was attempting to read his thoughts. Karic immediately filled his mind with schematics for the suspension equipment, mentally running through the theories behind his discovery as though delivering a lecture to a crowded auditorium.

The Fintil exhaled sharply, clearly annoyed. "It is quite impossible for now. I will not leave these three Fin until they emerge from their chrysalises." The Fountain waved at the encased bodies of the Deepwatch and his two acolytes. "And certainly not this one ..." The Fintil laid a slim golden hand on the casing of Utar's chrysalis. Even though Utar and his people knew themselves as Imbirri, it was clear the Fountain still considered them Fin, the Fintil progeny ... his children.

Silence ensued.

Uncomfortable, Karic turned his attention toward the hardened casings of the cocoons. "So these will hatch." He was amazed at the incredible transformation they would undergo.

"Yes." A wave of joy emanated from the Fintil, and he made no attempt to curtail it. Karic could feel the Fountain's alien emotion and realized with a shock it differed from human joy. He was swept up by a strange alloy of awe and exhilaration, and entered a landscape with vistas of feeling he had no words to describe, yet which evoked a sense of profound *belonging*: the blissful acceptance of the many, and the deep joy of surrender that came with integration into a complex social fabric where all had their place. This latter sentiment was foreign to his individualistic human mind. It was but a small glimmering of the immense cultural gap between human and Fintil.

The Fountain continued. "All three of these children are very much alive."

"How soon will they emerge?" asked Karic awkwardly.

The Fountain placed both hands on Utar's casing, gasping in delight. "There is such life in this one!" he said, schooling his thoughts. "Soon, human. Very soon."

The Fountain turned away from the bier and led Karic further into the dim light provided by the human's defensive shield. As they approached, the engineer could see his crew at work inside, assessing the damage to the lander. Once at the barrier, they stopped.

The Fountain turned to Karic, fully visible now in the bluish light. Karic was struck once more by his alien nature, the strange sentience he had taken for granted since their first meeting only hours ago.

"We should not be communicating in this manner," sent the Fintil.

"How else? It would take years to learn your language."

"The mind-touch of an Elder race such as the Fintil is too ... stimulating. We must minimize contact," said the Fountain, and Karic sensed genuine disappointment. "You, human, have a fine mind. The thoughts of your species do not travel as fast as those of the Fintil, yet your capacity for imaginative association is astounding. I wish we could have met in better circumstances. I truly do. And I have no doubt you will become a great people if ... given time."

Karic felt the Fountain's admiration overtaken by another, darker emotion, which was quickly hidden from him.

"I don't know how to thank you for all your help," sent Karic, his head filled with visions of a return to Earth.

"There is no need," replied the Fountain, turning to go. "Now I must activate the reactors beneath the darkened node. It is time this valley was once more filled with light, and energy."

Karic nodded and then the contact was gone. The Fintil walked swiftly through the darkness toward the entrance to the underground caverns. What was the Fintil hiding? Had his own relief, Karic wondered, at being rescued from the Awakener, at being given a chance to leave for Earth, blinded him to the Fountain's real plans?

Karic shook his head. He knew the Fintil would deliver them safely to their ship, and let them leave for Earth unmolested — there was no way the Fintil could have lied about that while linked to him mind-to-mind. But what else could the Fountain do to undermine them, without breaking their agreement?

Karic sighed. First they had to deal with the challenges of the here and now. He was looking forward to having light around them once more — it would make their work so much easier.

***

The Awakener sat on his throne, brooding. The interlaced canopy of the Tree, the ragged wound in the crown skillfully sealed with woven reeds and grasses, arched above him. The few remaining First lay prostrate before him, their bodies illuminated by the dull yellow gleam of the braziers set around the living dome. So many First were gone now. Some had fallen in the attack on the alien craft, others had succumbed to the Changes, while others were simply missing — Utar's two senior acolytes among them.

Instead of calming him, the familiar scent of the fragrant wood burning in the censers put him on edge. Yet another symptom of his unease. No matter what he did, how hard he tried to put the Imbirri back on course, nothing felt *right* anymore. *Nothing*.

Despite his determination to protect his people, more of the Imbirri had succumbed to the Changes.

When they had returned to the jungle to lay in wait for the humans, the Awakener had been shocked to find the encased forms of Imbirri littering the site of destruction. These were Imbirri who had fallen during his first attack on the alien's craft — he had assumed they had been destroyed by the raging firestorm. The sight of their bodies, so far into the Changes, sent a deep fear into him. He had longed to destroy them, but feared it would alert the humans to their trap.

Others had gone missing on the march back to the village, some stumbling only a short distance from the path before falling to the forest floor. He dared not stop. Instead, he had pushed his followers to the point

210

of exhaustion to reach their camp. As he had hoped, once within sight of the Tree, the rate of attrition slowed.

The Awakener counted each one of those fallen bodies in his mind. He vowed to return and burn every last one of them before he was finished. Yet these last acts of destruction must wait until the other aliens had been dealt with.

He shifted his bulk to the front of his throne then pushed himself to his feet.

"Rise! Rise! Gather the Imbirri together. We will share the Elixir before we set out to destroy the aliens," said the Awakener.

He sent Utar's five surviving acolytes to his enclosure to gather all the Deepwatch's instruments and materials. With all the ingredients before him, the Awakener prepared the powerful mixture himself. Buoyed by new confidence, he selected Utar's senior surviving acolyte, the gold New Bough, to become the new Deepwatch, and the four other remaining followers of Utar — all First greens — to be his new assistants. These five he made stand before him as he prepared the Elixir. "Watch and learn!" he said. "You will henceforth be the custodians of the secrets."

The five chosen First assisted the Awakener to the best of their ability. They were inept and clumsy compared to the vanished Otla and Munch. As the leader of the Imbirri watched the new Deepwatch, he was suddenly all too aware that although solemn and attentive, and swelled with pride over his new role, New Bough could never replace his friend. The dead Utar's powerful mind, and his ability to explore the myriad paths of the future, had been unique. The title of Deepwatch was a hollow honor for New Bough, who although outstanding among the First, could sustain only the most rudimentary mental bond. Although he would master the Elixir's preparation with time, he had no hope of mastering the artifacts of Cru as Utar had.

When the Elixir was ready, the Awakener and New Bough led the procession out from under the Tree. The voices of the First rose and twirled about each other in a rising harmony. Outside the enclosure, the Imbirri gathered for the ceremony. The chorus of song that greeted the Awakener was low and solemn, lacking the usual power and joy inspired by the celebration. He almost stumbled as he saw how few were left. That last time with Utar they had thousands, now … barely hundreds. Usually excited by the nearness of the mystery, and by the ritual, those who remained were unusually subdued.

As each of the huge beings came forward to take the Elixir, the Awakener grew more detached from the proceedings. For years beyond counting he had presided over his people, the powerful spirit of Utar beside him, Utar's presence as enduring as a mountain. It seemed inconceivable he was gone. Those uncounted centuries flooded into his head like a blissful, narcotic smoke, swamping his senses. He let himself dwell in that dream for a nostalgic moment, then pushed back the past. He had to remain intent on the goal before him: the destruction of all that had no place on this world.

The ceremony finished, and the song faltered to silence.

All the Imbirri waited. The twenty-eight reds who remained were eager, their bodies rigid with tension. The violence had fueled them like a drug. The purples, the strange obsessed purples, had all vanished. The golds hovered throughout the village, poised for his commands, yet aloof, while the hundreds of greens — the bulk of the remaining Imbirri — huddled close together, eyes dark with fear. *Had he become so terrible?*

All the Imbirri could sense the coming storm, and though many had no conception of the events that had taken place, all knew intuitively that their fate would soon be decided. Change, so foreign, was the invader. It walked silently through their ranks, touching each with a sickening feeling of fear — and a strange excitement so at odds with the peaceful, indolent life they had known for countless years, marked only by the passing of the annual Redwing Swarm.

Abruptly, the Awakener lifted his scepter and discharged the weapon in fury into the air above him. The gathered Imbirri drew back in awe from the Awakener's fearsome presence.

The blazing discharge of the scepter ceased and the Awakener's voice boomed out, filling the vacuum left by the extinguished power. "We go forth as a people to seek out the aliens and destroy them. Only then will the sacred spirit of Cru be healed."

The Imbirri sighed in unison, like the restless groan of a vengeful sea. A tide that would rise to engulf the aliens and their devices.

The Awakener signaled, and the First divided the massed ranks of the Imbirri into smaller groups for the trek through the forest.

"We must be silent and cautious as we move through the forest. It is only by surprise that we overcome and destroy the aliens," he said.

At length, the Awakener's army was arrayed. His urge to protect the Imbirri burned in his chest like a flaming sun. Surely *nothing* could stand between him and his goal.

As the ragged army was preparing to move into the jungle, two of his scouts — a pair of reds known for their swift feet — ran from the forest to stand before him. He signaled impatiently for them to speak.

"We have found the aliens."

The Awakener trembled with excitement. *It was as I thought.* All his plans now fell into place.

"They were in the darkened valley, as you said, surrounded by magical devices that glow with blue and green lights."

"Are all of the aliens there, including the winged one?"

"Yes. Yet also within the valley are three of the Imbirri, far gone into the Changes, one of the shells raised high on a platform of wooden stalks."

"Utar!" The Awakener's urge to discharge his duty of destruction could no longer be contained. "Take us to the darkened valley," commanded the Awakener.

The scouts ran ahead, and he signaled his First to lead the other groups from the village.

The destruction of Utar's remains would mean the end of a long chapter in his life. Yet he knew that until the remains of Utar were dealt with, a new future for him and the Imbirri would always be elusive.

The army of the Awakener melted silently into the tangled green, leaving only a single leaf swaying within the cathedral of its brethren, as though stirred on a gentle breeze.

Chapter 18

The Awakener walked alone through the silent ranks of his army. He was constantly in motion, spurring each of the smaller groups onward with the power of his presence. Around them, the deep greens of the jungle gave way to the duller pigments and broad leaves of the shadowed lands.

The force comprised the whole of the Imbirri people, welded together and driven headlong solely by his will. Most were simple beings, accustomed to roaming the verdant hills in endless, carefree repast. They feared the shadow-lands, those areas where the life-giving light of the towers did not reach. Now, as the ragged army moved further into the darkened zone, the more innocent of the Imbirri began to experience a numbing fear. Some turned to run, only to be caught and spurred onward by the more determined followers of the Awakener. Others slipped away …

The Awakener himself was growing more restless as his goal neared, time running faster as the crisis neared. Holding the scepter visible as a clear threat, he watched the marchers carefully for the slightest sign of the Changes. So far the effects of the recent Elixir and the unifying flame of their purpose had kept even a single Imbirri from succumbing.

The crystal ranges were soon lost from sight. The light in the sparse jungle fell rapidly until they were in deep twilight. They stumbled on through the rough terrain, the silent Imbirri drawing closer together for support.

Then the small army drew to a sudden halt.

Angry at the delay, the Awakener made his way to the front of the column, where the scouts were leading the advance parties. They had stopped on the crest of the hidden valley itself. When the Awakener reached them, the scouts sang in recognition, then pointed into the darkness below, explaining how the location of the bier could be reached. The Awakener could just make out the dim blue glow of the humans' protective screen. That distant point of light became the focus for his dark, boiling hate.

The Awakener was galvanized by the sight of the enemy. He climbed onto a high knoll in full view of his people. Here he spoke of revenge, of the future, of the need to surprise and destroy the aliens and all their craft. His speech was short and impassioned. As he made his way from the hillock toward the darkened valley, he had no doubt that the Imbirri — his people — would follow him. Yet as the Awakener marched into the pitch black, only his scouts, their rambunctious red caste-mates, and the braver of the First, remained at his side. When he turned to check on the forces arrayed at his back, he was bereft of melody. The rest of the Imbirri stood at the rim of the valley, fearing to cross from twilight to dark.

The Awakener was seized by an irrational fury. To be thwarted within sight of his enemies was unbearable. The passions that drove him captured him like a whirlwind.

So they feared the darkness?

They will fear me more!

His thoughts were lost within his howling mind, and in moments, he had done the unthinkable. He raised his staff, depressed the activating stud, and brought the weapon down on the heads of his people. The Imbirri screamed and fell down onto the earth of Cru, fully expecting to die.

Nothing happened.

The scepter was heavy in his hands. Cool, inert metal, empty of power.

Darkness surrounded the Awakener, pressing in like a stifling blanket. His emotions drained away, leaving him defeated.

He realized that within the darkness the scepter was useless as a weapon. At last he understood. Utar had commanded his acolytes to move his body here for just this reason. The Deepwatch had always been more gifted than him in the ways of magic. It was Utar who had divined the uses of the scepter, many ages gone by. Now the Awakener realized Utar had discovered many things, not all of which he had shared.

Slowly, the Awakener emerged from the valley into the twilight. Testing the weapon once more, he felt the comforting warmth of the energy within, reduced in potency, yet enough to achieve the destruction he desired. He sat on the knoll from which he had given his speech and laid the scepter across his knees. After a while, he signaled the Imbirri to attend him and sat in silence, staring into the eyes of these simple beings. All had been raised to sentience, yet not all were equal. Most had limited intellect, limited powers of the mind, content merely to eat, sleep and join in games and song. His eyes flickered with sadness and he wondered what he had become. Love had deserted his life. How much more pain would come to fill him before his task was done?

Utar had planned well, yet even so, the final confrontation would come. Turning toward the feeble glow of the humans' defensive shield, the Awakener schooled himself to patience.

The threat to the Imbirri would end. He swore it.

***

The Fountain roamed the darkness of the valley, deep in thought. There was much to do. Much to prepare. His metabolism, adapted for the extreme heat of the bright side, ran fast here on the dark side, compensating for the relative coolness. It put a strain on his ancient body, and forced him to consume increasing amounts of food. The mundane physical demand — that would have been so easily dealt with in the sophisticated Fintil city of Zenith — was an unwelcome interruption to his work here. He had to use raw materials and devices hidden below the valley to synthesize the right dietary factors ...

Suddenly, he stopped.

Just for a moment, he thought he felt another alien mind. *Brooding, waiting, watching ...* The dark, once so comforting with its elegant stillness, now seemed hostile. He raised his angular head and probed with his keen vision. The night side held no fear for the Fintil, whose bodies were capable of dealing with vast environmental extremes. Nothing. He opened his mind and swept the valley with his enhanced senses. Apart from the humans, the valley was devoid of sentient life. He clicked his mandibles with irritation and pushed the matter from his mind. There were much more important matters to be considered.

He checked the chronometer at his belt. The fusion reactors beneath the floor of the valley would be stirring in earnest now. In scarcely two hours' time, light would begin to fill the valley. Once the radiant energy emitted from the transmission node reached its peak intensity, he would shield the entire valley, protecting it from any rudimentary weapons the Imbirri might possess.

The Fountain turned his thoughts to the Pact, the ancient agreement among the advanced sentient races of Har Confederation, which he had unwittingly broken by communicating with Karic. What havoc would ensue from his careless actions? The humans were pre-transformation people, their society fractured and without of the unifying power of the mental bond. Now he had tainted them with the mind-touch of an Elder race, the Fintil. Worse still — the Fintil were not even one of the humans' benefactors! Never in his long life, or within the chronicles of the Har Confederation, of which the Fintil were a member, had the Fountain ever known such a serious error to have occurred. His mandibles ground against one another.

The Pact demanded that the Elder races have no contact with any pre-transformation species, and that under no circumstances should the young races of any single Confederation transgress into the space of another.

No matter how promising a new race seemed, they were kept in total isolation to develop their own path.

In the distant past the Elders were open in their contacts, helping each new race reach beyond the bounds of both their newly found sentience and their restrictive Timespace. That distant epoch was now called the Death of Hope by the Har historians. At the outset it seemed the brotherhood of races would extend and swell with seamless goodwill, yet within the period of mere centuries, the new races had thrown themselves

216

into conflict. System against system, league against league. It may have been fear, perhaps pride, or dreams of holy conquest spurred by ideals of racial superiority; the records of that bloody time were too scattered and fragmented to know. Billions died and worlds with them, ripped apart by weapons so powerful they rivaled the very forces of creation. After several millennia, the Elder races, at first too stunned to act, stemmed the tide of chaos. None of the transgressors were spared — and with their obliteration, their genetic potential was lost to the Universe for all time.

From that time came the Pact.

The memories were still vivid within the minds of the Elders, and in recent millennia even contact between the Confederations had dwindled, caution and reserve replacing the erstwhile joys of union.

What astounded the Fountain was the tenacity of these humans. Transgressing from their system across space as though it were a simple three-dimensional grid, traveling in straight lines! Despite himself, the Fountain laughed at the concept. It was perfectly logical from a simplistic point of view. And absurd beyond belief. The human race had more ingenuity and courage than common sense.

The Fountain growled. They were a pre-transformation species. If they should encounter another like them in their careless explorations ... The ensuing strife could be both bloody and tragic. If the Elders were forced to intervene in such a conflict, they would destroy both races without compunction. Harsh justice, born out of a time of abominations.

The Fountain grew tired of his wanderings. He turned and made his way back toward the human's encampment. As he walked, he noted a soft light was beginning to fill the valley. He smiled as he saw the jagged shape of the transmission node glowing softly in the darkness.

Alarmed, the small, mindless creatures of the valley were fleeing. The Fountain watched them as he strolled through the soft light. Adapted to the vanishing darkness, for the most part they would flee to their deaths, yet this seemed always to be the way. There must always be death for new life to emerge. He considered his plans for the humans. Must they be dealt with so ruthlessly? Perhaps it would be better to destroy them now and plead his case to the Council of Elders.

He chittered in irritation. *Enough of these dark thoughts.* He must focus on nurturing the new generation of Fintil.

His mind was fixed firmly on the birth of the three new Fintil as he strode through the fading darkness. He paused at Utar's chrysalis. *This one is the key to the Imbirri. He will lead them into the Change.* The Fountain focused his power and reached within the chrysalis to the sleeping mind within as he had many times since he had reached the valley. Utar was surrounded by confusion, but the Fountain gently eased his mind. The Fountain showed Utar how to focus his powers and grow accustomed to

217

his new body, hastening the transformation.

Light filled the valley, and with it came power.

***

A single tone sounded inside the lander's cabin. Then a small screen flared to life on Janzen's suspension set.

CRITERIA MET. PREPARING FOR SUSPENSION INTERRUPT.

Slowly, the fields sweeping around Janzen grew more insubstantial, until they were gone completely.

Janzen groaned, then reached into his pocket for his odin.

He stood.

"Activation command — *Janzen TYXJ 4327 JJXC VVFP.*"

One of the struts inside the lander started to quiver, then a long split appeared in the formerly seamless metal. A door slid open, revealing a hidden niche. A small, spindly robot stepped out, slowly raising itself to full height. Its wedge-shaped head swiveled toward Janzen.

"Report," commanded Janzen.

"All three targets are alive," said the small robot in a hollow, metallic monotone. "The lander has been moved to a new location. There has been the involvement of a new sentient factor called "Fountain". Probability confirms factor is likely an alien, co-operating with the three targets. Species: new."

Janzen grimaced. "Attack mode."

"Confirmed."

***

Karic was growing more anxious as the hours fled. The activation of the transmission node, despite the forewarning of the Fintil, had left him more unnerved than ever. At his side, he wore an XR32 recovered from the lander's core section. Around him, the sparse stands of fungi looked shrunken and ghastly in the light, their pale trunks like dead things. The ground, with its scant cover of grass-like fungi and thick, ancient humus, steamed as the rising heat drove off its moisture. Their hidden haven had transformed to an exposed wasteland.

Restless, the engineer walked to the bier and studied the black casing that enclosed the remains of Utar, now in the final stages of his transformation from Imbirri to adult Fintil. Utar had known that the darkness would protect them from the Awakener's staff. That protection was vanishing fast. The Fountain had powerful devices at his disposal, yet Karic suspected he was underestimating the Imbirri, still thinking of them as his simplistic children.

Experimentally, Karic reached out toward the Utar's chrysalis with his mind. He was soon lost within a dreaming sentience, infused with the potent energy of new life. The images he received were in disarray and yet there was no doubting the imperative running through all of them. *Hurry!* Utar was devoting all his power to emerging from his transformation as quickly as possible. Through the mind-bond, Karic was filled with the same urgency.

It was ironic. Utar had tried to destroy them all, and his attack on the *Starburst* led to the death of Evelle and thirty-two other crew. Karic had no idea how Utar had sent that deadly burst of radiation through space, yet he had. Then later, from the moment they had touched the soil of Cru, Utar had been their enemy. Janzen, in his attempts to rescue them, had given Utar and the Awakener every cause to despise the humans. Yet inexplicably the tables had turned. Utar had helped them escape, leading them to the sanctuary of the darkened valley. Utar had nothing to gain by leading them to safety — in fact he had much to lose. The humans' presence could only endanger his chances of transforming into a Fintil before destruction. So why had Utar helped them?

In the dreams and fugue-visions where Utar had first appeared to Karic, back on board the crippled *Starburst*, the Deepwatch had seemed a demon. On Cru he had been their tormentor. Yet now Utar seemed like the closest friend the humans had on this planet. The Fountain had pledged to help them and had already saved them from death, and worked miracles in their favor; yet even so, Karic did not trust him.

Karic turned from the bier and inspected the perimeter of the defensive shield carefully in the rising light. With the Awakener still at large, Karic would not relax until the *Starburst* was heading back to Earth. With the Fountain on their side, they had a chance; yet, both they and their Fintil guardian were still vulnerable.

Karic scanned the ridges above the valley. His eyes struggled to adjust to the half-light. The Imbirri people had long since ceased to be primitive in Karic's estimation and he was alert to the slightest hint of danger. The Awakener had ambushed them both times they tried to return to the lander, he had intercepted the pod as it first travelled to the darkened valley, and found their hiding place on the peak. The Awakener would be carefully planning his next move against them, and he would have no hesitation in destroying them if he could.

Karic walked back to the campfire they had lit outside the barrier shield and rejoined Andrai and Mara. They had discovered that fallen stands of the giant fungi dried up on the ground over time and could be gathered to make a good fuel. If anything, it burned a little too fast in the enriched atmosphere.

"No change yet?" asked Mara.

Andrai looked up from the fire where he was stirring a basic stew with a tiny spoon from one of the ration kits.

Karic shook his head, sitting by the fire.

The valley was quiet. The shriveled growths of fungi were deathly still, as though poised. *Waiting*. Karic shivered.

A figure appeared from the surrounding stands of giant fungi. Karic rose to his feet. His hand moved back to rest on the grip of the XR32.

The Fountain watched Karic carefully as he entered the encampment. The golden exoskeleton that encased his slender form glistened like brightly lacquered wood. The faceted eyes reflected the light like prisms, betraying no emotion.

Karic reached out toward the being with his mind, clumsily, attempting to make contact. Yet it seemed as though the space the Fintil occupied was vacuum, his mind unreachable. The Fountain seemed more alien than ever and Karic felt frustration and fear. Without the common bond of language, there was nothing that linked him with this strange being, no way to reassure himself he would not betray them. How could he communicate the pressing sense of unease that gripped him? The silence was as tangible as a wall of stone.

"He gives me the creeps," said Mara.

The Fintil turned and walked toward the metal structure and the underground caverns. As Karic watched him go, he realized his hand still remained on the XR32 at his belt and he let it drop. "I don't trust him either, Mara."

Within minutes, the light in the valley had risen to its full intensity. With a sound like thunder, a sheet of purple flame exploded above the valley.

Mara gasped, dropping her food onto the pale grass as she drew her weapon.

Andrai looked up at the translucent purple shield as it unfolded above, lost in wonder.

Karic pulled the XR32 from his holster and searched about him carefully for any sign of threat. Above them, the sheet of flame flattened with a roar, spreading out like a blanket through the thick atmosphere to cover the whole sky above them.

"Maybe we should move back inside the barrier," said Karic.

Mara nodded in agreement.

"It's some sort of defensive shield, boss," said Andrai.

Karic studied the sky. Andrai was right. The thick purple flame had stretched out like a thin, translucent veil above the valley, sealing it. Cursing, Mara walked back to the campfire and sheathed her weapon. The Fountain returned from the metal structure. He walked straight past them without the slightest hint of recognition. The tall insectoid creature stalked forward with an ominous focus, and Karic swallowed as he saw again the razored edges of his forelimbs, and the huge mandibles. It was an irrational fear, he knew, but humans and insects on Earth had an uneasy truce at best.

The three humans sat once more. For the first time in days, they began to relax. With the Fountain's shield above the valley, they should be safe from the Awakener. The conversation between them began to flow more freely, and the light around them began to seem like a gift, rather than a curse.

The Fountain reappeared a few moments later and sat nearby, resting with his elongated head slumped down onto his torso, his long legs folded back into grooves in the sleek abdomen.

Karic heard voices. *Hundreds of them.* Sweet, melodic voices — all growing closer.

The Imbirri!

The Fintil roused instantly, pulling himself up to his full height.

The Awakener swept into view through the sparse growth. He held the scepter like a bludgeon. A gold-crowned Imbirri walked beside him, as though in some position of shared authority. They led a massed group of Imbirri that was coming straight for them. The red-crowned natives — who Karic recognized as the primary attackers on the lander's first encampment — appeared at the flanks of the group like guards, eyes lit with a feral gleam, huge hands clenching and unclenching at their sides as though wringing imaginary human necks.

The Fintil held his ground, calmly reaching to adjust a device at his belt. A hum rose into the air, barely audible, but grating on the teeth.

The crowd of angry Imbirri was only paces away now. Karic backed away, awed by the size of them.

The Awakener growled as he saw the Fountain. He lowered the scepter and depressed the stud.

Nothing happened.

Karic sighed with relief. "The Fountain has somehow dampened the node's transmission. The Awakener cannot use his weapon."

He heard the familiar electric discharge of a defensive shield being cut. *Impossible.* He turned to see Janzen and a tall, silver-limbed robot step through a deactivated section near the control module.

"Janzen! *No!* Stay back!" called Karic.

The Fintil's head swiveled toward them.

Janzen pointed at the Fountain, and the robot's head followed the gesture. "Eliminate target."

"Acknowledged."

"*No!*"

The slender robot swiveled its thin, articulated arm toward the

Fountain and fired. A slender, hot beam shot out straight for the Fountain. The Fintil tried to move, but the beam sliced through him easily, cutting horizontally through his abdomen. His belt snapped, the devices falling to the ground, many cut into smoking pieces. With a shriek, the Fountain collapsed, silver blood flooding from the jagged cut, which was rimmed with green gore.

The low hum cut off abruptly. *The dampening field was gone.*

The Awakener attacked.

A blazing arc of fire lanced across the clearing. It narrowly missed Karic's group and struck the slender robot, lifting it from the ground and sending it back into the defensive shield, where it exploded in a shower of sparks.

Janzen ran for the shield but a burst from the energy weapon struck the ground between him and the lander, knocking him to the ground in an explosion of hot earth. He lay bleeding on the ground, unconscious.

Deadly fragments of rock and stone whistled past them. The three humans all tried to draw their weapons, yet only Karic managed to fire a rocket before they were subdued by a score of Imbirri and pressed to ground under the sheer weight of alien skin and muscle. The rocket flew through the clearing, narrowly missing the massed group of the Imbirri as they pressed in, to explode with a thudding concussion against the stalk of a giant fungus.

The Awakener stepped forward slowly, aiming the scepter at Janzen. But the executive was dead to the world, and the Awakener lifted the weapon without firing it, turning instead to the Utar's chrysalis. He trembled with suppressed emotion.

Karic struggled against the grip of his captors, managing to free his head for long enough to search the clearing for the Fintil. His heart sank as he saw the Fountain's crumpled form. A score of Imbirri now surrounded the body, busily scavenging any devices that remained intact. The robot's laser had cut him in two.

The Imbirri left the Fintil's twisted body lying alone and discarded.

Standing near the bier, the Awakener held the staff aloft. A soft rhythmic sound came from the weapon as the power within it slowly built. His huge eyes were fixed on the hardened shell that contained Utar's remains.

He drew himself up and looked about him in triumph. Karic needed no Imbirri guidebook to see the poise of the victor in the alien leader. He began an impassioned speech in the melodic language of the Imbirri. The other Imbirri listened in awed silence. *He held them all in thrall.*

The Awakener pointed to Utar's chrysalis, his tone now discordant and harsh. He clearly considered it an abomination. He leveled the weapon toward the remains of Utar. His face was alive with power, his eyes glowing bright yellow like twin torch beams, hypnotic. *So Utar will be the first to be destroyed*. Karic let his head sink into the rough Earth. He smelled the pungent, alien odor of the fungi grass, which had been crushed to a pulp beneath him.

Karic looked up. *There must be a way!*

Utar's chrysalis had long ago hardened to a sleek black casing, which had grown more brittle as it dried. Within, a form began to struggle against the skin, seeking to rip through the tough leather-like casing.

The Awakener reached for the stud that would unleash the pent power of the weapon. Nothing remained to challenge him. He was supreme on Cru.

Chapter 19

Karic did not struggle against his captors. Their combined weight, aided by the heavy gravity of Cru, was enough to snap his spine. It was difficult to breathe. In moments, Utar would die, before he could emerge from his chrysalis as an adult Fintil. And with the Fountain dead, the newly born Fintil was their last hope of surviving on Cru. There was only one thing he could do.

Ignoring the pain, he let himself drift into the fugue state. It was waiting for him. His vision swam with familiar patterns. He felt his mind expand, reaching out. He could sense the minds of the Imbirri that held him as dull centers of sentience, but he ignored them. His mind touched the Fountain. He was alive! Struggling to maintain consciousness. Karic twisted his head around. The Fountain was motionless, the jagged wound plugged by a rapidly hardening white resin. Karic marveled at the alien's resilience.

A wild plan formed in Karic's head. If he could distract the Awakener long enough for Utar to emerge and for the Fountain to recover … perhaps together they could stop the Awakener.

Karic reached out toward the Awakener, a ghostly tendril of spirit lancing through the Imbirri like a barbed harpoon. The Awakener gasped in shock and turned toward him. Karic gave him no time to react. He let his spirit swell, forcing the Awakener to link minds with him. A wave of outrage struck Karic across the mental link. The Awakener had none of the Fountain's sophistication and control and could not break the connection. Karic sensed the awesome power of the Awakener's determination. The drive to protect his people at all costs. It was the core of his being, his very purpose for existence.

As he had with the Fountain, he immersed himself in a haze of detail. His mind filled with endless schematics and the complex modeling exercises they carried out on the fusion drive before each test, where the slightest error might create a hydrogen bomb. Memories of the days of testing on the purpose-built shield generators, examining every single circuit, controller, and backup. All etched into his brain through the bright lens of the stim-drugs. He poured it all into the Awakener's mind.

An agonized groan escaped the Awakener's mouth. His finger hesitated above the activating stud, the scepter held immobile as he swayed under the assault. The bright flare of his eyes dimmed to black as his inner vision was swamped by the cascade of weird images.

The gold-crown Imbirri beside the Awakener sang a quick series of notes, and a small group of natives — perhaps those favored few who dwelt with the leader inside their sacred Tree — stepped forward uncertainly. They questioned the Awakener in their mellifluous native language, but when he did not respond, they grew silent, watching him with darkened eyes for any sign or command. The rest of the Imbirri waited patiently for their leader to choose the time of his revenge, content to watch the glorious moment suspended in time.

The Awakener's mind, having grown like a spreading tree through the centuries, now drew from deep roots that sank into the very soul of Cru.

Karic had a sudden sense of the power of the Awakener. He experienced the same awe and fear as a whaler of the 19th century may have felt as their huge prey turned on their fragile wooden longboat in fury. Instinctively, he tried to sever the connection. It was too late. The Imbirri's mind swelled around him, holding Karic in place.

A torrent of flame filled Karic's vision. White-hot pain shot along every nerve, from the tips of his fingers and toes to his head. His mouth opened in a silent scream. Once, on holidays years ago, he had been stung by a stingray. The nerve toxin had left him in excruciating pain for days. This was ten times that intensity. His brain was on fire with it.

Karic clung desperately to consciousness. He knew that every moment he distracted the Awakener increased their chances. Wave upon wave crashed down. Karic endured it all. He stood like a naked child against the Awakener's fury. Karic's strength was failing, while the Awakener, sensing victory, grew stronger. His power was immense. The Imbirri leader drew back, gathering for a renewed assault.

Karic's vision cleared for a moment.

The Awakener towered over him, the scepter held loosely and forgotten in his hands as he focused his huge, pulsing eyes on Karic.

The Fountain had crawled to the struggling form of Utar, pulling himself forward on slender arms, using his wings as crutches, dragging his thorax and severed abdomen behind him. His once sleek body was ruined and silver blood streaked his damaged torso around the resin plug. The Fountain drew himself up and rested against the chrysalis. His eyes glittered with determination. He laid his slim hands on the dark leather. The form within Utar's chrysalis ceased to struggle, calmed by the Fountain's touch. The gathered Imbirri drew back in fear from the Fintil. Some even cried out to the Awakener, but their leader remained silent, his expression rigid as a death mask as his mind descended on Karic once more.

Karic's strength flowed back. *My plan is working.* He turned to the Awakener, determined to hold him for as long as he could. His vision fled once more, lost in flames of white and orange. And the pain returned. His teeth clenched shut in a convulsive reflex, and he tasted blood.

Then a miracle.

Nearby, there was a sudden flowering of spirit. A wave of intense joy that flooded both his and the Awakener's mind. *The Fountain.* All three of them were linked mind-to-mind. The Awakener ceased his attack. Karic laughed with relief at the absence of pain.

Karic's vision cleared once more. The Awakener had turned to face the bier, the scepter loose in his big hand. Silence filled the clearing. Above them, the shield embraced the sky, shimmering violet.

The Fountain swayed back, lifting the razor tip of a wing to the tough casing. With a swift movement, the Fountain ripped through the enclosing sheath.

The Fountain sang out in a pure voice, a long series of notes full of power and beauty. There was a silent pause, as though the planet itself drew breath. Then Utar's golden form rose gracefully from the bier. He looked around the clearing with perfect, glistening eyes and extended his wings, which were still wet from the Change. They spread exquisitely, patterned symmetrically like stained glass. The facets caught the light in a dazzling display.

Utar's mind expanded, reaching out to them. Now all four of them were linked.

The scepter fell from the Awakener's slackened grip. His shoulders slumped forward in shock.

Utar looked at each of them.

"I have been Imbirri," sent Utar, his thoughts clear and dazzling. "I recall this, and all that I have been. Yet now I am ... changed."

"You are Fintil," sent the Fountain in awe. "Never before has one of our race remembered their pre-Change life."

The Imbirri around Utar looked upon him with fear and awe, trapped within his gaze. He turned to them and sang in the language of the Imbirri.

"I am Utar."

As though a storm had broken, the other Imbirri howled in fear and fled, leaving only the Awakener, the three humans, and the two Fintil behind. Karic felt a wave of blessed relief as his captors released him.

The Fountain used his wings to push himself upright. He carefully picked up the fallen scepter then turned back to Utar. "You ... you're *magnificent!* A male — and no innocent — you recall thousands of years of sentience!"

The older Fintil drew his ruined body toward Utar. "I am the Fountain."

Karic picked himself up off the ground and dusted himself off. He watched the Awakener warily. The big Imbirri's eyes were dark, and he was swaying slightly from side to side.

Utar and the Fountain shared in a silent moment of recognition, then the Fountain helped the newly born Fintil from the discarded casing and led him from the bier. There was a rapid mental communication between them that Karic was locked out of.

The Fountain turned to Karic. "One of you almost brought us to ruin, and yet, once more you have saved us all." Karic could feel the Fountain's joy, now that he knew the future of his race was assured, and his gratitude. "Your attack on the Awakener was impressive, and I am reassured. Your mind, human, is close to being fully developed. This could mean only one thing: your race is at the point of transformation. The Elders will take a much kinder view of this. Mental contact between the Fintil and a race without true mental powers — a pre-transformation species — would be a far graver crime."

Karic struggled to follow the Fountain's reasoning. *Transformation*, as the Fountain understood it, seemed to be related to the development of certain mental powers within a species, yet weren't his own simply an accident?

"You represent a seed from which a transformation will spread through the fertile minds of your planet. There is now hope that your race will be fully transformed before you encroach upon the star-systems of another confederation."

The Awakener's eyes flickered with yellow lights. The big Imbirri shivered, and the great folds of skin danced on his frame. His huge chest heaved with short, rapid breaths. He turned toward the two Fintil, his big face writhing in fear. His gaze settled on Utar.

The Fountain watched the Awakener carefully.

All four of them were still linked mind-to-mind, within the compass of Utar's power.

The Fountain smiled and turned away. "The next generation will now take over." With a soft cry of pain, the Fountain sunk to the ground, the pain in his body too much to bear any longer.

Utar walked forward gracefully. "Awakener. It is I."

The Awakener backed away. "No! You were killed!"

Utar smiled. "Come to me, my friend, and sleep in my embrace." He opened his slender golden arms.

The Awakener trembled. His eyes pulsed with sadness. "For so long I have buried the grief of your passing ... I tried to burn it with fires of revenge." The Awakener bellowed. It was a sad, mournful sound. "Utar, I have killed. So many Imbirri ... so many. Dead under my hand. Each face comes back to me like a curse. I just wanted to protect them. I wanted the Imbirri to live."

"I, too, was wrong. I saw that the path lay sundered. I saw the passing of the Imbirri as our end ... but it was not the dark tide, my old friend. It was the bright tide, drawing us into the future. Do not resist it. Do not resist."

The Awakener stood motionless as Utar gently folded his golden limbs around him, pressing his mandibles against the Awakener's lips in one last chaste kiss.

"Sleep, my friend. Sleep. And awake reborn."

The Awakener fell to the ground. His skin was already flecked with the thick, green mucus of the Change.

Mara and Andrai, helpless spectators throughout the confrontation, now came to stand with Karic.

Karic felt the familiar touch of Utar's mind.

"I am responsible for the damage to your ship and killing your comrades," said Utar. "This I regret deeply. Yet now I know my actions were part of a deeper destiny. We owe you much, human. Without you and the violence your arrival brought, the Changes banished for so long by our Elixir would never have been given a chance to emerge. The Fintil would have been lost to the universe as the Imbirri faded into death and stagnation."

Karic looked at the body of the Awakener, now consumed by the Changes, then at the Fountain. The ancient Fintil was in a deep swoon. The Fintil, once so powerful, now seemed broken and small.

"Will he survive?" asked Karic.

Utar walked over to the Fountain and prized the scepter gently from his grasp. "Do not concern yourself for the old Fountain. The Fintil Old Ones have the ability to shed their broken exoskeleton, growing another. Within a few sleep cycles he will emerge once more, whole."

Karic took a deep breath, letting it out slowly. "And the rest of the Imbirri?"

Utar turned his elegant golden head and swept the valley with his gaze, his mandibles moving to give the illusion of a smile. The jeweled eyes fixed on Karic's. "Those of the Imbirri who fled at my rebirth will soon succumb to the Changes. The physical drive to transformation has been building in the Imbirri for some time. The pheromones released here — and the use of Fintil telepathy — will now trigger an unstoppable cascade."

Utar and Karic shared a silent moment. A burgeoning joy grew from the newly born Fintil, encompassing them both like the breath of a god.

"Soon, this valley will be filled with new life. The new birth of our race."

Karic looked back toward Mara and Andrai. Mara's forehead was creased with concern and confusion. So much of this must have been frightening and strange to her. Andrai was stunned.

Utar broke contact with Karic and walked away.

With relief, Karic snapped out of the fugue state.

"What is happening?" said Mara, her voice tight with tension.

"The Fountain has been badly wounded, but he will survive. Utar has been reborn — and he has his Imbirri memories."

Karic looked over at the still form of Janzen and felt a rush of anger. Yet again, Janzen had almost destroyed them all. He walked toward him and stood over him. He felt like kicking the bastard. His face, arms, and chest were covered with blood. At first it looked bad, but most were small cuts except for a wound on his temple where a big rock had broken the skin, knocking him unconscious.

Mara pushed her fingers under his chin, feeling for the carotid pulse. "There's a strong beat. We should get him back inside the enclosure."

Carefully, the three maneuvered his inert form into the lander.

When they had him laid out, Karic took Janzen's odin from his shiny pocket sheath and put it on the floor.

"What are you doing, Karic?"

"What I should have done months ago." He brought the heel of his boot down on the data-glasses with a satisfying crunch. "Bind him and gag him."

"But he's wounded!" protested Mara.

"I don't care if he is dying. I will not give him the chance to activate any more hidden codes or programs. We *will* bind and gag him, Mara. And he will stay that way until we are on our way back to Earth."

"We should at least dress his wounds," said Mara.

"Agreed," said Karic.

Karic stared at Janzen, struggling against his fury. He watched in silence as Andrai and Mara cleaned and bandaged the cuts.

"Let me know the moment he regains consciousness. He has a transmission to make back to Earth."

Karic stalked out the cabin, burning off some of the anger and frustration as he paced outside. The defeat of the Awakener was not the end of the threat to their success here on Cru, and now more than ever they had to be cautious. Mara was both wary and frightened by his new powers. Andrai had not passed judgment — yet. He knew enough of leadership to realize that any deep division between them now could threaten their survival. He would need to reestablish the trust between them.

He had undergone a drastic change, his mind opening in a frightening way with new abilities. Yet he felt no fear of these new ways. Mara could have no conception of what had taken place. To her, it must seem bewildering, the silent conversations like the talk of ghostly statues. Yet the possibilities ... Could what the Fountain said be true? Would it be possible to mind-bond with Mara and Andrai? To not only share these abilities but to stimulate them, to give them to others? To begin this transformation the Fountain talked of? The use of the powers was exhausting, but also addictive in its intensity. Part of him ached to be able to share this remarkable gift.

Besides, there was only one way to truly make them understand. Karic had to mind-bond with them.

Chapter 20

Karic watched Mara as she balanced her plate on her knees. She looked up at the dark sky and sighed. After Utar's rebirth, they had taken a rest period and emerged for "breakfast" in the bright light of the transmission node. They had moved their campsite back inside the barrier. It was cramped. The shield itself reduced the air exchange, making it even hotter than the parched valley outside. But it was safe. Surrounded by these inexplicable, unpredictable aliens, they all felt the need for some security. Now, privy to the knowledge of the Imbirri-Fintil lifecycle, they were more aware than ever of the Fintil technology that surrounded them — soon to be reclaimed by a new generation of Fintil adults. If not for the vast terraforming of the dark side, and the radiant energy from the ubiquitous transmission nodes, it would have been a frigid, frozen wasteland here.

Janzen had never regained consciousness. Despite Mara's protests, Karic had put him into stasis. This time he had completely isolated the suspension gear from the ship's computer. There was no way he would be surprised by Janzen's tricks again.

Karic put down his plate, unsatisfied as usual with the protein-enhanced meal pack. Noting that both Andrai and Mara were also finished, he stood up. He watched them carefully as they sipped on their precious ration of reconstituted coffee. After a long moment, he cleared his throat, struggling for words, suddenly unsure. No. There was no other way. He plunged straight into it.

"By now you have probably both seen me using my mind to communicate with the Fintil."

"Telepathy," said Andrai.

"Yes, it is a form of telepathy. I ... well let's just say I never realized it, but I have a gift for it. It has been building up since the deaths on the *Starburst*."

Karic thought of the descent in the pod, the strange new way that the fugue state fused with the reality of the here-and-now — but there was no easy way to explain that.

"I guess it really snapped into place when I was taken by the Imbirri. That was the first time I used it consciously, to communicate with Utar. The Fintil also have this gift. According to them, it makes them what they call 'transformed sentients'."

"What do you mean by that?" asked Mara.

"Enhanced mental powers for a start. Beyond that, I'm not sure," said Karic. "But there's one thing the Fountain has said: if a species is on the point of transformation, once they experience the mental bond, their own minds will transform."

"And they will also be able to use this gift?" asked Andrai.

Karic nodded. "Yes."

"Why are you telling us this?" Mara paled.

Karic was silent for a long moment, then smiled. "Because I want to mind-bond with each of you."

Andrai nodded slowly, his eyes speculative as he considered the idea.

Mara edged away from Karic, then stopped, looking straight into his eyes. "God, Karic! I can't believe you are persisting with this!"

"You cannot possibly deny what you have seen," said Karic, gesticulating passionately with his hands, as though he could convince her with his conviction alone. "I *do* have this ability, Mara. I want to share it."

He stepped toward her eagerly, his mind — so alive with the recent contact with the Fintil — unconsciously reached out toward her. Her mouth opened slightly, and her eyes began to glaze over. A fraction of a second later, the contact was broken and her eyes darted around, as though looking for escape. Karic took another step toward her, and she leapt to her feet so suddenly her plate shot into the barrier, where it was deflected in a shower of sparks.

"*No!*" Mara ran to the lander and disappeared inside the hatch.

Andrai watched her go, his expression resigned. "If you think we should do this, boss, I'm willing to try," he said. "But I have to warn you — I am about as psychic as a rock."

Karic sat down in front of Andrai. The tech relaxed and closed his eyes. Karic reached for Andrai's mind. The surging rhythm that Karic knew so well rose from the unconscious depths of the tech's mind like a snake from the basket of a snake-charmer. Soon, their two minds rippled in sympathy. After all the mind-bonding with the aliens, it felt so *right* to Karic, like slipping on a glove. Humans were meant to communicate this way. Andrai's mind was uncluttered, as neatly organized as his tool bench on the *Starburst*. Karic felt a deep sense of peace within the man.

"Andrai, can you hear my thoughts?" sent Karic.

Karic felt surprise, then humor.

Yes. It seems you weren't crazy after all.

Andrai tried to send another thought. It was lost in a confused swirl of other competing cognition. Was this how the Fintil saw Karic's mind? He was lost in a storm of images and random thoughts that slowly cleared. He had the sense that with practice he could delve deeper, but that was not his intent.

Karic's temples pulsed with the effort of concentration. The strain of keeping the bond open was starting to tell. Although Andrai's mind was capable of the bond, all the energy that stimulated those crucial areas of Andrai's brain was coming from Karic himself. In effect, Karic's nervous system was powering two brains, each working at ten times their normal output. Once he realized this, Karic concentrated on stemming the flow of energy, to see if Andrai could sustain it on his own. As soon as the flow of energy ceased, the beautiful surging and flowing patterns that Andrai's mind had been radiating faded away. Within seconds, Karic could sense Andrai's mind as nothing more than a dull center of sentience, similar to the simpler Imbirri.

Karic broke the bond. He rubbed at his temples, which throbbed with pain. "Talking is easier."

"Wow! What a high." Andrai's eyes were alert, and he looked about him as though he had never seen the campsite before. "Everything is so clear. My mind. My mind is … is *singing*, Karic. Why did you stop?"

There clearly *had* been a transfer of energy. But would this be enough to nudge Andrai's mind into the transformation the Fountain had spoken of?

Karic stood up and looked across to the lander. "Andrai."

"Yeah, boss," said Andrai, sipping his coffee once more and watching the light from the transmission node with simple, innocent delight. "It's like a kaleidoscope!"

Karic fought down a sudden tension, and stuck to his plan. "I am going to try and bond with Mara. Can you wait here for me?"

Andrai gave Karic a frankly assessing look, and Karic realized that things had progressed further between Andrai and Mara than he had thought. "OK. I'll be waiting," he said eventually.

Andrai turned back to the transmission node and Karic started walking toward the lander. It had to be done. Besides, if there was ever going to be a chance to restore what was between him and Mara, this was it. His heart raced, and his eyes searched her out eagerly.

***

Mara watched Karic as he made his way toward the core section. From a distance, he looked like the same man she had always known. How she wanted to believe he was. She had at last acknowledged what she had tried to ignore: Karic was no longer just human, he was now something more. She had not wanted to believe it, but she had seen him talk with the aliens mind-to-mind and been witness to those strange moments when his eyes seemed to glow. Now Karic had begun to infect Andrai with this same change.

And he wanted to *mind-bond* with her? Of all the things she wanted to do since they ended their affair it was to put distance between them, not let him closer.

When he had reached for her moments ago, a pressure started to build in her mind, a surging rhythm like the swirling patterns of light that preceded sleep. As his eyes bored into her, he seemed close, as though he were standing only inches away, though he had not moved from the other side of the fire. The pressure had grown until there was a high-pitched ringing. It had been a sickening feeling, like her mind wanted to escape the boundaries of her vision, her reason.

Karic entered the lander.

She forced herself to begin some work at her station. Her hands shook too much to hit the keys. Behind her, she could feel him drawing closer and desperately strove to quiet her fear. Her instant reaction was to fight, to hurt him with a sharp remark, but she was tired of fighting. For months she had lashed out at Karic rather than deal with the complex knot of feelings he evoked.

She turned to face him.

For the first time since he left on that publicity tour with Evelle, she looked Karic in the eye and let herself feel the pain inside her. He had crushed her, destroying the delicate flower of their passion. She had never loved anyone before. After a life dedicated to science and ambition, driven by her domineering, yet distant parents, she didn't think she was capable of it. It had been such a joy. An incredible gift. She had not had the faintest idea how to deal with the desperate heartache she experienced when Karic left with Evelle on the publicity tour. The pain of it still nestled inside her, like a cancer.

All she wanted now was distance. Isolation. To reconnect with the foundations of her life and the only certainty she had known.

"Mara." Karic's eyes were at first hopeful, filled with the fire of determination. Then they became strange, expanding into the space around her.

"What's happened to you, Karic? What have these aliens done to you?"

His eyes resumed their normal focus.

"It began long before I came to Cru," he said, looking out the lander's viewport at the surface of the planet. "Being here in this world, and in the presence of beings such as the Fountain and Utar ..." Karic turned away from the sparse vista outside the lander and looked directly at her. The intensity was back in his eyes: a fierce hunger that frightened her. "It triggered some abilities in me. Things I would never have guessed were possible. Incredible things."

"Karic, listen to me. They have brainwashed you. You can't even see the changes in yourself. What have they told you? What have they turned you into?"

Karic took her hands and she let him guide her up out of the padded console chair to face him. Mara was conscious of Janzen's immobile form stretched out on the suspension couch — even though he would be incapable of perceiving them in any way. The cabin, strewn with boxes and supplies, seemed suddenly cramped. The bright, white lights reflected from the squared edges of the console's silvered surfaces like blades, stabbing into her vision.

His closeness was unbearable. But she had to endure it. If she truly wanted to take control of her life, she had to face him. Rejecting him had not ended it. It had only fueled his continued pursuit. She had to face down the past and see it finished. How far would she go to convince him it was over?

"Mara, these aliens have not made me do anything. They themselves have been reluctant to communicate with us. But, Mara," said Karic, unable to keep the passion out of his voice, "they are going to return us to the *Starburst!* Don't forget they are helping us back to Earth. They don't want us on this planet any more than we want to stay here."

"But we can't trust them!"

"Yes, Mara. I believe we can."

"Damn you, Karic! Why should they care about Earth, or the human race? This *transformation* you are talking about. It will destroy us. They know it. We are not ready for it. That's why they are letting you go."

That hit the mark. She could see the doubt in his eyes and felt a savage satisfaction, closely followed by guilt. She hated herself for being like this. That's why she just wanted him gone from her life.

She studied his face. A face that had always been honest and open, now gaunt with exhaustion, the cheekbones sharper than ever, his wavy brown hair wild and unkempt. She saw the lines of tension, the pain he had undergone. Karic pulled her closer. Their faces were inches away. She knew how much he wanted her. But as much as she cared for him, the passionate love she had felt was gone. It had died in the midst of her desperate heartache.

"I can't love you anymore," she whispered. "I'm sorry, Karic. But I can't. Not now. Not ever."

Karic bowed his head, touching the top of her head with his temple and breathing in the scent of her hair. "I should never have left you alone. You know I never betrayed you with Evelle."

"It's all in the past now. You deserve someone stronger than me, Karic. I reacted badly. I just couldn't help it.

"Just let me go." She was desperate to pull away, but she let him embrace her.

He pushed her to arm's length and looked into her eyes. "So I have lost you anyway." His eyes filled with pain and resignation.

Mara felt tears on her cheek and let them flow. She had to see this out. "Yes," she whispered.

His hands still held hers, his rough fingers softly playing over her own.

His eyes flowed over her face, her hair, her neck. His desperation filled the space between them.

Karic's dark brown eyes found hers once more, the ones she had once found so warm and enticing. Now his eyes were large … strange. His essence engulfed her, wrapping around her with ghostly fingers that made the hair on her skin stand up. Her heart beat like a wild bird trapped in her chest, but she did not flinch. If this is what is took, she would do it. She was strong enough to see it through.

Mara let her awareness flow outward. Their minds swelled like mist behind their vision and fled along the linked arms of spirit. She could feel Karic inside her, while thoughts and images from his mind flooded into hers — the Fountain's offer, the chance to explore space that he had forgone, his dedication to get her and Andrai back to Earth. She was filled with panic. *Her thoughts would also be this exposed.* Karic's mind reached for hers — eagerly searching.

"No!" She dropped Karic's hands and jerked back. The bond ripped away and her mind was hers again.

"I'm sorry Mara, I … I will not touch your mind again," said Karic. His head sank toward his chest.

"You know now that we are over for good," said Mara.

He looked at her with hurt in his eyes, and she felt cruel. "Yes. I know."

They heard the scrape of a boot on the floor of the lander and turned to see Andrai walk through the hatch. The blond tech was watching them carefully, light gray eyes flicking between them. "I … ah, thought you would be finished."

"No problem," said Karic. "We are."

"So, when are the Fintil going to get us back to the *Starburst*?" asked Andrai. His voice was uncharacteristically strained, and he seemed tense. Jumpy.

Karic took a deep breath and massaged the back of his neck with his hand. "We probably have a few days until the Fountain emerges from his cocoon with a regenerated body. Then we should be able to leave as soon as he can organize it. I'm sure the Fintil will be eager to get us off Cru for good."

"Seems a shame to leave. After all, we just got here," said Andrai with a quick smile. Mara touched him gently on the arm.

Karic tensed, a frown creasing his face for a moment. Then it was gone.

Mara leaned into Andrai's body, feeling the solid warmth. She was safe with him — and in control.

"I think we better leave as soon as we can. I wouldn't want to outstay our welcome," said Karic. "The old Fountain will regenerate, despite the damage to his shell, but what if something else should happen to him? Will the young Fintil honor the agreement?"

Mara hoped so. She wanted to leave Cru behind. To return to Earth and try and recapture some sense of a normal life.

"OK. I guess we better get back to work," said Karic.

Andrai and Mara began salvaging their data on the planet, which had been automatically backed up from both the pod's and lander's sensors onto the lander's hard-drives. She saw Andrai relax as he grew absorbed in the task. As they worked together, side-by-side, Karic grew increasingly restless.

"I'll be outside," said Karic, ducking through the twisted metal of the hatch.

Mara sighed with relief. *Thank God that's over.*

When he was gone, she leaned over and gave Andrai a warm kiss, feeling his soft lips beneath hers.

"So did you mind-bond?" asked Andrai. His eyes were lit with a peculiar gleam.

Mara hesitated, unsure how to answer. She and Karic had bonded, not long enough to communicate mind-to-mind, but long enough for her to realize what an intrusion it felt like. The surging rhythms seemed to boil in the back of her mind, waiting for a chance to leap outward. "Just for a brief moment. But it's not something I want to try again. I just don't think human beings are ready for that sort of honesty."

Andrai frowned, clearly disappointed.

"What's wrong?" she demanded.

"I … was just hoping you might want to try it with me?" Andrai left the question hanging.

Mara balked, her fear cresting like a wave. "We should finish this."

Andrai's face fell, but he turned back to his console without comment.

***

Karic was shaken by Mara's final refusal.

He stalked across the campsite and deactivated the defensive shield, leaving the safety of the shielded enclosure. He needed to get some distance. Just to see them working so well together … He knew it was time to put it behind him, and yet … if only he could truly mind-bond with her! He felt sure she would finally see what he felt. Felt sure it would change everything.

He growled deep in his throat. Despite his desires, he had to respect her wishes. He was her commander, after all. His leadership had to come first. He would not mention it again.

The valley was silent. The endless rustling that had filled the dark was gone — the myriad creatures having fled to the shadows beyond the valley. The huge fungi, which once seemed to swell and crowd together like mysterious beings, now appeared smaller, more spread apart, like sickly cactus in a desert of black, stony soil.

He had changed. He had abilities that gave him new strength. He could see more in the world, more within people, than ever before. It seemed natural. An extension of the same interactions that had always marked humanity. Yet there was a difference. It was harder to lie. Silence was the only deceit — the absence of truth.

Karic walked to the prone form of the Fountain. He gingerly touched the splintered shell. The bright coloration had faded from the exoskeleton, leaving it transparent. Beneath, he glimpsed the soft gold of another form emerging. New life. It surrounded them. Karic turned and walked to the bier. The chrysalises of Utar's two companions were darkening rapidly, hurtling toward rebirth as adult Fintil.

Stifling his fear, Karic walked toward the Awakener's cocoon.

The Awakener's huge body was now fully within the grip of the Changes. Even though the sticky green mucus had already hardened, the form continued to grow and stretch, swelling with power. It dwarfed the smaller cocoons of Utar's acolytes. Unnerved, he turned away.

He looked up to the dark blue sky above, thinking of the boundless mysteries of space beyond Cru. What had he given up to return Andrai and Mara to Earth? Had he truly lost his chance to explore space?

***

Mara stood beside the chrysalis of the Awakener, one slender hand on the heaving bulk of the black cocoon. Her heart hammered, and she fought to control her breathing.

It was the middle of her rest period, and she was supposed to be sleeping. Yet every time she had tried to reach for sleep, those surging, boiling rhythms would be waiting for her, filling the empty corridors of her mind with strange sensations. Visions of green jungles and hot suns. She had tried to let it loose, as though that would allow her to drift to sleep, but immediately her spirit had swept outward, locking onto the huge form of the Awakener's cocoon. She had tried to block it out, but could not. As though in a dream, she had deactivated the defensive shield — leaving it open — and walked barefoot across the ragged earth to kneel beside the chrysalis. Her mind was alive with an energy she had never felt before. A pent force suddenly unleashed. Now it swept around the huge form, engulfing it, embracing it. And the power coming off the huge cocoon fueled her own mind in turn.

She could feel the spirit within the chrysalis. It was drawing the essence of life toward it like a greedy child. The presence was strong and filled with a sweet, sad longing. Mara was momentarily overwhelmed with a feeling of incompleteness. Her womb was unbearably empty, aching like these transformed Imbirri for new life. Tears fled from her face and she keened like a banshee, lost within the mind-bond.

She longed to see the Sun. To stare through the softly swaying branches of spring at the full moon, to feel the subtle pull of her planet, and breathe the sweet air of *home*. To join with the spirit of Earth, taste her fruits and give birth. She had locked herself away behind steel walls. But she had not died. She had grown stronger. Mara ached for a child, and her tears would not stop.

Realizing the essence of the Changes was overwhelming her, Mara drew back into herself and opened her eyes. Yet the feeling was not to be so easily banished. Something in the essence of the Awakener had touched her, like a sister . . . yes, the spirit was definitely female. Mara drew herself away from the fallen form of the Awakener and returned to the campsite. On the verge of the defensive shield, she turned and watched the cocoon as it trembled and swelled. She felt a deep empathy with the being. What had the Awakener ever done except try to protect the Imbirri, her children?

Mara took a deep breath and reentered the shield, shocked that she had not thought to reactivate it. Inside the enclosure, she straightened her torn uniform jacket, tightening the fit around her using the smart seams, despite the oppressive heat from the transmission node. She worked her loose hair into a series of braids, focused on the stark metal hull of the lander, forcing herself back to reality before she entered the craft, before either of the two men could see her.

They all had their tasks cut out for them, and if working hard would bring them that much closer to Earth, then she would work like a demon. To think she may have never felt Earth's touch again ... Her feelings were overwhelming, but she could not give in. Not yet. If she did she would fly apart. Whatever Karic had done had released more than these strange gifts. She had to hold herself together.

Especially now.

In a little under two hours, they were going to rouse Janzen. Now *that* would be interesting.

Chapter 21

"You both ready?" asked Karic.

Andrai nodded grimly, while Mara tightened her grip on the XR32, her eyes fixed on the still form of Janzen.

"OK."

The suspension field surrounding Janzen had been cycling down for the last hour, and was holding at the last threshold, waiting for his command.

Karic tapped a short coded sequence into the manual keypad and the ghostly field vanished. "OK, Andrai."

Andrai stepped forward with a small vial and cracked it under Janzen's nose. The sharp smell of ammonia and a cocktail of other more exotic stimulants flooded the cabin. Karic blinked his eyes against the sting.

A few seconds later Janzen's eyes flew open. He looked wildly around the cabin taking in all three of them, then tried to sit up. For a few moments, he struggled furiously with his bonds. His face was as white as chalk, the plastered cuts stark against the pasty skin. His struggles ceased as recognition lit within his eyes. He sagged back and his face flushed red.

Janzen tried to talk through the gag.

"I'm going to remove the gag," said Karic. "But if you try anything — any communication with the computer — it will go straight back on."

Janzen nodded slowly, his eyes filled with familiar assurance and calculation as he looked at each of them in turn.

Karic loosed the gag and Janzen spat it out.

"Your mutiny is over, Karic," said Janzen.

"Really?"

"Yes. If you let me go, I will make sure they will go easy on you when we return to Earth."

Janzen waited for a reaction, but Karic returned his gaze with a steady resolve.

"Now. Get me out of these ties. Mara, Andrai. Come and untie these."

Andrai smiled slightly. Mara's look was icy.

Karic clenched his jaw to contain his fury at Janzen's blatant attempt at manipulation — after he had wanted all three of them dead and out of the way. He counted to five, then spoke in an even tone. "No, Janzen. You are not going anywhere. The only reason I've revived you is so you can make one more transmission back to Earth."

Janzen trembled. "What do you mean?"

"You forgot to delete your message log, genius," said Andrai.

Janzen suddenly surged forward, using his bulk to try and snap the bonds. He was a powerful man — the Davis geneticists had seen to that.

Karic grinned with a savage satisfaction as he saw the look of feral desperation in Janzen's blue eyes. The big man's breaths came in shallow gasps as he strained at the bonds, but his efforts were futile. Karic knew how to tie a knot.

"That's right, Janzen," said Karic. "We know what you said to them."

Janzen looked from one to another, seeking an ally. "You need me!"

"Why is that?" said Karic, keeping himself tightly controlled.

"You will never get off this planet without me. Release me now, or when the rescue ship arrives you will be left here to rot!"

Karic took a deep breath. "There will be no rescue ship. You are going to make one more transmission to Earth, telling them exactly what happened on the *Starburst*. The truth about the Tau Ceti Diversion and your knowledge of the X-ray source that killed the crew. You are then going to tell them about the Imbirri and the Fintil and make sure that no ships are sent. Not a single starship — and certainly no colonization fleet."

"But we need a rescue ship! We need it to get back to Earth."

"Not anymore," said Karic. "One of the Fintil, the one you almost killed — the Fountain — is taking us back up to the *Starburst*."

"No. *No*. This can't be. We have to colonize this world. Don't you see?"

"But this is not our frigging world!" Mara's eyes blazed. "Don't you get that?"

Janzen's classic features twisted into an ugly snarl. "It's our world if we can take it — that's the naked truth of history. You could share in the profits. I would see to it!" Janzen's gaze fixed on Karic. "It's too late anyway. You can't stop the fleet."

"Rubbish. You know how long it takes to prep a ship for an interstellar voyage. And most of the ExploreCorp fleet has been mothballed for over a hundred years. You can easily stop them. And you will."

"*Never.*"

"Oh, I think you will," said Mara.

"And why is that?" Janzen trembled with emotion.

"Because if you don't, we will. And when the Fountain takes us to *Starburst*, you won't be coming with us. I'm sure the Fountain would be only too willing to let you have a bit of local justice."

Mara turned to Karic. "I wonder what the Fintil punishment for murder is?"

Karic smiled grimly. "I would hate to imagine. One thing I know for sure, once all the Fintil are hatched, they will not take kindly to any alien on this planet. Not after everything that's happened."

"You can't do it." Janzen's voice, harsh from strain, was barely above a whisper.

Karic sat down on the couch next to Janzen, who jerked away from the contact, his blue eyes blazing at the familiarity. "Oh, we can. How do you think the ExploreCorp executive will respond to a joint transmission from all of us? A testimonial from three officers you claimed were dead? I'm sure the Fountain would be happy to join us. How do you think they would react to some footage of the transmission nodes, or of the Fountain's devices?"

Janzen glared at Karic, defiant to the end. The contempt in his eyes was tangible. Here, he saw Janzen Davis stripped of pretence, stripped of the charismatic mask and the carefully contrived conviviality that concealed his cold, manipulative mind.

"Who are you? All of you? Low-class drones! Do you know who you are dealing with? *I'm a Davis!*" Janzen's eyes blazed with an unshakable conviction. They had pushed him down to the grimy bedrock of his being. "Do you have any idea what sort of damage I can do to you — to your families?"

"You are a pile of shit strapped to a chair, you bastard!" hissed Mara. Her hand snapped forward to slap at his face with an open-handed palm, put Andrai caught her wrist.

"He's not worth it, Mara," said Andrai, his voice uncharacteristically harsh.

"Go ahead. Hit a bound man. I'd expect nothing less from platform-scum like you, Mara."

She shook off Andrai's hand. "I am what I made myself. Whatever you are was given to you on a silver platter, you prick."

Janzen snorted. "You are what I made you. Or do you think being assigned to the mission was an accident? I needed someone I could control."

Mara's lips drew back in a snarl, ready to fight, but Karic held up his hand to stop her. God help him, he wanted to pound on the bastard himself, but he would not give Janzen the satisfaction of provoking him.

"Enough delaying tactics, Janzen. Either send the transmission or I will leave you here on Cru," said Karic, his heart hammering with adrenaline.

"Do you really want me as an enemy, Karic? Help me colonize this world. The rewards would be immense. *Immense!*"

Karic looked at Janzen, saw the desperation in his eyes. The colonization of this world — the restoration of the Davis fortunes — had been a dream he had lived with so long it had become a delusion.

"Janzen. There is no colony. It's over."

Janzen trembled, sagging back onto the suspension couch. "No."

Karic's determination solidified like new steel emerging from the fires of revenge that forged it. "We *will* leave you behind if you don't cooperate. That *will* be fatal for you, have no doubt. So it's live or die, Janzen. A choice you never gave us. Decide now."

Janzen would not meet Karic's eyes. He mumbled.

242

Karic instinctively leant closer. "What was that?"

"Very well." Janzen's voice was barely above a whisper. Strangely controlled.

Karic felt a surge of relief.

Janzen lifted his head, tilting his chin up to face him.

"I'll do it." He looked at Andrai and Mara, his eyes assessing, calculating. His eyes flicked down to the XR32 in Mara's holster, measuring the distance. "Now let me out of these." His voice was soft, calm. Reasonable. He held up his bound hands.

Karic shook his head. "Oh, no. You will stay right where you are. And after the transmission, you are going straight back into stasis."

Janzen surged forward in a savage headbutt. Karic jerked back in reflex, and Janzen's forehead slammed into his lower lip and chin, rather than his nose, which had been the target.

"*Fuck you*. You overblown tech. Do you think you've got what it takes to fight the Davis family? Do you?" Janzen raved.

"The Davis family is finished, Janzen. We both know that," said Karic, touching his bleeding lower lip with a finger. "We've got you, Janzen. Got you cold. And you are out of dirty tricks."

He waved to Andrai. "Swivel the camera down. Janzen can make the transmission from the suspension couch."

Janzen's eyes bored into Karic's. What Karic saw there was pure hate. And a desperate hunger for power at any cost.

"Do we have the uplink?" he asked Mara.

"Yes, Commander," she replied.

"Start the record." Karic smiled at Janzen, knowing the blood would be staining his teeth. He wore it like a badge of honor.

All three of them glared at Janzen with cold determination, waiting.

Janzen began talking in a flat monotone, like he was dictating to his odin. The words came out in a swift flood, as though he wanted to get an unpleasant task over as quickly as possible. His eyes were glazed, looking into some strange world they could not see. More than a dozen times they had to stop the recording and force him to revise his weasel-words, but eventually they had it — everything. His admission to knowledge of the X-rays from Tau Ceti, and his plan to divert to the system from Epsilon Eridani despite of the risk — basically an admission of guilt in the murder of the thirty-three crew. His attacks on the Imbirri. His falsified reports back to Earth. The truth about Cru, its advanced inhabitants and their technology. Everything.

"Transmit it," said Karic. The lander's cabin, Mara, Andrai and Janzen — everything was outlined in a stunning clarity. He wanted to fix this moment in his mind forever. Justice at last for Evelle, for all those dead crew.

Janzen sagged back, defeated. "Put me under. *Do it.*"

"Finally. A command I can follow," said Mara. "Do you mind, Karic?"

He grinned, gesturing at the controls of the suspension couch. "Be my guest."

Mara's dark eyes fixed on Janzen. "Next time we see you, Davis, it will be with security personnel ready to take you into custody." She activated the fields. "Sweet dreams, scumbag."

As the shimmering, insubstantial fields wrapped around Janzen, his slumped body grew immobile, his defeated posture and haunted face frozen in place like some ghastly, living statue.

"And good riddance," spat Mara. "Now, can we get off this rock?"

***

"Karic, it's the Fountain. He's emerging from his cocoon." Karic and Mara looked up from the lander console to see Andrai in the hatchway, out of breath. He must have run to get there.

"At last," said Karic.

Mara's heart skipped a beat, and she shut down her terminal.

"Maybe now we can get back to *Starburst*," said Karic. "Come on!"

Mara maneuvered around the inert bulk of Janzen's suspension couch, careful not to contact the almost invisible fields. She followed the two men as they made their way through the barrier shield to the bier, where the Fountain had collapsed into his swoon days before. Those days had been tense, and filled with forced activity. In reality, there was little they could do until they returned to the ship. Utar had remained distant, and although they had seen him constantly moving around the valley, they had no further communication from him. It was as though the whole planet held its breath, waiting for the births.

Outside, Mara looked at the quivering form of the Fountain's chrysalis with mixed feelings. She still feared these enigmatic aliens. Even the Fountain, who should be their greatest ally. Beside her, Karic was tense, while Andrai's eyes were alive with wonder.

With a tearing sound, a long split formed in the casing: the Fountain emerged from his transparent cocoon, sleek body glistening in the light of the tower. Torso and limbs bright gold — almost reflective in their newness — and now showing striped highlights of green, red, blue and violet.

Karic stepped toward him. The Fountain turned to watch Karic for a brief moment before turning away.

"I don't think he's interested in conversation," said Andrai.

The Fintil took to the air with one powerful surge. He climbed rapidly, disappearing above them.

"Damn!" cursed Karic.

They knew their time on the planet was drawing to a close. Fate had led them to Cru, drawing them into the middle of a crisis for the Imbirri. But now the Imbirri were gone — transformed by the Changes — and the Fintil who would emerge in their place would not know them. They would be intruders, aliens who were forbidden on this ancient planet by the Har Confederation, of which the Fintil race was a member. Karic was silent and tense as they returned to the lander to continue working on the systems that ran the suspension gear.

Later, as Mara was outside the lander adjusting the uplink, she became aware of a presence nearby. She turned to see the Fountain just outside the shield. A shock of fear went through her at the sight of the tall alien. Mara had not seen him return from his flight, or heard him approach, but there he was, his new body glistening like a finely wrought, golden statue. Mara looked into the dark, glittering eyes — as perfect as jewels — and sensed the gentle power of his spirit swelling within him, as though waiting for a subtle signal from her before reaching outward. She was touched with a sense of an almost seductive, illicit possibility.

Her own mind still surged with strange rhythms, fueled by the rebirth around her. She had vowed never to mind-bond again, but the Fountain, unlike Karic or Andrai, would not pass judgment on her thoughts in the personal way her human companions would.

Mara subdued her fear and stepped toward the barrier.

The Fountain let his spirit swell toward her. She felt a wave of liquid gold, bereft of heat, yet charged with alien emotion.

The connection formed.

"I am ready to return you to your ship. But first I must wait for the rebirth of the Awakener as an adult Fintil. The time of the birth is very near and I dare not be absent," thought the Fountain across the bridge of minds.

Mara was spellbound by the intensity of the union, the wonderful simplicity of it.

"I understand," said Mara, awed by the experience. She tried to concentrate and focus on her thoughts.

The pressure of the Fountain's mind increased, pressing deeper. Mara felt images and feelings stir, rising to the surface, fleeing across the bridge toward him. Suddenly, she realized he was probing her mind, drawing forth her own memories and impressions against her will. She reacted instinctively, withdrawing her mind and severing the link.

The Fountain recoiled in surprise, then clicked his mandibles.

Cautiously, she let the bond establish once more. This time he made no attempts to probe deeper. The Fountain was irritated at the enforced restraint, she could sense it immediately.

"I will transport you to your ship in the large craft, the one you call the lander. The other must be left, and will be destroyed. Be prepared."

The Fintil stalked away.

Mara laughed, exhilarated. She had communicated telepathically with an alien! She felt dizzy and put her hand out against the metal struts of the uplink array to steady herself. Not only had she done it, she had controlled it. The Fountain had been unable to force her. She realized she would always be able to sense what others were seeing in her own mind as her thoughts crossed the threshold of consciousness between them. She would always be able to fight to keep the greater part of her mind her own. The potential for mental violation was still frightening to her, and in that way, the gift was a mixed blessing. Another jaded pearl from Pandora's Box.

She knew the human voice would never be replaced. Its warmth, its economy, was so natural, so easy ... and mental communication was exhausting. Yet the power to communicate in this way was transformative, allowing mankind to reach beyond boundaries that were otherwise insurmountable. Races and species with no common bond of language could use it to made their first contact, as had the humans and the Fintil — without danger of misunderstanding, with spirits joined in harmony ... It truly was the gift of a starfaring species.

Mara turned back toward the lander and saw Andrai approach across the clearing. He grinned and she returned his smile.

"Having a little chat?" said Andrai.

Mara laughed. "Yes."

"It's weird, isn't it?" said Andrai.

"I've got to tell Karic what he said. Can you finish adjusting the uplink?"

"Sure," replied Andrai, bending to the task.

Inside the lander, Karic was working on the final adjustments to the suspension gear. Three other couches were now set up beside Janzen's, taking up every piece of spare floor space. He looked up, eager for news.

"The Fountain spoke to you?"

"Yes. He is ready to take us back to the *Starburst*, but wants to wait until the rebirth of the Awakener. He insists we travel in the lander and leave the pod behind."

Karic's eyes shone. "He must mean to lift the lander into orbit. The core section computer already holds all the data. And it has the suspension gear.

"We should send all the data we have up to the *Starburst* through the uplink. Our presence on Cru may be some violation of the Fintil's code, but I am determined that our observations on this world reach Earth as soon as possible. I am not taking any chances."

"I'll let Andrai know," said Mara. "In a way, I'm glad we are staying for the birth. I want to see what the Awakener has become."

Karic nodded thoughtfully. "Yes, I am curious as well. Although in some ways, I would be happier if we were all gone from Cru before the Awakener emerges as a Fintil."

Mara knew what he meant. The Awakener *had* been their greatest enemy on Cru.

"I'll find Andrai and get to work transferring the data," said Mara.

"OK," said Karic. He gave her a long searching look, which she ignored. She left him alone inside the lander and rushed over to Andrai.

They were going home.

***

The Fountain swept through the clouds, reveling in the feeling of freedom. These were strange times. Strange and wonderful. He and his people had survived, and a new, reinvigorated generation of Fintil rapidly approached the time of their birth. His new belt was heavy with devices, some recovered from the valley near the Fintil cocoons — dropped by fleeing Imbirri as they succumbed to the changes — others replaced from hidden stockpiles beneath the transmission node. He would not be surprised again.

Around him the winds were cool, the sky dark, unfettered.

He had deactivated the shield over the valley, then increased the output of the fusion generators, pumping radiant energy through the transmission node in waves. This would draw in any Fintil birthed outside the valley.

The Fintil had to be allowed to develop in peace, and the humans dealt with as planned. They had proved to be dangerous, and divided in purpose, but he expected little else from a pre-transformation species. If not for the hasty bargain made with Karic on the peak, he would have destroyed them long ago. As it was, he had to adapt his strategy. Karic assured him the human who almost killed him had been subdued and placed in stasis, and would be dealt with by human justice on their return to Earth. He believed Karic's intentions were pure, yet mistrusted his ability to control the outcome. Other measures were necessary.

He had planned to send the humans on their way well before the new Fintil awoke, but he had not anticipated being injured and forced into an extended period of regeneration. He ground his mandibles together in irritation. Now it was too close to the time of rebirth to even consider removing them.

The Fountain had discussed the humans with the talented newly born Fintil, Utar, whom he had now adopted as his protégé, and knew he would support releasing them from the planet, yet the final outcome was far from certain. Once the new race of Fintil hatched he would no longer be the undisputed master of Cru. In the rigid Fintil hierarchy, it was the most senior female who ruled. It was possible she could sway the Fintil against him and have the humans destroyed.

His wings beat furiously with the thought, and he stilled them with an effort of will.

Unacceptable.

It was essential that the four humans be returned to their home world. He had removed the scepter and done everything in his power to ensure there was no technology that the newborn Fintil could seize that would seriously challenge the humans, yet still … what if the leading female should set Utar against him? He must prevent it at all costs. He must be ready to act.

He forced himself to be calm. All was going well. Now, the human female, the one called Mara, had the gift. It was a promising sign. The Fountain chittered happily. The next voyage of the human ship would be to Earth — carrying the precious cargo of transformation. Once in the midst of such cataclysmic change, the human race would cease to be a threat for a long, long time — if they survived at all.

Should more human exploration ships come searching through Cru's system, they would be turned away by a shield of illusion. Their sensors would show them an unstable system filled with deadly radiation. A system with nothing of interest or value. If these exploration ships should pierce Cru's deceptions and concealing shields — they would be destroyed without mercy. No trace of them would remain.

He was high above the valley. It was cold here, and the ceaseless storms of the upper atmosphere thundered above his head.

The Fountain shortened his wings and turned into a steep dive.

He had done all he could. One way or another, the problem of the humans would be solved. Then he would remain on as a guide for those that came after — the Fountain of knowledge. He would grapple with his crimes against the Har Confederation in due course.

The ground rushed toward him.

Below, hundreds of darkened cases were scattered across the valley floor — Imbirri cocoons — all dwarfed by the massive chrysalis of the Awakener, which quivered in the final, painful phase of the Changes.

He threw out his wings, pulling out of the dive, and soared low over the shriveled fungi.

The time of rebirth was near.

The shielded enclosure of the humans, shimmering blue within the sparse valley, was a violation of this sacred place. The old Fintil nodded gravely. It was time this sordid drama was ended.

The Fountain landed softly and fixed his eyes fondly on the writhing form of the Awakener.

"Soon," he whispered.

Chapter 22

Karic, Andrai and Mara approached their defensive screen, preparing to deactivate and dismantle the device. It was time to leave Cru.

The young Fintil were a familiar sight in the valley now. The first arrived singly or in small groups. Then, hours later, hundreds appeared at once. These must have been those born in the valley. They were magnificent. They circled the transmission node, singing and calling out as they flashed past each other. Together, they would form into groups or pairs, always moving. The more daring dove toward the bright mass of the transmission node, to pull away at the last instant. They shimmered as though lacquered, the light brushstrokes of brilliant color on their golden shells unique to each individual. Beautiful. Alien.

Karic's head thudded with tension. Freedom was closer than ever, yet the possibility of disaster boiled around them like molten sulfur. He knew the Fountain would let them leave — while the ancient Fintil was master of Cru — but could he maintain control after the rebirth of the Awakener?

Returning to the *Starburst* was only the first hurdle. Then they had to make it out of the Tau Ceti system. Only then could they look to Earth …

Would they be hailed as heroes? Would his own place among the next generation of starship travelers be assured? Or would their homecoming be the end of the odyssey that had propelled him through his life?

Had he challenged Janzen sooner, the crew — and Evelle — would be alive. They might still be waiting at Epsilon Eridani for news of a new target system. Perhaps they would be already heading there, a full crew in an undamaged ship.

Yet he had not. Instead, their path brought them to Cru — and a bitter harvest of betrayal, pain and death. Now, to survive, they had to return to Earth. To leave this living world; this inexplicable haven crafted with high technology on what should have been a hell planet of blistering heat and frigid waste. If only the Fintil were more open to them. If only they could stay and study what they had found. If only the *Starburst* were ready for new destinations …

Karic's hands tightened into fists at his side. He willed them open and forced himself to relax.

He keyed in the deactivation sequence for the shield.

The power cell in the main unit switched to standby with a low roar. One-by-one, each of the shield walls disappeared. The air filled with the smell of ozone as thousands of volts surged across the gaps in the final discharges. The indicator lights on the control panel faded and the rapidly changing digital readout grew static. Each of the shield components shrank and folded into its storage configuration, filling internal voids until they were rectangular ingots with a fraction their functional volume.

The camp was now fully exposed. In this show of goodwill, they were relying on their trust of the Fountain, and that he would honor Karic's bargain, as events moved outside their control.

Karic tried to appear calm, but his tension was obvious. "Let's get this gear into the core section."

Mara and Andrai quickly carried the equipment back to the lander.

Karic looked around him at the alien world and the golden-limbed Fintil above him, chittering together in an excited chorus as they flew circuits around the transmission node. They were a riot of color, most of the newborns' wings and thorax highlighted predominantly with green, yet others colored with bright highlights of red or purple. Always before when he had communicated with the Fountain, he had heard the Fintil's thoughts in his mind, a fact that made his Fintil speech somehow familiar. But these voices ... they were so alien. His stomach gave a sickening lurch, as though the ground had moved under his feet.

He took a deep breath and brought his mind back to the tasks at hand. Soon they would be back on the *Starburst*. She was keeping station above them, waiting only for the four remaining crew before the final burst of power that would propel them back across the dark leagues toward distant Earth. Of their equipment, now only the small satellite dish remained in position, providing the essential radio-link to the ship. He planned to remain in communication until their final moments on the surface, to confirm the ship's exact position.

They took the last of the rations from the lander and rested in its shadow.

"In a few more hours, we will be on our way back to Earth," said Karic.

"Seems hard to believe. You think the Fountain will live up to his promise?" asked Andrai.

"Yes," said Karic. *Provided he has the power to.*

Mara sighed. "Earth. It seems like a dream." She looked up at the sky and frowned.

Karic looked up at the heavy sky above, untouched by the passing of any sun. Winged shapes circled overhead. They were exquisite, and yet as he watched them, his sense of unease intensified. There were *so many* of them.

"It will be good to see Earth again," said Andrai. "But I would love to study some of this Fintil technology. Like that anti-gravity platform the Fountain used."

Over beside the bier, the Fountain and Utar stood in motionless vigil before the Awakener's massive cocoon.

"It must be close. Come on," said Karic, getting to his feet. He just wanted this over with.

They sealed the hatch and walked in silence toward the chrysalis.

There, they stood in silence with the two Fintil.

Karic had never felt more out of place.

It was growing hotter by the minute, the single tower in the center of the valley pushing out waves of heat and light. The humidity was almost unbearable, yet they endured, knowing they would soon be gone.

The dark, swollen capsule shook. All three of them felt the same mixture of excitement and fear. They had seen this before, and knew it signaled an imminent birth. Fintil began arriving, pushing forward to stand with the Fountain and Utar. Gradually, the humans were jostled to the back of the alien crowd by the Fintil. Karic kept his eyes on the Fountain's back, desperate not to lose sight of him.

***

The Fountain, sensing Karic's attention, turned toward him. He nodded to the human, and noted the return gesture from him. It was sufficient. Karic and the others disappeared into the rear of the crowd, each looking fearfully at the taller Fintil around them and their razor-sharp limbs. This was as it should be. They had no place near the birth.

The Fountain watched the young with joy and pride. This was their moment. A moment for the new Fintil race.

Unlike the birth of Utar, during which he had slashed open the tough hide of the cocoon wall to ease the transition, he made no move to interfere. He turned to Utar and felt another surge of pride. Here they stood together, both Fintil, ancient and young, as witness.

The Fountain touched Utar's mind gently. The young Fintil's memories of birth were still vivid. Utar watched with a deep sense of hope, longing to see his old friend once more.

Such vitality! *The raw passions of youth.*

The old Fountain pulled back from Utar's mind. He thought back to his own birth and found the images dimmed by time, but still charged with emotion. The desperation, the fear, the loneliness; and above all, the desire to be joined with others of his kind.

The struggle grew frenzied. Utar stepped forward, as though to help, but the Fountain laid a gentle hand on his to restrain him.

The darkened shell burst open.

The Fountain chittered with sheer happiness.

Sticky green fluid splashed across the clearing in a pungent fountain. The odor of birth filled the air, sweet and rich. Gold appeared amid the tangled muck. Then the razored limbs shredded the cocoon like wet paper.

She rose to her full height and extended her wings.

The children of the Fintil descended to the ground in massive numbers, drawn to her. Many wings beat against the thick air. There was a swift rustle as they furled, then the sound of slender, perfect limbs as they thudded onto the ground. The Fintil stood in glistening ranks, immobile. Entranced.

Although her head and upper torso were only slightly larger than a normal Fintil, her wings had a span of more than fifteen meters. Her huge abdomen was elongated and flattened, shaped aerodynamically like a single flaring wing. Her thorax and wings glistened with green highlights — the mark of a fertile female.

A Fintil Queen.

She dwarfed them, standing on magnificent legs in scale with her long abdomen. The Queen looked about her with huge black eyes, rainbows glistening in their depths.

The three humans tried to back away, but were trapped by the swelling crowd.

The Queen sang three earsplitting notes.

The humans fell to the ground in pain and covered their ears. The stentorian call raced across the winds, drawing Fintil from kilometers away. The crowd went into a frenzy and mobbed forward to reach her.

The three humans staggered to their feet and backed away through the press of golden bodies, ignored by the throng. One Fintil knocked into Mara, but Karic grabbed her wrist to keep her from falling. The Fountain watched them as they backed away from the crowd of newborns to sit on a hill in the shadow of a shriveled fungus. He knew the humans were suffering in the heat, but that could not be helped.

Utar was at the front of the crowd, as lost in the wild jubilation as the merest of them. For all his power and knowledge, he was one of the newly born, and like the rest of the Fintil, his body and spirit rejoiced with an intense, almost violent passion.

The Fountain strode gracefully through them, his head bowed in contemplation. The vibrant colors of his shell, more varied and complex since his latest rebirth, stood out against the gold shells of the other Fintil. He was lost in memories of his own birth when, like these young ones, he had celebrated the joy of new life. He had known no language, but had experienced thought as rapid as light that flashed in the crystal chambers of his new mind. His first mental contact had sent his heart soaring. To the Fintil, mental communication was a natural as breathing.

The energy and passion of the young Fintil were a joy to behold. When the Fountain had surged north toward the bright side at the time of his own birth, those who had the energy to celebrate such as this had been few. Even though great in numbers, perhaps as many as a thousand, they had been the crippled children of an aging culture, languid and without passion, their colors faded. His generation had been mostly without issue, the few such as himself the only fertile members of an ancient and dying race. But these children in front of him — they were *alive!* It seemed their long lifetime as intelligent Imbirri — rather than dumb Fin — had renewed their spirit. They had come forth from the cocoons in brilliant gold, eager for life, and the Fountain felt certain they would be fertile. It heralded a new age for the Fintil. They had lived as Imbirri for millennia, rather than the usual century of life as Fin. Perhaps the Fintil adult lifetime had also been extended. He would not survive long enough to know.

Then there was the Queen.

Such a sight. Her presence was overpowering and strong chemical signals filled the air. He fought his own instinctive urge to press forward. Never since the Death of Hope had a Queen been born amongst the Fintil. All of their females were capable of giving birth, yet a fertile Queen could lay down thousands of eggs in her lifetime. Zenith city would at last be filled with Fintil — perhaps in time even other cities would be removed from stasis to be inhabited once more. He thanked Fate that only one queen emerged. In their newly born state, a conflict between queens would have been unavoidable. It would have been a tragedy if one or both had been lost due to injuries.

The Fountain had known there was something special about the Awakener's cocoon from the outset, and he had set the conditions in the valley to keep the newly hatched Fintil here for this reason. The key was an acceleration of heat, making the newborns feel as though they were moving ever closer to the bright terminator — the dividing line between the night side and day side. Now, the entire Fintil nation had witnessed the birth. When the Queen took flight they could join together into a single formation.

One thing remained. Before they could fly to the bright side and a new life — a new age — for the Fintil, the fate of the humans would have to be resolved. He must get them off the planet. Yet certain protocols had to be observed. He must first put the matter to his new Queen.

The Fintil had settled around her in ranks. Each of the females came forward to touch wings and caress her. Then followed the males. First, Utar came forward. He spoke no words, yet there was a special recognition that passed between them as he touched wings to the Queen then withdrew. As the procession continued, the air was filled with the sound of their chattering, a senseless chitter and staccato that signaled joy and excitement. They were so innocent, untouched by knowledge, yet sentient. It was now that the knowledge of the Fountain was needed, to teach them their language, culture and history.

The Fountain could sense a rhythm growing in the noisy chatter. This first instinctual phase was drawing to a close. They had bonded with the new Queen and soon they would grow restless. Sensing his moment, the

Fountain stepped forward and waited for recognition.

***

The Queen was awash in a glorious sea of adoration. She could sense each of these glowing minds in turn and knew they looked toward her as a goddess. They called without words for her to lead them to a place of heat and brightness, where they might sing to each other and dance on the air.

Another of her golden race stepped toward the Queen. She could see he was not an innocent like the others. He had a sense of wisdom and age and his torso was splashed with colors more complex and vivid than the newly born. He did not come close; instead, he waited for her. She did not understand. Time was pressing. Could he not see that she must lead her people into the heat, toward the sun?

Utar also rose and stepped forward, approaching with reverence. She watched him as he came toward her, feeling a strong affection for him. He stopped. She felt his increasing closeness, even though he had not moved, then his voice spoke in her mind.

"My Queen. Do you remember me? I am Utar."

She concentrated, and thoughts raced like water-snakes in the newly flooded corridors of her mind. "I know you. Yet I ... do not remember."

Utar pressed her. "We were together for many years. We were the same — yet different. We were Imbirri.

"Do you remember?"

The pressure increased inside her. Then the memories exploded like a comet crashing to earth, its coldness heated to fire amid the shattering impact. *She was the Awakener.* These people who bowed before her were the Imbirri, her people ... and yet they were not. They were changed as surely as she had changed.

Her head moved swiftly as she examined herself.

She remembered now. She had fought the Changes, and had destroyed some of the Imbirri. This had been wrong. The Awakener looked toward this other, ancient one, and she recognized him. She had tried to destroy him also. How wrong she had been! She had tried to prevent a glorious transformation, and she felt an unaccountable joy that she had failed. Yet she remembered other things. The humans.

The intruders.

The Queen rose up to the full extension of her legs, flushed with power. Her gaze scanned the clearing until it fell on the three humans, cowering beneath the shade of fungi. Her rage found its focus.

"Destroy the aliens!" roared the Queen. Simultaneously, a mental command flashed into the minds of the Fintil.

The humans struggled to their feet as hundreds of Fintil rushed toward them — the tall red-gold warrior-caste in the lead — razor sharp limbs poised to strike ...

One human screamed, and they fumbled with their weapons. The heat had sucked the vitality out of them. Against the rushing wall of the Fintil, they seemed to be moving in slow motion.

The Fountain launched himself in front of the humans and spread his wings as though to create a barrier.

"Wait!" called the Fountain. The mental command flashed through their minds, and the young Fintil slowed their advance. They knew the Fountain, and had come to trust him, but this new Queen surely must be obeyed. They turned to her in confusion.

The Queen's wings thrummed in agitation. "Do as he says."

Karic and the others sank back to the ground.

"My Queen," said the Fountain with great respect. "I am the Fountain. The repository of all the history and wisdom of our ancestors. I am here to guide you, to advise you, and to serve you."

She turned toward him. "I had wished to destroy the aliens. Tell me more of them. Tell me more of us."

Her desire for knowledge was intense, and he felt his mind opened against his will like a distended, overripe melon, spilling forth a great flood of images. The story of the humans unfolded in a torrent, and she drank it in. The Queen captured all of these images as they flew past her like swift birds, using all the power of her spirit and all the surprising gifts of her new mind.

The Queen saw the great Fintil cities on the bright side, the wonders of their high technology, and the joys of sexual union. It was only then that she realized she had no sexuality before, that she had been a neuter Imbirri. The images continued. She saw the humans through the eyes of the Fountain, felt his initial outrage as he saw them facing the Imbirri across the clearing. She felt the Fountain's astonishment as he understood the Imbirri were sentient, not like the simple-minded Fin, the grazing beasts, that he had expected. She learnt more. Through the eyes of this ancient one, she saw and felt a thousand things. Understanding in brief moments the Fintil, the sacred planet Cru, the Har Confederation and their place in the cosmos. She learnt of the humans, the unwitting sacrilege they had committed by visiting Cru, and the twist of Fate that had seen them draw the Imbirri out of their slumber. She understood that without the destruction and conflict the humans had engendered, there would have been no way the Imbirri could have made the transformation. She, as the Imbirri Awakener, would have prevented it. She saw it had been the first of the Imbirri that the humans had wounded, born as a female, who had soared north to awaken the Fountain from his deep slumber.

The Queen also understood the danger that contact with these pre-transformation species could pose. Knowing now, as surely as the Fountain knew, the terrible judgment that the Elders of the Har Confederation could mete out to them, every hour these beings remained on the planet was a danger to the continued existence of the Fintil race.

Finally, the Queen released the Fountain from her mental grip. She looked up through the clouds, knowing that the alien's ship was waiting above. It must be removed.

The Queen touched the mind of the Fountain once more. "So we must let them leave?"

"I think it is best, my Queen. But have no fear. I have taken measures to ensure they will be no threat to the Fintil."

"Very well then. Remove them from Cru."

The Fountain raised his wings in ascent, momentarily overpowered as he looked into her eyes and was lost in the huge black jewels.

She felt a surge of tenderness for the old Fountain. He had performed so well for the good of Cru and the Fintil. He would be an asset in the years to come.

The Queen turned to the Fintil gathered around her. At some unseen signal, they gathered close, touching her, and she could feel their overwhelming need. She must lead them into the heat and the light. They must take flight. *Must* reach the great cities of the bright side.

"Utar! Stand by my side."

***

Karic, Mara and Andrai watched in awe as the Queen rose to her full height and loosed a thunderous cry. She rose into the air amid the drone of a thousand wings as the Fintil joined her, flying toward the bright side in a massive, bejeweled convoy.

The Fountain walked toward them with the same stately poise he always displayed, yet Karic could sense a new determination. He manipulated one of the small devices at this belt.

Karic felt a mind-bond form as the Fountain reached out. "Leave now while you can. Move into your *lander*. Abandon your other equipment."

Karic scrambled to his feet. "This is it!"

After the terrifying threat of the Queen, they needed no urging. The temperature and humidity had risen to extreme levels, and they found it heavy going. Finally, they made it into the lander's core section. They collapsed, exhausted, into the hot, cramped interior, momentarily overcome with fatigue. Karic maneuvered around the inert form of Janzen and the other couches to squeeze into a command chair. Forcing himself to concentrate, he checked the flight diagnostics.

"Will we make it to the *Starburst?*" asked Mara as she struggled into a chair and strapped herself in.

"We have plenty of oxygen. It is the temperature and carbon dioxide concentrations we have to worry about. As long as we get to the ship soon, we'll have no problem," said Karic. The carbon dioxide filters were shot.

As before, the Fountain summoned the flying platform. It arrived at tremendous speed, the squat, articulated body of its dormant attendant robot distinctive in its center. *So the platform is capable of escaping the planet.* Karic was awed. If humans could get their hands on this technology, it would revolutionize space travel. Once more, he felt a deep regret at leaving Cru. If only the Fintil were not so closed. They were like the Imperial China of history, and he and his crew were the visitors; except this time, they had arrived in dug-out canoes rather than square-riggers equipped with long-range cannon.

Karic tensed. "Brace yourselves!"

Andrai had only just finished strapping in when the huge robot in the center of platform unfolded itself. It eyed them once through its cylindrical oculars, then went into action. It took hold of the lander and lifted them deftly onto the floating platform. As soon as the lander was in contact with it, all sensation of gravity vanished. Karic watched the Fountain adjust his instruments, silently coveting, in one dark moment, all the secrets these beings held — wisdom that could be given ... or taken.

The Fountain activated the shimmering green field around the craft. Looking out through the lander's front viewport, Karic saw that this time, the Fountain himself was on the platform with them, also inside the field.

As they lifted rapidly into the sky, the field strengthened, enclosing the whole platform in a dome.

"Incredible. It must be air-tight," said Karic.

They soared upward through the atmosphere as though shot from a sling, swiftly disappearing into the dark purple vaults of Cru's immutable sky. The heavy storm activity, and the atmospheric drag on the platform and its insubstantial, enclosing dome sent it spinning wildly and there was nothing they could do except hang on. Karic had vivid memories of his perilous descent through the clouds to the surface. He certainly would not have expected he would be leaving like this.

Then all grew calm and dark. The stars appeared, winking into life in the viewport through the faint green haze of the platform's enclosing shield. It seemed a lifetime since he had seen them, yet now they spread out in a majestic display, thousands of dazzling points nestled around the lazy curve of the planet. Tears of relief and joy flooded down his cheeks. It was over. They really were going home.

They hurtled away from Cru at an unchecked velocity.

Andrai leant forward over the console, working rapidly. "I've linked with the main computer!"

"Ready for docking," came the voice of the Shipcom through the console speakers.

"How the hell are we supposed to dock?" said Mara.

Their velocity was slowing now, and they were truly weightless as the huge platform closed on their starship.

Cru continued to fall away behind them.

Appearing from the darkness like a vision of redemption, the *Starburst* grew before them. The dark gray metal of its massive superstructure slowly filled the lander's viewport as they approached, then expanded further until all they saw was the docking bay and the front of the rotating habitat. The platform slowed until it matched *Starburst's* vector, standing motionless relative to the huge ship. The green field swept out from the platform, forming a ghostly tunnel between the dome above the platform and the big doors of the main docking bay, which were forward of both the central hold and the rotating habitat ring. The huge robot lifted the lander, delicately straddling the gap between the platform and the *Starburst's* docking bay.

They held their breath.

Outside, the Fintil floated in space, inside the bubble of breathable atmosphere enclosed by the field.

Karic watched in wonder.

The Fountain turned toward them and pointed to the docking doors.

"Open the dock, Andrai."

"Are you sure, boss?"

Karic looked at the Fountain, once more amazed at the technology of the Fintil. It make humanity's greatest achievements look like flint axes. But that hardly mattered. They were still *their* achievements.

"Open it."

The docking bay doors drew back. Lights flickered on inside the dock. Karic knew all the hatches leading to the chamber would have been automatically sealed before it depressurized. Once the docking bay doors were fully retracted, the robot placed them inside the dock and left them there, suspended in the zero-g. The powerful grappling arms inside the dock extended under the control of the Shipcom. There was a shock of contact as the arms took hold of the lander, and they felt the vibration of the servo-motors through the hull. By comparison, the handling of the Fintil robot had been gentle. Even so, Karic was glad to be in the hands of technology they understood, and controlled.

Through the viewport, they watched as the docking bay doors closed on the void of space. He let out a slow breath, hardly realizing he had been holding it. "We're back! God *damn* it! We made it."

"Docking bay sealed," came the voice of the Shipcom a few moments later. "Repressurizing docking bay."

They waited in tense silence.

"Docking bay re-pressurized. Opening main hold doors," reported the Shipcom.

The huge doors to central hold opened and the battered core section was drawn into the main holding bay by a second set of articulated arms, then locked into place. After a series of quick checks, they released the lander hatch. The seal broke with a hiss, and in came the familiar scents of the *Starburst*: plastic, steel and ozone.

By the time they reached the control room and activated the computers, the Fountain and the flying platform were gone.

Chapter 23

Karic sat in the commander's chair, reassured by the feel of the solid metal arms.

"Let's go home," he said.

Mara was crying as she worked at her console. Andrai laid a hand on her back to comfort her in silence.

It was time for this to be over.

Free from the threat of radiation, the trip home should be straightforward. They had functioning stasis gear and a repaired ship. In less than a few days of personal time they would be back on Earth.

To accelerate from a standing start, the *Starburst* was designed to catch the energy from an anti-matter explosion on its magnetic sails. As it had done on leaving Earth, and on departure from Epsilon Eridani, the *Starburst* would fire an anti-gravity pellet at a small asteroid. The immense explosion of material would boost them up to relativistic speeds for the trip home. The fusion drive would continue to accelerate them, powering them through space to Earth.

Mara sniffed and cleared her throat. "The probe in orbit around Cru has given us data on a whole range of medium to small-sized asteroids in the vicinity. Many of them spiraling into Tau Ceti. Looks like the black hole has been disrupting the orbits of a lot of these small bodies."

"Anything useful for us?"

"Yes," said Mara. "I have already identified one that would be ideal for the anti-matter burst."

"OK. Lay in a course for the object. Program the release of the anti-matter with the Shipcom and set a secondary course for Earth."

It was a relief to be back in artificial gravity more akin to Earth's and each of them realized the toll the heavy gravity had taken on their endurance. They were exhausted, yet elated and relieved. Against all hope they had escaped the planet and were back in the familiar confines of *Starburst*.

Andrai checked and double-checked every conceivable system, searching the craft from the forward antenna to the aft observation bubble for the slightest fault; anything that could spell disaster for them as they lay helpless in the grip of suspension. He found nothing. This pleased Karic, for only Ibri had known the ship better than Andrai. Meanwhile, Karic wired the suspension sets in the lander into the main systems so that they were under the control of the Shipcom.

Hours later, they were all back in the control room.

"OK. It's time. Let's get into suspension. I want us out of this system as soon as possible.

"Computer. Implement a three-person shift rotation including Karic,

Mara, and Andrai. Janzen is not to be revived without my approval." In normal rotation, shift crews of two were taken out of long-term stasis every twelve months for a week of "live time", where they provided the key human oversight the *Starburst* needed. Solo watches were deemed too risky. With a "buddy system", they were able to monitor each other and provide help in the case of unforeseen accidents. With only three of them on active duty, Karic had decided that all of them should be revived for each consecutive shift.

Karic looked up at the screens, staring for a long moment at the dark bulk of Cru, now only a small disk in the middle of the star field. "Wake us all just prior to the anti-matter assist maneuver."

"Confirmed."

A question gnawed at the back of Karic's mind, but he pushed it away. He was exhausted and had no time for phantoms. The oblivion of suspension would be welcome.

"Put the consoles into sleep mode. Let's go." The holographic interfaces above each console vanished one-by-one, the projectors settling back into their niches.

Inside the lander, they maneuvered through the cabin to their jury-rigged suspension couches. The computer was programmed to wait until they were held immobile by the suspension fields — and their bodies were protected from any damage due to the massive acceleration — before it applied the full thrust of the fusion drive.

As the activation countdown proceeded, Karic looked across to Andrai and Mara, now side by side. Both had their eyes closed. Beside him was the still form of Janzen, his hands and face still patched with tape and bandages, his forlorn expression frozen in place. This was going to be an interesting homecoming.

***

They were roused by the Shipcom close to Tau Ceti. On the main deck, the blazing mass of the yellow-orange sun filled the screen.

"Shipcom, are all systems ready to commence the anti-matter assist?"

"Confirmed. Object targeted. Magnetic containment set to optimum configuration. Should I initiate countdown, Commander?"

This was it. The command that would take them home.

"Damn it to hell!" said Mara, slamming her hand down on her console. The floating icons of her console interface swirled crazily at the movement. A strand of dark hair came loose from her tightly woven bun and uncurled across her slender neck. She flicked it away angrily, her dark eyes fixed to her viewscreen. Andrai looked across at Karic, one blond eyebrow raised in a silent question.

Karic feared the worse. Was it some problem with the fusion drive? Or some crucial malfunction of the ship's systems? *No, please God!* Not this close to escape.

"What is it?" asked Karic evenly.

Mara took a deep breath to steady herself.

"It's that black hole. I know it's there. There is no doubt. I know the exact location, it's close by, very close. We even factored it into the orbital calculations for the target object."

"But?"

Mara clenched her fists. "Not only has it moved since my last set of observations, there is still no sign of the gas ring! It doesn't make sense. The damn thing should not even exist. It certainly should not be so close to Tau Ceti."

Something crystallized in Karic's thoughts. *That's* what had been bothering him. The device he had seen in Utar's mind! At the time, he had the sense that the Deepwatch had used the device to attack the *Starburst*, but had no idea what it was. Now he knew. The black hole *was* the device! He wracked his brains trying to remember the image he saw. A vast darkness, surrounded by huge supports. Impossible, surely, and yet ...

"Have you tried looking for visible light?"

Mara looked back at him blankly. "Well, I have been concentrating on the typical spectra —"

"Try it. Redirect all the sensor arrays that track visible light. *Look* for it. You know where it is."

Mara manipulated a series of glowing icons with short, deft movements. Then she batted the final icon up to the main screens, where it flared a brilliant yellow before fading into a grid. Moments later, the Shipcom started building the image.

"Oh, my God," said Mara.

Andrai left his console and walked over to join them. His eyes, lost in wonder, never left the screen. Karic was filled with a wild elation. They had to reach Earth. People had to know about this.

With every second, the definition on the image grew clearer.

It was gigantic.

Huge curved beams, visible only as they reflected the intense light of Tau Ceti, enclosed an ovoid space.

"But I am getting nothing on the other sensors, Karic," said Mara. "How can those materials be transparent to radiation and yet have structural integrity? I don't understand it!"

Material with no mass?

Inside the superstructure was a core of darkness, the size of a small moon.

"Are you getting any radiation?" asked Karic.

"No, nothing," said Mara. "It should be radiating huge amounts of energy."

"Wait, there is something. Another field, between the main supports. It's deflecting the solar wind."

"What if it's adsorbing the energy the black hole radiates?"

Mara shook her head and tried enhancing the image.

"There!"

"What is that?" said Andrai. "It looks like it's spinning."

"Trace amounts of gas. Probably trapped inside the superstructure. Spinning with the kernel."

Watching the gas, they could see that the dark core of the device was trying to shift its position, but was held confined.

"The field must be using its charge to contain it," said Mara. "But that does not explain how the black hole maintains itself. It would need to take on mass, just to stay intact."

Karic's mind lit up.

"You said it had changed position, didn't you?" said Karic.

"Yes," said Mara, chewing her lip.

"Well, what if it operated on a cycle? It moves in, close to Tau Ceti, the field opens to allow it to drag in enough gas to restore the mass it lost in radiation, then it closes."

"While maintaining the field that manipulates its charge to keep it in position," added Andrai.

"Yes," said Karic.

Mara's jaw dropped. "That would create a regular surge of radiation!"

"Just like what hit the ship," said Karic.

"So, if you had access to the device, you could alter the period of the cycle, and adjust the orbit and timing so the surge hit a specific location," said Andrai.

"Like the approach vector of *Starburst*," said Mara.

They were silent for a long moment, staring up at the silent bulk of the Fintil device.

"But that's impossible," said Mara, frowning. "How could Utar have used one of the most advanced devices of the Fintil?"

"How indeed," said Karic. His mind swept back to his first mental contact with Utar. After seeing the device in Utar's mind, Karic had seen other images: a confusion of colors, geometrical shapes and readings. What if the device was controlled mentally? Could Utar have somehow stumbled across it? It seemed impossible. The power of his mind would have to have been immense to reach across such as distance.

"Let's just be thankful that it has no gas ring now," said Karic.

"Look!"

The black heart of the device opened, yawning out like a funnel to fill the space between its massive supports. A sleek silver spacecraft, glistening gold in the light of Tau Ceti, shot out from the heart of the device at a tremendous speed. A moment later, the opening vanished.

That elegant silver ship was a Fintil spacecraft!

"Track the vector," shouted Karic.

Mara worked furiously.

"It's moving at over 0.8C, heading directly for Cru."

Eighty percent of the speed of light! Karic's heart raced.

"Of course," said Mara. "It's a wormhole gateway!"

Karic was lost for words, unnerved by yet another demonstration of the Fintil's ancient, yet advanced technology.

"What do we do?" said Andrai, watching the spacecraft as it disappeared from their screens.

"We go home," said Karic. "Shipcom. Initiate anti-matter assist."

"Confirmed."

"Come on," said Karic. "Into suspension."

Karic's voice shook as he gave the final commands to shut down the command deck.

***

As soon as they were roused from suspension, they hurried back to the control room. When the interface was back up, Karic addressed the Shipcom directly.

"Are we still at maximum thrust? Are all shields and systems operating within safety parameters?"

"Yes, Commander," replied the Shipcom. "The *Starburst* is traveling at nineteen percent of light-speed and still accelerating. Destination: Earth."

They cheered, dancing around the ship in a group of three, the voice of the Shipcom hardly audible over their shouts of glee. *"All operations are within normal parameters. The fusion drive is operating at peak efficiency."*

Finally, they settled back to their stations.

"Maybe it's time we broke into Janzen's private stores," said Andrai.

Karic laughed and tried to focus. He turned to Andrai. "Anything else?"

"Nothing, Commander. No anomalous readings or power fluctuations."

Karic deactivated his console and rose to his feet.

"That's it then."

Karic smiled. The *Starburst* had taken them to the stars and was on its way home. Now there was nothing to stop them from reaching Earth.

He felt a moment of pride. The suspension technology was the breakthrough that allowed them to traverse the stars in their own lifetime.

How passionately he had believed, in those early days, of the destiny of mankind — a destiny which would take them to the stars. Despite their contact with the hostile Imbirri and the aloof Fintil, he felt that passion more than ever.

The stars and life awaited them. He would not let the warnings of some tired outpost of a regressive spacefaring culture stop him.

"Well, I'm not wasting another moment," said Andrai, leaving the main control room for the central hold and the suspension equipment hardwired into the lander's battered core section.

"We made it, Karic. Thanks to you." Mara's voice was soft and low. "I need to talk to you."

"OK. I need to check the data storage one last time. Come with me to the commander's cabin."

Feeling no need for words, they made their way to the commander's cabin in silent companionship. The months they had slept through had given them no time to deal with the shock and loss they had experienced, and their ordeal was still fresh in their minds. Each of them was keenly aware of the empty chairs around them on the command deck. Thirty-three dead, their frozen and desiccated remains stored in the airless heart of the ship, Ibri left unmourned and unburied in the jungles of Cru. Memories of the outward journey plagued Karic. A hopeful, exciting time, when all thirty-eight crew nestled securely within the shell of Earth's best technology, feeling a deep solidarity that only absence would reveal. They were gone, lost like vapor to the void of space.

Karic had stored armfuls of heavy-duty data-disks in the commander's cabin, each crammed with information they had retrieved from the surface of the planet. They contained everything they knew about Cru: every instrument reading, each image and radio message, recordings of voice journals, and personal notes by Janzen and Karic. They had traveled over a hundred light-years and lost thirty-four lives in order to win this knowledge. It was priceless. Despite the apparent lack of any device planted on board the ship by the Fintil, he was taking no chances.

They had placed the data-disks in the commander's personal safe, a heavily shielded metal storage device fashioned from toughened armor. It was completely sealed from the ship and had its own power supply. Even if the *Starburst* was destroyed, and all the Shipcom's memory with it, this would survive. Only Karic knew the numerical code that would release the shield that protected it.

Karic checked the safe. Satisfied, he turned to Mara. "So what do you want to say?"

Their eyes touched.

"It's not what I want to say. I'm just sick of being afraid. I want to do it," said Mara. "I want to mind-bond with you. This time with no barriers."

Karic's heart raced. He reached for the fugue state and waited for her. Mara concentrated, but nothing happened. She screwed up her face in frustration. "It seems to be getting harder."

Karic reached across to her mind. With a shock, he realized it was once more dormant, like Andrai's. Somehow the presence of the Fintil — and their mental contact — had stimulated her mind while on Cru. Now it had grown quiet. Maybe she had closed the doors to her latent abilities herself. That did not matter now. He could supply the energy for both of them. He reached into the dormant, dreaming parts of her mind and poured that power into her, desperate to make contact. He had to know. Had to know her fully, at least once.

Her mind surged, swelled outward.

Karic gasped as their spirits met like two titanic walls of water, merging into one turbulent mass. Their minds lay open and unguarded. Thoughts and images swirled around them like pools of color. Karic watched Mara's mind, listening like a thief to her darkest thoughts. At last he understood her guilt, her pain — and the need to end it for good. At the same time, he could feel her reaching into his own mind, searching.

A sudden pain lanced through his temples. He could not keep this up. And now there was no point. The corpse of their love was long decayed.

Karic withdrew the mind-bond.

Despite the pain, a sense of lightness filled him and true freedom beaconed. At last he could let her go. At last he knew.

After coming to the edge of human space, his bond to humanity was stronger than ever. Yet, in another way, he was alone. There was no one standing behind him. No supporting hand on his shoulder. He had to find the strength to carry on inside himself.

Mara held Karic's gaze, ready for any recrimination.

"Thank you, Mara. Thank you."

"I loved you Karic, desperately. But our moments were always hidden things. At first that was the way I wanted it. Then it seemed you were ashamed of me. Touring off with Evelle. I thought you would go back to her."

"I never would have left you."

"I know," said Mara, bitterly. "I know that now." She had misjudged Karic badly, but it was too late.

"The truth is, Mara, I loved you both, in different ways. But you were my lover. It was over with Evelle. That tour was just something I had to do. I could not risk losing the *Starburst*."

"Instead you lost me," she said.

Karic bowed his head for a moment.

Mara felt a growth of joy in her: the relief of a heavy sadness expunged. Despite the sense of invasion, she realized that without this unwitting contact of minds — the brief moment of total knowledge and abandon — her feelings of bitterness and rejection would always have remained with her. Now she knew the truth, without a doubt, and that dark knot of twisted emotion was simply gone. Mara wiped the tears from her eyes. Was the human race ready for honesty this profound? What would this remarkable gift bring to Earth?

"Let's put it behind us. All I want to do is return to Earth. To smell the wind and feel the Sun, *our Sun,* on my skin," she said. "I don't ever want to leave Earth again."

"I can't wait to return either, Mara, but what I really long to see are the advances. We will have been gone almost a hundred and sixty years. Just think of the technology we could command! The starships! Just imagine if they have broken the light barrier?

"I long to see more of the cosmos. My time on Cru, as threatening and terrifying as it was, has only increased my determination to explore space.

"The Fintil were advanced, and they looked at the *Starburst* with contempt. But we did it, Mara. We have journeyed through the empty spaces, seen another world and communicated with the sentient alien life it supported." Karic grew thoughtful. "The Fintil were ill-suited as friends of humanity, but there must be other races in the stars, other living worlds waiting for us, other wonders to discover."

Mara frowned. "Do you really believe we belong out here after all you've seen? Weren't the lessons we learnt on Cru enough?"

Karic grew serious. "The Fintil are an ancient and arrogant race. Their knowledge was tainted with their own sense of superiority."

"We do not belong in space!"

Karic was silenced by her anger.

"We were aliens on Cru, in every sense of the word. Believe me, Karic, I know. Humans will never thrive on any world that does not have our sun, our moon, our sky."

Karic turned away briefly, then met her gaze with sad, yet resigned intensity. "The human race cannot continue to cram into the concrete cities of Earth, Mara. We have always needed new frontiers, always needed to grow beyond our limits. We need new worlds. Before we die and fade to nothing."

They stood in a silence filled with jagged edges.

The voice of the Shipcom startled them both. "The suspension equipment is on standby," said the computer. "Do you wish me to switch it off for you, Commander?"

"No. The remaining crew will be entering suspension shortly."

"Understood, Commander."

They moved in silence to the accessway, then up the narrow tube to the darkened central hold. They followed each other through the zero-g of the hold with practiced movements, finally reaching the lander. Inside, Karic helped Mara position herself on the makeshift couch, which cushioned and partially encapsulated their bodies while they were under the influence of the field. He watched as the cloud of energy grew thick like smoke around her, and her guarded expression froze in place.

Karic lay on his couch and let his body relax into the contours. His finger hesitated over the button that would send him toward the unknown future. His mind was in turmoil; and it seemed he could not bear to silence such an angry multitude of inner voices.

Karic honestly believed mankind had a destiny, and that it lay somewhere in the depths of space. Something had always drawn him out beyond the static revolutions of the worlds he knew, both the scientific and the corporeal; and he would continue to search until he found that destiny, as elusive as it may seem. His years spent developing the suspension field, working always against the derision of his colleagues, were simply a means to an end. And what were the Fintil's warnings anyway, if not simply the paranoia of an aging culture on the verge of collapse? Nothing would keep him from the stars. Nothing.

Karic felt a wave a tiredness wash through him. He settled deeper into the couch and let a warm, pleasurable feeling of relaxation take him. Before he could stop himself, or trigger the suspension field, he had drifted into sleep.

Karic dreamt of Cru.

He soared across the skies of the planet on wings of spirit, sent forth by the same winds that spawned the Fintil. He passed the terminator and reached the bright side, racing from each shining, jeweled city to the next. As he flew onward, he saw the golden Fintil busy at their tasks. They were rebuilding their future. The Fintil scientists with their large, purple-crowned, dome-shaped heads, were busy learning and extending their ancient technology, others worked as craftsmen, some — perhaps destined to be Old Ones like the Fountain — cloistered within the great libraries of their race, seeking knowledge, expanding their minds and their thinking, preparing to lead the race into a new era.

Of the Fountain, he saw nothing.

In time, he approached the greatest of the cities. He flashed through the brightly hued walls as though they were made of gas, led onward by instinct until he came to a circular chamber. High arches formed a dome high above him, while slender windows of exquisite design flooded the space with Tau Ceti's bright light.

Here lay the Fintil Queen.

She was attended by ranks of Fintil, while councilors and artisans waited patiently in the verges of the room for an audience. Unlike the queens of the insect world, she did not give forth an endless stream of eggs. It seemed the time for her to give birth was still distant. The room was flanked by ranks of the tall, austere warrior caste, their narrow angular heads, armored thorax and abdomens colored a vibrant, threatening red.

She had lost none of her elegance and frightening power.

Utar was at her side, overseeing the myriad minor matters that came to the attention of the Queen's court.

Karic let himself drift down toward the Queen and Utar. He examined them with great curiosity, wondering how these shining, sophisticated, metallic beings could have been birthed from the simplistic Imbirri. As Karic approached, Utar looked up suddenly from the glowing device in his hands. He met the human's eyes with an intense, yet unreadable expression. Karic felt the touch of the Fintil's mind on his own. He also sensed the awesome power of the Queen's mind, now focused elsewhere.

"The curiosity of your race will be its end, human," spoke Utar to Karic's mind. "How you found us here is beyond me. And I warn you — if the Queen should know of your presence ... forces would be unleashed against your world that your race could not hope to resist.

"Flee! Before my duty compels me."

Karic felt safe, convinced the scene was a dream and not truly real. "I will leave you, Utar, but tell me before I go, is mankind forever doomed to disaster as we reach outward to the vastness that surrounds us? Surely there is a place for us somewhere in the depths of space?"

Utar spoke to his aides in a rapid staccato. He excused himself from the presence of the Queen, then walked casually toward the less populated regions of the expansive chamber, feigning tiredness. Karic followed him. At last free from company, Utar turned toward the human. Some of his fierceness had gone.

"Karic, what can I truly say to you? There are worlds for you, and yet you will not reach them before disaster strikes your race. The basic precepts by which you reach outward are flawed."

"What do you mean?"

"I have said enough. It's forbidden."

Karic was enraged. How dare this specter speak to him of forbidden truth! Mankind was destined to know all truths! Karic had been taught by his own mentors in science and engineering that nothing should be hidden from the inquiring mind, and he believed this. It defined who he was.

"If you know, what gives you the right to withhold the knowledge from us?" asked Karic.

Utar grew angry once more, turning his huge, glittering eyes on Karic. His body stiffened as if to take flight ... or strike out.

"What do I know of Truth? I foresaw a new beginning for our race, and my prophecy was borne out, yet now ..." Utar relaxed his posture. "Now

I am only one of the many. Once I was the Deepwatch, now I am one of the subservient mates of the Queen, bound to take the place of the Fountain when he finally expires, which will be all too soon. I envy your freedom."

"Utar, you are one of the leaders of an advanced race. You have access to knowledge and a high technology. The universe is yours to explore as you will. Lead the Fintil beyond Cru. Reach outward!"

Karic felt Utar's sadness. "Once we were changeless, Karic ... lost in innocence. There was only the joy of Union, the magic of song — the Elixir. Now, time presses on me.

"The jungles in which we wandered for so long seem cold to me, now. So cold," said Utar sadly.

"The others?"

"Only the Awakener has the memories, and she chooses to forget."

Karic was frustrated. If only he could take a fraction of the knowledge these beings possessed, or gain the merest words of guidance from them, then the mysteries of space would yield to him.

"Surely there is something you can tell me? Anything. What path to take? Where to search?"

Utar raised his wings in fury, almost leaping into the air.

"Be gone!"

A mental wave hit Karic like a physical blow. The golden light of the chamber vanished and he was swallowed by darkness.

Karic awoke to the voice of the Shipcom.

"... been asleep for one hour, Commander. Do you wish to return to your cabin for an adequate rest period, or enter suspension with the other two crew members?"

Karic shook his head, feeling a savage pain behind his eyes. He rubbed his temples. "No. I will enter suspension now."

"Would you like me to activate the field for you, Commander?"

"That will not be necessary," said Karic, depressing the time-delay button with a savage stab of his finger.

As the field drew around him, and his final thoughts began to slow, it occurred to him what a remarkable gift they had gained. No matter where in the cosmos they roamed, with the ability to communicate from mind-to-mind, the barriers of language need never prevent them from meaningful contact and dialogue with an alien species. They would know each other fully, in moments.

Understanding would be quickly attained.

Conflict would be instantaneous and violent ...

***

As Karic was drawn finally into stillness, a glowing sphere appeared in the air above his suspension couch. It hovered close to his inert body for a time, then sped toward each of the others in turn, finally settling to a distant corner of the room, unnoticed by the Shipcom or the ship's sensors. It drew what little energy it needed from the surrounding lights and electrical systems. Its patience was unlimited. It had waited for almost ten thousand years as the Fintil slumbered in the guise of the Imbirri. It spun slower as it entered its own kind of slumber, alone with its alien thoughts.

And the *Starburst* sped on through space, toward Earth.

Chapter 24

Karic felt a touch on his arm. An urgent voice spoke in the distance. He rose from the depths, finally breaking through the dullness to see Mara above him.

"Karic!" Her face was flushed with excitement. Andrai was at her side, filled with the same reckless energy. "Earth, Karic. We've made it back!"

They had taken shifts together on the way back to Earth. Memories of the last time they had spoken, seemingly only days ago, were sharp in his mind, and his heart softened to see Mara so filled with unrestrained joy.

Still a little disoriented from the revival process, he pushed himself off the couch with too much force and sailed up toward the lander's padded ceiling. Mara and Andrai grabbed his arms to steady him. Both seemed to have been alert for some time. In accordance with his standing orders, Janzen remained in stasis.

"We have Earth on the viewscreen, Commander," said Andrai.

Karic was annoyed that his two crew had roused before him. "How long have we been out of suspension?" he asked sharply.

"Suspension fields cut forty-seven minutes ago, boss," said Andrai. "We were roused right after the deflectors powered down. You were in such a heavy sleep we thought it best to leave you to wake naturally."

Karic grunted. "Magnetic braking: was it successful?"

"Went like a charm," said Andrai. "We are on track for Earth orbit."

Karic stretched, the movement causing him to drift up into the air though the zero-g. He took hold of the side of the couch to stabilize himself.

"Don't you think it's time Janzen was revived?" said Mara, the thin line of a crease appearing on her forehead.

Karic looked over at Janzen, still clothed in the same ExploreCorp field gear he had been wearing during the lander descent, now stained with blood and sweat. The damage he had caused. The *lives* he had cost. Karic took a deep breath. Mara was right. It was time to rouse him. Soon, he could be handed over to Earth authorities for trial.

"You're right. Shipcom, bring Janzen out of suspension. Notify me when he is ten minutes from emergence."

"Confirmed."

He forced himself into action, pushing across the chamber to lander's hatch. "Are we receiving the beacon from the ExploreCorp station?"

"No, not yet," said Andrai.

Based on the last transmissions they had received — on arrival at Tau Ceti — ExploreCorp had dropped their fleet and headquarters right back into low Earth orbit, abandoning their stations in the Lagrange fields — but that news was eighty years out of date.

"Anything from Earth at all?" said Karic.

"Negative," said Andrai, his light gray eyes shadowed with concern.

They had been broadcasting all the way back from Tau Ceti, but had received nothing from Earth. At first Karic had assumed it was a targeting error, or a fault with their jury-rigged equipment. But he and Andrai had both checked the transmitter and receiving arrays. There was nothing wrong with the gear.

As they drew closer to Earth, Karic's unease had grown.

Earth *should* have been receiving their transmissions and *Starburst* *should* have been getting a well-targeted response … but they were not. Perhaps there was some sort of interference outside the ship, disrupting the signal or deflecting it. But what could do that? In their last shifts, Mara had concentrated on finding any rogue astronomical bodies in their path big enough to have a gravity lensing effect, but had come up with nothing.

Their last news from Earth had been disturbing enough. Karic had discovered the transmission by chance on one of their shifts, checking records to see if they were being received but not registered through a computer glitch. Janzen — up to his usual tricks — had managed to bury the record before he descended to Cru in the lander. Karic could see why. Another habitable world, named Kestrel, had been found by a rival company and ExploreCorp was on the edge of ruin. Karic now understood his desperation, but nothing could ever excuse his actions.

Karic led the way through the ship to the main control room. This moment, the reentering of the Earth system, had been something they had feared would never come. The *Starburst* had been away from Earth for almost one hundred and sixty years. Would ExploreCorp still exist? What changes had the planet, and the United Earth government, undergone in that monumental span of years? Would the astronomers of ExploreCorp, of Earth, still be looking for them?

Karic paused briefly in the doorway of the main control room. He was captured by the beauty and clarity of the image of Earth suspended in the twilight of the ship's command center.

Their home world.

Their birth planet seemed so fragile, so unprotected compared to the heavily cloaked leviathan of Cru. Karic found himself on the edge of tears. It would have been easy to give in to the same reckless joy that had seized the others, but he did not have that luxury. He was commander of the *Starburst*. He forced his emotions under control. They could not be sure what reception they would receive.

The three crew took their stations, the dimly-lit room cast into soft relief by the blue and white colors of Earth and the glowing icons of the console interfaces.

"Lights."

The harsh incandescent glare brought the dull steel panels and crowded consoles into sharp relief.

"Keep hailing the ExploreCorp station and Earth on the standard frequencies, Andrai.

"Mara, see what information you can gather on the solar system in general. Intercept a spectrum of electromagnetic communications and see what sort of space-going traffic is out there. I need some sort of indication of what to expect. I don't want to renter Earth orbit if there is any danger to us."

Mara nodded and set about her work. The first flush of excitement was gone now. Both she and Andrai were nervous, subdued by Karic's caution.

His head swam with a sense of unreality. The *Starburst* — his baby — had taken them to a living alien world and back. Despite Janzen, despite the damage to the ship and the threat of the Fintil, it had also carried them home. He felt enormous pride in both her and their own achievements.

Would he ever venture into space again? He had to. He *must*. What they had seen so far was only a taste of the universe. *Life was everywhere.* He knew it now. Life was a property of matter, evolving as surely as star systems from the basic matter of existence. Wonder awaited humanity. It could not end here. Once they told their story, once Earth knew of the advanced race on their doorstop, how could they not reach outward? Maybe not to the dangerous Fintil, but to the score of other races that must be there. His excitement grew. As the bringer of the news, surely he would be at the center of this new drive outward. He was still the same young man — scarcely a year older for all the distances they had covered.

They had masses of data. Everything they had recorded in the Tau Ceti system — including all their images of the massive device orbiting Tau Ceti, and the Fintil spaceship emerging from it. They had footage of the unique life of Cru, of the Imbirri and the Fintil. Somewhere in that storehouse of information would be clues that could advance Earth's science by millennia. How could the mission be judged anything but a success?

Time passed, with both Andrai and Mara busy at their stations. He had so much to tell those who had sent them forth, or more correctly, their successors; about their sojourn on Cru, their experiences with the Imbirri and the Fintil. A thousand memories crowded into his head, but he pushed them away. He tapped the side of the commander's chair impatiently.

"Commander. Janzen is ten minutes from completion of the revival process," reported the Shipcom.

"Understood." Karic stood, eager to be in motion. "Keep trying to make contact. I'll be back soon."

Karic made his way back through the ship, up into the null gravity of the axis. His mind seethed with questions. Had any of the other exploration craft returned? Had Earth colonies been established on Kestrel or any other planets, and if so, how did they fare? But the question that really burned in his mind: had there been contact with other alien life, other sentients, and did these aliens possess the gift ... were they *transformed?*

Karic passed through the twisted airlock into the lander's battered core section. He pulled himself down onto a couch and waited. With the end of this drama nearing, Karic felt a stab of anxiety. As the one who had seized control of the mission, it was he who would be called on to justify his actions. The records of their time on Cru would be crucial to his case. He knew that if Janzen ever gained the upper hand, he would be merciless. To the public he would play a tragic hero — the sort of role his bioengineered looks were made for.

The suspension field disengaged.

Janzen was instantly alert, but bound as he was, could not leave the couch. To the former commander, it would seem only moments ago that Karic and the other crew had forced him to record the transmission back to Earth confessing his crimes and canceling the colonization mission. Blond hair disheveled, his piercing blue eyes hot with outrage, he looked at Karic. The man was still imposing, yet Karic had lost all the respect he once had for him.

"We are back in Earth system, Janzen. Only hours from Earth orbit.

"I am going to take off your gag, but you will stay bound. You can sit with us in the control room ... or stay confined to your quarters. Your choice. At no time are you to give commands to the Shipcom, or access the computer system." He looked at Janzen steadily. "And believe me, I'll be watching."

Janzen nodded.

"At the first hint of trouble from you, I will put you back into stasis. Understood?"

Karic untied the make-shift gag, pushing it into his pocket. He removed the restraints securing Janzen to the couch and freed his legs, but left his hands tied.

Janzen looked away. "I would like to clean up and get a change of clothes."

Karic tried to gauge Janzen's motives. He seemed subdued. "OK. I'll have to watch you."

Janzen turned to Karic, sudden anger flaring in his eyes. Then it was gone. He slid off the couch and pushed off with his legs. He drifted stiffly through the hatch. In Janzen's quarters, Karic untied his hands so he could wash and change into a clean, standard-issue officer's uniform. Surveying himself in the mirror, Janzen's eyes fell on an odin in his storage rack.

"I'll take those," said Karic. "And any others you have."

His jaw clenched as he handed the odin to Karic. No others were forthcoming. Janzen opened a drawer, which shone with a collection of assorted jewelry and decorated combands. He picked out a platinum-encased communicator, chased with gold and gems.

"No, Janzen. I'll take all those as well. I'll get you a standard issue comband." There was no telling how they had been modified.

He tore the expensive communicator off his wrist. "Enjoy it while it lasts, Karic. Because once we are back on Earth, I'll …" Janzen clenched his jaw shut.

"You'll what?"

Janzen remained silent. He handed over all his jewelry and the collection of communicators to Karic. A quick search of the storage compartment yielded three more odins, which Karic took without comment.

"Put out your hands."

Janzen stared back at him, defiant.

"If I have to ask you twice, I *will* put you back into stasis."

Janzen extended his hands and Karic tied them securely. Karic led the way back to the control room, shepherding Janzen down the access tube on its lift platform, which was used to move heavy equipment or non-ambulatory personnel between decks.

Andrai and Mara looked up as Karic exited the accessway hatch, then directed Janzen to a dead terminal in the corner of the control room. They exchanged a quick look with each other, but remained silent.

Karic took his seat in the commander's chair. "Any word back from ExploreCorp, Andrai?"

"No. I am picking up a tremendous amount of EM noise." Andrai met Karic's gaze. "Even so, our signal should be loud and clear."

The *Starburst* was equipped with a powerful communications array. This close to Earth it should be swamping local signals, but still they were not getting through. It was baffling. Soon they would be close enough for visual contact.

"Try a broad spectrum broadcast," said Karic. *Somebody out there must give a damn!*

"What have you got for us, Mara?"

"I have managed to filter out the interference and classify most of the background signals. Based on the radiation I am receiving, there must be thousands of fusion drives in operation in the system," said Mara.

Andrai blinked. "Wow. So many spaceships."

"Thousands?" said Karic, astounded.

"The exact figure is closer to three thousand confirmed. The signals extend from the orbit of Venus to well beyond the asteroid belt. I can't get any accurate readings further out."

Three thousand fusion drives! When they had left orbit in the *Starburst*, the ship had contained one of five working fusion drives. The other four were prototypes. Research work had been progressing on the new anti-matter drives that were to be used for the nine interstellar craft that followed *Starburst*, but none were yet in existence. It did not surprise Karic that Mara had not detected any anti-matter drives in the vicinity. Even with advanced techniques, manufacturing anti-matter was just too damned expensive to support widespread use of the technology.

"Anything else?" asked Karic.

"There is a conglomeration of signals from the whole Earth-Moon axis, everything from radio and EM to laser signals."

"Stretching between the Earth and the Moon?"

Mara nodded. "Yes."

A thrill went through Karic, and for the first time, he was beginning to get a sense of the tremendous changes that had occurred in their absence.

"Are we close enough for high-resolution visuals of the Earth and Moon?"

"Yes." Mara sat forward in her seat, her face alive with excitement.

"Let's see them."

Mara movements were almost fevered. The distant shot of Earth was replaced by magnified views of the Earth and Moon, appearing together on a split screen.

"Oh my God!" said Mara, her shocked gaze fixed on the picture of the Moon.

Karic felt goose pimples rise on the nape of his neck.

The Moon was crisscrossed with glowing threads of amber, blue and brilliant white: transport conduits, stretching for thousands of kilometers across its face like a tracework of fine scars. They connected hundreds of cities that dotted the surface like a collection of jewels, their bright lights undimmed by the cloak of atmosphere.

"We have been away a long time," said Andrai.

Karic uttered on oath under his breath. The first Moon mining settlements — little more than bunkers — were scarcely twenty years old when the *Starburst* left. They had been small operations with a high degree of automation. Now the Lunar population must number in the millions. The tens of millions!

In contrast to the Moon, the Earth's image was unchanged from the familiar one they remembered. This was comforting, and yet alongside the startling transformation of the Moon, it was also somehow disturbing. Earth would also be starkly different, but in hidden ways. What awaited them there?

"Who cares about the Moon? Can you not even get ExploreCorp from this distance?" asked Janzen, who clearly thought they were incompetent.

"Ahh," said Andrai. "We are finally getting something."

Janzen snorted and turned his hand around to examine his nails. Karic could see his chest heaving. The first contact with ExploreCorp would be crucial. It would tell them immediately if they had received their transmissions from Tau Ceti, and if they were going to support Karic's decision to remove Janzen from command.

"Put it through on the overhead speakers," said Karic.

The message boomed from the speakers above them, the Shipcom rapidly compensating for the enormous strength of the signal.

"… approach, identify yourself immediately. Repeat. Starship on Earth orbital approach, identify yourself immediately." The message continued to repeat.

"Shipcom. Broadcast on received signal frequency. Target source. Transmit my voice only, on cue."

"Acknowledged, Commander. What message should I send?"

"This is the ExploreCorp exploration vessel, *Starburst*, inbound from Tau Ceti. Please identify yourself."

The received message continued to repeat for long minutes, then it abruptly cut off.

They cheered, overwhelmed with relief. The cessation of the signal could mean only one thing. Their message got through!

After a short time delay, they were hailed. "*Starburst*, this is Free Colonies Station Fourteen. You are to proceed directly to our orbital position for debriefing. Is this understood?" The voice was heavily accented and the English halting.

"Commander, they are transmitting coordinates," said Andrai.

"To what location?" asked Karic.

The tech quickly processed the data. He looked up from his console and met Karic's gaze. "They correspond to an orbital position over the Moon."

Karic cleared his throat. He touched a small icon floating above the console to cue the transmission. "Free Colonies Station, are you the legal representative of ExploreCorp?" He touched the icon once more to indicate the end of the message.

"*Starburst*, I am Oric Bennet, the Director of this Station," the voice was different, deeper and more confident, yet still heavily accented. "The Mega-Corporations off-world assets became property of the Free Colonies government after the Embargo of 2190 and Earth's surrender. The Free Colonies took responsibility for the unreturned exploration ships sent by the Mega-Corporations, including the *Starburst*. In effect, the Free Colonies owns your ship and all the data you have retrieved.

"Am I speaking to Commander Janzen Davis?"

Janzen's head snapped around to Karic. "They are bluffing. ExploreCorp withdrew all its assets into low Earth orbit."

"I know!" said Karic, his face hot. "Stay silent unless I ask you to speak."

Karic leaned forward. Once more, he used the icon to cue the transmission. "Janzen Davis has been relieved of command. My name is Karic Zand, and I am the commander of this vessel."

There was a pause, which stretched too long. "Very well, Commander Zand. You are directed to take your starship to the coordinates specified, there to await further instructions."

Karic swallowed. He knew of the tension between the Free Colonies and Earth government from the transmissions from Earth. But experiencing it firsthand was a whole different level of reality.

"With regret, I cannot comply. We are bound for Earth orbit, where we will be endeavoring to contact the legal representatives of ExploreCorp."

"Divert immediately," came the voice of Oric. "A squadron of fighter craft have been dispatched to escort you. If you deviate off the flight plan we have supplied you, your ship will be destroyed. Do you understand?"

Blood thumped in his head. Mara and Andrai sat motionless at their stations, their eyes fixed on him.

"Plead systems failure," said Janzen. "It will give us time to get to ExploreCorp and the Earth government."

Karic surged to his feet. "*I said be silent!* One more word out of you and I *will* put you back in suspension."

He paced the deck.

"*Starburst*, you have still not diverted your ship. Our fighters have orders to fire on you."

Chapter 25

Karic could not let *Starburst* be taken by some provisional government. The data she was carrying was too precious to be locked up in some political dispute. How could he keep the fighters at bay and give themselves the time they needed to reach Earth space? In a flash of inspiration, he had it. As infuriating as Janzen was, he was on the right track. The system might be flooded with fusion drives, but nothing they had seen would be like the *Starburst*, with its complex magnetic containment systems for the drive plasma. It was first generation, with all the flexibility of a prototype.

"Andrai, can you introduce a random fluctuation into the magnetic containment fields? Not big enough to put us off course, but enough to flood nearby space with high-energy plasma?"

"Of course."

Andrai drilled through the holographic interface, manipulating key icons to make the adjustments. He swept them away with a gesture, then turned to smile at Karic. *Done.*

Karic cleared his throat, then tapped the broadcast icon. "Director Bennet. I regret to inform you that we have had problems with our fusion drive's containment field for some time. Many of the crew have died from radiation sickness. I urge you to keep your ships distant. I am sure your short-range fighters would have little in the way of shielding," said Karic, ending the transmission with another tap of his finger.

"I am picking up the fighters," said Mara. "Coming in fast on an intercept course. Six small fusion-powered craft. Heavily armed."

There was silence from the Free Colonies station.

"What now?" asked Andrai.

"We wait and see."

The three of them looked at the images of the Earth and the Moon, each growing larger on the screen above them. The orbital traffic was visible now. Mara adjusted the images and they watched in amazement as she showed them the massive stations that filled the Lagrange fields, worlds in their own right.

What would Earth be like?

"*Starburst*, this is Free Colonies Station Fourteen. You are to deviate from your present course and enter lunar orbit as instructed. Under no circumstances are you to enter space controlled by the Earth government."

"Mara, where are the fighters?"

"Still coming in. Hold on … they are decelerating!"

"It's working!" said Andrai.

Karic shot Janzen a look of triumph, but the former commander had sunk down on his chair, his eyes unfocused.

Another message boomed from the speakers. *"Starburst.* This is your final warning. Attack craft are in position with orders to destroy you if you exit the neutral zone into Earth territory."

"Earth territory?" echoed Karic. The Earth he left behind had been a peaceful place. There were minor conflicts, but in most parts of the globe, war was a memory. Neutral zones, territorial borders defended by armed craft; these seemed unwelcome intrusions on the future from mankind's violent past.

"A squadron of ten ships is moving out of Earth orbit toward us," said Mara.

"Finally." Karic unclenched his fists, unaware that he had been holding them closed.

A powerful radio transmission boomed through the cabin. *"Starburst,* maintain your course. This is Commander Salek of the Solar Federation. We have jurisdiction in this matter."

"Solar Federation," snorted Janzen. "Wishful thinking. They only control Earth now."

"The Free Colonies ships are turning," said Mara. "They are on their way back to their station."

Karic sank back into his chair. A wave of tension flowed out of him. *Thank God.* "Andrai. Restore the magnetic containment."

"Roger that." Andrai grinned as he worked the holographic display.

"Welcome to Earth, Commander Karic," came Salek over the speakers. "Your ship appeared on our sensor grid only hours ago. We had no idea you were inbound to the system until we intercepted the Free Colonies transmissions to you. It was almost like you were operating in some sort of stealth mode."

Karic and Andrai looked at each other in nervous silence.

"Have ExploreCorp and Earth received our signals from Tau Ceti?" asked Karic. He waited anxiously. Across the control room, Janzen watched him with taut intensity. The signal's time-delay stretched out into an eternity.

"Negative."

Karic clenched his jaw. How could this be possible?

"Nothing was received from *Starburst* after your last transmission from Epsilon Eridani. Given the intense radiation we are now reading from the Tau Ceti system, we assumed you must have been lost. You are the last, sir."

"The last?" Karic's hands tapped out a restless tattoo on his thighs as he waited.

"The last of the ten interstellar ships that were sent out to return. Your arrival will cause quite a scene."

"Can you tell me where ExploreCorp has its operations now,

Commander? We need to dock and debrief." He felt a tightness in his stomach. He needed to find out if it was he — or Janzen — who would be led away from the airlock in restraints.

"Negative," came the reply. "ExploreCorp folded decades ago when the first reports came in on Kestrel."

"No!" It was a tortured cry, torn from the throat of Janzen. He surged to his feet. "There must be still something! Let me talk to him."

"No."

Janzen advanced on Karic, drawn to his full height, his arrogant poise reminiscent of the powerful executive that once controlled *Starburst*. "The Davises will still have power here, Karic. *I* will still have power. If you ever want to command a ship again, let me talk to him."

Karic had learned the hard way not to give an inch to Janzen. His determination hardened. "Andrai."

"Yes, Commander."

Janzen's face fell.

"Take Janzen back into the lander and put him in stasis. Indefinitely."

"You can't do this!" shouted Janzen as Andrai led him away, but the real power, the real fight in him had gone; torn away with the last of his assets.

Speaking with Salek was frustrating, and each time-delay chaffed at Karic.

"You have chosen well to return to the seat of Solar civilization, Commander Karic. Earth government will look after you.

"You did well to bluff the Free Colonies. Some of these provincial governments will try anything to get hold of the data you have. Off-world colonies are still big business."

Karic rose slowly from his chair, his heart racing.

"How many off-world colonies do we have, Salek?" Karic paused and swallowed. "Have we broken the light barrier?"

There was another pause, then Salek replied, clearly impatient. "We have three colonies, although Kestrel is the only direct Earth-analogue. As for the light barrier: it remains. But the anti-matter drives are up to 0.41C."

Andrai reentered the control room. He nodded to Karic and took his station.

Salek continued, his tone harsh. "You are required to surrender the navigational control of your craft. On behalf of the Federation, I now request you give my computer access to your Shipcom and we will guide you directly to the orbital position of the main Solar Federation station."

He hesitated. Earth was their chosen destination, yet after so many years charting their own destiny, to surrender control seemed wrong. "OK, Andrai. Give them access."

Andrai methodically set the commands then turned to nod at him.

Karic opened the channel to Salek once more. "We have given you access. Bring her in gently," he said, his throat tight with emotion. Soon the adventure would be over. He would be in a foreign century, an engineer once working at the cutting edge of technology, now almost two centuries out of date. What would the future really hold for him now? Would he be able to track down his family's descendants?

"We are receiving another transmission from Salek," said Andrai.

"*Starburst*, your Shipcom is not responding. Please release control to us."

Puzzled, Karic shot a look at Andrai, who shrugged. "They should be in."

Karic reopened the channel. "Salek. You should have control, but we have been experiencing problems with our communication. Please forward the course corrections and we will code them from this end."

There was a delay. "Confirmed."

"We are receiving the vectors now," said Andrai.

"OK. Implement them." Karic looked at the image of Earth on the screen, his neck tight with tension.

"Commander, the ship is not responding to my change in course," said Andrai with a note of panic.

Karic went to Andrai's console, his thoughts for the future banished instantly.

"Computer, why have you not implemented the current course corrections?" said Karic.

"Cannot access. Memory fault ... processor failure." The Shipcom's voice grew steadily more inhuman — a sign of rapid deterioration. "Navigation algorithms ... not accessible."

A cold feeling gripped Karic. *The Fountain!* It was sabotage. Karic paced the deck. Why let them leave Cru at all only to destroy them now? It did not make sense.

"Mara, go down to the drive room, see if you can get direct control of navigation."

She sprinted out the door.

Andrai worked frantically. Icons flashed and spun as he manipulated the interface, throwing key diagnostics up onto the main screens.

"What's happening, Andrai?"

"The ship is maintaining its original course toward Earth orbit. All the navigation and control systems appear to be in perfect working order, but they are not responding to any input."

Karic reopened a channel to the Earth fighters.

"Commander Salek, this is Karic. Our main Shipcom is down, and we have lost navigational control of the craft. We are locked into an orbital approach, but we have no way of knowing if the ship will achieve orbit."

A long silence ensued. There was no doubt in Karic's mind that Salek was weighing the likely truth of their claims, and considering how he could take external control of their vessel. Karic suspected that Salek was not prepared to destroy the ship, and in the end, the Earth Commander had little choice but to work with them — after all, they were not bluffing.

Karic had visions of the ship falling into the atmosphere of Earth, the fusion drive set to detonate like a massive hydrogen bomb, heralding a disaster for their homeworld. Could the Fountain have been cruel enough to let them travel to within sight of Earth before destroying them? No. He could have destroyed them at any time. The Fountain had given his word he would return them to Earth and not threaten their lives — and Karic had felt the truth of that. No. He had other plans for them. *Plans that included blocking all their transmissions!* Of course. He was a fool not to have considered it before. With the wormhole device at his command — utilizing the singularity near Tau Ceti to achieve instantaneous travel through space — the Fountain could have easily sent a ship through space to disrupt their first transmissions, placing another device on the ship before they left orbit to ensure that any subsequent transmissions were neutralized. *Stealth mode indeed.*

Salek's voice blared over the speakers. "Karic, I have command of three heavy-lift low-orbital spacecraft. We will position them on your hull. If you fail to achieve orbital velocity on your final approach, we will push you back away from the planet and keep you there while our engineers board your craft and deactivate your fusion drive.

"Hold tight, *Starburst*. We will monitor your progress. Salek out."

Karic raised his comband to his mouth. "Mara, any luck with the drive?"

"Negative, Commander," replied Mara through the open channel, her voice small and thin as it issued from the tiny speaker. "None of the manual controls are responding. All accessways into the main drive area have been sealed tight — it looks like some sort of weld. We won't get in there without cutting equipment."

Karic froze. *Welds?* Something was actually on the ship! "Mara. Return to the main control room." Whatever the Fintil had placed on the ship had not finished its work, he was sure of that. "Computer, what is the status of your memory?" The big screens flickered.

"The Shipcom's down," said Andrai.

Together, they started a manual computer diagnostic. A visual display of the Shipcom's main processors, memory storage units, sensors and conduits flashed into existence on the main screens.

"Damn!" said Karic. "Half the system is gone."

Memory was being wiped out at phenomenal rates. As he watched, he could see nodes sliding into blackness on the display. Empty. Most of the software could be restored but the rest … It was disappearing before his eyes.

All their data from the mission!

Karic watched, helpless to prevent the destruction, struggling to understand. What could he do? His gaze was fixed on the screen above him as two isolated sections of architecture were disabled with brutal efficiency. Then, gradually, he began to observe a pattern. The targeted areas of memory were all in the same physical location on the ship. The damage was not originating within the system. It was external. It was their saboteur, working with inhuman speed and efficiency.

"Mara. Where are you?" called Karic, through his comband.

There was nothing but static. She should have returned to the main control room by now.

"Maybe she's in a dead spot," said Andrai, talking about the many areas of the ship where the radio signals would not penetrate.

Karic grimaced.

"There's a pattern to this," said Andrai.

"Yes. Something is moving physically through the ship," said Karic, pointing at the viewscreen above them. "You can see its location as it moves from section to section."

"Yes. If it was a computer virus it would have moved from the Shipcom to the main archiving areas then out to the peripheral processing units, but it's jumping around everywhere. It went from the Shipcom modules in the main hold directly into the lander computers."

"Which aren't directly connected, but are both in the central hold."

Andrai stood, drawing closer to the viewscreen as he traced out the pattern. "From the central hold it proceeded directly to the main fusion drive area, then on—"

"Mara was in the fusion drive area!" Karic gripped the back of Andrai's chair. "Where is it now?"

"It's moving through the atmospheric processing units."

What was it and how could they fight it? He did not dare use anything as dangerous as an XR32 inside *Starburst*. The ship security detail had high-voltage electrical stunners. With luck, they might be powerful enough to disrupt the electronics of a robotic device — assuming what they faced was anything like their own technology. They had to try something.

"Andrai, take a stunner and see if you can intercept it. I am going to find Mara and warn her." If that thing had not already found her.

They armed themselves with stunners from the small armory on the main deck, then raced into the ship.

Karic climbed the shaft into the zero-g of the ship's axis, alert for any danger. He cursed the Fountain. If any harm came to Mara, he swore he would take his revenge on the arrogant Fintil, regardless of the awesome technology at his command.

He found Mara floating prone and unconscious in the accessway to the fusion drive. Her dark hair was damp with sweat, fringe plastered to her forehead, her face flushed. He cradled her, calling to her, desperately trying to rouse her. Even her uniform was soaked through. Her eyelids flickered open, and she pushed him away.

"What happened, Mara? Can you remember anything? What attacked you?"

As her vision cleared, she focused on Karic, and a look of confusion came over her face. "Karic ... have we reached the target star?" She looked around her at the accessway, then back at Karic. There was fear in her eyes. "What am I doing here? I don't remember ... *anything*."

Terror gripped Karic as he finally understood the purpose of the Fountain's device. It had the capacity to wipe out all forms of memory, *even human memory*. His heart beat like a drum, flooding his body with adrenaline. It was hard to think. To clear his mind.

"Karic, what's the matter?"

"Mara, listen to me carefully. Do you remember the accident, the deaths, the planet Cru, the Imbirri ...?"

Mara concentrated, then cried out in agony. She collapsed into a ball, clasping her head as she bounced around in the zero-g. Karic steadied her. Her body was rigid with pain.

"The Fintil," she gasped.

Sweat broke out on her forehead, then as abruptly as it had began, the pain left her.

Mara met his gaze. "I remember some things Karic, but the planet ... *Fuck!*" She paled. "I can't remember anything about the planet, or the star system. I get vague images of the aliens, but nothing more. What's happened?"

A look of concentration and determination came over her face and the pain started again. After a few moments, she cried out and sagged against him, weak, but conscious. Karic guided her back through the ship's axis to the lowest level of the habitat, where the sleeping quarters were. He took Mara to her cabin and secured her in her harness.

"Rest, Mara. Rest. We will be back on Earth soon."

She fell into a deep, exhausted sleep. She must have fought the device with every ounce of her strength. Still, she had lost.

Karic's terror turned to fury. Somehow he *had* to defeat this device. He could not let everything they had achieved — everything they had sacrificed — come to nothing.

Think. *Think!*

He had to ensure that the last, untouched records of Cru, which lay secure in the Commander's cabin, were not destroyed. But how to deceive this Fintil device?

Karic turned toward the commander's cabin, even more wary than he had been before. He raised the comband to his mouth. "Andrai, where are you?" He had sent him against this thing, whatever it was.

"I am following the Fintil device, tracking it through the damage it is causing, but it's moving too fast. I can't catch it."

"Break off the pursuit. I want you to meet me in my cabin, but take a route that leads you as far away from that thing as possible. Under no circumstances are you to try to confront or destroy it, understood?"

"Yes. On my way."

Karic walked slowly along the corridor to the commander's cabin, bouncing in the low-g. If the device had the capacity to destroy specific sections of human memory, it also had the capacity to read and understand it. If it got control of him, it would be able to lift the safe's deactivation code from his mind, and the priceless data would be gone.

If he could distract the thing for long enough, Andrai may be able to take the disks and beam the contents directly to the computers of the Solar Federation. Once inside a network of that size, there was no way a single device could track down and destroy all the data.

Karic entered the cabin, unconsciously scanning the cramped confines with his senses. Andrai entered behind him. The tech's blond hair was wild, and he was out of breath, but his light gray eyes were clear and focused. Karic drew him further into the room and explained Mara's condition.

"It wiped her memories?" Andrai said, astounded.

Karic nodded gravely. "I think I understand the Fountain's intent now. He wanted us back on Earth, but with no memory of Cru or the Fintil." He also wanted Mara and Andrai to be transformed by their contact with Karic. To act with him as harbingers of an unstoppable transformation for humanity. But that would not happen. The Fountain had judged the whole human race based on the power of Karic's altered mind; but as a human, he was unique. Mara and Andrai, like most of humanity, although responsive to his mental bond, could not develop his abilities through contact. "Once we were back in the Earth system, all records of the location of Cru, the planet itself, the Imbirri and the Fintil were to be destroyed."

"Including our own memories," said Andrai.

"Yes."

Andrai drew a breath. "Is it possible one of the Fintil is concealed on the ship? To be able to wipe out human memory, this thing would have to be partially sentient."

Karic did not want to speculate. They would discover the exact nature of the intruder soon enough. "How much longer do we have before it destroys every last vestige of memory storage on the ship, including our high-density backup media and holo-disks?"

"At the rate it's moving, it probably already has."

A shot of fear went through Karic. If its first task was complete, it would be coming for them.

"We don't have much time, Andrai. It's imperative that we transmit a record of our journey back to Earth, and that one of us remembers exactly what happened on that planet. For our sake, and for mankind's. I don't trust either the Fintil or the Har Confederation."

Karic looked into Andrai's eyes, gauging his strength. "I want you to take the data backup disks to the main control room and broadcast the contents to the Solar Federation. Then I want you off this ship. Take one of the pods and head straight for the surface with the disks."

"But boss — you should be the one who survives this. Let me face this thing. You take the disks. Take them and run. Don't wait to transmit them. Just launch a pod and go."

Karic shook his head. "No, Andrai. I will have to fight this thing like a Fintil — with my mind. I am the only one who can. You have to be the one to take the data, before it takes you."

Karic walked over to the safe to retrieve the disks. He jolted to a standstill when a beam of focused white-blue energy appeared from midair. It sliced into the safe's shield. At first, the barrier resisted. He covered his eyes as the beam flared brighter, and edged away from its increasing heat. There was a flash, then a detonation that threw them off their feet and slammed them into the bulkhead behind them. Karic grunted at the impact, winded. Most of his velocity had been lost in the impact, but he still bounced off the metal and floated back into the cabin. He struggled for a breath amid the fume and smoke, seeing Andrai still beside him.

"No!" The safe! The Fintil device had vaporized everything inside the armored chamber. The last records of Cru were gone.

Karic and Andrai scrambled back to their feet and drew their stunners, turning in a circle.

"Andrai! Run for the pods! Go!"

"I can't let you face this thing alone."

Andrai gasped in pain and fell to his knees, holding his head. His eyes rolled and he fell unconscious to the floor.

Only Karic was left. Initially, he sensed nothing. Then he felt a sharp tingling across his skin. The sensation broadened out across his body. Invisible needles lanced through him, moving back through his nervous system from extremities to the brain stem. The stunner slipped from his fingers and tumbled to the floor in slow motion.

The Fintil device gripped his mind and he grunted in pain. A high-frequency vibration pulsed into his skull, triggering a chemical release, shaking loose a flood of memories. A hot needle punched into his forehead, seeking to shatter those memories like painted glass.

This was the ultimate violation.

Karic stumbled into the charred and smoking remains of the commander's safe, slashing open his knee on a shard of metal. Pain stabbed into him, but was lost in a rising swell of rage. Desperately, he sought some way to pull away from the device, yet failed. It seemed to have no substance at all, perhaps constructed of some sort of transformed matter. Unwilling to be defeated, he reached out toward its artificial mind.

Karic felt a surge of energy as the mental bond was formed. Then he was suspended in a space filled with glowing shafts and dials, each shimmering and shifting like holographic visions. He understood where he was and what he faced. The device had more than advanced artificial intelligence; it had the capacity to interface directly with a sentient being.

More hot needles stabbed into his brain. The device was completing its task. If he did not act soon, all his memories of Cru would be gone. He reached out toward the floating icons, sending powerful and directed thought-commands, seeking to deactivate or disable the device. Nothing worked. His time was running out. Karic faced thousands of glowing icons, each a different color and shape. How was he to find the right one and then send the correct message toward it?

Another wave of pain hit him as the device probed deeper.

He floated through the space, distant from his body and without form. There seemed to be no pattern to the arrangement of objects. Somehow, he had to extract order from the chaos. He wandered through the myriad shapes as though through a forest, completely at a loss. Then he looked up. Darkness. *He was thinking like a human*. To command the device, he had to think like a Fintil. With a burst of mental power, he leapt into the air on invisible wings, rising above the confused mass to view it from above. As he rose, the shapes grouped together to form a single glyph. A stylized spiral. Its colors moved through the spectrum from deep red to bright violet at the central icon, a slim oval. It was here that Karic directed his thought-command.

Stop program.

There was a last stab of pain, then his mind was released. Karic was back in the room. The ruins of the safe smoked and hissed. Andrai was prone on the floor. A bright globe hovered above his head. Its rapid spin slowed as it powered down. He sensed the device waiting for further commands. Receiving no instructions, it faded into invisibility.

His eyes fluttered, and darkness rose to claim him.

Chapter 26

Karic walked slowly along the plush, carpeted corridor.

The main station of the Earth-controlled Solar Federation was huge. He watched the moving landscapes on the wall-screens with a sense of wonder. It was hard to believe this was a space station. It seemed more like an up-market hotel. A self-contained habitat almost a kilometer in diameter and twelve kilometers long. Despite the luxurious surroundings, he still found himself aching for a *real* view — a glimpse of the stars or perhaps an artificial garden or food-production area — but he had not seen a single viewport on the station, which felt odd to him. The Station's busy inhabitants seemed perfectly content inside their artificial environment. But he had little time to puzzle over 24th century civilization.

To his left walked Olek Durez, his appointed counsel for today's hearing. To his right, a security guard. He was a prisoner. His fate, and the fate of the others, would hinge on the hearing. Olek was a tall, thickset man of middle years. His well-proportioned, symmetrical face would have been called handsome in Karic's time, yet in the 24th century, he was merely average. It seemed beauty was something purchased here, the illegal genetic enhancements of his time now routine procedures undertaken by concerned parents with no more thought than agreeing to a pre-natal ultrasound. He grinned. *Even Janzen's looks might be below average here.*

Both Olek and his guard had a barcode on their inner left forearm around five centimeters in length that glowed against their pale skin with a faint blue luminescence. At first, he thought it was a common style of decoration, but then he saw every single person here had the strange tattoo — some glowing in other colors. Karic wondered what it signified, and with the extensive debriefings and court preparations, had not had a chance to ask.

They reached a branching in the corridors.

He felt Olek's hand on his arm, his touch gentle, as though in sympathy. "This way, Mr. Zand."

Olek led the way down a long corridor, indistinguishable from the rest.

Karic had been roused by the Earth rescue team some hours after the final battle with the Fintil device. He was relieved to discover his memories of Cru intact. Of the device itself, there was no sign. The *Starburst* had been shunted into orbit, the fusion drive shut down manually by the Solar Federation recovery team. Karic, Mara, Andrai and a disoriented Janzen had been taken onto the Station under heavy guard. They were separated and subjected to intense questioning.

They reached another intersection, and Karic saw Andrai and Mara being led to the hearing from an approaching corridor. "Andrai! Mara!" He waved. They smiled and returned the gesture. Dressed in clean ExploreCorp uniforms from the supplies on *Starburst*, they were a welcome sight. Andrai's hair had been closely cut, and he was clean-shaven — it was the most presentable Karic had seen the tech since his *Starburst* screening interviews before crew selection. Mara's hair was artfully coiffed, and she was wearing earrings and carefully applied make-up with an off-red lipstick. It made her seem even more remote and distant than usual. It also made her look so dated — like a living portrait from the past. The faultless complexions of the 24th century, the product of genetic enhancement and advanced cosmetic medicine, needed no artificial concealment. The earrings at least would pass without comment, perhaps seeming understated in an era where displaying a profusion of jewelry — most of it concealing computing power — was common.

"Try and maintain a certain decorum, Mr. Zand. The judge will be watching you closely for signs of instability," came Olek's soft voice. He saw Mara and Andrai's minders speaking to them as well, no doubt telling them not to talk with Karic before the proceedings.

Karic gritted his teeth and kept his eyes ahead. After all they had suffered together, being separated so abruptly after their rescue had been hard to bear. When Andrai and Mara's group joined his, they exchanged frustrated glances, but being hemmed in by their minders there was no chance of conversation. As they turned a corner, they saw the big, gold alloy doors that led to the chambers. Two fresh-faced guards, looking muscle-bound in their tight-fitting black Solar Federation uniforms, flanked the entrance.

Approaching from yet another corridor came Janzen, also with a security guard and an advising counsel. Karic was pleased to see he was getting no special treatment. Janzen was dressed immaculately, if a little out of date. Someone had obviously transferred all his personal effects from the *Starburst*. The fine tailoring and rich colors of his clothes reinforced his patrician posture, even if he did not own more than one damaged, outdated starship. Restored in confidence, he looked down his nose at Karic when they met in front of the doors. "Today you will find out exactly what happens when you cross a Davis, Karic. They will lock you up for so long you will never see the light of day again."

"That's enough, Mr. Davis," cautioned his counsel, a thin man with a soft, effeminate face and high, reedy voice.

As they waited in tense, uncomfortable silence for the chamber doors to open, another group approached along Janzen's corridor. They were dressed in rich, bright fabrics, some shimmering with enhanced light displays and hints of 3D imagery projected into the space around them — the current height of fashion. At the center of the group was an older man and a young woman, both dark-haired, with smooth olive skin and serious demeanors. Both wore heavy jewelry — earrings, chains and wristbands glinting gold and silver from myriad facets and set with gems. They wore an advanced generation of odin that Karic had never seen before, even on his interrogators, merely an ultra-thin band above their eyebrows that projected a holographic display. The image appeared as a scrambled patchwork of ghostly color to Karic, but he knew it would be clearly visible to the wearer, and only appeared that way to him because of some sort of visual encryption that would be decoded by the wearer's glasses. The man and the woman were flanked by four advisors, with another two burly men walking a step behind. *Personal security.* The whole group, even the hired muscle, would have been at home at a 22nd century red carpet event, their looks and physiques impeccable. Everything about them reeked of wealth. The man at the center of the group gave Karic a frankly assessing look, while the woman's attention was elsewhere. Karic saw her lips move without sound and realized she was talking inside a noise blanket so seamless not even a trace of interference escaped. One of the door guards approached them. The older man talked swiftly and impatiently to him, after which the guard backed away.

Janzen's face lit up. He gave Karic a triumphant smile and marched over to them. His heart sank. *So the Davises have come to the rescue.*

The doors opened with a thud.

"Stand back, please!" called out a door guard.

Another group filed out of the chambers, a single man surrounded by tight security, and two counselors who nodded amiably to Olek as they passed.

Olek looked at his watch, betraying impatience. Karic took a deep breath. So this was all routine. Just another case, perhaps with a twist, but just another case all the same.

He looked over at Janzen, who had rejoined his counsel and was talking heatedly. His face was flushed red and he was seriously upset.

Across the room, the older man and the woman had shut down their odins and were now both looking at Karic with unabashed interest. The woman absently tapped the right corner of her mouth twice. Karic blinked as her lip color flashed to a vivid green, then to a dull purple. *Implanted genes that express color, probably controlled by the release of key chemicals from computer-controlled implants.* Karic suppressed a sense of irrational fear. Was he truly home, or somewhere alien? This was just cosmetics — he had yet to see the real changes on Earth.

"Enter now, if you please," said the second guard.

Inside, the room was smaller than Karic had expected. The walls were plain, the ubiquitous wall-screens of the Station absent. It had low ceilings and rows of basic seating covered with synthetic gray fabric. The judge was dressed in thin black robes, and seated behind a wide desk with imitation-wood paneling. His balding head shone in the overhead lights. Considering the advances in cosmetic technology, Karic assumed the judge must think the bald dome made him look impressive, perhaps stately. His looks could still have made him a 22nd century vid-star. Two men sat with him, one to his left in civilian clothes, one to his right in an immaculate Solar Federation uniform. Each was scrolling through compact e-readers in last minute preparation. Karic fought the disconcerting illusion that none of this was real, simply a play conducted by a cast of fine-looking actors for their own amusement — and at his expense. He fought down the fear, knowing it arose from his own secret terror at having no control over his fate.

The bailiff stood up and looked over the crowd. "Please be seated."

At the door, the SF security men were turning away the advisors and guards of the rich-looking man and woman, who were forced out while their employers entered the room and took their seats at the back without objection.

"The court is now in session. Honorable Judge Yanel presiding." The familiar legal phrasing helped to focus Karic. *Perhaps not so much has changed.*

Karic turned to give Andrai and Mara, seated behind him with their minders, a nervous smile before turning back to the judge.

Yanel took one last look at his e-reader then set it down. "Hmmm," he said, finally looking up at the crowd. "Case KZ354A," said the judge, his terse voice picked up and broadcast around the room via hidden microphone. He looked up at the wall clock. "We seem to be running late, so let's keep the oratory down to a minimum."

The judge looked at each of the counselors, who nodded immediately in response. *No prizes for guessing who rules the room.*

"Right. This is a hearing only. An unusual case. Commander Janzen Davis and sub-Commander Karic Zand, both of the exploration ship *Starburst* — ExploreCorp, now defunct — have laid charges against each other. Brief summaries please, gentlemen." Yanel nodded at Janzen's counsel to go first.

Karic watched as the thin counselor stood. "These are the charges Mr. Davis wants brought against Mr. Zand: Unlawful assumption of command. Insubordination. Thirty-four counts of murder. And a long list of specific grievances." He read mechanically, swiftly, than sat. Janzen's face was tight with tension, his blue eyes intent, mouth a thin line in his perfect face. He did not look at Karic.

Olek stood up. "The charges Mr. Zand wants brought against Mr. Davis: Gross Dereliction of Duty after being lawfully removed from command. Disobeying direct orders. Attempted murder. Thirty-three counts of murder." Olek looked over at Janzen's counsel and smiled. "*And a long list of specific grievances.*"

Yanel tapped his desk thoughtfully with his right index finger. "Many of these charges might have been of interest to ExploreCorp had its corporate structure still been intact. As it is, it has no legal successor. Only a long list of unsatisfied debtors.

"The only charge of interest here is that of murder."

Yanel paused and looked directly at Karic and Janzen. "There is no doubt that deaths have occurred. The bodies of thirty crew and three officers were found in storage on the *Starburst*. One officer. Err ..." Yanel looked down at his e-reader. "Ibri Haus. Reported missing.

"I have the statements of both Janzen Davis and Karic Zand here. I have read through them in detail."

Yanel took a deep breath and looked them over silently for a moment. "Honestly, I'm perplexed. Here we have two differing, seemingly wildly exaggerated reports. Alien insectoids. Advanced species. Black hole devices ... It reads like fiction. From what I understand, the radiation counts are too high for any possibility of life in the Tau Ceti system."

Yanel put down his e-reader and looked across to the man on his right. "Has the Solar Federation concluded its investigation, Colonel Rimsky?"

"It has, your honor."

"And your findings?"

"There is no doubt the *Starburst* took heavy radiation damage. This much is consistent with our readings of the Tau Ceti system. All the deaths on the ship are the result of radiation-induced failure of the suspension systems and direct tissue damage from radiation."

"And there is no doubt?"

"None at all, your honor."

"And your additional findings?"

"The Shipcom was found to be severely damaged and contained no command memory, and no data. There is simply no evidence."

"No record at all? What of the claims regarding these transmissions from Tau Ceti?"

Rimsky shook his head. "Nothing was ever received, your honor."

"And the surviving crew?"

"Mara and Andrai are suffering from memory loss consistent with a probable malfunction of the suspension gear."

"And what of Karic and Janzen?"

Rimsky smiled. "For that, I will defer to my honorable colleague."

Yanel turned to the man on his left. He was the oldest of the three men on the panel, with hair artfully streaked with gray at the temples and lines around his eyes and face that had not been erased by cosmetic procedures. He seemed bored by the proceedings.

"Dr. Valdof. What are your findings?"

Valdof cleared his throat. "We have examined both candidates thoroughly, using every test at our disposal to assess their mental state."

A sheen of sweat broke out on Karic's forehead, which cooled instantly in the dry, recycled air.

Valdof spoke with a slight accent, something vaguely Eastern European. Although what that signified in the 24th century, Karic had no idea. "Although appearing lucid, it is significant that their delusions diverge so radically, while placing each other in the role of wrongdoer. These two non-existent transmissions are a prime example. Each contains the missing evidence that would incriminate the other. It's the classic centerpiece of the paranoid delusion — providing all justification and proof, and yet insubstantial upon analysis.

"After careful assessment, it is our conclusion that physical damage to the brain sustained in the return from Tau Ceti, combined with the psychological stress of the conditions, and the tension between the commander and sub-commander, induced fantasy scenarios that played out their internal feelings."

"So you see little basis in fact for these ... fantastical stories?"

"No, your honor. Spaceflight ... The stresses on the human brain are enormous. We have seen this before: in the return of the *Ulysses* in 2278. There the entire crew seemed to have been affected."

"And again, no evidence was recovered?"

"No. *Ulysses* was badly damaged. They had lost suspension entirely, so they were old men and women by the time they made it back. How they survived on biodome crops and recycled water, I have no idea."

The bailiff cleared his throat. "Excuse me, your honor. The time?"

Yanel grunted. "Yes." He looked squarely into the courtroom. "Well. I see no justification for proceeding with either of these two sets of charges. The question to be decided is, can these four be released on their own recognizance?"

The judge turned to Rimsky.

"Well, your honor. I have discussed this with my honorable colleague Dr. Valdof, and we both agree that Andrai Wright and Mara Montes should be released immediately. They are quite sane and no danger to themselves."

"They will have a pension I believe?"

Rimsky cleared his throat. "Yes. And they will be free to apply for service in the SF corps if they wish to pursue a military career. We are always looking for skilled people in the Space Service."

"What of Zand and Davis?"

Valdof leaned in to answer the question. "I was going to recommend that they both be remanded to an institution where they can receive treatment for their conditions."

"And now, Dr. Valdof?"

"My recommendation stands for Janzen Davis, who seems to have no close family left alive. Or at least no family with any interest in identifying themselves."

"And for Zand?"

"We have come to an arrangement that he will be taken into the care of his own family."

"Very good," said Yanel, sweeping his gaze across the courtroom. "And is the family of Karic Zand present in the court?"

The older man Karic had seen in the corridor stood. "Yes, your honor."

Karic's eyes widened. Those were not Davises. They were his own family. He turned and met the man's gaze, which was still wary. No wonder. *They think I'm insane.*

Janzen was crying. He had completely collapsed onto his table, his shoulders heaving as he wept. The guard beside him had one hand on his arm, clearly ready for anything.

"Please identify yourself for the court."

"Jureth Lein Zand."

Karic felt his legs go weak. His family. *His own family.* He had given up hope. Tears coursed down his cheeks, but they were tears of sheer joy.

The judge sat upright, Valdof and Rimsky were also suddenly alert. "*The* Jureth Zand. Of Offworld Enterprises?"

"Yes."

Comprehension flooded the judge's face. "Of course! Karic Zand was the inventor of the suspension technology." He looked back at Karic with new respect. "You're *that* Karic Zand. I had no idea ..." Yanel took a deep breath, cleared his throat, then looked back at the clock. His jaw tightened.

"Well, Mr. Zand," said Yanel, addressing Jureth. "Are you willing to take Karic into your custody and ensure he has every care until he should recover from his err ..." He looked at Karic, unsure for the first time in the proceedings. "His illness?"

"Yes, your honor. My factors have already completed all the applications."

Yanel hit the desk with his gavel. "So the court rules. Bailiff, clear the court. Next case!"

Valdof and the SF investigator exited swiftly through rear doors.

Andrai and Mara raced to Karic. They wrapped their arms around him, both laughing and crying in relief. Mara's careful makeup was streaked with tears, but to him, she looked more beautiful than every single, perfect face around him.

Jureth and the younger woman walked over to Karic. He could see the family resemblance between them, the smooth features, dark hair and olive skin. Jureth stopped a few paces away and smiled at him. "Karic, let me introduce my niece, Rosa."

The young woman smiled and extended her hand. Karic shook it in a daze. She had his grandmother's green eyes, dazzling in a smooth, perfectly proportioned face. The room swam around him as his eyes misted with tears of relief.

Karic turned to watch Janzen being led out of the courtroom. The tall man he had once called a friend looked back at him, but there was no recognition in his eyes, just a forlorn hopelessness. Then he was gone. His crimes had gone unpunished, but then the loss of his power and position in the Earth system — that was probably the hardest punishment that could be meted out to a man like Janzen. But more importantly, with the loss of his power, he became that much less dangerous to those around him.

"Are you ready?" asked Jureth.

"Yes. Can Andrai and Mara accompany us?"

"I don't see why not."

It all fit into place. Karic had never signed the suspension technology over to ExploreCorp; instead, he had let them use his invention under license. Ownership would have passed to his surviving family.

"This way," said Jureth stiffly indicating the exit and the retinue of six, who waited outside.

"Oh, Uncle. Don't be so formal." Rosa took Karic by the arm and led him out. The gentle touch was welcome. "Suspension technology is the core of Offworld Enterprises, Karic. There isn't a single ship that leaves orbit without our hardware. Your invention transformed our world."

Jureth turned to one of his aides. "Is our Flyer prepped and ready?"

"Yes, sir."

"Very good. We'll be back in Boston in thirty minutes, Karic." Jureth smiled for the first time. "I'm sure you and your crew could all do with some relaxation after one-hundred and sixty years on the job."

***

Earth was beautiful. The cities were green, elegant and understated. The vast landscapes of concrete — the huge ugly towers he remembered — had been replaced by underground networks of astounding complexity. Those structures above ground were all elevated, leaving the ground below them free to live and flower. Silent transports flew through the air under full computer control. The air was clean, the skies clear, and the waters of the Earth renewed.

Karic sipped his drink and watched as Rosa, slim and graceful, dived into the big swimming pool on their open terrace. Above him, the sun was hot and huge. The sky pale and limitless. It would take some getting used to after Cru.

The Zand residence rose high above Boston, overlooking an idyllic vista of green and widely spaced towers like a scattered array of artworks in glass and steel. The suburbs he remembered were long gone, demolished in the name of progress, and their remains ploughed into the renewed Earth. This *was* an alien world.

The society was more rigid than he remembered. The hereditary rich flaunted their wealth in a way that would have been abhorrent to the liberal sensitivities of his time, forming an oligarchy of entrenched power whose elite families had a constitutional basis for membership on United Earth advisory and enforcement councils. It was an aristocracy in all but name, tolerated by wider society only because the wealthy and ambitious social climbers of the middle-class knew they could buy their way into it.

The population was greater than ever. Despite strict and limiting birth controls, the Earth was still dealing with the legacy of centuries of unrestrained and frenzied growth. In the big cities, most of the people lived and worked in subterranean Urban Zones. The privileged few dwelt above, and only they had the wealth for frequent travel, or could afford the fees charged for access to the great World Heritage areas or other Environmental Precincts. The rural Production Zones were controlled by hereditary land-owners who retained some measure of social and cultural control, and it appeared the city-country divide was greater than ever.

Karic had visited one of the middle-class Urban Zones under Boston. The corridors and shopping centers were pleasant, and the brightly lit squares and park spaces had overhead screens that depicted faultless images of the surface sky. All of it projected a numbing gestalt of suburban and corporate environments. Most of these wealthy areas were integrated with the surface landscapes at their highest level, giving free access to the open air. But still, this was only part of the vast underground structure that housed the population. The tip of the social pyramid.

When Karic had insisted on exploring further, the tolerant smiles of his family had become strained. Eventually, they relented … with conditions. He was allowed to visit the deeper Urban Zones, but only protected by Zand minders. Here, Karic had seen the true face of Earth. The seamless genetic enhancement of upper classes was absent, replaced instead by the vast human lottery he remembered — short, tall, weird, ugly, dysfunctional — the whole gamut of humanity. There, he saw the disfigurement of industrial accidents worn casually like work-wear, just another burden to be borne by those without the wealth for advanced treatments. The harried workers, with pale skin and haunted eyes, hurried past him through cramped tunnels and squares, all lit by vid-screens that broadcasted an endless mix of advertisements and calming landscapes. It was there, in the shadows, that he began to see the seeds of the discontentment that had triggered the system-wide civil war between Earth and the Free Colonies, which had fractured human society. These disenfranchised men and women were the losers.

The level of enforced control in Earth society was frightening to Karic. The ubiquitous wall-screens lost much of their charm when Karic learned they also functioned as cameras, part of a computer-controlled network that continuously monitored the population.

There were other areas where not even his security team would venture. Karic had seen enough to know what he would find there. The slums of this world, rife with crime and misery, hidden out of sight below the lofty towers of the wealthy and their perfect skies. Yet even these people would have some say in their future, surely?

No.

Although democracy survived, the right to vote had to be purchased — either though a tightly controlled loan scheme, or by vital public service, such as time served in armed services or other hazardous duties. The gap between the wealthy elite and the Insiders — those that spent the bulk of their lives in the artificial environments of space or the Urban Zones — was vast. Most of the low-paid workers and social rejects of the underground slums never had a chance to cast a single vote in support of any reforms ... Karic shuddered. No wonder they had given up looking for windows. There was nothing to see beyond them but more darkness.

And here he was in the Zand tower, in the lap of his own inherited privilege. He touched the Timezone marker on his inner wrist. The glowing barcode with its embedded processors still stung from the procedure. Karic was still reeling from the knowledge that his own invention — the suspension technology — had caused massive social upheavals. In the early years after its discovery, misuse had been rife, leading to a global economic crisis as financial institutions collapsed. Early users had frozen themselves in time, growing rich on accumulated investments, jumping into a new future.

The social impact of stasis technology had been huge. Offworld travelers had returned to a foreign society decades distant from their cultural origin. They were "out of their time", with loved ones either dead or bizarrely aged compared to their memories of them, and fought a losing battle to adjust. Out of all of this had come the legal basis for the registration of Timezones: whole communities registered to keep step with each other, forming viable social units. Members within a single Timezone had to stay in sync, the planet-bound going into stasis to match their age and context with those who travelled off-world. There were now complex rules that governed assets, to halt the abuse of financial institutions using the technology, and other rules to allow individuals to transfer between Timezones. Clever processors hidden under the Timezone marker's barcode recorded biological 'live time', uploading data to central databases every time it was scanned.

Still — there had been untold benefits from the suspension technology that went beyond space travel. Terminal patients could be held in stasis until treatments were available. Those injured in accidents held frozen in time until help could arrive, or organ replacements grown.

And the Zand Empire got a piece of it all.

And genetic enhancement ... Karic's head swam. The colonists that had left the solar system for new worlds had been modified for their new environments. While here on Earth, citizens could legally apply for the most bizarre and radical procedures. These were usually cosmetic, following the more extreme dictates of flesh-shaping vogues among the rich.

He had found it hard to engage with this modern world. Rosa and Jureth had insisted on him attending a round of high-society soirees to introduce him to an endless array of Zand business associates. They were decadent affairs, well stocked with social climbers and the dissolute rich. He had quickly backed away from the proposals to use his wealth in various Earth-bound schemes — Karic had never been interested in wealth as an end in itself, and in that way was profoundly different from his living descendants. He had been propositioned by many beautiful women — and men — who had been attracted by his wealth, and intrigued by the novelty of this "primitive" man out of his time. The fluid sexuality of this new elite ground against the values of his own time. The Zand servants watched their masters at play with the stony indifference he had seen in the low-class Urban Zones, an assumed manner that masked impotent resentment, making him realize this sort of sexual play was a game for the idle rich. It had been academic in any case — his internal struggle to adjust had made even the most casual liaison untenable.

Mara and Andrai had stayed with them only one month. As soon as their applications into the SF forces were processed, they had left for training on the stations in orbit. They were eager to start again. Faced with the same hole in his memories, Karic would have been the same.

He had mind-bonded with both of them. Sharing his own memories. They were profoundly affected, and had seen through his eyes the real events on Cru. Even so, they had refused to jeopardize their own future by supporting his story. At this demonstration of his mental powers, they were awed. Even so, neither of them spoke of it again. As he suspected, the abilities that Mara had begun to show on Cru were now fully dormant. The altered genes in Karic's brain had awakened something in him that evolution had yet to bring forward in the human race. The Fintil seemed to think it was inevitable, a hallmark of evolution as primary as the ability to communicate through speech, or sentience itself. Was he now alone with his gift? Were there others like him who hid their abilities?

Of the others who now supported him, not a single person — not even in his own family — had been willing to believe the truth. He had soon learned his best strategy was to stay silent and act "reformed". He had access to considerable wealth, but he was restless on Earth. After all that he had strived for ... there had to be more.

Setting foot on another living world like Cru had changed him forever. The Earth was at once more precious and smaller. It was nothing but a taste of what space had to offer.

He had passed all his psychological evaluations for six months running. Technically, he was free. But the SF interstellar program would not touch him. He was tainted. Outdated.

By the standards of the 22nd century, the people of the 24th were wealthy. While it was true that the beauty and wildness of the surface had been restored — a testament to the utopian dreams of the Environment movement — this came at the cost of individual freedom. Karic could understand why off-world colonies were such big business. The Earth government was harsh and uncompromising, the people heavily controlled in every aspect of their lives.

In Karic's view, Earth was inward looking and lost, her people trapped within her cities, lost in a descending spiral of cultural burn-out. Controlled by suffocating layers of bureaucracy and a rigid social structure that was edging toward a crisis.

He was pulled out of his reverie by a soft tone from his odin. He picked it up and slipped it on, a thin band held across his forehead by loops over his ears similar to those on conventional glasses. He was still getting used to them.

"Mr. Zand?" A visual of Markem, one of Jureth's aides, appeared in front him, as though the Zand business manager was sitting at his desk right there on the wet poolside tiles.

"Yes, Markem."

"Good news, Karic. Davis has agreed to our last offer."

Karic sat forward. "When can we take possession?"

"Within the week."

"Excellent. I would think the Federation will be pleased to have it off their hands."

"Instructions?"

"Move her to low orbit transfer station 738. Proceed with the program of repairs and modifications I forwarded to you last month. I'll be up to supervise within the week."

"Understood. Markem out." Markem and the desk vanished.

302

Rosa climbed out of the pool, smiling as she toweled herself off. Her one-piece outfit rippled with an ever-changing array of colors that complemented her olive skin. She was framed against the charming prospect of the Boston skyline, manicured green below and blue sky above. Karic was struck again by her unblemished beauty.

She walked toward him. "You got her?"

"Yes!"

"Congratulations. But you know there are better ways to spend your money."

"I know. But I need to do something off-world. At least for now." Karic took another sip of his drink.

"You will need to change Timezone," said Rosa. Her voice was flat, failing to conceal her disappointment. Karic's decision meant that an irrevocable divide would open up between him and those he had come to know on this new Earth — as they aged and he did not. But he would not be alone. He would be now encouraged to form social bonds within the new Timezone. He had other plans.

Karic put down his drink, slipped off the odin and walked across to Rosa. She stiffened as he embraced her.

"I'm soaking wet," she said.

Karic broke away and smiled up at her — she was as tall as walkway model. "Thank you for everything. I could not have done it without you."

The corners of her mouth tugged up into a smile and she touched his wet shirt. "Look at you now." She walked toward the open glass doors of the tower level beside them, calling over her shoulder. "Honestly, Karic. I'll get the servants to bring you a towel and something dry."

Alone now, Karic looked up at the blue sky, as though to force his vision up through that concealing vault to the welcoming darkness beyond. To the stars.

The *Starburst* was his. With a few repairs and modifications, she would be ideal for the rapidly growing He3 trade out of Saturn. Reserves on the Moon were already getting scarce. It seemed like packhorse duty for an old thoroughbred like her, but it was that or being sold for scrap, and he could not bear that. Besides, he knew her intimately. He could feel useful on her, while he brought himself up to date on almost two centuries of scientific advancement. He would transform her into his own yacht, cruising with her across the Solar System, building his wealth.

Long hauls like that would let him leap-frog into the future via the miracle of suspension technology, waiting for the years to go by. Waiting for his chance.

Above him, like a distortion in space, hovered the Fintil device. It was always with him. He knew that now. Forever invisible, spinning endlessly, forever waiting. It was likely quiescent — its original purpose as programmed into it by the Fountain now halted by his command — yet he could not forget the terror of those last few hours on *Starburst* before they reached Earth. He could never think of the ghostly device as harmless; no, it was more like an executioner on standby, waiting for its next command. All his attempts to work it had proved fruitless. Yet, somewhere within it, was every piece of information the *Starburst* had gathered. Memories. Proof.

Transversing Free Colonies space was risky — but lucrative. Earth was thirsty for fusion power, and hungry for the He3 that fueled fusion space-drives.

And he was hungry for space.

Epilogue

Karic jerked awake. It was years now since his return from Cru. Since he had left Earth on *Starburst* for the outer system. Yet still the dream would return.

He was trapped in the punishment pit. Alone with the heat. The pain. The insects. The stink of refuse. Utar would come to taunt him, his huge head morphing between Imbirri and Fintil as he spoke to Karic mind-to-mind: *This time, there will be no escape.*

The huge form of the Imbirri Queen would appear, her mouth opening in a dissonant scream before her huge body smashed down at the bars of the pit, snapping them like twigs ...

He wiped the sweat from his eyes.

"What is it, Karic?" came the sleepy voice of Kat, his lover. She had been with him since their stopover on Titan. Hitching a ride back to Mars in comfort. She was sweet and young. He tenderly lifted a strand of her dark blonde hair with his fingers and brushed it behind her ear. His eyes fell to the jagged scar on her left cheek and he smiled. The fiercely independent and egalitarian people of the Free Colonies despised Earth's decadent leadership. They eschewed the cosmetic perfection of Earth's elite, viewing it as an outward sign of moral weakness. That did not mean they avoided genetic enhancement − if anything, they were more adventurous in changing themselves for their challenging environments. Kat had no Timezone marker − registration was voluntary in the Free Colonies.

"Nothing. Just a dream. Go back to sleep," he said.

They were in the main stateroom of the *Starburst*, docked at Free Colonies Jupiter Station, orbiting well outside the deadly radiation belts of the gas giant. Merchant ships, led by entrepreneurial captains like himself, were given free passage to allow the movement of vital supplies and materials. Starlight filtered in through the wide panels above them. He could hear a lonely cricket in the biodome nearby.

He heard Kat's breathing slow and knew she had drifted back to sleep.

"Captain Zand?"

Karic rolled over and grabbed his comband.

"Captain Zand. Come in?"

Karic slipped the band over his wrist and raised it to his mouth. "Yes, Conroy."

"You have visitors. SF brass."

"Out here?" said Karic, puzzled. "You serious?"

"You bet."

Conroy was his third in command. He was hard-case, tough, but competent. He was running the ship while Karic took a well-earned break, and the rest of the crew took leave on Jupiter Station. "How many?"

"Two."

"Weapons?"

"None show up on the scan."

What could the Federation want with him? "OK. On my way. I'll meet them at the entry port."

Karic dressed, then made his way up through the ship to the main dock. A telescopic access corridor joined *Starburst* to Jupiter Station at her axis, allowing her to keep spinning her habitat.

He stood at the airlock, his heart racing.

"They are requesting access," said Conroy, across the link.

"Let them through."

"OK."

The inner airlock hissed open.

It was Andrai and Mara. Both of them were wearing the black and gold uniforms of a colonel in the SFSS, the Solar Federation Space Service. Hair cropped close in military style. They had married soon after joining the corps. Karic had lost touch with them after leaving Earth, but had followed their progress through his own contacts in the service. The couple had two young girls back on Earth, five and seven by now. To swing two successive birth permits, they must have certainly impressed their superiors.

"I see you haven't wasted any time moving up the ranks," said Karic.

Mara smiled. "I think you forget how much time you spend in suspension, Karic. It's been ten years."

Andrai and Mara pushed themselves forward through the hatch, moving easily in the zero-g. They looked around briefly at the *Starburst*, turning back to him without comment. He felt like embracing them, but their stiff manner and the SFSS uniforms held him back. Besides, he did not know what they wanted. Yet.

"Well, why don't you come down to the main floor?"

"You have made some changes, I see," said Andrai as they negotiated their way through the central hold to the main accessway. His manner was self-assured, and he wore his authority naturally.

"Yes. We had to lose most of the hold space to make room for the He3 storage."

"It's strange being back on this ship," said Andrai.

Mara's brow creased with tension, and she looked at Andrai in disapproval. He caught the look and remained silent.

Karic led them to his private office which, like his staterooms, adjoined the biodome. Through the big polymer-glass panels, they could see the ranks of greenery, recently watered, glistening in the artificial light.

"Take a seat." Karic patted Andrai on the back. "How have you been?"

Andrai shot a quick look at Mara, but said nothing in reply.

Karic cleared his throat. "Can I get you anything? Drink?"

"No, thanks," they chorused.

There was a period of uncomfortable silence.

"You are a hard man to find, Karic. We have been trying to contact you for the best part of a year," said Mara.

Karic shrugged. "Saturn's a long haul. You know that. What brings you out from Earth? I imagine SFSS officers are a bit unwelcome this far out."

Andrai and Mara exchanged a grim look.

"The Federation reached an agreement with the Free Colonies for an amnesty. But that's not what we are here to talk about," said Andrai. His voice was harder, more serious than Karic remembered. But then it had been years. Ten years in which Karic had spent less than a year out of suspension.

Andrai reached into his coat and drew out a sealed envelope. "This is a commission for you as a full captain in the Solar Federation's off-world program." He placed the envelope on Karic's desk. "We are offering you command of the *Stargazer*."

Karic was stunned. "But why now? Why me?"

"We have lost contact with the colony on Kestrel. Transmissions ceased from the colony five years ago. We need a brave and capable Commander, Karic," said Mara. "Someone with special skills. Special ... experience."

They looked at him in silence.

Mara's gaze hardened. "We pushed hard for this, Karic. We need you to lead this one."

"But you have capable commanders. Experienced commanders. There's more — what aren't you telling me?"

"The last transmissions were ... strange," said Andrai. "We have only fragments, but it looks like there was some alien contact. Something got to those colonists."

"But they were well defended on Kestrel." Karic thought rapidly. "You need more than a capable commander. You need someone desperate enough for a suicide mission."

Mara gave Andrai a quick look. He nodded.

"Karic, only we know what really happened at Tau Ceti," said Mara.

Karic studied her. "Have you remembered more?"

She shook her head slightly. "Enough."

"Enough to know that we would never have made it off Cru without you. We need someone who can deal with — and communicate with — whatever they find," said Andrai.

"And someone who will take a mission despite the risks," said Karic.

Andrai and Mara did not reply. They knew what the answer would be.

"Where is she?"

"In Earth orbit. She can be prepped and ready two weeks after you take command," said Mara.

"What is she running?"

"State of the art anti-matter drive. Magnetic breaking. 0.53C," said Andrai.

Karic's heart thumped in his chest. This was it. The chance he was waiting for. He looked out through the viewport.

At the stars.

"Sign me up."

THE END

About the Author

Being able to escape into the realm of the imagination was handy growing up as the youngest in a family of eleven. Chris continues his fantasy and SF writing habit from his home town of Brisbane, where he lives with his lovely wife Sandra and three children, Aedan, Declan and Brigit. He has a fourth-dan black belt in Moon Lee Tae Kwon Do and also enjoys movies and exploring narrow alleyways. Chris is very passionate about music, if a little inconsistent, and loves singing and playing classical guitar.

Chris publishes a regular blog on his website discussing everything from the latest developments in space science to the art of writing.

Check out the free downloads and other cool stuff at: www.chrismcmahon.net!

www.ingramcontent.com/pod-product-compliance
Lightning Source LLC
Chambersburg PA
CBHW021409110726
47901CB00008B/2113